EXPIATION

Book Four of the Shadeward Saga

by Drew Wagar

EXPIATION

Book Four of the Shadeward Saga

by Drew Wagar

FIRST EDITION
First published by Fantastic Books Publishing 2020
ISBN (ebook): 978-1-912053-98-8
ISBN (paperback): 978-1-912053-37-7
ISBN (hardcover): 978-1-912053-35-3

Thanks To:

My family continues to be of the greatest support behind the creation of these books of mine. I owe them all thanks for their patience in putting up with my … ahem … 'creative' moods. Writing a book is an undertaking of weeks, months and years, time that has to be carved out of other things. So, to my wonderful wife Anita, sons Mark and Joshua, and to Abbey – thanks for letting me do this. It's very hard work, but it is what I want to do.

To Anita (again!), Jason Hall and Steph Wyeth – proofreaders extraordinaire. Plot-holes, spelling, grammar, scientific accuracy, the list goes on. I rely on them to call out errors in the story for me to correct before it is published. Many changes are incorporated before the book is released due to their insight and oversight, including additional scenes and dialogue.

To David Stevenson, my 'informal' science advisor on all things related to the Lacaille 9352 system. His 'proper' (as in non-fiction and scientific) books are a gold mine of information on the properties of exoplanets.

To Mae, my editor, who goes through my manuscripts and suggests modifications which improve emphasis, pace and clarity. It's rare she stumbles with her suggestions, so this story is much improved due to her work.

To Dan at Fantastic Books Publishing for encouraging me to get to the end of this now quite lengthy saga – we made it! This is a saga which doesn't fit into your traditional genre classifications and is all the better for it, but this is a problem for some publishers. Not so FBP!

And thanks to you my readers, a circle which continues to grow. I know you share the love of storytelling from the past from which these new stories are inspired. It's been an honour and privilege to meet many of you in person and I hope to meet many more of you in due course. More books will come, even if this story ends here, there is much more to see and do in the universe of Shadeward, and there will be another 'Drew Wagar' book about it!

Author's Note

So here we are my friends, fellow travellers in space and time. This is the end of this series; quite a bittersweet moment.

The initial idea for the Shadeward Saga came to me in late 2010. Being a keen amateur astronomer, I wanted to write a story on a scientifically plausible world, but one where the traditional trappings of science fiction; spacecraft, laser beams, space battles, hyperspace and so on, weren't the focus of the story. Any science had to be as realistic as possible, no random suspension of the law of physics for dramatic effect.

I've always enjoyed post-apocalyptic stories too, but was often intrigued to know how civilisation bounced back after such events, a topic not usually covered given most stories focus on the devastation rather than the aftermath.

So with Shadeward the science is real, the world is plausible, perhaps even likely. Exoplanets like Esurio will doubtless exist out there in the universe, even if Esurio itself is not present around Lacaille 9352. Mayura, the 'hot Jupiter' planet used in these stories for time-keeping, is also a common feature in many star systems of this type. The weather and surface conditions of Esurio are based on real scientific data. There's no magic here.

The devastation featured in the Shadeward Saga, two-fold, has happened in the dim and distant past, so long ago that the current residents are largely unaware of what occurred. The civilisation they find themselves part of seems to them to be all that is and was. Only slowly do they begin to determine that they came from another place, with other values and concerns.

This saga thus takes place at a time when civilisation is on the cusp of emerging from a feudal state, on the brink of a renaissance, where the powers of religion and enlightenment both have an equal chance of dominating the future.

This premise is, or certainly seems to be, unique. It's drawn fans from the worlds of science fiction and fantasy. I'm rather proud of the fact it straddles genres, pulling themes not just from science fiction and fantasy, but thrillers and romance too. That makes it untouchable by a traditional publisher, so huge thanks go to the team at Fantastic Books for taking on such a risky project and believing in it.

But to all of you who have read and enjoyed this series thus far – the biggest thanks goes to you. It's been an honour and a privilege to write these stories and then hear people talking about the characters, the scenes and the adventures I've penned (or keyboarded!). It's hugely rewarding for an author to listen in on these conversations, fascinating to see what depth or interpretation people weave into their reading. Sometimes it's what I intended, but, more often than not, I find myself surprised by the different views people have. None of these are wrong – they're just … different. I have a view of the world and people I create; you, as the reader will have another. That's part of the wonderful bond between writer and reader. We both create the world we see in our imaginations.

Others too, have commented on the sense of realism my characters have. This is something I spent a lot of time on, trying to ensure the people in these stories are relatable. They're not perfect, they make a lot of mistakes, get impatient, annoyed and cross. They love, they hate, they argue, they fight. They're just like us, they just happen to live on a different world.

It will be a wrench for me to leave these characters behind. Like you, I've spent a lot of time in their company, and they almost feel like real people. Many of the comments I've been sent via email, social media and in reviews echo these feelings. We care for fictional characters, feel for them, laugh and cry with them. Perhaps that allows us to get in touch with our own emotions in a personal and private way.

This truly is the end of this saga. I've worked hard to wrap up all the threads, give closure to the mysteries I've created and give each character a suitable finale appropriate to who they are and what they've done. The stories of Kiri, Meru, Zoella and all the others end here and won't be revisited; I'm not a fan of stringing things out.

But there will be more stories in the Shadeward universe, perhaps a prequel describing what forced us away from home, or perhaps stories of the other worlds that were colonised alongside Esurio. There will be more characters and more adventures. The fates of those spheres, out there in the darkness of space, are yet to be told.

Regardless, my type of storytelling will continue as it has done; stories that run chronologically, not applying sleight-of-hand literary tricks, but straightforward to read. The complexity then lies with the characters, what they do, the drama, the action and the politics that are weaved together. That's my style, or 'voice' as it's sometimes called.

If you like it, there's plenty more to come. Thank you for supporting me thus far.

Drew Wagar,
April, 2020.

"She needed a hero,
so that's what she became."

Lacaille

In order to effectively administer the colony it was decided that some of the colonists would be given additional technological capabilities within their biological makeup.

Various criteria determined that female colonists with the appropriate temperament were selected and enhanced, providing them with significant abilities. The primary purpose was to allow communication between colonists via the augmented booster, without any other equipment being necessary. The planet's magnetic field was used as a medium for the transmission, with individuals themselves acting as a relay mesh, rendering more traditional radio technologies, which were subject to major interference over long ranges, obsolete. The technology was designed to align itself with reproductive processes, ensuring that subsequent generations would benefit from the enhancement, even if the knowledge of how it worked were to be lost.

The original administrators of the colony worked under strict guidelines to ensure their abilities were governed and used effectively. The settlements prospered for many generations, the necessary knowledge being embedded in song, tradition and writings.

The booster itself was designed to be self-regulating, but it could provide status reports and updates to the administrators in case of any variance outside of its ability to manage. When such events occurred, the administrators would be automatically summoned via their in-built communications mechanism.

The booster itself was the core of Esurio's terraforming and stabilisation systems. If it were to fail the impact on the planet's terraforming stability, the ability to defend against Lacaille's radiative flux and the lives of the colonists themselves would be put in jeopardy.

The original colonists who retained knowledge of the technology involved in creating and maintaining the booster could see that the long term viability of Esurio depended on keeping the booster functional for periods of time that dwarfed human lifespans. Over the course of several tens of rounds it was determined that artificial intelligence and automation were insufficient for this task and some kind of human oversight would be required.

The problem was eventually solved in a controversial manner. Whilst this was being carried out, several further adjustments to the environment and the augmented abilities of the administrators were undertaken.

It was whilst those adjustments were taking place that the first flare hit Esurio. It was not anticipated, either by the semi-automated systems that had been set to guard the colony or by the colonists themselves. Lacaille 9352 was not catalogued as a flare star and no flare had ever been observed from the time of its discovery until the present time. Thus the calamity that overtook the colony was as unexpected as it was devastating.

Over nine tenths of the colonists were killed in a devastating holocaust. Most were outside when the flare hit and died as a result of exposure to lethal levels of ultraviolet radiation. Still more were caught by deadly firestorms caused by the pulse of infrared that emanated from Lacaille during the flare.

In the immediate struggle to survive the aftermath, the intentions of the original colonists were lost and the nascent civilisation on Esurio collapsed. Through many generations those who survived began to spread once more across the planet. History became mixed with legend, the origins of the population only dimly remembered. A barely recognisable culture staggered back. It was far different from what had gone before, surrounded by the broken remnants of the past.

What little technology remained was perceived as magic or religious power, its origin misunderstood. Thus wars were fought, empires rose and fell. Thousands of rounds passed. Civilisation emerged from a dark age longer than those known on the forgotten homeworld but, as always, those who understood even a little of the past grew to be great and powerful.

The powers of the original colonists were still present, yet they had also adapted in the long rounds since they had first been gifted to the people. The booster still operated, unattended, forgotten by all, and yet still its automated systems continued to discharge the task its long vanished makers had designed it to perform.

The controversial means by which the booster had been set to operate were stable for thousands of rounds, but, as time continued to erode its ability to function effectively, even those means were found to be insufficient. The booster was failing, it required assistance from outside, from those who still had the administrative gift from long ago.

Only now, so many generations since any such communication had been received, those administrators knew little of their past and perceived the summons as dreams, fears, or messages from a Goddess that neither existed, nor cared for the salvation of those on the planet below.

But without their help, the booster would fail.

And with it, all human life on Esurio.

Prologue

Round 2287, Eleventh Pass

It was clear that even the herg was tired. Dirt cloyed its nostrils and its fans were drooping in the heat. The road beneath its feet was baked hard and cracked dry. Astride it, wrapped in a cowl and thin fabrics to keep out the worst of the wind-blown dust, was a rider, huddled down in the saddle.

The rider patted the flank of the beast, urging it on. The herg snorted and resumed a slow amble. Before them a shade forest was rising, promising relief from the heat and the unending blaze of the star above, Lacaille.

As the herg moved forward, the rider checked the road behind for any other travellers. There were none.

The path wound into the forest. Within, the rider guided the herg to a stream, allowing it to drink its fill of the water that flowed there, before dismounting carefully cradling a bundle that was then lowered gently to the ground.

The rider straightened, pulling back the cowl.

It was a man, his brown hair streaked with grey, his skin weathered and lined. He wiped his brow with the back of his hand and took a deep breath, all the while looking about himself.

At his feet, the pack he had lowered to the ground wriggled. A cry issued from it.

'Alright little one, water is coming.'

He unwrapped the pack, revealing a baby, swaddled in wrappings. Curly brown hair framed big brown eyes that stared up at him. At the sight of his face the baby smiled.

The man cradled the child in his arms as he sat beside the stream, scooping water into its mouth by hand.

Once the child was sated, he lowered it once more and drank his own fill, all the while keeping a close eye on the road ahead and behind.

Satisfied, he picked the child up again and strode to the herg.

'Just a little further now,' he said. 'And our long journey will be over.'

The child gurgled happily in his embrace as he vaulted up on to the herg. It snorted in irritation, but he ignored it, steering the beast on to the track by the reins.

The path unwound before them, the tall shades on either side. The man looked up, seeing the light of Lacaille filtering through the few gaps in the canopy. Nargs, small black insect-like creatures, buzzed about him, and he flapped his hand to clear them away.

He had been travelling for almost a pass, riding across the land of Scallia, heading sunright towards the coast. His destination lay but a few marks ahead. Already the path was improving, showing signs of being used and cared for. About him, the land was rising, drying out once more. He had turned away from the lowlands and their dangerous bogs, he knew of the dangerous creatures that infested them.

The forest ended at a boundary. A stone wall with an open gate marked out a field in which hergs were grazing. The path led alongside it, wider now, easily enough for two carriages to travel abreast. The river was flowing adjacent to the path, at the base of a narrow valley, with fields either side.

Ahead was a building, grand in the nature of such things. It was a hall, surrounded by a well-tended courtyard. The man directed his herg onwards towards it, bringing it to a halt outside. He could see a pond off to one side, underneath the lee of the hall. A faint aroma of wholesome cooking drifted on a breeze. His stomach rumbled in response.

He dismounted nearby, tying the herg to a fencepost and making sure the sleeping baby was secure on the creature's back.

He walked around the perimeter of the hall, seeing a couple of young children sweeping the courtyard. Beyond them was a gardener, with a pair of apprentices assisting him. They were busy working, clearing pathways and tending to the creepers and vines that ran up the side of the building. The scrape of brooms, the sounds of shears clipping and scythes being swung reached his ears.

A servant saw him and approached.

'A good stretch, sir?'

'I hope so,' the man replied.

'Might I be of assistance?'

'I seek Lord Tarq,' the man replied. 'I hear he lives hereabouts.'

'Why,' the servant replied, 'this is his hall, sir. May I announce you?'

The man nodded. 'You may, I have travelled some way to meet him.'

'Might I ask your name?'

'My name is Guerrun. Guerrun Sandatch.'

'A moment.'

The servant retreated within the hall. Another man walked out, limping and leaning on a stick. His face was pale and jowly, the skin marked by a pox.

'Greetings to you traveller,' the man said. His voice was rough, but not unpleasant. 'What is your business at my hall?'

'Do I have the pleasure of addressing Lord Tarq?' Guerrun asked.

'You do,' Tarq replied, looking at him, his eyes narrowed.

'I understand you house and care for children,' Guerrun said. 'I was recommended to you by those in Serenia.'

'Aye that be so,' Tarq said, 'We take in those upon whom misfortune has ventured. Many have lost their fathers to the sea, or their mothers to sickness and disease. They work though, from the youngest to the oldest, 'til they can make their own way in the world.'

'Would you take a babe? A girl?'

'A babe? Tarq frowned. 'No. Too young, sir! A babe cannot–'

'What if there was payment?' Guerrun interrupted. 'Forgive me, but I am in haste.'

'Payment you say?' Tarq said, licking his lips. 'I would not wish to insult you, sir. But such care would not be cheap.'

'Name your price.'

'Ten koins a pass,' Tarq said, without a pause. 'For nursing such a young 'un.'

Guerrun sighed, but nodded.

'Agreed,' he said. 'I will pay you for half a round now, then I will return.'

'A hundred …'

'Yes.' Guerrun led them round to where the herg was secured. He took a satchel from the saddle and counted out the money into a small bag, holding it out before him. Tarq reached for it. Guerrun pulled it just out of reach.

'I will expect her to be well cared for. Food, cleanliness, washing, medicine. She will want for nothing, is that understood?'

'It is sir, I will instruct my best maids to look after your daughter.'

'She is not my daughter,' Guerrun said. 'I am her … guardian.'

'She will be well cared for.'

Guerrun nodded and dropped the bag into Tarq's outstretched hand. Guerrun turned to the herg, gently lifting the baby out of the sling in which it lay. A faint cry of protest sounded from it and it wriggled in his arms. Guerrun gently comforted the child, planting a kiss on its forehead.

'There there …'

Tarq whistled and two women emerged, moving to his side, their heads bowed.

'We are to tend to this child,' Tarq said. 'See to it that a cot and linen are prepared. Summon a wet nurse at once.'

'Sire.'

Both the maids bowed. One immediately skipped away. The other held her arms out towards Guerrun.

Guerrun handed the swaddled child over to her and she took it in her arms, rocking it back and forth.

'She is a treasure, sir,' the maid said. 'We will tend her well, do not fear.'

'So I trust,' Guerrun said.

'What is her name?'

'She is called Zoella,' Guerrun answered and then looked at Tarq. 'I will return in half a round as promised. You will care for her, or I will hear about it.'

Tarq swallowed, but nodded.

Guerrun took a deep breath, kissing his fingers before placing them on the child's forehead.

'Bless you, little Zoella,' he said. 'I will be back.'

Guerrun jumped astride the herg and spurred it up the path at a gallop, leaving Tarq and the maid standing outside the hall.

CHAPTER ONE

The Border of Drayden and Scallia

Round 2307, Third pass

She had no idea how long she'd been there. She propped herself up on her elbows, coughing up water and spluttering.

I'm alive! I escaped!

She was lying on the edge of the river, washed up on the bank. Her clothes were ripped and torn, full of sand and dirt.

That priestess, she was going to kill me ... she tried ...

Gemma shook her head and wiped the muck out of her eyes. She coughed again, pulling herself up to her knees and looking around.

The river was a gentle bend behind her, the banks soft and shallow, water lapping about her. It was a far cry from the foaming torrent she had thrown herself into.

But it worked. I got away ...

Gemma recalled how a young priestess had saved her from the torture inflicted on her fellow prisoners. How she had feigned unconsciousness as she was carried out and how she had been flown out of the city of Daine on the back of a dach.

She brought the young priestess to mind. There was one particular vivid memory; blue eyes and dark black hair.

At great risk to herself the priestess had smuggled Gemma out of Drayden and flown her to the borders, leaving her there to make her own way into Scallia and to freedom.

Gemma remembered what she had said.

'I've come as far as I dare. You must make your own way now.'

Gemma nodded, shedding the heavy riding gear. The priestess handed her a sack of provisions.

'Be quick, it is only a few stretches march to Viresia from here,' she said. 'Hide in the forests and don't let yourself be seen in the open until you are close.'

'Thank you,' Gemma replied. 'For everything.'

'Just stay alive,' the priestess answered. 'That is the only thanks I need. Beware the priestesses. Don't use your gift if you can. It will bring attention to you.'

'But what of you?' the woman asked.

'Do not fear for me,' she replied.

Gemma hoisted the sack. 'Why?' she asked. 'Why did you save me?'

The priestess licked her lips.

'For Scallia.'

Gemma frowned.

'There's no time to explain,' the priestess said, gesturing for her to go. 'I am of Scallia myself. Quickly! We may have been followed, run and hide.'

The memory faded. It left more questions unanswered.

Gemma still didn't understand what had happened. How could a priestess be of Scallia? What did the woman mean? Maybe she had been stolen from Scallia too and had become a priestess? Whatever it was that had driven her to this daring rescue, Gemma was grateful to her.

Then she shivered, recalling what had happened next.

A second priestess had appeared once the first had gone, this one with a shock of red hair and fierce expression.

Gemma had tried to run, but pain savagely cramped up her thigh. She had fallen, rolling into the tall rushes at the edge of the river, hearing the rushing water nearby.

When Gemma had looked up, the second priestess was there, her staff jutting forward at Gemma's throat. That memory was full of fear.

'Don't move,' the priestess said. 'I'll make this painless.'

'Please, don't hurt me! Please …'

Gemma saw the priestess roll her eyes and then stretch out her hand, palm outwards.

She's going to torture me … kill me!

Gemma had tried to scream, but found she couldn't. Her whole body was caught in the priestess' strange power. Then, like a burning knife cutting into her skull, she heard words.

Who are you?

Gemma … my name is Gemma … please!

Why did she rescue you?

I don't … I don't know …

There was more pain, but she couldn't cry out.

Why did she rescue you?

Gemma hadn't been able to stop the priestess from invading her memories. The conversation was replayed. Gemma could sense the red haired priestess' astonishment at what she had found in Gemma's memory.

Then the priestess' mental grip slackened.

Gemma didn't pause. She stumbled to her feet and ran.

The river wasn't far away. She reached a rocky edge, pausing before throwing herself over the precipice. She felt the priestess clasp at her mind, but the grip was faint and unsure. Wind roared in her ears …

She hit the water hard, it was freezing and the current dragged her along and down. There was the brief sensation of pain, perhaps the priestess had tried to attack her again, but then it was gone. Soon there was nothing but the chill torrent churning about her. It was all she could do to drag her head above water to catch a breath before she was swept under again.

Her body crashed against unseen objects. Every moment she expected to be dashed against a rock and for her life to end. Every time she came up gasping she thought it would be her last, her arms and legs ached as she struggled.

Just as she thought she would drown she felt the current slacken and then …

She forced the memories out of her mind and sat up.

I must have passed out and washed up on the bank.

She took a good look around her. The river was wide and slow now, the water lapping around her. She felt stiff and bruised, but a quick check seemed to indicate she wasn't hurt, nothing was broken. She could feel the warmth of Lacaille on her, drying out what remained of her clothes.

She felt her heart hammer in her chest.

That priestess might be looking for me. I've got to get away. Got to hide.

The first priestess had told her to travel shadewards into Scallia. She looked behind her to see the warm disk of Lacaille visible over the opposite bank. Before her the forest was thick and dense. She got to her feet, nursing her stiff legs and staggered into the vegetation. Within, it was dark; she had to wait for her eyes to adjust to the gloom. The tall shades carried on as far as she could see. Wearily she began to walk.

* * *

Lord Crenech stood atop the veranda of his home. It was a grand affair, mimicking the architecture of the capital city of his homeland, Viresia in Scallia. Built of white stone on the banks of a river it overlooked his lands, a series of well-cultivated fields bordered by the deeper forests of Scallia which stretched out sunward and shaderight to the limits of vision. His lands bordered another land to the sunward, that of the priestesses. Drayden itself.

Not that there is much distinction now. Scallia belongs to them.

He looked to the shadeward. A few dozen marks away lay the capital itself. Viresia was an ancient city, built in ages long forgotten, using techniques that no crafters could match in modern times. Much of it was empty and abandoned; it housed far fewer people than it could hold, and fewer now than in recent rounds.

The priestesses saw to that.

Scallia had been its own kingdom just a round before. Old King Marek had ruled for many rounds, a time of relative peace, though the king had a strange mercurial side to him. He had always counselled complete obeisance to the wishes of the Drayden priestesses to the sunward. He always obeyed their commands to send the cream of their young women to that strange land every five rounds.

But the priestesses had not been satisfied with the last tithe. They had demanded more and came to enforce their mandate.

And with the news of their arrival, Old King Marek had breathed his last.

His son Ioric had taken over, a man many Scallians had great respect and fondness for. Much of the aristocracy were less enamoured, for Ioric was a man of few words and straightforward thinking, whereas his father had ears for their schemes and politics.

And then the war came.

Lord Crenech hadn't been present in the city when the priestesses had descended and the fires rose, he'd ridden in on seeing the fires. The battle had been short and brutal, all was lost before he'd even arrived.

Viresia was left in flames, King Ioric and his half-brother Torin were dead and, according to the stories, his daughter, Lady Liana had been kidnapped never to be seen again. Hundreds of refugees had spilled out of the city and into his lands, looking for shelter and food having lost everything in the attack.

It wasn't long before the lords were summoned by the priestesses. Crenech had looked on while Lord Sequon defied the will of the high priestess herself, a woman who called herself Nerina Helios.

Sequon had faced her down and paid the penalty, the others had watched as he was crushed down to his knees, tortured and despatched by the high priestess' otherworldly powers. None had dared to defy her again.

So she thinks.

Crenech permitted himself a smile.

It was clear that direct confrontation was not the way. The priestesses' abilities were way beyond anything anyone in Scallia could hope to counter. Sequon had been brave, but foolish. He'd achieved nothing but his own death. If the priestesses were to be resisted, it had to be by more subtle means.

Crenech had overheard some talk about a conflict with an island far out in the sea to the sunright; that problem was occupying the priestesses.

Perhaps something has not gone to plan …

The priestesses who remained couldn't be challenged directly, but it was easy enough to ensure they were kept busy with the minutia of Scallian administration. The priestesses' intentions were the same as before. They were seeking more young women like themselves, now with a great deal of urgency.

Crenech knew of the old five round tithe. How high born girls from each aristocratic family had been summoned by order of the king and sent to Drayden, never to be seen again. Young women were still being caught by the priestesses and wrenched from their families, subjected to some strange check and then either being released or taken away by dach, presumably to Drayden.

According to the rumours, many women, regardless of where they were born, had the potential to manifest powers such as the priestesses displayed.

The priestesses are taking our women … our kin, then brainwashing them, indoctrinating them in their ways, turning our own against us.

Whatever this power was, it was the core of the priestesses' purpose.

If we could retain these powers, perhaps we could defy them and reclaim our homeland from them.

And such, behind closed doors, had been the thinking of the lords of Scallia.

Crenech looked up, seeing one of the dachs circling in the sky above. It was descending in sweeping arcs. He quietened his thoughts, unsure of whether the priestess above would be able to hear what he was thinking. The limits of their powers weren't known.

But at least I knew this one was coming …

He strode forward across the veranda, waiting for the large creature to land. It came down with a heavy thump, raising a gust of wind as it back-flapped its wings to reduce its speed. The priestess aboard leapt down with a lithe movement and strode towards him. She was dressed in leather armour as was custom for the priestesses, though it was covered in a dark cloak. She held a staff, the priestesses' primary weapon, in her right hand. Crenech knew it was called a kai.

'A fine stretch,' Crenech said, with a bow.

'I come to search your lands,' the priestess replied.

'Again?' Crenech asked. 'You did so barely a pass ago, no more girls have been born or come of age in such a short time.'

The priestess stepped closer, her expression one of annoyance and arrogance.

'Do you defy me?' she snapped.

'Not at all,' Crenech replied. 'I merely fear you will waste your time.'

'My time is not wasted,' the priestess replied. 'Prepare food and water and follow me.'

Crenech bowed and gestured for her to proceed. The priestess strode across the veranda and entered his house, Crenech following behind. He gestured to his staff and they went to prepare provisions for his visitor.

'How goes your search?' Crenech asked.

'Well enough,' the priestess snapped at him.

'I heard some talk of trouble in faraway lands,' Crenech said. 'I hope it has been dealt with.'

'We will deal with them in the same way we have dealt with Scallia,' the priestess returned, her pace not slackening. 'Resistance to our rule is foolishness.'

So … not dealt with yet. Interesting.

'Viresia was humbled in a single stretch,' Crenech observed. 'Surely these adversaries of yours have already been subdued?'

The priestess glared at him, but didn't deign to reply.

So, there do exist some who can defy the priestesses! Who are they, and how have they managed it?

The priestess continued her walk through the halls and corridors of

Crenech's house. Wherever she encountered a woman she would stretch out her hand, her fingers reaching forward. The women would stand obediently, knowing any defiance would be punished with a pulsing headache. The priestess was disappointed with each one, turning on her heel with a tut or a sigh before moving on, with Crenech trying to keep pace behind her.

She came to the end of her search of the rooms.

'Are there no others?' she demanded.

'None within the household,' Crenech said. 'Stablehands and urchins in the fields perhaps, if you wish to …'

The priestess turned to him. 'I will not traipse through muck and filth. I will be back in five stretches, have every woman in your household from the youngest to the oldest assembled for my inspection at the first chime on that stretch.'

'All of them?' Crenech asked in dismay.

'Every single one,' the priestess replied, emphasising each word with a curl of her lips. 'And they should be clean as well.'

'Of course,' Crenech said. 'It shall be done as you request.'

The priestess turned on her heel, striding away, her dark gown billowing out behind her. The servants who had brought food and drink scattered out of her way. She ignored them completely and strode to the veranda, mounting her dach. With a sharp cry it arched its back and, with its wings flapping mightily, rose out of sight.

Crenech watched it go before picking up a ripe corcun from a table and crunching down into it, a grin upon his face.

A waste of time for you perhaps, but I have learnt something from your visit.

He finished the fruit and gestured for the rest of the repast to be cleared away. Then he strode into his house and down into the halls below.

'Open the cellars,' he asked two of his staff.

Two heavy trap doors were lifted out of the stone flooring. Crenech grabbed a torch and descended into the depths below via a ladder.

'She gone,' he called. 'It's safe.'

Dimly lit by the torch Crenech could see dozens of barrels stacked in rows, alongside many racks holding bottles in ordered columns. As he stood there, figures emerged from the shadows. Women and girls, some dressed in smart attire, others in the garb of common folk and farm labourers.

One woman approached him. He embraced her, hugging her close. It was his daughter.

'How is everyone?'

'Scared, bored, wondering if they're going to be caught,' his daughter answered. 'Sitting in the dark is horrible.'

Crenech nodded.

'She'll be back in five stretches, most likely sooner,' Crenech replied.

'How long can we keep doing this?' his daughter asked. 'Surely one stretch they will find us, and then …'

'There is hope,' Crenech said. 'This stretch I learnt that they have failed to subdue some other land they have waged war upon. It appears they are in some distress. This is why they search so hard. I think they have been frustrated in their attempts to attack this other city.'

'How can this be?'

'It seems there are those that have the power to resist the priestesses,' Crenech said. 'If we can but contact them somehow …'

'Scallia might be freed again,' his daughter whispered. 'Can it be true?'

'I will be trying to find out more,' Crenech replied. 'But such information is hard to come by, and dangerous to seek.'

'Be careful!'

'We must all be careful.'

* * *

Gemma stumbled over the roots of a shade, losing her footing and falling to her knees in the soft loam. She stopped to catch her breath, looking about her in dismay. The forest seemed unending.

She had no idea how long she'd been walking for, only that she was keeping Lacaille behind her and heading shadeward. Her stomach was growling; she hadn't eaten since the priestess had rescued her and the pack of provisions had been lost in the flight from the second priestess. She didn't have anything, not even a knife. She'd hoped to come across a few raw melps or tupes, but the shades were thick overhead, blotting out the light from Lacaille, the forest floor gloomy and bare.

She got to her feet to take her bearings.

She sniffed. There was a faint smell on the air she didn't recognise, sweet yet sharp. Her stomach rumbled again in response. Whatever it was it smelled like food. Maybe a stash of sweetbuds? Some luck after all? She got a sense of which direction it was coming from, somewhere ahead, and set off.

The smell grew stronger about her, she could feel her mouth beginning to water in anticipation. The shade canopy above seemed even thicker now, it was hard to tell which direction she should be heading, Lacaille's light was blocked by the trunks, branches and cups above.

The smell was thick now though, whatever it was couldn't be far ahead. She stumbled into a small clearing, bereft of shades. She squinted in the gloom, seeing a vine hanging down before her. She moved closer, seeing a thick liquid dribbling down it.

She reached out, running her hand against it, the sticky liquid dribbling over her finger tips. Definitely the source of the smell. She tasted the liquid, it was sharp but sugary, sticky and gloopy, like a syrup. She looked up, the vine hung down from the darkness above. She paused to look around, straining her senses in case anything was there.

Nothing was moving or making a sound.

She began scraping the syrup into her hands. It was a messy affair, but the syrup was good to eat, satisfying her hunger. It would keep her going for a while as she kept travelling, perhaps she might find more of the vines along the way.

Her hands were coated in the stuff by the time she had scraped away what she could reach. As she was licking the last of it from her fingers she felt a stinging sensation in her ankle. She looked down, wondering whether she'd been bitten by something, only to see a thin silvery thread had wrapped itself around her.

She stumbled back, trying to kick it off, but it held fast, elastic and stretchy. She tried to pull at it, but as she did so more tendrils appeared around her, almost invisible in the gloom, snaking their way around her arms and wrists.

She yelled and pulled away, trying to back out of the clearing. She turned, running into a veil of tendrils that had appeared across her path, those too wrapped themselves around her arms and thighs with a faint stinging sensation.

She fell, only to find herself suspended above the ground in the tendrils' grasp. Screaming in horror she flailed, trying to break the thin tracery that had caught her, but she could get no purchase on the tendrils, they just stretched a little and returned to the same position.

More of them spun out around her, binding her fingers together in a sticky mass of white, stopping her from tearing at them. She squirmed, helpless, feeling her body being hoisted up into the air.

As she rose she was rolled over on to her back.

She stared upwards.

Something hung from the shades above her, a vague shape in the darkness above.

A vast beaked bud, surrounded by a cascade of tendrils, was opening. She screamed, heedless of the noise she was making as she thrashed around, helpless in its grasp. The bud peeled back revealing a dark maw several hands wide. Liquid dripped out, splashing on to her. Some of it touched her clothing. She stared in terror as it started to smoke.

It dripped on to her skin, burning her. Her screams rose another notch, shrieking out in hysteria.

The silent shades about her did not react. Creatures foolish enough to wander into the grasp of a snare were a common enough occurrence in the depths of the forest. And the result was always the same.

The snare would feast, slowly, yet surely.

Then more tendrils descended, wrapping themselves about the struggling girl, soon she was enveloped in them, her screams muffled, the numbing anaesthetic stings slowing her movements.

She was only jerking spasmodically now.

Above, the snare prepared to feast upon its catch.

* * *

Lord Crenech had set runners to keep him informed as to the whereabouts and activities of the priestesses in Viresia. They came back at intervals through the stretch with news.

Only three priestesses had been seen in the city. The others had been summoned away, perhaps due to the problems encountered elsewhere. Nothing new had been overheard as to what those problems were, but the priestesses seemed to be very agitated, exchanging short words with each other, uncomfortable with the situation.

Crenech nodded to the latest one as he gave his report. He was a young man, but with a sensible manner about him. Joachim had become a trusted pair of eyes, ears and hands in the last round or so. He had come into Crenech's service when his parents had been killed in the attack on Viresia.

'Just three?'

'Yes sire,' Joachim replied. 'The others left two stretches ago aboard their dachs and haven't returned.'

Crenech nodded. 'You've done well. Send one of the others to Viresia upon the next stretch and tell them to keep their eyes and ears open for news.'

Joachim nodded.

'Is there something else?' Joachim asked.

Crenech grinned. 'We're taking a short trip sunward. I'm going to ride to the shadeward borders, to check on the outlying hamlets, see if there are any rumours from beyond our lands. We won't be long, three stretches at most. Have a pair of hergs saddled and provisions made.'

Joachim nodded and left.

Crenech walked out on to the veranda once more, looking across his lands.

The priestesses' grip is unsure. If we could but learn of these folk that have somehow defied them! How has that been achieved? Some weapon the priestesses are scared of? Or perhaps other folks have found a way to counter their magic? If so, might we ally with them and throw off the shackles imposed upon us by these women? How to reach them?

The sunward edges of his lands bordered those of Drayden. A few traders came and went between the two. There was the possibility of some news. It was worth the trip. He leant on the balustrade for a spell, watching the comings and goings of his people.

Joachim led two hergs out ready for the trip. Crenech could see his sword was buckled to the saddle of his, along with two pannier bags loaded with water and food. The young man stood waiting for him below.

Crenech turned to see his daughter standing at the threshold of the veranda.

'You ride out?' she asked.

He nodded.

'I must find out more,' he said. 'If there is anything to be found.'

She nodded.

'Have faith,' he said. 'The priestesses are not as strong as they would have us believe. Something ails them, worries them, that works to our advantage.'

'If they should find us …'

'Keep to our plan,' Crenech said. 'They have not found you in the passes since the battle and they grow impatient and careless.'

His daughter looked unconvinced.

Can I blame her? Having to hide in the darkness for chimes at a time to avoid being found?

He walked over to her, pulling her into a hug.

'I know it is hard,' he said. 'But I would not run the risk of you being taken away to Drayden. We do not know what they do with those they take, but none ever return.'

He felt his daughter shudder in his embrace.

'No Father,' she said. 'You are right. We will follow the plan. Just … don't be long!'

He hugged her close.

'I will be back as soon as I can. I'm taking Joachim, he'll keep an eye on me,' Crenech said with a chuckle. 'The runners will continue to update us. Look after our folk. The priestesses are not due again for a few stretches. I will be back before then.'

'Make sure you are.'

'I love you,' he said, stepping back and placing a kiss on her forehead.

'And I, you.'

He turned and walked away, signalling to Joachim. The younger man helped him up on to the herg. Crenech give her a brief wave as he set the beast to canter off sunwards, Joachim following behind.

The road was easy for several chimes. It was well-travelled as the farmers that worked his lands were often moving their produce to and from his estates or onwards to Viresia itself. Beyond that the road led deeper into the shadeward forests.

The weather was fair, Lacaille shining peaceably in the sky for now. Two of the terrifying flares had hit, but the second one had been less fierce than the first, and his people now knew what to do. Hiding within their homes was the best defence, ensuring nothing flammable was nearby, failing that, the shade forests were the next best thing as the shades themselves seemed to cope with the sudden bursts of light by extending their cups to shade the ground below, protecting their own trunks.

Afterwards, the cups would shrivel and die within chimes, but new ones would grow within a couple of stretches and the shade forests would return to normal. The rotting husks of the old cups would be consumed by the creatures of the forest.

Clearly the shades are ready for the flares …

Other creatures seemed to know what to do too. The hergs retreated into the forests, as did the fellins and cainer. Marsips fled to their burrows. No one knew where the wild dachs flew away to, but they had been seen since, high up in the sky. Many people had seen the beasts' third eyes, usually sightless, staring around as if measuring something. It seemed they all could tell when a flare was due and knew what had to be done.

A stretch's ride saw them to the forests close to the border. Ahead Crenech could see a familiar farmstead belonging to an old friend of his family, the land having been gifted by his ancestors long rounds ago. Smoke was rising from a hole in the roof of a ramshackle building, but as he rode up Crenech was surprised to find no one was home.

Crenech and Joachim tied their hergs to a gate and walked inside, seeing a pot of stew bubbling away on a fire, with places set on a rough table for dinner, but there was no sign of anyone.

'Where are they all?' Joachim asked.

Crenech came out, a frown creasing his forehead.

Strange.

Hergs were still in the fields about him, but were clustered away from the forest fringes, packed together in a herd. Everything seemed unusually still.

Crenech walked to his herg, unbuckling his sword from the saddle and taking another look about him.

'Come on,' he muttered. 'Something's amiss here.'

Joachim pulled his own sword from its scabbard and stood alongside him.

They heard shouts and some kind of commotion from the forest ahead. Raised voices reached him alongside the sounds of trampling undergrowth. Crenech stepped forward and drew his sword.

Brigands perhaps? If they have hurt any of my people they will live to regret it!

But the figures that emerged from the forest were familiar. Crenech saw his old friend surrounded by his family, together they were carrying something between them, wrapped up in a bundle, struggling with its weight. He squinted, it looked like a body.

Sheathing his sword he ran forwards, the family seeing him and then recognising him. Joachim followed close behind

'My Lord Crenech!' the lead man said.

'Fareth!' Crenech replied. 'I came unannounced, my apologies! What has happened?'

'Someone caught in a snare,' he said, gesturing to the body. Crenech could see it was wrapped in linen. 'We heard the screams and cut them down. Likely too late …'

'Get them to the house then,' Crenech said. 'I have some medicines with me, let's see what can be done.'

Crenech and Joachim pitched in with carrying the body. It wasn't heavy, whoever the person was they were small and lightweight. Within the house, space was made and the body lowered to the ground.

The linen was unwrapped to reveal a body swathed in the fine silky wrappings of the snare.

'What were they thinking getting close to such a thing?' Fareth asked. 'Travellers know to avoid them …'

'Frequent travellers, yes,' Crenech said, pulling a knife from his belt and cutting at the tendril coils. 'Did you find anyone else? Anything with them?'

'Nothing,' Fareth said. 'We just heard screams and went running. They were alone, no pack, no provisions, nothing.'

'Strange indeed.'

Crenech's knife cut through the sticky material and the family helped pull it away. A face was revealed, a young woman with pale skin and blonde hair.

'A girl …' Joachim said. 'She looks familiar. I'm sure I've seen her before.'

Fareth bent his ear to her mouth.

'She's breathing,' he announced.

Crenech used his knife to cut down the side of her body and the family continued to pull at the tendrils until they were all removed. The girl's body was battered and bruised, with a nasty burn across her midriff.

'Get that cleaned,' Fareth instructed. 'Snare venom for sure. Make up the fire too!'

Her clothing was tattered, a simple grey smock, ripped and torn in places and coated in the tendrils of the snare. She was skinny too, as if she'd gone without food for too long.

Before long her wounds were cleaned and dressed with fresh linen.

'I'd say you got to her just in time,' Crenech said.

Fareth nodded. 'Half a spell more and the snare would have eaten her.'

Crenech noticed something and bent forward to look closer. He picked up the girl's limp wrist and turned it over, examining her palm and fingers.

'Interesting,' he said. 'Not a farm worker I would guess.'

'Yeah, skin's too soft, a maid? She's definitely not worked outside, that's for sure.'

'She's a waif of a thing,' Crenech said. 'I'd say she'd never scrubbed a floor or carried a pail in her life. Look at her skin, other than the bruises it's all smooth, her fingers are soft, fingernails neat. Not the type to go wandering in the wilderness.'

'So what was she doing out there?' Fareth asked. 'And on her own?'

Crenech looked at Joachim. 'You think you've seen her before?'

Joachim frowned. 'I don't know her, but I'd swear I've seen her in Viresia at some point. I can't place her though.'

The girl stirred, her eyes blinking open, dark and wide with fear. She panicked for a moment, a scream dying in her throat as she looked at the people clustered around her.

'It's alright,' Crenech said. 'You're safe from the snare.'

The girl looked at him, her breath coming in short gasps.

'It caught me …'

Crenech nodded. 'Nasty things,' he said. 'You were lucky to be found by these good folk.' He gestured at Fareth and his family. He saw her look around at them and then swallow.

'Thank you,' she managed. Her voice was soft, her accent refined. It was familiar enough too, she couldn't have come from far. Her pronunciation was Scallian.

A girl of breeding? Why was she out there alone?

'What's your name, child?' Crenech asked. 'And what happened to you?'

He saw her tense and swallow again.

'Please,' she said. 'Tell me where I am? This is not Drayden is it?'

'Drayden?' Crenech asked. 'Nay, lass! You're in my lands now. This is Scallia.'

The girl relaxed, her eyes closing with a deep sigh. Then she was crying.

Crenech looked at Fareth, who shrugged. He took the girl's hand.

'What happened to you?' he asked, trying to make his voice sound as gentle as possible.

'I escaped,' the girl managed to say.

'Escaped?' Joachim asked. 'From where?'

The girl made an effort to stop her sobs, sitting up and wiping at her eyes. After a few deep shuddering breaths she looked up at Crenech.

'From Drayden,' she said, her eyes wide and dark. 'From the priestesses!'

Then she fainted.

* * *

The girl had been given food and water and had revived in the warmth of Fareth's small house. She'd slept for half a stretch before waking again, ravenous for more food. Crenech broke out the provisions he had brought with him and shared them around. Then he, Joachim and Fareth sat with her.

'This is Fareth, a well-respected man of these parts,' Crenech said, introducing his companions. 'It is he and his family that rescued you from the snare.'

The girl looked at him and nodded. ‘You have my humble thanks,’ she said. ‘I thought I was dead.’

‘This is my servant, Joachim,’ Crenech continued. The girl looked at Joachim, but said nothing.

‘And I am Lord Crenech,’ Crenech finished with a smile. ‘These lands belong to me.’

‘Lord Crenech?’ the girl said. ‘Of Viresia?’

Crenech nodded. ‘Yes, the same. And who are you?’

‘My name is Gemma, my Lord,’ she answered. ‘I am the granddaughter of Lord Sequon, he took me in after my parents died in the plague …’

‘Then that’s where I saw you,’ Joachim said. ‘In the Viresian courts … ’

‘Sequon?’ Crenech exclaimed. ‘Then you’re one of the chosen tithe sent to Drayden a round ago?’

‘Yes my Lord. Prince Torin took us …’ She stopped at the look on his face.

And she has escaped from Drayden?

Crenech sat back and thought for a moment.

‘Can you tell me of Lord Sequon?’ Gemma asked. ‘Is he well?’

Crenech rubbed his chin.

‘Alas,’ he said, softly. ‘Lord Sequon is dead.’

‘Dead?’ she wailed. ‘How? Why?’

‘Killed by the high priestess herself,’ Joachim said. ‘After the city fell.’

The girl’s eyes were wide now. ‘The city? Viresia is fallen?’

Crenech nodded. ‘The priestesses defeated us in battle, Viresia is theirs now, though it still stands.’

Tears flooded her eyes at his words.

‘Then there is no escape from them …’

‘Much has happened since you were sent away,’ Crenech said. ‘But first … how did you escape from Drayden, are there others?’

Gemma shook her head. ‘No others, none but me.’

‘Then how?’

‘One of the priestesses set me free,’ Gemma said. ‘She smuggled me out of their city, flew me to the borders sunward of here on a dach. I walked from there, hoping to reach Viresia.'

Crenech frowned, shaking his head in confusion.

'Why would a priestess do such a thing?' he asked.

'She said she saved me for Scallia,' Gemma said. 'And that she was of Scallia herself.'

'Of Scallia?' Joachim echoed. 'A priestess? How can that be? Who was she?'

'She was young,' Gemma replied. 'Maybe five rounds older than me, but powerful, strong in their ranks, a warrior of their people.'

Crenech was leaning forward now.

'What was her name?'

Gemma looked up. 'She called herself … Kiri.'

CHAPTER TWO

Amaris, Capital of Amar

Round 2307, Seventh pass

A dimly lit cell.

Two women; two sisters.

One was bound in place by ropes at her wrists, arms and neck, defenceless, bloodied and hurt. The other stood nearby, holding a long blood-stained metal staff aloft, striding back and forth.

The kai, the weapon of the priestesses.

Kiri and Zoella. Sisters united only by a bond of hatred.

Zoella lifted the kai.

'And you killed Ren,' she screeched, howling her pain and misery. 'He was just a boy …'

The blow from the kai went wild, catching Kiri across the face. Kiri's head was knocked back against the chair and she slumped in her restraints.

Zoella grabbed forward with her other hand, lifting Kiri's chin again. Zoella saw blood flowing from her lips. Kiri's eyes rolled in her head, unfocused for a moment before she managed to look at Zoella.

'Not my fault,' Kiri whispered. 'I didn't want to hurt him …'

'No,' Zoella screeched, tears burning her eyes. 'Always lies. Always murder. Now it stops … stops forever!'

Zoella let go of Kiri and stepped back, raising the kai above her head, a screech of unbridled rage coming from her.

She saw Kiri look up at her, realising what was to come. Zoella saw the fear and hopelessness in her blue eyes, the dread …

Now die!

In a vicious swinging arc, Zoella brought the kai down.

'No!'

Something thumped into her, knocking her sideways. She lost her grip, the kai clattering to the floor. She slammed into the wall, stunned by the impact and sank to the floor, dizziness whirled about her. She blinked, trying to clear her vision.

Someone else was there. Rage boiled up within her.

You! How dare you interfere! How dare you …

Meru stood before her. He'd picked up the kai and was holding it out before him, pointing it towards her.

'Back off!' he yelled.

Zoella got to her feet, staggering. Meru was standing between her and Kiri.

'Get out of my way,' she snarled.

Meru shook his head, tears in his eyes. 'I won't let you do this.'

'Don't you see? She must die!' Zoella screamed at him. Anger, betrayal and sorrow fought for dominance in her mind. Anger won. She raised her hands towards him.

'No,' Meru said, raising the kai. Zoella stepped forward.

Don't make me hurt you! Because I will!

Meru was already swinging the kai. She heard him yell as her mental blow crushed around his mind, saw him stagger with pain.

It was too late. The blow from the kai was clumsy, but it connected with the side of her head. Bright lights flashed in her vision and then darkness swamped her.

* * *

Meru dropped the kai and ran to Zoella, pulling her up.

'Zoella!'

There was a cut on her temple and a bruise was already growing. She was unconscious, but she was still breathing. He lowered her to the floor as gently as he could.

No time, got to get out of here or …

Meru straightened and turned, pulling a knife from his belt. He stepped over to Kiri's prone body, still tied to the chair.

She was barely breathing. Her head had fallen forward, her body slumped in the ropes.

'Kiri? Kiri!'

She didn't respond. Her face was battered, one eye almost swollen shut, blood trickling from her mouth. A rattling gasp came from her, but that was all.

Meru cut the ropes around her ankles, waist, wrists and neck before moving forward to pick her up. Her body fell into his arms, lifeless.

As gently as he could he pulled her forward, lifting her up before swinging his arms under her. She yelped in pain and he felt her body spasm in his grip. Her head fell back, her eyes closed and her arms limp. Meru turned, staggered and made his way out of the cell with Kiri in his arms.

* * *

Coran gasped as the pain in his head evaporated in an instant.

It had been agonising, as if his head had been caught in a vice and crushed. Beside him Mel was crawling to her knees and Daf and Creg were pulling themselves up, Fitch likewise.

'We've got to stop her,' Mel managed.

'How do you suggest we do that?' Coran said, wincing. 'She has the same powers as the priestesses and she's clearly not afraid to use them on us.'

'She's hurt, upset … angry.'

Coran nodded, getting to his feet and pulling Mel up beside him. 'She's not the only one.'

'Aye,' Fitch muttered. 'And she's totally out of control.'

'Come on,' Coran yelled, pulling them all towards the exit.

All five raced downwards, their footsteps echoing on the stone flooring. They found the door, the two guards insensible on the floor. Coran was ahead and raced into the cell, skidding to a stop within.

Kiri was gone. Gore was splashed around the chair. Zoella, her face sprayed with blood, was lying dead or unconscious on the floor. Mel went straight to her, crouching down to check.

'She's alive,' Mel said, cradling Zoella's head in her lap. 'Coran … it's not her blood …'

'Then where is Kiri …?' Coran demanded.

Fitch inspected the chair where Kiri had been secured. He pulled at the ropes, holding up their ends.

'Ropes have been cut,' he said. He stooped to pick up the kai. It, too, was blood-stained.

'What happened?' Coran asked. 'Where is she? Daf, Creg! Kiri must have escaped somehow, go look. She can't have got far in that condition.'

The two big men retreated out of the cell. Coran heard their footsteps thump outside.

Mel stroked the hair out of Zoella's face. Coran could see a bruise across Zoella's right cheek and a cut across her forehead. He crouched down next to Mel.

'Zoella? Can you hear me?'

Zoella moaned and stirred, her eyelids fluttering.

'Can you hear me? What happened? Zoella!'

Her eyes opened and she looked around at them, her face a picture of bewilderment and confusion.

'She has to die … she should die.' Zoella's voice was a croak.

'What happened?' Coran demanded. 'Zoella, tell us what happened!'

Her expression crumpled. Tears formed and dripped down her cheeks as she sobbed, her body shaking in Mel's embrace. Coran watched as the girl slumped in Mel's grip.

'Zoella …' Mel said. 'You must tell us.'

Zoella tried to speak, but it was several moments before she was able to say anything.

'She's gone,' she stuttered in between choking sobs.

From outside a noise came, reverberating through the walls of the cell. Mel, Fitch and Coran stared at each other, recognising it immediately; the sound of engines, whirring up to speed.

'The medical transport,' Fitch whispered. 'Meru …'

'Shades,' Coran said. 'Mel, stay with her.'

Coran and Fitch raced from the cell, leaping up the stairs four at a time. They both ran across the Senate forecourt only to see Daf and Creg before them, both staring up into the sky.

The silhouette of the medical transport was already receding into the golden disk of Lacaille.

* * *

Meru waited until the altitude indicators levelled off. The medical transport was already above the clouds and heading sunwards. He throttled back the engines and triggered the autopilot. Sandra's tones responded as he expected.

'Maintain a sunward course,' he instructed.

'Autopilot engaged. Course zero, mark zero.'

'And Sandra,' he said. 'Switch off the radio and the remote flight controls.'

'Neither action is recommended …'

'Just do it!' Meru snapped.

Sandra's voice was as inflectionless as ever. 'Radio and remote flight control capability has been deactivated.'

Meru undid the flight harness and got up, satisfied for now. He walked backwards into the mid-section where the medical bays were housed.

Kiri was still there, lying where he had left her, unconscious in one of the surgery bays. She was secured by the straps he'd tied around her. Gently he loosened them, easing her around until she was lying on her back. He looked her over and swallowed.

'Shades …'

She was in a bad way, her face was swollen and a mixed colour of blue, black and yellow. Blood was congealed across her face. There were bandaged wounds up and down her body, stained with blood. The fingers on her right hand were bent at unnatural angles. Her breathing was coming in ragged gasps, wheezing as her chest rose and fell. Zoella had beaten her to within an inch of her life.

At least she's still breathing.

He activated the medical system as Caesar's training had instructed. Instruments popped out of the trays above the bay and he clipped them on to Kiri's arms. A moment later the small devices flashed and screens lit up above him. Sandra's voice sounded nearby.

'Scan underway, please standby.'

Meru waited, watching as a series of graphs and indicators appeared on the screens. He recognised some of them and could see they weren't telling good news. A pulsing flash of light flickered across Kiri's body, starting at the head and working down her body.

As the light moved it paused, Sandra's voice sounded again.

'External scan. Multiple lesions. Head trauma detected. Broken jaw. Three broken ribs. Broken femur. Penetrative wound to right thigh muscle and epidermis. Broken finger bones in right hand. Broken right wrist. Sensor input data follows. Blood pressure eighty two over sixty. Pulse fifty two.'

The lights flickered. Meru watched the graphs. They were all heading downwards.

'Indicators falling. Significant discrepancy from norm noted. Internal organ scan commencing.'

'Quickly!'

'Internal haemorrhaging detected,' Sandra's voice intoned.

'What does that mean?' Meru demanded.

'Internal organ damage has been noted,' Sandra replied. 'Blood loss is accelerating.'

Meru could see the pulse indicator was dropping. Kiri's skin was pale, and growing whiter with every passing moment.

'Blood pressure dropping outside of tolerance,' Sandra intoned.

'Heart rate continuing to drop. Atria and ventricle depolarisation in progress.'

'Do something!'

'Subject requires surgery,' Sandra said. 'Activate autonomous mode.'

Meru stared at the instruments, looking from one side of the displays to the other.

'Where? How do I ...?'

'Autonomous control is activated by selecting the mode descriptor from the available list of ...'

Meru jabbed at the screens, searching for the commands as Sandra read them out.

'... then select the appropriate routine from the selection provided.'

The monitors flashed red and an alarm blared. With horror, Meru saw the pulse rate drop to zero. The tone from the monitors became a constant drone.

'Cardiac arrest detected.'

'No!'

He jabbed at the controls again.

'Autonomous mode selected. Engage triage routine?'

'Yes!'

Cables snaked down from the roof of the bay. One moved towards Kiri's head. Meru watched in shock as two small nodules forced their way into her nose. The tube bifurcated further, expanding itself to cover her mouth. He heard a surge of pressure as air was forced into her lungs, saw her chest rise.

'Artificial respiration engaged.'

A series of mechanical appendages appeared next. They were metal, hinged and jointed in multiple places. Meru watched as they descended close to Kiri's chest. There was a bright flash of light and Kiri's tunic was sliced open. More appendages joined in pulling back the tattered shreds of the clothing and then placing two large metal fasteners on to her exposed skin.

'Cardio stimulation in progress. Stand clear.'

Meru stepped back.

There was a sharp buzz. Kiri's body jolted, her back arching for a moment before slumping to lie prone in the bay.

'No response, retrying.'

Again Kiri's body lurched and fell back.

'No response, retrying.'

'Please …' Meru whispered.

Kiri's body lurched a third time. There was no change to the constant tone of the monitor. It hummed, insistent and unarguable.

'No response,' Sandra said after a moment. 'Unable to proceed. Vital statistics continuing to drop. Time of death recorded as …'

'Try again,' Meru shouted. 'She's not dead. She's not!'

'Repeat cardio stimulation will not be effective,' Sandra intoned. 'Discontinuing resuscitation attempts. I am sorry, Meru.'

'No …'

The metal appendages detached and the tubes retreated back into their housings.

Meru grabbed Kiri's hand. It was cold. Her chest fell as her breath sighed out of her. Then she was still and silent.

Meru could hear nothing but the tone of the monitor.

'Kiri?' he whispered.

He closed his eyes, remembering how it felt when she had used her gift to speak into his mind.

Kiri! Don't leave me. Please!

The tone remained, steady, sure … mocking him. He searched deeper in his memories, wishing he had the power to push into her mind as she had into his.

You must be able to hear me, come back, come back!

The tone was interrupted and began pulsing again.

Bewildered, Meru opened his eyes and looked around at the displays. 'Sandra?'

'Spontaneous cardio reactivation detected. Reason unknown. Pulse rate now stabilising at nominal levels. Proceed to internal surgery?'

'Yes, yes!'

Meru stepped back as the tubes reappeared and the mechanical appendages made short work of the bandages that had been wrapped around Kiri. Yet another appendage appeared, this one containing a cylinder with a needle at one end. The needle pierced Kiri's right arm. At the same time another was fastened into her left, fluid began to move down it.

'Blood type AB-negative confirmed. Adjusting antigen mix.'

Then a bright beam of light flashed across Kiri's abdomen. Meru watched in horror as an incision was made and then the appendages proceeded to pull the flesh apart. Tiny manipulators entered her body. Blood trickled from the wound.

He swallowed, feeling sick, lightheaded and dizzy. He had to turn away and staggered across the room to lean against the bay on the other side.

'Surgery is proceeding normally,' Sandra said.

'Oh good,' Meru said, and sank to the floor.

* * *

'Stole it?' Henoch exclaimed.

Coran nodded. 'Nobody else can fly it. It has to have been Meru. He was aboard under medical care himself.'

Henoch and Janaid had heard the medical transport take off and had come running. By the time they reached the plaza where the machine had stood it had disappeared over the sunward horizon.

'But why?' Janaid demanded. 'And where is he going?'

'The witch girl that was washed ashore,' Coran said. 'He's taken her.'

'But she was locked in the cells,' Henoch said. 'She was to be tried for her crimes, we were only just discussing what to do early this stretch …'

Henoch stopped at the look on Coran's face.

'What's happened?'

'There's been–' Coran began.

'Zoella tried to kill her,' Fitch interrupted.

'What?' Janaid asked. His expression was bewildered. 'The young woman with the mental powers?'

'Fitch …' Coran said.

'Snuttin' near beat her to death,' Fitch added. 'I'm guessing Meru intervened.'

'Zoella wanted revenge,' Coran said. 'For past wrongs, hurts …'

'And you let her?' Henoch demanded.

'No,' Fitch replied. 'She used her powers to force her way past us and then to deal out her own justice.'

'But there are laws that must be applied,' Henoch said. 'We can't have people taking things into their own hands, it would be chaos. Where is she now?'

Coran turned to see Mel emerge from the building behind.

'Zoella?' he asked.

'Out cold,' Mel said, looking at the four men. 'Looks like she took a blow to the head, there's a big lump on her head. I guess that must have been Meru. Zoella is still in the cell for now. Otherwise, she seems fine.'

'Fine?' Fitch scoffed. 'Other than her trying to crunch our brains … yeah she's absolutely dandy.'

'You goaded her on,' Mel snapped.

''Cause she was right about the witch,' Fitch said.' But then she lost it and tried to do away with us. She needs to be locked up permanently.'

'Agreed,' Henoch said.

'We can't imprison her,' Mel protested.

'She used her powers on you?' Henoch asked. 'Then certainly she should be locked away, the law is clear. I understand her motivations, but to assault …'

'Zoella was overwrought,' Coran said. 'Ren's death, she and the boy were close …'

'She's traumatised,' Mel said, with a glare. 'Locking her up will do her no good. Let me talk to her …'

Coran shook his head. 'No, that's too dangerous. We've no idea what she'll do when she wakes; we have to take precautions.'

Henoch nodded. 'Agreed. Guards!'

'Alright!' Mel said. 'If we're going to do this, let me do it rather than those brutes.'

'Tied hand and foot,' Fitch said. 'And a blindfold. Seems to stop the witch's powers if they can't see.'

'She's not a witch!' Mel snapped.

'I don't see no difference,' Fitch replied.

'That's because you don't care about anyone save yourself,' Mel said. Fitch's right eye twitched.

'Enough,' Coran said. 'Bind her up while she's still out. Then, nobody is going anywhere near her …'

Mel was shaking her head.

'You must let me stay with her,' Mel said. 'She can't be left alone. She's distraught, upset, hurting …'

Coran shook his head. 'No way, what if she attacks you?'

'That's the deal,' Mel snapped, jutting out her chin. 'Or I won't let you tie her up.'

Coran looked at Mel's expression, it was clear there was no more room for negotiation.

'House arrest then,' Henoch said. 'That will suffice until we determine what must be done.'

Coran nodded. 'One of us will be outside at all times. If there's any hint …'

'Help me take her to our house,' Mel said. 'We'll use one of the upstairs rooms. I'm not having her lying in a cold cell, she's not a prisoner. She needs our help.'

Fitch and Coran exchanged a look, but complied.

'And what of Meru?' Henoch asked. 'We need to bring him back.'

Coran nodded. 'Fitch, get down to the *Mobilis*. Let's hope the radio is working, see if you can raise Meru. Tell him there'll be no recriminations if he comes back. The witch-girl won't be harmed and that we've … dealt with Zoella.'

'Aye, Captain.' Fitch nodded.

Coran turned to Mel. 'Let's get her to the house.'

* * *

Meru had climbed into the medical ship's cockpit to check the instrumentation whilst he waited. The medical ship was still flying straight and true, heading sunwards. A couple of chimes passed before Sandra's voice interrupted his reverie.

'Surgery completed. Subject is now stable. Please acknowledge.'

Meru swung around and walked to the medical bays.

Kiri was lying there as before, but already Meru could see a remarkable improvement. The cuts and wounds were reduced, somehow knitted together, though it was still clear where they were. The incision on her abdomen was obvious, but it was small, neat and sealed. The bruising around her face was still pronounced, but even that was fading. The fingers in her right hand had been set and were strapped together. Her leg and wrist were also strapped tight. Even her skin had been cleaned, the blood stains washed away. Restraints held her in place by the ankles, wrists, chest and head. Her left hand was covered, as always, in the tight-fitting leather glove she always wore.

He crouched down near her, smoothing the black hair from her face. Her breathing was slow but regular and there was colour back in her skin. He ran his fingers across her cheek.

So weak and frail, so unlike how she was. But she's alive, she's going to be alright.

His breathing quickened, stirred as it had always been by her presence. He remembered when he had first seen her, standing in the dusty courtyards outside of Viresia, calling King Ioric out to fight her. Then she had seemed only the brutal warrior, fearsome and intimidating. He had still admired her.

Later he had been on the receiving end of her brutality himself.

But then things changed.

Some shared understanding had grown between them without either being aware of it, through the trials and adversity of that first flare they had grown into a strange shared experience. She had the chance to capture him, but she had spared him. He had seen an unexpected tender side to her, beneath the warrior there was compassion and gentleness.

And then …

He remembered her in the dimly lit chambers of a room in Taloon. She hadn't been gentle then, but burning with lust and desire, and no less determined to get her own way. But she remained mercurial, unpredictable. She had been thrown into a frenzy when Zoella had refused to work with her. His heart pounded when he recalled her scream when he had abandoned her to return home.

Kiri had raged against Amar. She had attacked them along with the other priestesses. She had fought them; brought death and destruction upon them.

If I had stayed with her then, maybe that wouldn't have happened …

Meru's head dropped until his forehead was resting on the edge of the medical bay.

And to save her I've betrayed my friends, abandoned my home and fled. I am a traitor, just like Zoella said! Saving a priestess of Drayden, the enemy. I'm alone …

He trembled at the thought. Brief images of Coran, Mel and the rest of the crew swamped his mind.

My parents …

More images. Then one final mental picture. Accusing, angry, lips pursed in disapproval, hurt and anguish.

Zoella …

Pangs of guilt and shame lanced through him, his blood ran cold for a moment. He was alone, cut off from his friends and his own people. Then rage boiled with him as he thought of Zoella's brutal attack.

She tried to kill Kiri in cold blood! She was defenceless, and they didn't stop her …

He couldn't allow it. Not Kiri. He trembled and then looked up.

Kiri's face was before him, now serene and calm. Looking at her drove the pain away and he was lost in admiration once more.

Just look at her. She's not the evil woman they say she is. She is worth it ...

He stretched out his hand to stroke her cheek once more, brushing the dark hair away from her face. He stayed that way for long moments before the beeping of the medical bay instrumentation interrupted his dreaming.

'How is she?' Meru asked.

'Would you like a status report?' Sandra replied.

Meru nodded. 'Yes, give me a status report.'

One of the console screens flashed up a series indicators. Meru peered at them.

Subject identity unknown, no subcutaneous transponder detected.

'Her name is Kiri,' he said.

'Noted,' Sandra said. 'Subject identified as Kiri.'

Sex, female.

Estimated age, 22 rounds, 4 passes.

Pulse and Blood Pressure below stat but within plus minus 25% thresholds.

Blood chemistry below stat but within plus minus 5% thresholds.

Respiration nominal.

Subject sedated post surgery.

IV painkillers, anti-biotics and anti-inflammatories continuing.

Warning! Nano-infusion at 832% of maximum values.

Warning! Post operative. No strenuous activity to be undertaken for seven stretches.

Meru frowned.

That phrase! Nano-infusion ... that's what Caesar said about Zoella ...

'What is nano-infusion?' he asked.

'Nano-infusion is the augmentation or replacement of biological functions for administrators,' Sandra replied. 'It is typically used to support immune deficiencies or provide additional physiological and or psychological capabilities.'

'What does that mean?'

'Please restate the question.'

'What sort of capabilities does this nano stuff give?'

'In addition to supporting immune deficiencies, nano-infusion is designed to provide mesh communications, authentication and authorisation, remote telemetry and knowledge management.'

Meru blinked. He had no idea what Sandra was talking about.

'So why does Kiri have so much?'

There was a characteristic pause. Meru could only assume Sandra was sifting through her vast stores of knowledge.

'There is no previous record of excessive nano-infusion levels in an administrator.'

'Is it dangerous?'

'There is no data on the subject, however scans have not detected any contraindications. Subject Kiri remains stable and recovering from sustained injuries. She will regain consciousness in approximately two chimes.'

'You said she was an administrator,' Meru asked. 'What does that mean?'

'Subject Kiri is identified as an administrator due to the nano-infusion signature,' Sandra answered. 'This means she has leadership, governance, control and communication responsibilities as per Esurio founding statute.'

Just like Zoella ... an administrator ...

* * *

Zoella had been carried to the house by Daf and Creg under Mel's watchful eye. There Mel had seen to her, bathing the bruise on her head with a cold compress. Zoella looked pale, but otherwise unhurt. She had not regained consciousness.

Mel sat by her side, looking at her.

She hates me for my part in Ren's death. I can understand her grief, but she was such a gentle soul, what has made her so hard and cruel in such a small space of time? How did she come to the point she could murder in cold blood? Such hatred ...

She stroked Zoella's wavy brown hair back from her face.

There was a creak from behind her. She heard a key turn and then the door opened. It was Coran.

'Any change?' he asked.

Mel shook her head. 'Still out cold. I guess Meru hit her pretty hard.'

'I imagine he was forced to,' Coran said, looking down at Zoella. 'He probably had only a moment before she would have turned her powers on him. Judging by the blood in that cell she almost killed that witch ... Kiri ... whatever her name is. She may not even have survived.'

Mel nodded. 'Did Fitch ...?'

Coran shook his head.

'No answer,' he said. 'Looks like Meru has the radio switched off on the medical ship. Fitch couldn't get hold of him.'

Mel held her head in her hands.

'Where's he gone?' she asked. 'And more importantly, how are we going to get him back?'

'For now,' Coran said, 'we can only hope he tries to get in contact with us. Perhaps when he feels he's got this girl of his safe, assuming she's alive, he'll be willing to talk.'

Coran looked at Zoella again.

'Do you know what was going on between these three?' he asked. 'Zoella seemed kind, gentle and then ...'

'Just completely lost it,' Mel agreed. 'Ren's death pushed her over the edge? I don't know. She and Meru had definitely had words and this Kiri girl was right in the middle of all of it. They got mixed up in Taloon, picked up more refugees ...'

'Sounds to me like this Kiri has addled Meru's brains,' Coran said. 'He's risking life and limb to save her.'

Mel looked up. 'That's what love does.'

Coran sighed. 'Well, there's nothing much we can do until he gets back in touch. What about her?'

'I'm guessing it's shock,' Mel said. 'Lots of stuff going on. Zoella said Kiri was her sister. Meru slept with Kiri. A right old mess.'

'I'm no expert on these things,' Coran said. 'But Zoella and Meru weren't … well, it's not just a jealous rage …'

Mel shook her head. 'No. Zoella and Meru were friends, but not like that. Pretty sure of it anyway. No, this is something else. Zoella's not jealous, this was pure hatred … never seen anything like it. She'd become incensed … she wasn't like that before. Something changed in her like a switch was flipped.'

Coran nodded, remembering Zoella's frenzied expression and the way she attacked them.

'We'd better hope we can flip her back,' Coran said. 'Zoella and Meru never got to the Obelisk. We need her, we've still got to deal with that somehow.'

Mel nodded.

'What about this other girl,' Coran asked, 'and the children who came with her?'

'Zoella said her name was Ira,' Mel said. 'All of them seem to be mute, they have some kind of sign language, but I don't know how to use it. Zoella had learnt to talk to them.'

'So we need Zoella for that too,' Coran said. 'Stay with her, let's hope we can reason with her when she wakes up.'

* * *

Kiri blinked. Her vision was blurred. Strange colours flickered above her and faint sounds came to her ears. She had no idea where she was. For a moment all was confusion.

Come to kill me?

Something like that.

Memories surfaced. Pain and agony. Being hit. She gasped.

A woman, a woman with a staff, hitting her repeatedly. A blur of motion.

Sister! Zoella!

The words flickered into her mind and she let out a yelp of fear.

Meru ... please ... help me!

A voice sounded, but she couldn't make out the words. A face, fuzzy, unrecognisable.

She's going to ...

The voice brought back other memories. A shout, a scuffle. Her body being hoisted up. More pain and then blackness.

Meru?

She blinked again. Meru's face swam into focus before her.

'Lie still, don't move.' His voice was soft and gentle.

'Where ...?' She looked around, bemused at the coloured lights all around her.

'You're safe,' he said. 'We're safe.'

'She was going to ...' Kiri's voice was high with fright.

She felt his fingers brush across her forehead. 'I know, but we escaped. It's alright. It's just you and me now. You're safe.'

She tried to move, but she felt Meru's hand press down on her.

'Don't,' he said. 'You were hurt, you need to rest.'

The memories were clearer now. The confrontation with Zoella. Her sister's murderous intent ...

'You rescued me?' she asked. She tried to move, but found she couldn't. Something held her in place.

'Wait a moment,' Meru said, reaching and pressing something above her. 'Restraints to keep you safe.'

There was a faint hiss and Kiri felt something move around her.

'There, you can move now. Just ... slowly. Be careful.'

She moved her hand up towards him, frowning as it felt heavy. It was secured in an ornate bandage, holding her fingers in place.

Zoella broke them ...

Meru took her hand in his, his palms wrapping hers.

More memories. The fight on the wall. Nerina, Rihanna ...

They betrayed me ...

The man with the hat, fighting to defend the machinery.

He fought well, a worthy opponent ...

The boy.

She gasped, the memory horrific to recall.

I killed him. I killed that child. Why was he even in the fight?

'Kiri?'

Her face crumpled into despair, tears flowing down her cheeks.

Like Tia, so like Tia, but my fault, I did it!

She felt Meru gasp her hand tighter. She tried to pull it away but she was too weak.

No ...

But there was nothing she could do about it. Memories surged around her, Meru could see everything. Their memories entwined.

The boy. His name was Ren. Meru knew him. Meru had been rescued by him. He was part of the crew of the metal ship. The *Mobilis*.

Anger!

Kiri heard a gasp. Meru let go of her hand.

She looked at him. His mouth was open; she could see he was shaking.

'I didn't mean to kill him,' she breathed. 'I didn't know, I just ...' He voice tailed off at the look on his face.

He hates me for it, for what I've done. Killing that boy.

'Show me,' he said, grabbing her wrist, squeezing so hard it hurt.

Kiri moaned, but she was too weak to resist.

The pain in my leg. Stabbed! Spinning around. The knife at my throat. A knee in my thigh. The agony! Roll, stop the knife ... blood! A child? Horror ...

Meru's grip on her wrist relaxed.

'Ren?' Meru whispered. 'He was just a child.'

'You must hate me,' she said, looking at the anger on his face. She swallowed, sensing the rage and fury building in him. He was trembling, shaking with emotion.

He's going to end me ... I can't blame him. The boy was his friend ...

She pursed her lips, looking away, accepting her responsibility. She had killed the boy, it was only right that she should make amends. He was like Tia, an innocent …

Without me Meru can go back to his people, Zoella has her revenge, my death would atone for it, at least in part!

'I understand,' she whispered. 'Please, just … make it quick …'

'What?' he said, after a moment, his expression bewildered. 'No, not you … you mustn't think that …'

She shivered, looking at him.

'It wasn't your fault,' he managed. He was shaking his head. 'It was theirs. They put him in harm's way. Why would they do that?'

Tears coursed down her cheeks. She was gasping for air, the sobs snatching her breath away. The sadness didn't relent; something had broken in her, a torrent of pent up rawness that swamped her thoughts. She could only see him, his own face wet with tears.

What has happened to me?

With the little strength she had she beckoned him down towards her. Kiri's thoughts surged; sudden gratitude at being alive, still having a chance to change things, a chance to put things right …

You saved me … I thought I was going to die!

The answer was immediate, full of regret and pain.

'I should have stayed with you when I had the chance. It might have stopped all this. Can you forgive me?'

Forgive you? Of course! I should have been honest with you … I lied … I'm sorry.

She felt his hand upon her cheek.

'I won't leave you again.'

I know you won't.

There could be no lies, not via this strange connection between them. She could feel his thoughts, his regret and self-recrimination. She could also sense the grief and anxiety of betraying his friends and home. She understood what he had given up for her.

Likewise, her own feelings washed across them both, unrestrained. Her regret over lying to him and forcing him to leave, her own loneliness, pain and anguish over being betrayed by her people, the horror of killing the boy, but the joy of being wanted, being loved, a solace that took her back to the warm comfort she remembered from her long lost mentor, Charis.

The effort was exhausting. She sank into whatever it was she was lying on, weary from the strain. She closed her eyes, she could feel the pulse of Meru's heart through his touch. Neither of them moved for a spell, to overwrought to speak.

* * *

Zoella stirred.

She blinked, her eyes staring upwards. She could see nothing but a blur. Screams howled in her mind.

Murderer! Killer!

Snatches of memory flashed around her. Meru, his expression torn and hurt.

I won't let you do this!

Blood. Blood on her fingers. Kiri's blood. Kiri who had caused all the hurt, Kiri who had killed Ren.

She has to die!

Rage boiled in her, a redness sweeping her vision. Kiri had escaped. Kiri wouldn't answer for her crimes!

It would be murder by our laws! Is that what we're sinking to?

Zoella twisted and turned, but the voices would not let her be. Mel, trying to be reasonable, but wrong! So wrong!

Nothing stopping us from sticking an axe in her right now …

Yes! The strange man with the stupid hat was right. Kill her, kill her now!

Back down, Zoella …

The captain. He thought he was in charge. Who was he to tell her what to do? He didn't know what she had suffered. How could he? Ignorant man!

You can't stop me, none of you can.

Redness subsumed her. There was nothing but fury.

* * *

Kiri wondered whether she might have fallen asleep, she wasn't sure. She came to notice lights and coloured panels were all about her. Above her head was a strange bulkhead, all metal, festooned with lights and little hatches and compartments.

She felt stronger than before, more alert, less tired.

'Where are we?' she whispered.

Meru stirred alongside her.

'You're aboard a ship,' he said, his voice low. 'A flying machine. A medical ship.'

'One of the flying machines?' Kiri's eyes opened in wonder, focusing on the lights about her, they were glowing against the roof and walls, pulsing on and off around her.

She sat up.

'Careful!' Meru said, supporting her. 'You're injured, broken bones, you mustn't strain ...'

Kiri looked down at herself. She was lying in a bed of sorts, a soft material that had somehow taken the outline shape of her body. Her right hand was wrapped in the strange ornate bandages, keeping her fingers immobile. Her leg and wrist were likewise bandaged securely. She could see the wounds on her arms and legs were treated, cleansed and healed. There was a thin red welt across her stomach. There was a little pain, but it was more of a general ache throughout her body.

Her clothing was nowhere in evidence.

She looked at Meru, raising an eyebrow and tilting her head to one side.

'The injuries,' he stammered. 'It was ... I mean, the machine couldn't ... I'll get you some clothes. There are some in the sleeping quarters ...'

She laughed.

'Don't bother,' she said. 'After everything, I don't think I have much to hide from you.'

'Are you warm enough?' Meru asked. 'Sandra said …'

'Sandra? Who's Sandra?'

'She's the voice of the ship,' Meru said and then looked up. 'It's hard to … Sandra, why don't you explain?'

Before Kiri could say anything more she heard a strange woman's voice, it was oddly metallic and distant, but clear and precise. She had heard it once before, in Meru's crashed flying machine, back in Drem.

'Sandra is the designation given by Meru for the onboard voice interface facility of semi-autonomous vessels.'

'Oh,' Kiri replied, looking at Meru.

'Just introduce yourself,' Meru prompted.

'But there's no one there,' Kiri whispered.

'Just try it,' Meru said.

Kiri frowned for a moment, but then spoke. 'Hello Sandra, how are you?'

'Hello Kiri,' the voice replied. 'I am operating within normal parameters, thank you. You have recovered from surgery and are now recuperating.'

'Sir … gerry?' Kiri asked.

'Sandra … fixed you,' Meru said. 'You were hurt, inside.'

Kiri looked down at her stomach, seeing the red welt.

'You had extensive injuries,' Sandra said. 'All damage has been repaired.'

'Can I get up?'

'That is permissible,' Sandra replied. 'However caution is advised.'

Kiri swung her legs out and down until her feet were resting on the floor. It was cold to the touch of her bare soles.

The whole machine is made of metal …

She sat there for a moment, regaining her equilibrium.

'Alright?' Meru asked, sitting alongside her.

She nodded. The truth was she already felt dizzy. She took some deep breaths to clear her head. Then she stood up.

And regretted it.

She felt light headed, the room wobbled before her eyes and she swayed. She felt Meru's arms about her waist and she sank back against him.

So weak! I've never been so weak …

'You need to rest,' Meru said, his voice close in her ear. 'Sleep.'

She nodded. Even though she had just woken, sleep sounded wonderful.

'There is space available in the living accommodation in the rear of this vehicle,' Sandra said.

Kiri looked and could see the corridor leading away. It was mere paces away.

'I'm not sure I'll make it …'

'I'll carry you.'

'I don't need to be carried …' she said, pushing him away and trying to stand up on her own.

She saw Meru watch as another wave of dizziness washed over her. She staggered and he caught her. She sighed.

'Last time I was hurt this bad I wouldn't let you carry me,' she said, a faint smile on her face. 'I guess I should learn from my mistakes.'

That seems like so long ago. We were mortal enemies then, forced together in the ruin of the first flare when Shanza died …

Meru gently picked her up. It felt good to be carried, but alarming in the same measure. She had never felt the desire for such closeness before and part of her was horrified by how much she enjoyed the comfort of Meru's embrace. Her fierce independent spirit railed against it. She forced herself to relax and allowed her head to rest against his shoulder. It felt right in a way she could not describe.

She watched as he carried her through a narrow corridor. Beyond, a room opened out before her. She could see large panelled windows beyond which lay thick vegetation of a dark-hued green. Rain water was trickling down the glass on the other side.

'We're not flying …' she said.

'I've landed the ship,' Meru explained. 'We've flown hundreds of marks sunward.'

Kiri squinted through the window.

'Where are we?'

'I'm not sure, I don't think anyone has ever been here before.'

She could sense the weariness in his voice.

'How long have you been awake?'

'It's past the eighth chime. We've been gone a stretch and a half already.'

'You've been awake all that time?'

'Yeah, had to ...'

There was a pair of beds in the room, each underneath the windows. Kiri found herself lowered into one.

'You need to rest,' Meru said.

'So do you,' Kiri replied. She could see the dark rings under his eyes. He was exhausted.

'I'll just get those ...'

Panic washed over her; unexpected and alarming in its intensity. She reached up toward him instinctively, without even thinking.

No. I can't be alone. Not now, not ever.

The reaction was visceral, strong and startling. She gasped, her body trembling.

'Hey, it's alright.'

Stay with me. I need you.

Her gaze was locked on his.

He lay down on the bed alongside her. Kiri wriggled across and he draped his arm across her. She luxuriated in the warmth from his body. Within moments they were curled up together; both exhausted, both weary, but both drawing comfort from their shared closeness, bodies entwined. Sleep stole up on them and smothered them in its welcome shroud.

After a moment Sandra dimmed the illumination in the room and shuttered the external windows.

Lost in their dreams, neither Kiri nor Meru noticed.

* * *

Zoella's eyes were open, and her mouth was moving, but no sound came out.

Mel leant forward cautiously.

'Zoella?' she whispered. 'Can you hear me?'

There was barely a response. Zoella's body twitched, her shoulders tensing. Her breath snapped in and out in rapid flurries, her eyes moving in her head. But no words came, no recognition.

'Zoella ...'

Mel smoothed down Zoella's hair and pressed a damp towel to her forehead. Zoella flinched. Mel waved a hand in front of her, but Zoella's eyes didn't focus, they just kept staring upwards. The shivers continued.

Mel grabbed the girl's hand, pressing against her fingers. There was no return gesture. Mel stroked the back of Zoella's hand. Zoella stopped moving, her eyes still open and staring up.

Tears formed in Mel's eyes.

'I'm sorry about Ren,' she said, stuttering between her sobs. 'Dear little Ren. We all loved him, all of us ...'

Zoella twitched again, but then lay still.

'You must know I didn't mean for him to die. He was so brave, he wanted to do something. He was the only one who could fly the ships, he was so good at it. Without him we would have lost the battle. He saved Fitch's life, he probably saved all of us ...'

Mel squeezed Zoella's hand again. There was still no response.

'Zoella ... Please come back to us ...'

CHAPTER THREE

Sunward of Amar

Round 2307, Seventh pass

Coran saw Fitch beckoning from the deck of the flying cargo transporter. The big vessel was blackened and burnt after the defence of Amar, parked just outside the city limits.

'You want the good news, the not so good news, or the bad news?'

Coran raised his eyebrows.

'I'll take the good news,' he said.

'Well, that's mixed up with the bad news,' Fitch said with a shrug. 'I haven't been able to raise Meru at all. Reckon he's ignoring us.'

'Reckon you're right,' Coran said. 'So?'

Fitch grinned. 'That's where the good news comes in. I know where he is.'

Coran's expression brightened. 'You do? Where? How?'

'Used my noggin,' Fitch said. 'Come have a look.'

Fitch gestured to the bridge of the big machine. Coran clambered in behind him.

'These infernal machines have another one of those funny voices,' Fitch said. 'Meru's gone and called it "Sandra" of all things, but it turns out to be quite useful.'

'Go on.'

Fitch pointed at a display.

'It's a map,' he said and then raised his voice. 'Sandra, show me the position of the medical transport.'

On the screen before them, Coran could see the map zoom out, widening in all directions. He could make out Amar, where a small collection of dots was marked.

'Those are our machines,' Fitch said.

As the map continued to widen, the Scattered Isles and the coastline of the continent to the sunward and shaderight came into view. Another dot was marked on a small island some distance sunward of Amar. A pulsating circle of light ringed the dot.

'That's where he is right now,' Fitch said smugly. 'And we can track him wherever he goes.'

'How?' Coran asked.

'Tell 'im, Sandra.'

Coran recognised the odd female tones of the onboard voice.

'All autonomous vessels carry transponders allowing triangulation of location. Position is accurate to within a quarter of a mark.'

Coran looked at Fitch. 'You figured that out?'

Fitch looked aggrieved. 'I'll let you stew on it next time if that's your attitude.'

Coran grinned. 'You've done good.'

'There's more,' Fitch said. 'Sandra, status report on the medical transport.'

'Medical Transport has landed at indicated co-ordinates. All telemetry is normal. Two occupants are aboard.'

'So Meru's alright,' Coran said, with a sigh. 'And he has that girl with him.'

Fitch nodded. 'Nice cosy little love nest, eh?'

'Can we call the transport back?'

Fitch shook his head. 'Sandra says no.'

'The medical transport's autonomous flight mode has been disabled,' Sandra said, by way of explanation.

'Meru isn't stupid,' Coran acknowledged.

'Not that stupid, anyway …'

'He probably figured we would try to call him back.'

Fitch nodded.

'So that was the good news and the bad news,' Coran said. 'What's the not so good news?'

'Reports from the fisherman seem to favour that those scorchin' witches weren't all wiped out in the flare. Seems they may have retreated to the Scattered Isles.'

'You reckon they'll come back?' Coran asked.

'I wouldn't if I were them,' Fitch said. 'I'd get home, lick my wounds and then think again. But no real telling what they might do.'

Coran nodded. 'We need to get out there and find out what they're up to.'

'Which brings me to the last thing,' Fitch said. 'Sandra says the flying machines are in a bad way, they need some fancy word ...'

'Maintenance,' Sandra prompted.

'Yeah that ...' Fitch said.

'Let me guess,' Coran said. 'We need to take them back to Caesar's hangar to fix them.'

'That would be the fastest route,' Fitch acknowledged. 'They're busted up pretty bad so it seems, but Sandra says they can fix themselves given enough time, just not quickly.'

Coran cursed and thought for a moment before letting out a deep breath.

'What about the *Mobilis*?'

'She was banged up pretty bad too,' Fitch said. 'But's she's a tough old trouper. Reckon Mel will have her seaworthy in a few stretches. If you can spare her that is ...'

'I'll see what I can do,' Coran replied.

'So ... er ... how is our resident witch?'

Coran shook his head. 'Mel says she's just ... gone away inside her mind somewhere. She's just lying there, staring at the ceiling. Doesn't respond to anything. Mel's staying with her, hoping that she'll snap out of it ...'

'She might never come back,' Fitch said. 'Some folks who see too much, something snaps in their brains, they just wither away and ...'

'Not Zoella,' Coran said. 'We're going to get her back. Somehow ...'

* * *

Kiri blinked awake. She was lying where she had fallen asleep, a blanket draped across her. She stretched and sat up, looking around. Meru was nowhere to be seen, but she could hear a sizzling sound from somewhere nearby. A delicious aroma reached her nostrils and her stomach rumbled.

Cooked herg!

A tunic and trousers had been placed at the foot of the bed, she grabbed them and dressed herself. She got to her feet, taking a moment to gather herself. Her body felt stiff and sore, but she felt far better than she had. The restraints around her fingers were gone. She turned her hands over, flexing her fingers. They were stiff, but they were working.

Healed already …

She walked towards the sizzling sound, finding herself in the mid-section of the flying machine. It was some kind of galley. Meru was already dressed, cooking. As she watched he replaced a knife alongside a set of others on the wall. She looked at it in surprise, it stayed put, somehow sticking in place.

He turned as she entered, and smiled at her.

'You're looking much better.'

'I feel better,' she said. 'That smells good …'

Meru handed her a plate of food and a fork. She accepted it and began eating.

'How are you feeling?' he asked.

'Good,' she answered, between mouthfuls. 'Sore, but …' Her voice trailed off.

'I'm sorry for what happened,' Meru said. 'For what she …'

Memories returned to her. Zoella's fury and the pain, but even that was blotted out by stabbing guilt. The blood, the boy's life ebbing away beneath her. She'd killed him, just a child …

'I'm the one who should be apologising,' Kiri interrupted, her voice shaking. 'That boy …'

Meru shook his head. 'That wasn't your fault.'

I killed him ... his blood is on my hands. If I hadn't, Meru wouldn't have been forced to run ... Zoella wouldn't have ...

'And what happened to me wasn't yours,' Kiri said, unable to repress a shudder. 'She was going to kill me ...'

Meru nodded. 'I've never seen her do anything like that before, it was like she was mad ...'

'It's this power. I've felt that rage,' Kiri said, bowing her head. 'It's like something inside takes over ... when I've lost people ...' She looked up. 'I understand why she wanted to hurt me. This power, it's made me kill before.'

'Torin,' Meru whispered.

Kiri nodded. 'Him ... and a guard before that.' She looked pale. 'The rage, the hatred ... it takes over. I tortured them and I enjoyed it. I wanted to inflict pain, it felt good ...' Her voice cracked.

'I remember,' Meru said.

Kiri swallowed. She had tortured Meru too once, forced her way into his mind, hurting him, enjoying the feeling as she did so.

'I ...'

'Look, we could keep apologising for past wrongs forever,' he said, trying a smile.

Kiri didn't return it. Her mind kept flashing the image of the boy over and over in her mind. She heaved a sigh, forcing the memory away.

'I don't know what to do,' she said.

'Do you know what happened to the rest of the priestesses?' Meru asked. 'I don't remember anything, I must have been knocked out in the crash.'

'There was a flare from Lacaille,' Kiri said. 'Unexpected, no one saw it coming. I threw myself into the water. It was dark and cold. My next memory was being hauled up by a crowd of people, beaten and thrown in a cell, then ...'

Meru squeezed her hands gently.

'I saw none when we left,' he said. 'I'm guessing they fled or were destroyed. The invading ships were wrecked, burnt and smashed, and the city smouldering. Seems we … the Amarans … won.'

'They betrayed me,' Kiri said, thinking back and shuddering, her voice distant. 'On the walls of Amar. The high priestess Nerina and the others. They were waiting for the right time, to take my powers. I only just escaped but …'

She held out her hands, looking at them, turning them over and then running her fingers across her palms.

'… my powers are weaker. Nerina took them. I'm less strong.' She looked up at Meru. 'But the rage isn't there now. I don't want to hurt people any more. I'm not like them …'

Meru took her hands in his.

'Then we're both alone,' he said. 'You can't go back to your people and I can't go back to mine. That leaves just you and me.'

Kiri looked at him. Images of the boy came back. Blood, pain, screams …

He's isolated on account of me, because of what I did. Because I'm still alive … He's left his people behind. That's not fair … I should have died there … either at Nerina's hand or Zoella's. Meru would be … and he still can be!

She looked up, eyeing the set of kitchen knives that hung on the wall.

'Then you should turn this flying machine around and go back,' she said.

'No …'

'You can't give up your friends and your people for me,' she said. 'Leave me somewhere, it doesn't matter where …'

'No way …'

'Meru, you have a home, parents and friends. You have to go to them, they still love you. You can still fix things with them. Say I overpowered you and escaped, say anything that makes sense …'

'I am not leaving you.'

'You have to,' Kiri said, tears growing in her eyes. 'I can't go with you, can I? I killed that boy, whether it was an accident or not … I killed him.'

'It was a fight,' Meru countered. 'He attacked you, you defended yourself …'

'They will never forgive that and they'll never forgive you if you protect me. I've seen what you'd be giving up, your friends, your parents … I will not ask that of you.'

'That's my choice to make,' Meru said.

Kiri shook her head.

No, Meru. I won't let you …

She got to her feet, lurching across the small galley. Meru saw where she was headed.

'No!' he cried, scrambling after her.

Kiri managed to grab one of the knives and was turning its edge towards her throat as Meru caught her wrist.

'Don't do this!' he shouted, struggling to twist the knife out of her grasp.

She was weak, but her grip was still firm. They thrashed back and forth, both trying to gain control.

'Drop it!' Meru yelled. 'Don't …'

He turned her wrist and then crunched it down on the table. Kiri yelped and the knife clattered to the ground. Meru kicked it away and grabbed her wrists, pulling her around.

'I am not leaving you,' he shouted. 'I didn't try so hard to save your life just for you to throw it away!'

She wouldn't look at him.

With one hand he turned her head to him.

'I love you.'

The strength went out of her body. He felt her go limp in his grasp. She sucked in her breath, gasping.

'Meru … no …'

'Whatever happens,' he said, pulling her close, 'whatever the future holds, you and I will face it together.

Trembles shook her, conscious thought was banished, tears blurred in her eyes. Kiri sobbed.

* * *

'Anything?' Coran asked, peering around the doorway into Zoella's room.

Mel was still sitting with her. She shook her head.

'She twitches and moans every so often,' Mel said, 'like she's caught in a sleepterror or something. Her eyes are open, but she can't see or hear us ...'

Coran looked at Zoella. She still looked pale, her unseeing open eyes unnerving; her expression blank. As he watched, he could see her body twitch, her neck twisted at an unnatural angle.

'I don't know what to do for her,' Mel said, holding the girl's hand.

Coran sighed. 'There may not be anything we can do for her. Mel ...'

'I'm staying with her.'

'Mel,' Coran repeated. 'I need you to work on the *Mobilis*, the ship is ...'

'I said I'm not leaving her.' Mel turned, an angry expression on her face. 'She needs care.'

'We still need to deal with the Obelisk,' Coran replied. 'Meru's out of contact, the flying machines are broken down. I need our ship. You're the only one who can fix it ...'

Mel was about to answer when the door creaked behind them. Both looked around.

The white-haired girl stood there, her pale pink eyes watching them. She was small and petite, her expression worried. Mel wondered how old she was, a bit older than Ren for sure, but not yet fully grown.

'Ira?' Mel asked.

The girl nodded. She opened her arms to them. Coran and Mel got a brief image of Ira kneeling down next to Zoella. It was clearly a request.

'I'm not sure ...' Mel said.

'Can't do any harm,' Coran said. 'Maybe she can help.'

Mel nodded, releasing Zoella's limp hand and standing up to make way.

Ira smiled and moved forward, crouching down by Zoella's side. She closed her eyes and then placed her hands on Zoella, one on her chest and the other on her forehead.

Zoella flinched at the contact, but then her eyes closed.

* * *

Zoella watched as Ioric's flesh was ripped by the vast dach, its teeth bloodstained and raw.

Torin screamed as he was mutilated. Blood flew.

Raga jumped and was slain. His body crashing down on the ground to lie limp, twisted and broken.

Over and over again the images assaulted her mind, each one more lurid and horrific than the last. Every time the perpetrator of those crimes strode through the flaming wreckage of Viresia to gloat over her.

Kiri, her dark hair waving in the wind, her eyes bright blue, staring down with contempt, her weapon clenched in her black gloved hand.

But then it was her turn.

Die cursed witch!

Kiri staggered back, reeling. Zoella struck out, pummelling at the hated figure before her, unrelenting, mental blow after mental blow.

A fog … confusion.

Kiri was now tied in a chair, slumped, beaten, half unconscious.

The metal staff was in Zoella's hand. She looked down at it.

Blood. Kiri's blood.

Just one more strike.

'That's right,' a voice said. 'Kill her, it is the right thing to do.'

Zoella turned to see a pale woman standing to her right. She was dressed in the dark gowns of the priestesses, a kai held in her hand. Zoella gasped, the high priestess … Nerina of Drayden.

'You have the power,' Nerina said, stepping forwards and then moving around Zoella, her gaze never leaving Zoella's. Zoella spun to look at her.

'Kill Kiri,' Nerina continued. 'You are the stronger, it is you who have the greater power. Kill her, show everyone how strong you are!'

Zoella looked at Kiri's bloodied form, still lying helpless before her.

She smiled, raising the staff.

'No!'

She turned at the cry. It was Meru.

How dare he interfere?

She blinked. His features were blurred, indistinct, hard to see. She frowned.

It wasn't Meru.

A girl stood before her. Zoella recognised her.

Ira?

The girl nodded.

Let them go, Zoella. You must let them go.

Zoella shook her head.

She killed them, she must pay! I will never forget Ioric, Torin or Raga. She slew them!

Ira's voice came at her again.

Vengeance will not bring them back. You must let them go. Come back to us Zoella.

Zoella snarled.

No! She must die!

Ira gestured to either side of herself.

Zoella gaped as she saw other figures appear alongside Ira. Her heart clenched.

Ren …

The boy spoke.

I wanted to fight! Proud you'd be if you'd seen! I flew, I stabbed that girl good and hard.

Fitch appeared alongside him, patting Ren's shoulders.

He saved me. Wouldn't have been here without the boy, got to give him that.

Zoella gasped as Ioric appeared next to them. She cried out in grief and love. He looked at her.

I understand your hatred, my precious niece. But you'll end up digging

two more graves if you continue like this. Remember me with fondness, not with vengeance. This is not the Zoella I remember, the gentle soul who saved me from the molossc and who served me so well in Viresia …

Something nudged her. She looked down, seeing Raga lick her hand. The big carn barked and nuzzled her leg.

Beyond them all she saw Meru. He said nothing, just looked at her, his expression unreadable.

Ira stepped before all of them.

Come back to us Zoella!

* * *

Kiri was still trembling. She was crouched on the floor of the galley, Meru holding her close. Meru took one of her hands in his. They sat in silence for a spell, then another. Kiri's trembles ebbed, her breathing slowed.

'The last person to say they loved me …' she began. 'They died, Meru. I swore I'd never cry again until all this was finished.' She wiped at her tear-stained face. 'Look what you've done.'

'Who was he?' Meru asked.

Kiri shook her head. 'She … Her name was Charis, and she rescued me too.'

'When was this?'

'It's long story.'

'We have time,' Meru gave her a squeeze with his arm.

Kiri took a deep breath and told Meru about her upbringing as an 'only' in the slums of Drayden. The death of Tia and Choso, how she'd almost been stoned to death. How Charis had found her and saved her, nursing her to health.

'She believed in Lacaille as a goddess,' Kiri said. 'Even though she was wrong, she was a good woman. Kind, gentle. She trained me as a healer, but …'

Kiri related how she had accompanied Charis to Varda. How Torin had shot Charis with a crossbow. How Charis had died in her arms.

Meru listened without interrupting.

Kiri held up her left hand, slowly pulling off the black glove. Then she turned her hand around, showing Meru the scar on her palm and the tight twisted skin on the back.

'This scar,' she said. 'Torin shot me, right through the palm. It still hurts even now. More when I think of her.'

Meru ran his fingers over the scar before taking her fingers and giving them a gentle kiss.

'We could fix this,' he said. 'Stop it hurting.'

'Fix it?' Kiri asked.

Meru gestured at the medical bays behind them.

'The machines aboard, they can fix anything,' he said. 'I'm sure they could take away the pain and the scar … if you want to?'

Kiri looked at her hand, flexing her fingers, clenching them into a fist.

'No,' she said, after a moment. 'It reminds me of her, the sacrifice she made. It might sound silly, but it's … part of who I am.'

Meru nodded.

'This Charis … sounds like she was a wonderful woman,' he said.

Kiri nodded.

'She gave me some advice,' Kiri said, shaking her head. 'I should have heeded it.'

'What was it?'

She looked up at Meru.

'Don't meet violence with violence.'

'Wise words,' Meru said. 'We could all do with heeding them.'

Perhaps if I'd listened, none of this would have happened.'

Meru pulled back, moved around and faced her.

'Stop blaming yourself for everything,' he said, a sterner tone in his voice. 'Torin lied about the treaty, if anyone was responsible for the attack on Viresia it was him. Your priestesses lied to you, betrayed you. Lacaille did its thing. None of that was your fault …'

'But …'

'Ren's death …' Meru began, blinking back his own tears. 'Horrible yes, shouldn't have happened … it was a tragic accident.'

Kiri swallowed, wiping at her nose. She nodded, pulling the glove on to her hand.

Meru stood up.

'Come on,' he said, holding out a hand and pulling her to her feet alongside him. 'Enough of the past. We've got work to do.'

She frowned.

'Work?'

'The Obelisk,' Meru said. 'We're not going back, so we might as well go on.'

Kiri thought for a moment. 'Yes. That machine I saw in your mind … Caesar. The Obelisk needs fixing, it called to me. It needs me. But I don't know where it is …'

'I do,' Meru said. 'Look.'

He led her forward into the cockpit of the medical ship, gesturing to the co-pilot's chair. They both clambered into the seats.

'Sandra,' Meru called. 'Map of Esurio please.'

A panel between them lit up with a coloured map. Meru poked at the screen.

'We're here,' he said, pointing at a small flashing triangle. 'Sandra, can you show the location of the Obelisk?'

The map zoomed out, revealing Esurio to be a sphere. The curvature was plain to see. Another dot appeared.

'The Obelisk is located here,' Sandra said. 'Co-ordinates zero, zero, the substellar pole.'

'Changes must be made,' Kiri whispered.

'What?'

'That's what it said to me,' Kiri said. 'Changes must be made. Lacaille must be sated, all must be set right or death and destruction will blossom, fires will come more devastating than you have known … I thought it was talking about our task appointed, that we had to attack Amar as our religion demanded, but …'

'It was calling for help,' Meru said. 'Zoella and I were on our way to it when we got diverted to Taloon. Zoella even managed to speak to it.'

'How?'

Meru shrugged. 'She just sort of concentrated ...'

Kiri thought about it for a moment and then closed her eyes.

Obelisk?

There was nothing. She frowned, pushing her thoughts out further.

Obelisk. It is me, Kiri! You called me your faithful one, servant of Lacaille. I am here, can you hear me?

The voice she remembered spoke, echoing around in her mind.

Administrator Kiri, Obelisk responds. Contact has been established. Access is granted.

Shocked, Kiri opened her eyes.

'I can hear it,' she said, staring at Meru.

'Ask it for a status report,' Meru said.

Kiri concentrated again.

Obelisk, please give me a status report.

Acknowledged Administrator Kiri. Status report as follows. Axial alignment is now out of tolerance. Thermal load is out of tolerance. Cooling facilities are operating in emergency mode ...

Kiri relayed what she was hearing to Meru, her expression taut.

Magnetic power distribution will fail permanently in approximately fourteen stretches. Without realignment, atmospheric erosion will reach critical values.

Kiri had no idea what she was repeating, but concentrated as the Obelisk continued.

Flare generated ultraviolet. X-ray and microwave radiation exposure will rapidly increase to fatal levels as ozone layer depletion rises exponentially. It is imperative a repair maintenance team proceeds to the substellar pole, co-ordinates zero zero, immediately.

Kiri let out a gasp as the Obelisk's imperious voice stopped.

'Tell it we're coming,' Meru instructed.

Obelisk, we are coming to you.

Acknowledged Administrator Kiri. What is your estimated time of arrival?

'It wants to know when we'll get there,' Kiri said.

Meru looked blank.

We'll be there as soon as we can!

Acknowledged Administrator Kiri.

Kiri shook her head as the contact faded in her mind.

'Did you understand any of that?' she asked.

'Some,' Meru said.

'Tell me on the way,' Kiri said. 'I understood enough to know time is running out.'

Meru nodded. 'Buckle in,' he said, pulling the harnesses about him. Kiri copied his moves.

He flipped up a series of switches.

'Sandra, please plot a course to the Obelisk.'

'Course plotted.'

Meru took a deep breath. 'Let's go then, as fast as we can.'

* * *

Zoella's eyes had closed, her breathing deeper and more regular. Colour had returned to her cheeks and she was no longer twitching. Ira leant back, lifting her hands away.

'Is she …?' Mel began.

Zoella stirred, her eyes opening. She looked around her.

'Zoella?' Mel whispered.

Zoella looked across at her.

'Mel?'

Mel went to her side, grasping her hands. 'Yes, Zoella. I'm here. Ira and Coran too … How are you?'

Coran stepped up behind her.

'I …' Zoella blinked. Her expression looked confused. Mel, Ira and Coran watched as she looked about herself, her eyes moving rapidly.

She sat up and looked at them, her hand going to her mouth in shock. 'No …'

'Look at me,' Mel instructed firmly. 'Zoella, here! Look at me.'

Zoella turned to look, her face haunted, going pale once more.

'But I … what I did,' Zoella said. 'I hurt you, how can you …?'

Mel pulled her into an embrace. 'It's alright.'

Mel felt Zoella grip her, feeling the girl trembling in her arms. After a moment Zoella drew back.

'Where … where is Meru?'

Mel looked up at Coran for a brief moment. She saw his jaw tense.

'He's gone hasn't he?' Zoella said. 'With her … This is all my fault! I'm sorry …' Her voice rose with hysteria. 'I don't know what happened … A madness took me … I didn't …'

'Hey,' Mel said. 'You're with us, that's what matters for now.'

'Ira?' Zoella asked. The girl smiled at her, signing something with her fingers.

Zoella looked up at Coran.

'But … Meru …'

'We'll find him,' Coran said to her. 'We'll get him back.'

* * *

Coran and Mel had returned to the *Mobilis*. The ship was a mess, blackened dented and smelling of smoke. Coran had set to work with Daf and Creg trying to clean things up while Mel went straight to the engines. Several spells later the ship was at least serviceable, but it looked severely beaten up. There were leaks along the hull and it had a slight list to starboard which they weren't able to correct. Looking down the hull Coran wondered if the keel had been twisted with the impact it had suffered in the defence of Amar. The ship just didn't look right.

Daf and Creg had turned their ample muscles to the hand pumps and cleaned out the bilges while Coran had finished cleaning up the bridge.

A sudden thrum from below decks indicated Mel had fixed

something. The wire mesh sails above him crackled with ’tricity and some of the lights flickered on.

‘Now we’re getting somewhere,’ Coran muttered to himself and jumped down on to the deck, heading aft.

The engine covers were still open, one of the engines turning over slowly.

Mel was watching it, her arms folded.

‘You got it working?’ Coran called.

Mel shrugged, ‘Yeah. Guess I’m better at fixing things than people.’

Coran climbed down beside her.

‘Don’t be hard on yourself,’ Coran said. ‘You sat with her, looked after her, tended her. More than you had to after what she did. I appreciate what you did. So will she.’

‘I couldn’t fix her.’

‘Each to their strengths,’ Coran said. ‘You’re the best snuttin’ engineer on the whole of this world. Don’t forget that.’

Mel shrugged. ‘I guess.’

‘So, how is she?’ Coran asked.

‘Zoella, or the *Mobilis*?’

Coran smiled. ‘The ship!’

Mel sighed. ‘Pretty banged up. Using her as a ram did her no favours.’

‘So I saw,’ Coran said. ‘Daf and Creg worked at the pumps, but she’s definitely taken a battering.’

‘I managed to swap over a lot of the busted parts when we were in Caesar’s hangar,’ Mel added. ‘But it’s her general condition. The keel is sound enough, but some of the bulkheads are cracked, bolts and rivets are popped all over the place. Bow has a massive dent. She needs more patching …’

‘Is she seaworthy?’

‘I need more time.’

‘Yes or no?’

Mel glared at him. ‘Yes, but barely. We can’t do no more smashing into things.’

Coran nodded.

'We need to get back out there, find out what's going on … fix the Obelisk.'

'I hear you,' she said. 'But even if the ship does hold together, if the 'tricity goes like Caesar said it would, we'll be stuck out at sea …'

The clumping sound of boots echoed across the deck. Both of them looked up to see Fitch approaching.

'What's up?' Coran asked.

'Meru's on the move again,' Fitch replied. 'That infernal woman's voice said that the medical transport is in the air.'

'No joy getting hold of him I suppose,' Coran said.

Fitch shook his head.

'No, still not answering the radio. But I think I know where he's going.'

'Where?' Coran and Mel asked, simultaneously.

'Got the track plotted,' Fitch said, eyeing them both. 'He's heading directly sunwards.'

'He's heading for the Obelisk,' Mel exclaimed. 'Must be.'

'But he needs Zoella to fix it,' Coran said. 'Doesn't he? Caesar said …'

'Caesar said something about Zoella,' Mel said. 'Don't you remember? Meru started talking about it … Nano something. Caesar called her an administrator. Zoella has the gift, so does that witch, Kiri. Maybe …'

'She's an administrator too,' Coran finished.

'And Meru thinks she's going to help him fix it?' Fitch asked. 'After she just tried to do us all in?'

'Meru might have explained it,' Coran said. 'If the Obelisk fails we all die, Amarans, Scallians, Witches … all of us. Maybe Kiri understands that …'

'So what are we going to do?' Fitch demanded. 'We can't just sit here and hope Meru and that witch make it there.'

'We can't use the flying machines, they're busted,' Mel said. 'And the *Mobilis* will never catch them up.'

'And we might still have the rest of those witches camped on our doorstep,' Fitch said. 'We've got to secure Amar too.'

Coran nodded.

'Agreed. A recce of the Scattered Isles is the first priority,' he said. 'We need to get hold of Meru, confirm what he's doing and see if there's any way we can help.'

'He won't answer,' Fitch said, with a shrug. 'I've tried. Snuttin' stupid kid.'

'If he won't answer the radio,' Mel said, 'There's nothing we can do.'

'There's another way of getting hold of him,' Coran said, grimly.

Mel and Fitch looked confused. Then Mel's eyes widened and she shook her head.

'No, Coran. You can't ask her to do that,' she exclaimed. 'Not after what happened.'

'Who?' Fitch demanded. 'Do what?'

'Zoella said she could spy on Kiri before,' Coran said. 'Maybe she can speak to her and relay a message.'

Fitch chuckled. 'I'd love to see her face when you ask her to do that.'

'Coran, you can't!' Mel said.

'Do I have a choice?' Coran replied, getting to his feet. 'We need to talk to Meru. You two get the ship patched up as best you can. We'll be leaving soon as you're done.'

* * *

Coran strode back to Amaris from the harbour, heading for the house they had been assigned by the senate staff. Coran saw Senator Henoch standing at the gates, clearly hoping to speak to him.

'Captain Coran!'

'Senator.'

'Any news of my son?'

Coran grimaced. 'We've not been able to contact him, but the flying machine he took is in the air once more. Meru must be flying it.'

'Is he coming back?'

Coran shook his head. 'No, he's heading sunwards. We think he's going to attempt to fix the Obelisk.'

'And what of the witch with him?'

'All we know is that she's alive too.'

'How are you going to get him back?' Henoch demanded.

Coran turned to him. 'Right now, I'm not.'

'What?'

'Meru's got the best chance of fixing the Obelisk,' Coran replied. 'He's nearly halfway there already. If the Obelisk isn't fixed the flares will get worse, we'll all die.'

'Then … what can we do?' Henoch said. 'You said you couldn't contact him …'

Coran sighed. 'That's why I'm here, there's something I've got to try.'

'The other girl, the one that's lost her mind?'

'She may be able to send a message,' Coran explained. 'These powers …'

'Are extremely dangerous,' Henoch replied. 'Are you sure this is wise?'

'I don't think I have a choice.'

Henoch nodded. 'I appreciate your efforts in all this, Captain. I apologise if I seem impatient. I'm just … worried …'

'I will get hold of Meru,' Coran promised.

'I'd have him back safe,' Henoch said. 'But abducting a war criminal, breaking her out of jail? This girl assaulting you? Such a mess – and I am bound to uphold the law.'

'Let's get them back before we worry about the legalities,' Coran said. 'If you'll excuse me …'

Henoch stepped aside. Coran turned and walked into the house, climbing to the upper level. He walked into the room where Zoella had been put, knocking on the door.

'Come in,' Zoella's voice called.

Coran took a deep breath, pushed open the door and walked inside.

Zoella was sitting up, dressed in a simple nightgown, with a bandage strapped across her forehead. She still looked pale, her brown eyes wide as she looked at him. She was gaunt and thin, her eyes sunken, with dark rings around them.

'May I?' he said, gesturing to a nearby chair. She nodded.

Coran watched her for a long moment.

'How are you doing?' he asked.

'Better,' she said, her voice a whisper. 'How are the crew?'

Coran puffed out his cheeks. 'Still pretty nervous I think,' he said. 'And I can't blame them.'

Zoella swallowed, pulling her knees up to her chest and wrapping her arms around them. 'I'm sorry. You must all hate me.'

Coran shook his head. 'Scared is more the thing. You were pretty terrifying.'

Coran watched her expression. She seemed contrite.

'You remember what happened?' he asked.

She nodded, miserably. 'Yes. All of it. What I did, what I said. It was unforgivable. I was …' She looked away. 'I don't know what happened to me. Lost control … struck out … hurt you … all of you.'

'We couldn't stop you,' Coran said. 'You swatted us away like we were just nargs.'

'It was pure rage,' Zoella said. 'Ren was murdered …'

'Ren was killed,' Coran said, his voice firm. 'Not murdered. He wanted to fight for Amar. Mel and I did try hard to discourage him, but truth be told, we needed him. No one else save Meru could operate those machines. So we let him fight. He probably saved us all. Then …'

Zoella's expression hardened. Coran saw her lip curl.

'She killed him.'

'Kiri?' Coran asked, keeping his voice level. 'Yes, she killed him; in self-defence. Kiri was fighting Fitch. Ren stabbed her and she defended herself. Then she was captured. We had her locked up; she was going to stand trial for everything she'd done. Then you took matters into your own hands. Now she's escaped, Meru is an accomplice to a crime and all three of you are in a heap of trouble with the council. It's just as well we don't have a death penalty.'

Zoella looked away.

'I understand what you felt,' Coran said. 'Fitch and I wanted to do the same thing, but not at the cost of attacking our friends. Just as well Mel had the courage to stand her ground. We talk, we debate, we argue, but we don't attack each other, force our will upon others.'

Coran could see Zoella's expression crumpling, but he kept going.

'This gift of yours makes you incredibly powerful. You just bashed us aside. Is that your way, Zoella?'

'No,' Zoella cried. 'It's not …'

'Because if it is, if that's what you're going to do,' Coran continued. 'You can't be part of my crew. You can't stay. It's too dangerous. The Amaran council wants you locked up …'

Zoella was sobbing now.

'I'm sorry,' she said, desperation in her voice. 'It was rage … it came from somewhere inside me … hatred for her yes … anger with Meru … grief over Ren … Mel promised to look after him … all of those things, but …' She looked up. 'It wasn't me, something … it was …'

'Can you control it?' Coran asked. 'Will it happen again?'

'I don't know,' Zoella replied, stuttering through her sobs. 'I don't want it to.'

Coran nodded. 'An honest answer.'

Zoella wiped at her eyes. 'It happened once before. When Viresia was attacked. Kiri duelled with my queen, tortured my prince and struck down my carn Raga when he tried to defend me. A rage took over; like a part of me that's so furious. It makes me want to hurt, want to inflict pain, it's horrible, burning hot anger that just …'

'Triggered by this witch, Kiri,' Coran said. 'She's your problem.'

Zoella nodded.

'Who just happens to be your sister,' Coran added. 'What happened in that cell? There was blood everywhere.'

'I took her staff and I beat her,' Zoella said, her body shaking. 'Tortured her like I saw her torture others. I was going to kill her – I wanted to! The rage I felt … She was terrified, I saw it in her eyes. She cried out. I was about to finish her. Then Meru …'

'Both of them were gone by the time we got there,' Coran said, softly.

'Do you know what happened to her?' Zoella asked. 'What happened to Meru? He pushed me aside, hit me before I could turn on him. That's the last thing I remember.'

'They're both alive,' Coran replied. 'It seems Meru managed to get Kiri to the medical ship, I guess he saved her life. We're able to track the ship, but we can't get Meru to answer the radio. He's switched it off. I'm guessing he figures it's not safe to come back.'

'Because of me,' Zoella said.

Coran didn't answer. Zoella's head fell forward.

'We think he's heading towards the Obelisk,' Coran said, after a moment.

Zoella looked up and frowned. 'But he won't be able to fix ...' She swallowed. 'Her?'

Coran nodded.

'Could Kiri have the same instruction from the Obelisk?' he asked.

Zoella shrugged. 'Meru said she'd heard it call her, I guess so.'

'I need to speak to him,' Coran said. 'If Meru is going to the Obelisk ...'

'But you said the radio was switched off.'

'Yes.'

Coran watched her face go even paler.

'You want me to talk to her?' Zoella said. Coran could see her fingers trembling.

'That's it exactly.'

'I can't,' Zoella said. 'I hate her, we will fight ... the rage will come back!'

'I need you to do this, Zoella,' Coran said, his voice calm and even. 'I need to speak to Meru. I need to know what he's doing and whether there is anything we can do to help. You're the only one who can relay a message.'

'No, don't make me do it ...'

'I need you to control this hatred. I need you to speak to her, to Kiri.'

'She will refuse. It won't work!'

'You must try!' Coran shouted the last words.

Zoella flinched away from him.

Coran waited for a moment before he spoke, his voice stern. 'Prove to us you can put this aside. Prove we can begin to trust you again.'

Silence hung heavy between them.

'It's the only way we can get Meru back,' Coran whispered, breaking the stillness. 'Will you do this for me, Zoella? Will you do it for him?'

Zoella swallowed and then drew a long shuddering breath.

'Alright. I will try.'

CHAPTER FOUR

Airea, Capital of Taloon

Round 2307, Seventh pass

Rihanna stood above the dying priestess, seeing her struggle to breathe, gasping for air. She was injured inside, the few healers had tried to save her, but nothing further could be done. She knelt down and grasped the woman's hand in hers, feeling the life drain from her.

Rihanna felt guilt, anger which burned and rolled within her. She gritted her teeth, her lip curling as she thought of the attack on Amar and the loss of so many priestesses.

Nerina's responsibility … Nerina's greed … Nerina's fault!

Rihanna had watched as the battle unfolded. Nerina had assured them all that Amar would be defeated easily, but the inhabitants of the island had put up a spirited and effective defence. Where they had expected to overthrow the island in the manner of previous battles, Amar had its own aerial force, a fleet of flying machines from the ancient past they had used to counter the priestesses' dachs.

The more traditional weapons of the Taloon army had likewise been thwarted, their ships had been set upon by the metal vessel, many struck down by strange explosions. Even as they approached the harbour of the city, more contraptions rained fire down upon them.

But it was Lacaille herself that truly turned the battle …

The sphere above had blazed with fury, almost as if it disapproved of their actions. The ships of Taloon were set ablaze, the priestesses retreating before the flames, far out to sea.

That will be hard for Nerina to explain! Many truly believe in the goddess Lacaille … Kiri did …

That brought Rihanna's thoughts around.

Nerina had been grooming Kiri, there was no other word for it. Driving her with promises of authority and giving her access to teachings and power; fattening her up for the inevitable tearing. Kiri had even suspected it, taking Rihanna into her confidence.

Kiri actually trusted me. I saw it on her face … the betrayal. It was only then when she knew I still truly hated her …

Rihanna smiled, that sweet morsel of vengeance had been a long time in coming.

Kiri had taken Rihanna's position as favourite in the eyes of the priestesses. Nerina had been cunning. She knew this, and had reassured Rihanna in private as to her intentions. Kiri was to be allowed to grow her gifts and Rihanna was to deceive Kiri into trusting her, only for Nerina to take her powers from her.

Nerina should have taken her before, not there, in the midst of battle. But Kiri was weak, hurt, exhausted …

Rihanna had watched in satisfaction as Kiri was struck down, but as the flare had begun to flame around them, Kiri had run, throwing herself into the sea. There to be drowned.

So Nerina had assumed. Did she die? If not, the Amarans will have her as a prisoner. Either way she is beyond our reach. Nerina took some of her gift, but not all of it. It is lost to us now. Nerina has what she wants, she is unassailably strong, none will defy her …

Rihanna turned, sensing a presence behind her. She looked up to see Nerina standing there, her figure silhouetted against the light of Lacaille. She was as pale as ever, perhaps even more so, the light of Lacaille adding no colour to her face; her eyes dark. Only the silver streak in her hair caught the light.

'Dying?' Nerina asked, the word harsh and cold.

Rihanna nodded, looking down at the supine priestess alongside her.

'Take her gift,' Nerina said.

Rihanna shook her head. 'No … she's …'

'Take it,' Nerina said, her voice chill. 'We cannot afford to waste it. Do it now.'

Rihanna swallowed. She turned to the priestess before her. The woman's eyes were closed, her face pale, her breathing ragged. As Rihanna watched she opened her eyes, hearing Nerina's words.

Rihanna sensed the horror and betrayal well up from her.

She fought for our ideals, for Nerina's plan and at the end all that matters is …

Rihanna hesitated, staring at the woman's face.

'Now!' Nerina called.

There is only one path left for me now … loyalty … complete loyalty to Nerina. My choice is made.

Rihanna dropped the woman's hand. She cried out before Rihanna's fingers pushed against her face. Rihanna forced her way into the woman's mind as she had been taught. The gift, the precious gift, still glowed before her. She reached out, pushing past the horror, the betrayal; the last vestiges of anger and shock were all that was left.

The gift swirled around Rihanna, lighting her from within, sparking through her mind and body and invigorating her senses. She clenched her eyes shut in ecstasy. Lust flared and Rihanna took the last essence of the woman's power. Nothing remained.

Rihanna moaned in delight as the new power shuddered through her body, addictive and engorging.

When she opened her eyes, the woman's body was still, the breath had gone from her. She was dead. Rihanna stood up.

Nerina was looking at her.

'Better,' Nerina said.

Rihanna's gaze was harder, she pushed her remaining doubts aside. There was no place for the weak or the infirm. Strength and power was all that mattered.

Nerina is right. The gift is the concern! Nothing is as important. We must seek it out everywhere and control it …

A smile touched the edges of Nerina's mouth.

'Take whatever else you can from the dying,' Nerina said. 'When you are done, we will leave.'

'All of them?'

'Every single one,' Nerina said. 'The first reward for your service. Taloon awaits us and I have something for you there.'

Rihanna nodded.

* * *

Vandare heard the bells sound in the city of Airea, ringing from the whitestone parapets of the city. He walked out into the sunshine, squinting in the sudden brightness.

He could see the guards pointing upwards, his own gaze followed as he joined them. The flying dachs could be seen, circling down towards the city.

'The priestesses return,' he said, frowning. They had departed on the ships of the fleet along with King Karquesh, but there was no sign of the ships. 'Something has happened.'

The dachs dropped, fanning out around the leader as they swept in to land in the courtyard before the royal palace. Vandare summoned the guards and they strode out to meet them. Vandare was counting them as the great beasts settled before him.

Less than half return … and they return without our people … where is King Karquesh, where is the fleet?

Vandare gestured to the guards and they fanned out on either side of him, five men each side.

Before him, the priestesses had dismounted. As they walked towards him, he recognised their leader, the high priestess herself, Nerina. Next to her was another woman, younger, but no less fierce looking. Both carried their familiar metal staffs. He recognised none of the others and there was no sign of the woman that had first come to Taloon on behalf of the priestesses, the one that had killed King Karquesh's cousin, Taryen.

Kiri, what has happened to her?

'Vandare of Taloon,' Nerina said, stepping up to him.

'High priestess, Nerina,' Vandare said, bowing before her. 'We did not expect you back so soon, what has transpired?'

'The battle did not go well,' Nerina said, her voice clipped and short.

'The fleet?'

'All but destroyed.'

'Destroyed?' Vandare echoed in dismay, hearing the guards about him mutter in agitation. 'What of our King? What of Karquesh?'

'Slain in the battle,' Nerina said, looking at him.

'But victory was assured!' Vandare said, his expression slack. 'These Amarans were to be defeated easily …'

'And so they would have been,' Nerina said, interrupting him. 'They were saved by a flare from Lacaille. Ships were set ablaze before they reached the city, my people burnt from the skies. Without it we would have been victorious.'

'But you are the servants of Lacaille, are you not?' Vandare asked. 'Was this not her will …?'

Vandare caught the worried look the other woman shot Nerina. Nerina's voice was cool.

'The will of Lacaille is not something to be discussed with men,' she said. 'We have returned, my people need care after their travails. Ensure it is done.'

Vandare nodded, licking his lips before speaking. 'Everything will be done as you desire, High Priestess, but these are ill tidings. King Karquesh left no heir … in such a situation there is little precedent for ceding authority …' He shook his head. 'The affairs of state will be complex.'

'On the contrary,' Nerina said, gesturing to the woman beside her. 'The situation is simple. Rihanna here will govern Taloon, under my supervision.'

'But,' Vandare spluttered. 'We are a sovereign nation, an ally of Drayden. Our treaty …'

'Was with Karquesh,' Nerina said. 'The situation has changed. If you must have royalty, then you will have a queen. Rihanna will be that queen.'

Out of the corner of her eye Nerina saw Rihanna turn to her in surprise.

'This is not acceptable!' Vandare said. 'Our laws, our people are governed by …'

'Not acceptable?' Nerina asked, her eyes narrowing.

'No,' Vandare said. 'With the greatest possible respect …'

He saw Nerina gesture to Rihanna. Rihanna stepped forward, her staff raised.

'Guards!' he called.

The men about him drew swords and spread out, flanking him.

'Do not seek to defy me,' Nerina said, her voice still and quiet as ever.

'I must,' Vandare replied. 'I serve Taloon, we are not a vassal of Drayden.'

'You are now,' Rihanna said. Nerina smiled at her.

Rihanna held out her hand. One at a time, in rapid succession the men about him yelled out, clutching their heads as agony consumed them. Vandare watched in horror as they collapsed to the floor, blood seeping from their noses and ears. Each one convulsed, their screams cut off, before lying still.

Rihanna pointed at him. He tried to turn and run, but found he couldn't move. His legs went out from underneath him and he fell forward on to his knees. Rihanna and Nerina strode around and stood before him, looking down upon him with contempt.

'Swear your loyalty to Queen Rihanna of Taloon,' Nerina said. 'Or we will find another who will. Make your choice. I know you understand this, Vandare. You are not a fool.'

Vandare looked at the bodies of the men about him and then at Rihanna. He swallowed.

'My service,' he said, taking her hand and planting a kiss on it.

Nerina nodded at Rihanna.

'You will make such announcements as are necessary,' Rihanna said. 'Bring your nobles to me, there is much they must understand.'

Vandare bowed his head.

'It will be done … my queen.'

* * *

The priestesses were accommodated within the palace. The staff within accepted the news without question, ensuring their needs were catered for. Fresh clothes, hot water, food and wine were brought for them.

'Taloon is yours,' Nerina said to Rihanna. 'A reward for your service.'

'It is an honour,' Rihanna replied.

'Take what you will,' Nerina said. 'I want the fleet of ships rebuilt to strength as soon as it can be achieved. I will rally our strength in Drayden. We will attack Amar as soon as we are ready, our strategy altered.'

'The people here may revolt,' Rihanna said.

'Continue to make an example out of them as you have already done,' Nerina said. 'They cannot resist our powers, they are our playthings, for us to do with as we wish. Take the women, kill the men. They will quickly learn the new order of things.'

Rihanna smiled and nodded.

'You will return to Daine?'

'I shall,' Nerina said. 'There will be those who doubt my leadership. They must be dealt with too. Drayden, Drem, Scallia, Taloon – all ours. And Amar will fall. All lands will be subject to Drayden.'

'And you will be Empress of Esurio,' Rihanna said.

Nerina smiled. 'Yes, you speak the truth indeed. I will exceed even Elena's grasp. The priestesses rule will be supreme and we shall have peace at last. Tithes will be sent, our position restored and reinforced. Never again will men defy us, they will know their place. Women will rule, as it was always supposed to be. The elements fulfilled, Lacaille's will done, the task appointed complete.'

'And Kiri …' Rihanna added.

'You did well,' Nerina said. 'Concealing our intentions from her. Her face when you betrayed her!'

Rihanna smiled. 'She trusted me. I felt her pain as she realised the truth. I only wish …'

Nerina nodded. 'Her death was unsatisfactory. Yet, I took much of her power. Had she lived she would have been weak and easy to tear, a shame Merrin could not have taken her as a mindless whipping girl. She will have to take her frustrations over Charis out on someone else now.'

'Her powers are what was important.'

'Indeed,' Nerina said. 'And those are mine.'

'You're sure she is dead?'

'I would have sensed her otherwise,' Nerina said. 'She is gone; drowned in the waters of Amar. Her body food for the creatures of the sea … or carrion rotting on the shore.'

'Could she have been captured by the Amarans?'

'And would they have saved her?' Nerina said, shaking her head. 'More likely they would have made an example out of her. Paraded through their streets before a public execution. A short lived celebration of their supposed victory. No, Kiri is gone, think of her no more.'

Rihanna nodded.

'You still have doubts?' Nerina asked. 'Have you sensed something?'

'No. But Kiri had a way of … staying alive,' Rihanna replied. 'No matter what hardship she faced.'

Nerina smiled.

'I have taken what I wanted from her,' she replied. 'If Kiri lives and you find her, take what is left for yourself. Then kill her, or bring her to Drayden so your mother can vent herself upon her. Regardless, she no longer matters, it is the other one that counts now.'

Rihanna cast her mind back to the battle on the quays of Amar.

'The maid?'

Nerina nodded.

'Yes … the maid,' she answered. 'It was she who fought Kiri to a standstill in Viresia. The same one who defied you in Nireus. Kiri said she met her in Airea too. She was there on the quay, in the flying machine, still strong enough to resist us. She is very much alive and her power is potent. It is her we must seek, the reason we must take Amar.'

'So you can take her,' Rihanna said.

Nerina nodded, looking at Rihanna.

'You wish to take her for yourself?' Nerina asked.

Rihanna shook her head.

'Oh but you do,' Nerina said, with a smile. 'Ambition is not bad thing, Rihanna. I applaud it. If you are strong enough, you will be high priestess … nay, Empress … in time.'

'Succeed you?' Rihanna asked.

'Why not?' Nerina asked, with a smile.

'But what of my mother?'

'Merrin?' Nerina laughed. 'She has always been capable, both in administration and bearing children with the gift, such as yourself. But she is no leader, strength and spirit is what is required there.'

'But …'

'If you want to stand by my side,' Nerina said. 'To take on this mantle at the proper time, you must be strong enough. Prove yourself.'

'Prove myself?' Rihanna asked. 'More than I have already?'

'Kiri is dealt with. Taloon will occupy you for now, Queen Rihanna,' Nerina said with a chuckle. 'All challenges enough, but when you're ready a final hurdle remains before you can stand alongside me.'

Rihanna swallowed.

'Yes,' Nerina said. 'Now you understand. The time will come, be ready.'

* * *

Nerina was gone the following stretch, returning to Daine with half of the priestesses that had flown in from the attack on Amar. Rihanna was left with the remaining half of their force, with instructions to subdue Taloon and rebuild the fleet. She set to work immediately.

Vandare had already communicated the news to the nobles of Airea. They had assembled before Rihanna and obsequiously pledged their fealty without complaint. Rihanna smiled at their fawning attempts to win her approval, inwardly despising them.

'I shall be crowned,' she said to Vandare after she had dismissed them all. 'Crowned in the manner of your people, with all due ceremony. I expect the people to honour me thusly. It will take place upon the next stretch, all the nobles will swear their loyalty in public.'

'And if any refuse?' Vandare asked.

'They will answer to me,' Rihanna said. 'I will see to them … personally.'

Hurried arrangements were made. The courtyard before the palace was dressed in ribbons, all manner of traders and workers slaved throughout the stretch to ensure preparations were complete. Within the palace things were just as busy preparing dresses, food, wine and music.

The chimes of the following stretch rang out across the city.

The crowds had gathered, but they stood mute behind the ropes that bordered the piazza before the palace.

Rihanna, flanked by her priestesses, stood at the far end, a red carpet stretching out before them, with the great phaunts lined up each side of them. Trumpets blared and they began to march forward.

Awaiting them on the steps of the palace, Vandare stood, flanked by the nobles of Airea. All were dressed in their bright flamboyant outfits, with garish colours and enormous hats.

Rihanna took her time walking down the carpet. She looked straight ahead, flanked by her priestesses, some of their dachs swooping overhead. Triumphal music was playing, but there were no cheers from the crowds of people around them.

Rihanna arrived at the end of the carpet where Vandare awaited her. The music faded. Vandare spoke, his voice raised.

'King Karquesh is slain,' he intoned. 'Taloon fondly remembers our fallen leader, but we now look to the future. Taloon has allied itself with the realm of the priestesses, Drayden. We welcome a new monarch from amongst their ranks. We are blessed by Lacaille herself, for she has seen fit to bring us priestess Rihanna of Daine, here to be crowned our queen.'

Trumpets sounded. Two young girls brought a dark purple velvet cushion out between them and stood alongside Vandare. Upon it lay an ornate crown.

Vandare turned and took it, nodding to Rihanna.

She knelt before him.

'By the powers vested in me as servant to the monarchy of Taloon,' he said. 'I crown you, Rihanna.'

Vandare placed the crown upon her head. It was heavy, pressing down on her with a surprising weight.

'Rise my Queen.'

Rihanna got to her feet. Vandare and the nobles bowed to her.

There was some sort of commotion behind them. Some of the phaunts trumpeted.

Rihanna turned to see a large troupe of men walking into the piazza in rigid formation, twenty abreast in several rows.

'What is this?' she demanded.

'The army of Taloon,' Vandare said. 'Your honour guard.'

The men wore thick leather armour over their bodies, necks and heads. Rihanna could see they marched with swords at their belts and pikes in their hands.

They marched down the centre of the piazza towards the palace, coming to a halt in their formation.

A man, dressed in a more decorated uniform, marched down their flanks, turned smartly and walked to the middle of the group and then turned on his heel to face them. At some unspoken command, the pikes were lowered and the men stood to attention.

'The army of Taloon,' the man called out. 'Stands ready for her majesty, Queen Rihanna.'

'Captain of the guard,' Vandare said to Rihanna. 'For your inspection.'

Rihanna nodded, stepping out towards the ranks of men. The other priestesses spread out around her. She walked towards them.

Without warning, out of the ranks of men, crossbow bolts flew. Rihanna saw two of her fellow priestesses slain before she could react. Their dachs screeched in fury above.

Treachery! Kill them!

The armed men before them yelled, breaking ranks and running towards the priestesses, pikes outstretched and swords drawn. They closed, their swords rising ready to cut down the women, still in a precise military line. Others hung back, reloading the crossbows ready to unleash them again.

But the priestesses were trained too.

At Rihanna's imperious mental command, they unleashed their own wrath. The crown slipped from her head and was lost in the fray.

Many of the men fell screaming as the priestesses turned their mental powers on them. Others found that the priestesses' staffs could be used to deadly effect at close range. Few of the men even managed to land a blow, the priestesses able to sense their movements and counter them as if they could tell where they were going to attack before they'd even begun.

The dachs descended too, their talons outstretched and ripping into the ranks of men, grabbing some of them and wrenching them up into the air only to drop them and see them dashed against the pavements far below.

In dismay the men reloading the crossbows saw their companions cut down in moments. Seeing they could not be ready in time, they abandoned their ranged weapons and pulled out in their own swords, turning to the attack.

Swords crashed, screams rent the air as men fell one after another, the priestesses now striding forwards, Rihanna in the lead, cutting down each man as they brought their attack. The men had never faced such speed, fury and precision before.

Now the men's resolve failed. They fell back, trying to protect a single man in their group. Rihanna signalled for the attack to pause.

'Bow to your queen,' she snarled at him.

'Taloon will not bow to Drayden,' he answered. 'And you are not my queen.'

Rihanna hoisted her kai and strode towards him, battering down the men that stood between him and her, despatching each with a furious strength leaving broken necks and crushed bodies until she stood across from him.

She held out her kai, raising it above his head.

'Bow,' she hissed.

She saw him take a final look around at his fallen comrades, a hundred men at arms, cut down by less than twenty of the Drayden priestesses, who all stood behind Rihanna, their staffs ready. Other than those who had been slain in the initial hail of crossbow bolts they were all standing uninjured, calm, showing no sign of exertion.

He shook his head.

'Never.'

With a yell he swung his sword at her.

Rihanna parried, twisted and struck at his chest. He doubled over and the kai crashed down upon his neck, ending him. She grabbed his sword from his lifeless hand and skewered him through the chest with a shriek of rage.

Before anyone else could react she grabbed him by the collar, dragging his body through the dead or wounded bodies of his companions and on towards the steps of the palace, leaving a trail of blood in her wake. Screeching an instruction to the remaining priestesses she coiled a rope around his neck and with their help hoisted him up into the air to hang from the platform, the sword still impaled in his body.

His body swung there, turning to and fro before hanging still, the sword dripping with blood, sagging from his chest, hilt down.

Only then did she turn to the shocked people and the nobles around her. She saw Vandare was lying on the ground, with some of the nobles around him. He too had been injured, a crossbow bolt embedded in his shoulder.

None spoke.

She gestured to the bodies of the men before her in the courtyard.

'Kill any who remain alive,' she muttered. The priestesses nodded and walked forward, ending the lives of the wounded.

Only then did Rihanna step forward. She found the crown amidst the bodies and placed it upon her head once more.

'I am your queen!' she raged, using the gift to amplify her voice. 'Let none of you have any further doubts as to my power or my intentions. Those that defy my rule will be punished as he has been. I will leave his body there to be consumed by the nargs as a lesson for you all. The same fate awaits you if you do not pay homage to me.'

No one spoke. No one moved.

'You will return to your tasks. You will work. You will rebuild the fleet and tend to your duties. Do this and all will be well. Fail to do your duty …'

Then there was silence all about her, all were staring at the carnage.

Vandare was on his feet, helped forward by two nobles either side of him.

'Bow before the queen,' he shouted out in his deep voice.

For a long moment nothing happened, but then Vandare's words seemed to penetrate the minds of those around him.

Rihanna watched as the nobles lowered themselves to their knees alongside him. Then, in a rolling wave, the people edging the piazza did the same.

'Hail the queen,' Vandare shouted. 'Priestess Rihanna, Queen of Taloon!'

Slowly at first, but then in a rising crescendo, the chant was taken up.

'Priestess Rihanna, Queen of Taloon!'

* * *

There were no further reprisals.

The people of Taloon returned to their work, whether it was the hydroponic systems below the city, or the tasks above ground. In the harbour the quays were busy as new ships' keels were laid. The work kept the people busy for the most part.

Rihanna ensured the taverns and eating houses were well stocked. Other than the odd sporadic outbreaks of violence, which were subdued, there were no complaints. It seemed that few of the populace cared who was in charge, as long as they had food, work and a roof over their heads.

The rotting corpse of the army captain, moved away from the palace itself, might have continued to have an effect. Swarms of nargs had infested the body and folks stayed away from it.

'I am pleased,' Rihanna said, when Vandare provided her with an update.

'Your majesty,' Vandare said, bowing low.

'A welcome turn around,' she said. 'How long will it be before the ships are constructed and the fleet replenished?'

'Construction at such a rate hasn't been attempted before,' Vandare said, cautiously. 'The materials, transporting them …'

'How long.'

'The first ships will be ready in ten passes,' Vandare replied.

'Ten?' Rihanna replied. 'Half a round? No, that is not acceptable. They must be built quicker.'

'It cannot be done,' Vandare replied. 'That is already far faster than the rate at which the shipbuilders would work and there are only so many with the necessary skills.'

'Do they require further motivation?' Rihanna asked.

'Only so much work can be completed in so much time,' Vandare replied.

'It is not enough,' Rihanna said. 'Redouble their efforts. If they wish, I will arrange to tour the shipyards.'

'I will do what I can to convince them,' Vandare replied. 'Will there be anything else?'

Rihanna turned to regard him.

'Your injury, is it healing?'

Vandare nodded. 'It has been treated and dressed.'

'Not too painful I hope.'

'It is bearable.'

'I appreciated what you did in the piazza,' Rihanna said. 'The situation could have been … much worse than it was.'

'I did what I thought was best,' Vandare replied.

'You have accepted the transfer of power then?' Rihanna asked.

'If I have learnt anything in my long rounds,' Vandare replied. 'It is that power is an ephemeral thing. It changes when least expected. It is best not to resist change when change is inevitable.'

Rihanna smiled at his words.

'Then you have accepted that the priestesses will rule from now on?'

'My concern is for the people. If they are well treated and cared for then all is good. I will accept any ruler who guarantees their wellbeing.'

'I do not intend to be a tyrant,' Rihanna replied. 'But I will not tolerate disobedience. The will of Lacaille has been thwarted for long enough. It will be thwarted no longer. Long ago it was ordained by our founder, Elena, that all lands should be subject to our rule. We have control of Scallia and of Drem. Now Taloon belongs to us too. Only Amar has defied us, and they will fall.' She looked at Vandare. 'That change is also … inevitable.'

'There are lands to the sunward too,' Vandare said. 'We have fought with them in the past. Kerun for instance.'

'They will bow to us too, in time,' Rihanna said. 'Do not doubt it. Perhaps we will make them a province of Taloon. Something to occupy the army, perhaps?'

'Such a thing would greatly please the people here,' Vandare admitted.

'Once all this is achieved we will have peace,' Rihanna said. 'Do not doubt it. Esurio will be one, whole and calm, as it was in the times of the Voren Empire.'

Vandare nodded, but didn't reply.

'Only this time,' Rihanna said. 'There will be no emperor, but an Empress. We women will rule with wisdom and strength, as it was supposed to be from the beginning. Esurio will be united.'

'As you say, my queen,' Vandare said.

She gestured for him to go, returning to her watch from the palace balconies.

CHAPTER FIVE

Sunward of Amar, heading sunward

Round 2307, Seventh pass

Kiri dozed in the co-pilot's chair. There was little to do. Meru seemed to be comfortable with the flying machine. He didn't have to do too much either; the machine was more than capable of managing itself.

Kiri glanced around her.

A round ago and this was all magic, myth and legends out of the past. Now here I am, sitting in a machine straight out of those stories ...

She shivered, her thoughts turning to the priestesses.

Nerina, Merrin and Rihanna ... they have schemed all the way through. Schemed and had Charis killed to foment a war, perhaps they killed old Launa too! Nerina wants everything ... Nerina always gets her way ...

The words mocked her now. Nerina had got her way, with her at least.

She has stolen much of my power ... she tutored me so my powers would be all the stronger when she finally decided the time was right. She will be unstoppable now.

But the people of Amar had defied her and lived. Kiri remembered the battle, the fierce and determined defence of the city that had taken the priestesses by surprise.

What has happened to them? Were the priestesses all killed in the flare, or have they survived?

She thought about opening her mind to try to search for them, but then decided against it. For now, as far as they knew, she was dead. It was better not to reveal she was alive.

Something crackled in her mind. A presence, a feeling, a crisp metallic tang that put her on her guard.

She gasped in horror, a gasp that turned into a stifled scream. She curled up in her seat, shaking, her eyes clenched shut. She heard Meru's voice calling out.

'Kiri? Kiri! What is it?'

Kiri couldn't answer. She saw brown eyes staring at her. Eyes she had last seen with a murderous vindictiveness staring down at her, intending to end her life. Zoella!

Go away!

Her reaction was visceral, she tried to blot Zoella's presence out, but it was insistent and powerful.

You must listen to me …

No! How dare you? Leave me alone! Get out of my mind!

'Kiri, what is it?' Meru demanded from alongside her, a worried expression on his face. 'Please, you're scaring me!'

Kiri managed a shuddering breath.

'It's her …'

Meru's friends need to speak to him. This is the only way. Tell Meru to switch on the radio … please!

'Zoella?' Meru asked. 'What does …?'

Anger rose in her, fierce and burning. Kiri directed it across the link.

I will tell him. Get out of my thoughts!

Kiri …

Get out! Get out! GET OUT!

The link severed. Kiri cried out, shuddering into sobs.

'Kiri!'

She opened her eyes. She was in the flying machine. She could see clouds, blue sky, the arc of Lacaille just visible above. She tried to calm herself, taking deep breaths in and out.

'Kiri?' Meru's voice was full of concern.

'I'm … it's …' She swallowed. 'I'm alright.'

'What did she try to do?' Meru demanded. 'Was she attacking you?'

Kiri shook her head.

'It's your friends,' Kiri said. 'She said they need to speak to you, but you've switched off …'

'Switched off the radio,' Meru said, heavily. 'So they got her to relay a message.'

Kiri nodded.

'I can't believe them … How could they, knowing …' Meru swallowed.

'Maybe …' Kiri began, catching her breath. 'Maybe you should speak to them.'

'I don't want to speak to them,' Meru snapped. 'They let Ren get killed, they didn't stop Zoella trying to kill you. Some friends they turned out to be!'

'Perhaps they couldn't stop her,' Kiri said. 'And it sounded important.'

Meru looked at her. He sighed.

'I'm sorry, this is my fault. They need to know what we're doing and without the radio … Coran's used the only way he knows how. I left them no choice. I didn't mean to …'

'I know,' Kiri said. 'Just … speak to them.'

Meru took a deep breath and flipped the switches on the radio.

'Alright. Let's do this.'

* * *

Zoella's eyes opened. She gasped, blinking rapidly. She looked up at Coran.

'Well?' he asked.

'She said she would tell him,' Zoella said, swallowing. 'She wouldn't listen after that. She hates me, she was furious.'

Coran sighed and nodded, getting to his feet.

'I don't think we could hope for much more,' he said. 'Thank you for trying.'

'Coran …'

He stopped and looked at her.

'Yes?'

'There's … something else you ought to know.'

'Oh yes?'

'When I was … wherever I was … I saw … I saw Nerina …'

'The high priestess?'

Zoella nodded. 'She was goading me on to kill Kiri, I saw Meru and he stopped me again … it was a dream but … it felt real.'

'So …?'

'I think she sensed me,' Zoella said. 'I don't think it was just a dream, or a sleepterror. I think she might know about me … know where I am …'

'These powers give you away,' Coran said.

Zoella nodded. 'Kiri and I could see through each other's eyes at one point. I can't do that with anyone else … I don't think I can anyway, but Nerina is so powerful she might be able to …'

'To spy on us.'

Zoella nodded.

'And she wants me,' she said. 'She wants to take my gift like she has taken everyone else's. The more power she has, the more unstoppable she will be.'

Coran pursed his lips, thinking it through.

'Doesn't change our immediate plans,' he said, after a moment. 'I'd better get to the *Mobilis*, in case Meru does switch the radio on.'

'Can I come with you?' Zoella asked.

Coran pursed his lips. 'No, you can't. The Amaran council has forbidden it.'

'The council?'

Zoella's face had gone white.

'Yes,' Coran said. 'They won't have you wandering around given what's happened and I can't say I blame them. You have to stay here.'

'But …'

'Count yourself lucky that you're not in a cell,' Coran added. 'You can thank Mel for that kindness.'

Zoella looked bereft and didn't answer.

'Listen,' Coran said. 'I will talk to them. But I can't promise anything.'
Zoella nodded, and then began to cry.

* * *

Fitch was sitting in the bridge of the *Mobilis*, listening to the crackling hum of the radio. Strange whistles of sound rose and fell, punctuated by thumps of static. There was nothing new. He dozed in the warmth of Lacaille.

Then there was a staccato buzz, a deep throbbing tone which cycled over and over again.

Fitch opened his eyes and sat forward.

'Hello?' he said.

He tweaked the dials on the radio. The tone altered, warbling back and forth before …

'… to *Mobilis,* are you receiving me?'

Fitch moved across. 'Meru? That you, boy?'

The voice was thin, but understandable.

'Fitch?'

'Yep. Can you hear me?'

'I can.'

'Coran's going to be mighty pleased to hear from you,' Fitch said, standing up and waving. 'He's coming, I can see him legging it down the pier. How you doing anyway?'

'I'm alright.' Meru's voice was tense. 'Let me know when Coran is there.'

Fitch rolled his eyes and waited.

Coran vaulted into the bridge.

'Is he …?'

'Right here,' Fitch said, raising his eyebrows. 'Waiting to talk to you.'

'Will you excuse us?' Coran asked.

'Yeah, I know when I'm the unwanted cargo,' Fitch grumbled and stepped outside. Coran waited until he was out of earshot.

'Meru?' Coran asked. 'Can you hear me?'

'I can hear you,' Meru's voice sounded sullen.

'Are you alright?' Coran asked. 'We've been trying to reach you ever since …'

'We're fine,' Meru replied, emphasising the first word. 'No thanks to you.'

Coran's voice was guarded. 'You don't know what happened here, Meru.'

'I know you let Zoella almost kill Kiri,' Meru replied. His voice was bitter. 'I know you let Ren fight.'

Coran took a deep breath.

'We had no choice with Ren,' Coran replied. 'And he volunteered. I wasn't happy with it, but without you he was the only one who could fly those scorchin' machines. He wanted to play his part and he did. We didn't kill him … that was that girl you're with.'

'Kiri acted in self-defence!'

'She attacked Amar,' Coran said. 'That wasn't self-defence. Or did you forget that?'

'She doesn't deny it,' Meru fired back. 'But she deserved a fair trial, not murder.'

'I agree,' Coran said, keeping his tone level. 'So does the Amaran council.'

The radio went silent for a moment, with nothing but the faint crackle of static.

'Then …'

'Zoella took matters into her own hands,' Coran said. 'She did her mental thing on us; me, Mel, Fitch … even Daf and Creg. Knocked us out. We tried, but we couldn't stop her. By the time we got to the cell you were both gone.'

'You didn't mean to kill Kiri?'

'I won't lie Meru,' Coran said. 'The thought did cross my mind, and Fitch's too for that matter. But Mel stood up and defended her right to a trial. We agreed. Zoella didn't.'

There was another gap in the transmission.

'I had to take her away,' Meru said. 'Otherwise …'

'I hear you,' Coran said. 'I understand you and her are …'

'Yes, we are.'

'Is she with you now?'

'Yes, she is.'

'Then I can't say too much,' Coran said.

'You can trust her,' Meru replied. 'She's changed …'

'She's a witc … a priestess, Meru! An enemy of Amar,' Coran replied. 'I can't trust her.'

'She's left the priestesses,' Meru said. 'She's no longer one of them. They disowned her, abandoned her, tried to kill her too …'

'Can't take the risk,' Coran said. 'Now …'

'Don't ask me to come back,' Meru said. 'Because I'm not.'

'Meru,' Coran countered. 'Think this through; you're making yourself an accomplice to a war criminal. Lacaille knows how many laws you're breaking. The Amaran council …'

'I don't care about the council,' Meru said. 'I'm not coming back.'

Coran clenched his eyes shut for a moment, thinking rapidly.

'I already figured that,' Coran answered. 'Alright. What I want to know …'

'You want to know what we're doing,' Meru said. 'We're going to the Obelisk. Kiri has already spoken to it; she can do whatever it was that Zoella was going to do. We'll get there and fix it, like we first planned to do.'

'Makes sense,' Coran said. 'Do you need anything from us?'

'No, we're fine.' Meru's voice was abrupt and hostile.

Coran sighed.

'You plan on just leaving it like that then?' he asked, his voice bitter. 'That's it is it? After all we've been through together? What about your parents? Thought you were part of my crew, Meru. Sounds like I was wrong.'

There was another long pause. Coran could just hear a whispered conversation at the other end, but he couldn't make out the words. It seemed Meru and Kiri were debating something.

Meru's voice came again.

'I'm sorry,' Meru said. 'I don't mean to defy you. Even Kiri says I should turn back ...'

'Listen,' Coran said. 'We're your shipmates and there's people here who care about you. You don't just put that aside, boy. Now, it makes sense for you to head to the Obelisk. I'll trust your faith in Kiri. Not much we can do from here anyway. That's your responsibility, get that Obelisk fixed.'

'We will,' Meru said. 'We promise.'

Static crashed across the radio transmission, drowning out Meru's voice. Coran waited until it faded away again.

'If you manage all that,' Coran said. 'That will go in yours and Kiri's favour. If you decide to come back, I promise her a fair trial here, all above board. Zoella will be kept out of the way. That's my responsibility ... but it's your choice.'

'We understand,' Meru replied. 'How is ... well ... everyone else? The crew, my parents ...'

'Glad you asked,' Coran said. 'The crew's fine, bit shocked and battered. Amar took a lot of damage, a lot of folks killed, but we survived. Mel's working on the *Mobilis*, the ship's pretty banged up, but we'll get her running soon enough. Your parents are safe but worried, they want you back ...'

'Tell them not to worry. What about the priestesses, and the fleet?'

'Ships were burnt up in the flare, not many of their crews survived,' Coran answered. 'And those that did are locked away. As for the priestesses, maybe you should ask Kiri.'

'I already did,' Meru said. 'She doesn't know.'

'Well, then that makes three of us,' Coran said.

'And how is ... Zoella?'

'I'm not sure I can answer that,' Coran said. 'She was in a pretty bad way, lost her mind for a spell. I didn't mean to cause any extra ruckus, but there was no other way to get hold of you ...'

'I understand. I didn't want to hit her, I had no choice …'

'Truth be told we're not quite sure what to do with her right now,' Coran said. 'Everyone is pretty much scared of her. The council has her under house arrest. You left me with a right problem.'

'Sorry.'

'The more I learn about these powers the less I trust them. We're playing with fire. Be careful.'

'I will.'

'Listen Meru. Concentrate on the Obelisk. One less thing for me to be concerned with. I want regular catch-ups on the radio, clear? This time each stretch will do nicely.'

'Aye, Captain.'

'And the same deal as last time. No diversions, no detours, no little quests to satisfy your curiosity. Are we clear?'

'As crystal.'

'How close are you?' Coran asked.

'Difficult to tell. We should be able to see the edge of the vortex soon,' Meru replied. 'Weather is still clear now though.'

'Good,' Coran said. 'We'll get this sorted. We're a crew, remember?'

'Yes. And thanks.'

'Don't mention it. I'll speak to your parents for you. Good luck. We'll speak soon.'

The radio crackled and the signal was lost.

'You can both stop eavesdropping now,' Coran called out.

Mel and Fitch peered over the door jamb of the bridge. They had been crouched below. Neither looked apologetic.

'I'm glad he's safe,' Mel said. 'You did well with him.'

'Captain needs his crew,' Coran said. 'And if Meru can fix the Obelisk with that girl's help, so much the better for all of us.'

'So,' Fitch said. 'The witch girl who swore to end us all comes over here, firebombs us, kills one of our crew, wipes out half our people, smacks me around the head and breaks my arm, seduces Meru, makes off in one of our flying machines … and now we're trusting her to save the life of everyone.'

Coran nodded. 'That's about the shape of it.'

Fitch sighed. 'I could have shipped out with a sensible crew.'

'Where would be the fun in that?' Mel asked. 'By the way. I've had an idea. Checked it out with Sandra and she says it will work.'

Coran turned. 'Oh aye?'

'You know when we were becalmed that time when the 'tricity failed?' Mel asked. 'And how the *Mobilis* was struck by lightning in the storm at Drem?'

'Not likely to forget it,' Coran said, remembering how they had all got into trouble out in the Strathian Sea. 'Touch and go for a while.'

'The flying machines have these big … things,' Mel said. 'Sandra had a word for them …'

'Bat…er…rees,' Fitch added.

'That's it,' Mel said. 'Sandra said they can store 'tricity for emergencies, even if the source isn't working. The *Mobilis* probably even had them at one point.'

'So?' Coran asked.

'We can take some of the batteries from the big flying machine and put them in the *Mobilis*,' Mel said. 'Then, even if the 'tricity does fail again, or we have to travel through a storm, we can stow the sails and keep going. As long as we have a full charge we'll …'

'Be able to keep moving,' Coran finished for her. 'How long will it take?'

'A reckon a couple of stretches if you can give me Daf and Creg.'

'They're yours,' Coran said. 'I want to be able to cast off as soon as you're ready.'

Mel smiled and jumped down from the bridge, yelling instructions to Daf and Creg.

Fitch waited for a moment. Coran turned to him.

'What?'

'Well, you was doing so well at fixing all our woes, I figured you'd be addressing the big one next.'

Coran sighed.

'Zoella.'

Fitch nodded. 'She's a danger to us all.'

'That she is,' Coran said. 'But she's part of this crew too.'

Fitch looked alarmed. 'You mean to bring her back on the ship?'

Coran rubbed his chin.

'I need to speak to the council first,' he said. 'Let's talk about it after last chime. Tell the crew.'

* * *

The medical ship was heading sunwards, cruising across the thick shade forests of the continent. The shades were growing in size. Some were enormous; their bowls perhaps thirty hands in diameter, dwarfing anything that Meru or Kiri had seen before. The vegetation below looked thick and dense.

'We're going to struggle to find somewhere to land,' Meru said, looking out of the cockpit windows. 'This forest seems to go on forever.'

Kiri was looking out of the other side.

'It's beautiful though. Such lush colours.'

She was right. The cuplike bowls of the shades were coloured with all sorts of patterns and splashes of colour. Some were a bright garish green, so unlike the familiar red and dark hues they were used to.

'I wonder why,' Meru said. 'There's got to be a reason.'

Kiri laughed. 'Always questions with you, isn't it?'

'I'm a curious person.'

Kiri nodded. 'Yes, you are.'

'Hey!'

Lacaille was climbing higher into the sky as they continued on; they had to crane their necks forward to see it out of the windows. It wasn't far from being overhead.

Kiri turned to Meru.

'Those people of yours are good friends,' she said. 'Are you sure you're doing the right thing?'

'We have to fix the Obelisk,' Meru said.

'You know what I mean. You've no intention of going back to them, have you?'

'If I take you back you'll stand trial,' Meru said, looking at her. 'An enemy of Amar, you killed Ren, even if it was in self-defence. What do you think they'll do to you?'

'We should face it,' Kiri said. 'I'd have no fear with you beside me. I have committed crimes, I should answer for them. I don't want you to lose your friends and family on account of me, you know that.'

'I won't risk losing you again,' Meru said. 'Not for them, not for anyone.'

Kiri tried to say something, but the words wouldn't come. She reached across and grabbed his hand, squeezing it tight. Their conversation lapsed and they watched the landscape unroll beneath them for a spell.

Kiri pulled her hand back and scratched an itch on her nose.

'Do you really think we'll be able to fix this Obelisk when we arrive there?' she asked. 'I mean … I don't know anything about it. What am I supposed to do?'

'Caesar said it would be able to tell us … tell you … what to do,' Meru said. 'That's all we've got.'

'I don't even know what this Obelisk is supposed to do when it is working.'

'It's some kind … I don't know, like a shield,' Meru said. 'It protects us from the flares, makes the 'tricity for all these machines … and it has something to do with the powers you have. Something our ancestors built generations ago to keep us safe.'

'And administrators, 'Kiri said. 'I heard it, it called me administrator Kiri …? But I'm not an administrator, so what does it mean?'

'I'm not quite sure,' Meru said. 'But people like you, with this gift … Caesar calls all of you administrators. You have something in you.'

'Something in me?' Kiri looked horrified.

'Your powers, your abilities,' Meru said. 'Something makes that possible. Sandra, can you explain what an administrator is?'

Both listened as Sandra responded.

'Administrators are selected members of the population required to undertake leadership, governance, control and communication responsibilities as per Esurio founding statute,' Sandra said.

'The priestesses have a caste of administrators,' Kiri said. 'They organise things, keep records, make lists and so on. But I was never one of them. I was a healer, then a warrior. It sounds like the administrators were supposed to be in charge ...'

'That is correct,' Sandra replied. 'Administrators share responsibility for the welfare of all colonists upon Esurio and the operational governance of protective systems such as the Obelisk. Administrators have the signature nano-infusion complex that provides mesh communications, authentication and authorisation, remote telemetry and knowledge management.'

Kiri looked blankly at Meru.

'Yeah, that's where it gets weird,' he said. 'I have no idea what most of that means. I think the nano-infusion thing is what gives you your gifts, but it seems clear people with this power were supposed to run things.'

Kiri was thinking it through. 'So the priestesses were sort of right ... we were always taught we were supposed to be in charge.'

A thought occurred to Meru.

'Sandra, are only women administrators?' he asked.

'That is correct,' Sandra replied

'Why?'

'Esurio governance records indicate that only female colonists were selected for the administrator role.'

'So,' Kiri said. 'Women were given the gift, they were supposed to look after all Esurio, keep things working. How long ago was this?'

'The date is round 2307,' Meru said. 'Maybe it was that many rounds ago.'

'Thousands of rounds?'

'That's when we first got here, after all.'

'Got here?' Kiri asked. 'What are you talking about?'

'Caesar told me some other things; you'll find this hard to believe.'

'All of this is hard to believe!' Kiri laughed.

'Do you remember back in Nireus?'

'Yes.'

'There was a light in the sky, high above the clouds.'

Kiri shrugged.

'There were lots of strange lights in the sky. Lots of tiny dots. They were cold and hard, I didn't like them. So what?'

'This one was moving. I asked Caesar about it. I'd calculated some numbers on it and they didn't make sense. He didn't want to tell me, but Zoella forced him to.'

'And?'

Meru swallowed.

'That light is a ship, a ship that came from a place called Earth. It's how we got here.'

Kiri frowned. 'Got here?'

'To Esurio.'

Kiri shook her head. 'I don't understand.'

'We don't come from Esurio,' Meru said. 'Us, people, folk. We come from another place, another world. Think about it, all the creatures have three eyes, we only have two. They all have fans to cool themselves, we sweat. We sleep … and they never do.'

Kiri thought about it for a moment.

'This isn't our home? We come from another place? Up in the sky? What did you call it?'

'Earth.'

'Strange name. Where is this … Earth?'

'So far away it sounds impossible,' Meru said. 'It's one of those dots in the sky you don't like.'

Kiri blinked, trying to work it out.

'That makes no sense at all,' she complained.

'We came from Earth,' Meru said, trying again. 'It's very far away. We came in a ship and arrived here on Esurio.'

'But … why?' Kiri asked.

'Something went wrong on Earth,' Meru said. 'Caesar wasn't very clear, but we couldn't live there any more, so we came here.'

'And you're saying all that happened 2307 rounds ago?'

Meru nodded.

Kiri thought about it.

'So what went wrong?' she asked. 'Why don't we all know about the Obelisk and the ship and the flying machines and this Earth place and everything else?'

'I'm not sure,' Meru said. 'But I have an idea.' He spoke up. 'Sandra, when did the first flare hit? What round?'

Sandra's voice responded. 'Round 341.'

'And since then?'

'Subsequent flares occur at intervals of 491 rounds. The current flare is the fifth to have occurred since records were kept.'

Meru nodded. 'Caesar said there was no other access to his hangar after that round until we turned up to talk to him. We found the body of a woman … her name was Sandra, I named the voice after her. She died in that first flare. I don't think our ancestors were ready for it.'

'So … all this stuff they could do, all this cleverness … lost?' Kiri's voice was hushed.

'We found bodies in Caesar's tunnels,' Meru said, nodding. 'Burnt to a crisp. That woman left a message saying the heat was really bad, she'd lost contact with the Obelisk, she was trying to save everyone, but had to seal herself in. She died alone. Everything we've found, our ship, these flying machines, all of it … it's all from back then. Some of it works, some of it is broken …'

'But if they couldn't deal with the flare,' Kiri said. 'How can we? We don't know …'

'People have survived this long,' Meru said. 'Somehow we've survived all the flares that have happened since. Enough of us to keep going anyway.'

The flying machine vibrated around them. Meru grasped hold of the controls until the turbulence faded away.

'The priestesses have books,' Kiri said, after a moment's thought. 'They call them the Elements. They speak of Lacaille growing angry, a blackness crossing her face because of the Nirians and their machines. Cold smote the land followed by storms of fire long ago. That must have been the last flare.'

'I remember you telling me this when we first met,' Meru said. 'You spoke about Elena and the Voren Empire.'

'Elena was supposed to have lived back then,' Kiri said, recalling what she had been taught. 'At the end of the empire. She founded our faith, had gifts of incredible strength. The Elements say that the men of Nireus defied Lacaille. There was war. Elena fought them and beat them, sending the survivors into exile … your people. The flares stopped, but the empire was gone, destroyed in the conflict. And we were taught that the evil was unfinished, Lacaille would be angry again … which led to …'

Meru nodded. 'Everything since.'

Kiri looked downcast. 'It was supposed to be the will of Lacaille. I used to be so sure of it, but it was just half-truths, bits of legend. Women are supposed to be in charge, but looking after everyone, not just themselves like we have. We only wanted the gift for us.'

Kiri stopped and looked out of the windows of the flying machine. She took a deep breath.

Meru reached across and held her hand.

'You know, for having your whole world turned upside down in the last pass … losing everything you believed, everything you trusted in … you're doing pretty well.'

Kiri laughed. 'Three rounds ago I was raking through litter and hunting marsips so I didn't starve. It might have been different if I'd been raised a priestess. Back then it was enough just to stay alive. You learn to take one stretch at a time.' She paused for a moment. 'Then I thought I was special, that Lacaille had chosen me, singled me out. Zoella was right when she accused me in Taloon. I did see myself as Empress, thought it was my destiny …'

'And now?'

Kiri shrugged.

'It's so strange … I just … I just don't want it any more. I don't want to fight, I don't want control … I can't explain it. It's not just knowing that all that religion was wrong, it's something else …' Her eyes widened. 'Ever since Nerina tried to tear me …'

'Tear you?'

'When the priestesses take the power from another,' Kiri said. 'I couldn't resist her, she was unstoppable … I only just escaped and now …'

'Your gift …'

'Weaker … not like it was … and the rage is gone …'

Kiri stopped, she looked out of the windows again.

* * *

Coran sat across a table from Senators Henoch and Janaid.

'Truth be told,' Janaid said. 'I'd rather you did take her with you. I've no idea what to do with her. She'll have to be locked up for the safety of everyone.'

Henoch nodded. 'If she loses her mind once again she'd run amok here,' he said. 'No one has any idea what she's capable of or how to stop her. These powers she has …'

'I can't guarantee my crew will have her back aboard,' Coran said. 'What she did … they may not forgive her, or even give her another chance.'

Henoch exchanged a look with Janaid.

'But you say you need her?' Janaid asked.

'A precaution,' Coran said. 'Meru is on his way to this Obelisk, the witch-girl Kiri with him. They intend to fix the Obelisk. He believes he can trust her, but I have my doubts. If he isn't successful or that trust is misplaced we need someone with these powers to talk to the Obelisk. If the Obelisk isn't fixed, based on what we know, we all die. Zoella may be our only choice.'

'A risk either way,' Janaid said with a nod.

'It seems clear that you must take her,' Henoch said.

'I can't force that choice upon my crew,' Coran said. 'I'd be putting their lives at risk. Zoella is quite capable of killing us all should she lose control again.'

'And she lost control due to grief?' Henoch asked. 'The boy who died?'

'So it seems,' Coran answered. 'Grief mixed with a desire for vengeance on Kiri. Lots of history there.'

'Then the choice belongs to your crew,' Janaid said. 'And whether they can find it in their hearts to give her a second chance.'

Coran nodded.

'If they will not accept her,' Henoch said. 'She stays here under lock and key. We can take no risks. She will be a prisoner, in a secure cell, not your house.'

Coran sighed, but nodded.

'Will you give her over to me for now?' he asked. 'I will vouch for her and be responsible for her actions.'

'You've done much for us,' Henoch said. 'If you think you can redeem her, then yes.'

'I will ask my crew,' Coran said. 'If they decline, I will hand Zoella back to you.'

Janaid and Henoch nodded.

'Agreed.'

* * *

Zoella heard a knock at her door. She got to her feet, hearing the bolts on the outside unlocking. Coran appeared in the doorway.

'Come with me,' he said.

'Where are we going?'

'To the ship,' he replied. 'The council have handed you over to my care.'

'Oh … thank you!' Zoella said.

'Don't be thanking me too quickly. I'm going to explain our position to the crew. Meru and Kiri have gone to the Obelisk. I want to help them, and to do that, I need you.'

'I will do whatever you say,' Zoella said, earnestly.

Coran nodded.

'It's the crew you have to convince, and accept any stricture they place upon you. I will not force them. What you did …'

Zoella nodded.

'Will you let me speak to them?'

'I will,' Coran said. 'But understand this. If they will not let you back aboard, then you will stay here, answerable to the council and subject to their laws.'

Zoella swallowed.

'They'll keep me locked up.'

'Aye, that they will,' Coran said. 'Likely in a cell, blindfolded. So, choose your words carefully.'

* * *

'What is that?'

Meru had been watching the instruments. He looked up hearing Kiri's voice, scanning the horizon ahead. In the distance was a curving wall of cloud reaching far up into the heavens. It was still hazy and indistinct, but he could sense the scale of it. Above the forest hung a dark grey and oppressive looking belt of cloud stretching all the way across the horizon. Above that the clouds towered into the sky, widening out from the base and reaching out towards them. As they watched they could make out more and more detail, the cloud wall seeming to roll towards them.

'It's the edge of the vortex,' Meru whispered.

A bright pulse of light flickered from the cloud base, outlining shapes in an eerie bright purple before fading.

Kiri looked at him.

'We have to go in there?'

Meru nodded. 'It's a huge storm that surrounds the Obelisk, like a giant whirlpool of cloud. But we'd better set down before we try flying into it. Too tired now. We need to be as alert as we can.'

'What about over there?' Kiri said, pointing.

Meru could make out a green area between the huge shades. It was still full of vegetation, but it was wide enough to set down in.

'Let's hope the ground is solid,' Meru said.

'There's nowhere better we've seen.'

Meru slowed the flying machine and jostled it into a hover above the clearing. The shades rose up above them as they descended.

'They're huge,' Kiri said, in awe. 'They must be almost a hundred hands high.'

'Everything looks like it's bigger,' Meru said. 'Those plants, look … and the flowers. Enormous.'

Meru toggled the machine's undercarriage and was rewarded with a faint clunk as it lowered into place. They continued to descend, his hands clenched on the controls, ready to pull the ship back up if the ground wasn't firm. Greenery rose about the windows.

'Still not down,' he said, watching the controls.

'Can't be far …'

The flying machine jolted, canting to one side. Meru levelled it out, reducing the thrust downwards.

'I think we're down,' Meru breathed, waiting for a moment before shutting down the engines.

Kiri opened the co-pilot's door.

'Wow …'

A blast of heat swept into the cabin, the air outside was thick and humid. Meru watched as she stepped outside.

'It's so hot!' she said. 'And these plants. They're like the ones in Drayden, but they're huge.'

The vegetation outside Meru's door was too thick for him to open it, so he scrambled across and clambered down beside her.

She was right. He recognised some of the plants, but they were five or ten times the size he was used to, on a scale that matched the enormous shades nearby. All the vegetation around them was taller than they were, underneath the ground was firm and dry.

'I feel like a marsip,' Kiri said. 'Like I've shrunk.'

Strange calls sounded around them, rumbles and hoots that filled the thick air. A buzzing noise sounded above them. They looked up to see a narg that was almost two hands long.

It buzzed above them, regarding them with its three eyes, its head turning this way and that before it rose up and flew away.

'Did you see that?' Kiri said. 'It was huge …'

There was an echoing boom from somewhere in the distance, they felt a tremor in the soil beneath their feet.

'That sounded big too,' Kiri whispered.

'I don't think I want to know what that was,' Meru said back.

'Maybe we should stay in the ship until it goes away.'

'I think you're right,' Meru replied. 'Let's get some food and rest.'

* * *

Coran looked around at his crew, they were all sitting in the *Mobilis'* cramped mess room. All of them save Zoella.

'You've probably all figured why I called this little meeting,' Coran said. 'Got something we need to decide.'

They were all looking at him expectantly. None said anything.

'We've come through a few stretches of rough seas,' Coran said. 'We won a battle, we lost a friend. One of our crew mates is down in the sunward Lacaille knows where, and the other …'

'Tried to do us all in in a murdering rage,' Fitch finished for him.

Coran nodded.

'The council have put her fate in our hands,' Coran said. 'If we take her back aboard, it will be our responsibility. If we decide we won't, she stays in Amar under lock and key until …'

'You're not seriously thinking …' Fitch began.

Coran held up his hand.

'That's what we're here to discuss,' he said. 'All things being equal she'd not be stepping back aboard, but things aren't that plain.'

Everyone was listening to him.

'Zoella did help us contact Meru and set that towards straight,' Coran said. 'Meru's in the company of this Kiri girl … same one as attacked us and busted Fitch's arm. They're heading for the Obelisk.'

'Can we trust her to fix it?' Mel asked. 'She's a priestess after all …'

'Trust her?' Fitch asked. 'You daft? Of course we can't trust her.'

'Meru's vouching for her,' Coran said. 'That's all I've got. There's been something between those two ever since we left Nireus.'

'She might just be stealing him away,' Fitch said. 'We've seen some of what these priestesses can do, how do we know he's not just under her spell?'

'We don't,' Coran said.

'Then we need a backup plan,' Mel said. 'If Meru doesn't fix the Obelisk then we'll have to do it ourselves …'

'And we can't do that without …' Fitch said. 'Oh great.'

Fitch and Mel looked at each other, even Daf and Creg breathed in sharply.

'Exactly,' Coran said.

'She can't come back on the ship,' Fitch said. 'I ain't sailing with her. No way.'

Daf and Creg were shaking their heads as well. Mel looked doubtful.

'I don't think we can trust her,' Mel said. 'What she did …'

'I know what she did,' Coran said. 'She did it to all of us …'

'She snuttin' near killed us,' Fitch said. 'If Meru hadn't caught her in that cell she would have killed that witch-girl … shame she didn't really … but leastways she's out of her mind. What happens if she goes all sideways on us at sea and takes a fancy to squashing our brains? None of us can stop her, she's proved that already …'

'Pains me to say it,' Mel said. 'But Fitch is right about that.'

'It's definitely a risk,' Coran said.

'But we need someone with those powers to fix the Obelisk,' Mel said. 'If Meru and Kiri don't make it for any reason …'

'Like you said,' Coran agreed. 'A backup plan.'

'What about that other girl?' Fitch asked. 'The mute one. Can't she do it instead? She's not gone do-lally, has she?'

'Ira can come with us,' Coran said. 'But Zoella's the only one who can translate her hand speech. Doesn't help, and Ira's too young anyway.'

'The girl is a menace,' Fitch said. 'I ain't getting my brain crushed. Not for no one.'

He folded his arms and glared at Coran from underneath his wide-brimmed hat, the tip of his nose protruding and catching the overhead lights. Daf and Creg nodded.

'She was trying to get at Kiri,' Coran said. 'Vengeance, she wanted to kill Kiri. Zoella loved Ren, we all did. We all thought the same.'

'Don't deny it,' Fitch argued back. 'I'd have stuck an axe in the dratted witch, but not by stepping over the dead bodies of my crewmates first.'

'I hear you,' Coran said. 'I have misgivings myself. I could make the call, done it enough in the past, but this is your safety we're talking about and I can't guarantee it. You'll have to make up your own minds.'

Mel frowned.

'What do you mean?'

'We vote,' he replied. 'If it's not unanimous, Zoella stays here.'

'Then she's staying,' Fitch said. 'I'm not sailing with her …'

'Let's listen to what she's got to say for herself first.'

'She's here?' Fitch demanded.

'I'm vouching for her,' Coran said and then pulled a wooden cudgel out from underneath the mess table. 'And if there's any trouble, she'll get a dose of traditional medicine. Ready?'

Fitch exchanged a look with Mel. She looked at Daf and Creg. They all nodded silently.

Coran leant back and rapped his knuckles on the door.

The door clicked and opened. Zoella stood there, outside in the corridor.

Mel, Fitch, Daf and Creg looked at her and then looked at each other. Everyone recoiled.

'Let's just stay calm,' Coran said. 'I've spoken with her, she has something to say to all of us. Will you let her speak?'

Fitch muttered something under his breath. Daf and Creg were looking towards Mel. Mel stared at Zoella for a long moment before nodding.

'Come on in,' Coran said to Zoella. 'You can sit here with me.' He tapped the bench alongside him. Zoella walked in and sat next to him.

Coran saw her swallow, her hands were clenched together, he could sense her trembling beside him.

'I …' she began, before looking down. Everyone waited as she gathered herself and looked up.

'I'm so sorry,' she said, her voice cracking. She looked around at each of them in turn. 'I know I hurt you all. You all took me in and then I did this …'

She was pulling at the tips of her fingers, twisting them this way and that.

'I truly, deeply regret what I did,' she said. 'I don't want to hurt anyone ever again …'

'Except Kiri,' Fitch said, unfolding his arms and gesturing at her. 'You want to kill her, don't you?'

'Fitch!' Mel snapped, elbowing him in the side.

'No,' Zoella said. 'He's right. I tried to kill her, I did want to kill her; make her pay for everything she's done. But there was this rage, a rage that just took over, almost as if I was watching it and it wasn't me. I couldn't control it. I hated the way I felt. I hurt you all, and because of me Meru's run away …'

'We did get hold of him,' Coran said. 'Your contact with Kiri made him call home. We can speak to him again.'

Zoella nodded, a sob escaping from her, before she got herself under control again.

'I don't want it to happen again,' Zoella finished.

'Neither do we,' Fitch said. 'And it's lovely you're all apologetic like. Question is, what about next time? Reckon we're best leaving you with the council. Let them lock you up and throw away the key.'

Mel glared at Fitch again, but Zoella leant forward and stared at him.

'If you decide to leave me with the council,' she said. 'I'll go willingly. If you decide I have to be put to death, then just do it …'

'Zoella!' Mel said, grabbing her arm. 'There'll be no talk of death …'

'These powers are truly dangerous,' Zoella cried, looking at her. 'I don't want to hurt you … any of you, ever again! I will die first. If I can't control them …'

Her voice faded out. Silence fell for a long moment.

'Well, that's the big question,' Fitch said, glaring at her. 'Can you?'

'I don't know,' Zoella said, fresh tears coming to her eyes. 'All I can say is I will try.'

Fitch sat back with a dissatisfied sigh, looking around at the others and shrugging his shoulders.

'What about Kiri?' Mel asked, her voice soft. 'She's helping Meru in your stead. They're heading to the Obelisk to fix it. If you do come with us, seems likely you'll cross paths with her again. What then?'

Zoella trembled.

'For all the things she has done,' Zoella said. 'All the hurt she has caused … taking justice into my own hands was wrong. I see that now. She should stand trial for her crimes, under your laws here or back in Scallia, but I will let others work out her fate. It shouldn't be me. Just keep me away from her, that's all.'

Zoella fell silent. Coran looked around at his crew.

'You've heard all there is to hear,' Coran said. 'It's a vote. Will we accept Zoella back aboard or won't we? I vote yes – I think we need her, going into unexplored territory, the obelisk and all. Mel?'

Mel placed her head in her hands and rubbed her cheeks before looking at Zoella.

'I'm sorry about Ren,' Mel said.

'I know you are …' Zoella said, fresh tears coming to her eyes, her voice cracking. 'I didn't mean to accuse you or hurt you …'

Mel pulled Zoella into a hug across the table. Zoella's sobs echoed around the closed space as she hung on to Mel, shuddering in her grasp.

After a moment she pulled back from Zoella and looked up at Coran. 'I think we should give her a second chance.'

Coran nodded.

'But there must be precautions,' Mel said, looking back at Zoella. 'For you … and for us.'

Zoella nodded, meekly. 'I'll do whatever you say.'

'Fitch?' Coran asked

'Don't like it,' Fitch grumbled. 'Don't like it at all. But you say there's no other way to fix the Obelisk …'

'That's right,' Coran said.

'And I can't see a way around that conundrum,' Fitch said, folding his arms again. He looked at Zoella. 'I say you should be secured away whenever you're not being useful. Locked in your cabin, and someone should be on duty keeping an eye on you whenever you're out and about.'

Coran looked at Zoella. She nodded.

'Agreed,' Coran said and looked to Daf and Creg. 'Gents?'

Both of the big men moved forward to stand either side of Mel. Daf and Creg nodded at Coran.

'That's settled then,' Coran said. 'Zoella, grab your stuff and tell Ira what's happening. I want to be ready to leave harbour in the next stretch. Jump to it everyone.'

The chairs squeaked on the floor as everyone departed. Zoella smiled a thank you at Coran and allowed Mel to lead her out. Fitch hung back at the entrance.

'You know what I'm about to say,' Fitch said.

'I do,' Coran said.

Fitch nodded.

'So… what we going to do if she does go berserk?'

'Have a rifle loaded,' Coran said. 'Keep it on the bridge, safety on. If needs be …'

'Aye Captain,' Fitch said. 'I was worried you were going soft.'

'I have no desire to shoot a young woman.'

Fitch grinned. 'Then just as well you have somebody without an excess of sentiment aboard. Soft touches, the lot of you. Leave it to me.'

Coran grabbed his arm.

'Only if she really loses it, Fitch.'

'I'll deal with it, Captain,' Fitch answered, before stepping out of the mess room.

Coran sighed as he watched him leave.

CHAPTER SIX

At the edge of the Vortex

Round 2307, Eighth pass

Kiri woke early, pulling on her clothes and walking forwards into the cockpit. Meru was still asleep. Nothing had changed outside, the vegetation still held close around the windows. She pushed open the passenger side door, feeling the heat hit her as she did so.

She listened for long moments. No sounds came to her ears, but there was a faint smell on the air. She sniffed.

'What is that?'

It seemed to be coming from the boundary of shades not far from her. She wanted to have a look at the magnificent plants close up, so much bigger than the ones she had known in Drayden.

Carefully, making sure she could retrace her steps, she moved through the greenery towards the edge of the copse. The smell was faint, but still there, a perfumed aroma that she could almost taste; sweet and tangy.

She reached the edge of the shades, stepping out of the greenery and underneath their enormous cups. It was dark here, the shades blotted out all the direct light from Lacaille. She couldn't see far, it was dark and gloomy, the heat still oppressive. She could already feel herself sweating.

She frowned.

'What is …?'

A crunch of vegetation from behind startled her. It was Meru.

'What are you doing?' he complained. 'You shouldn't go wandering off on your own. We don't know what's out here, it might be …'

'Shhhh!' Kiri admonished. 'Look.'

Meru blinked in the gloom. Then he began to see. The shades were glowing. He gasped in surprise.

'Wow …'

'It's like the jars of moss-glow,' Kiri said, looking around her in awe. 'But so much more …'

Above them, the delicate traceries of plant life cascaded upward, flickering and twinkling about them. Plants were growing on the ground below the shades, glowing in the gloom.

'Generating their own light,' Meru whispered. 'It must be because Lacaille's light is blocked out by the shades, it's always dim down here.'

Kiri touched some of the plants, as she did so they changed colour from green to red. A trail of lights flashed across the forest floor for a moment before fading out again. A wave of warmth rose around them as the lights faded.

'Did you feel that?' Kiri asked.

Meru nodded. He knelt down and poked one of the glowing green plants. Its illumination went red at his touch and he felt a blast of heat from it. The trail of lights flickered in the gloom. Other plants around them flickered red too. They waited for a few moments and the heat and redness faded, and the green glow returned.

'It's like they're talking to each other,' Meru said.

'And that scent,' Kiri said, sniffing the air and stepping further into the shade wood. 'Can you smell it? It's lovely.'

Meru turned to follow her, likewise sniffing.

'It smells like …' He wafted his hand in front of his face. 'Coran's Ochren.'

'Ochren?'

'It's a drink, a strong drink,' Meru said. 'Burn's your throat if you're not used it.'

'It's coming from over here.'

Before he could stop her Kiri had walked further into the forest of shades.

'Wait … we don't know what's in here … and we mustn't go too far from the ship.'

'I know what I'm doing,' Kiri replied. 'Don't worry! Look …' She gestured behind her. 'We can still see the light … we can follow that back. I just want to see …'

'Kiri … no.'

'Come on, don't be scared.'

'I'm not …'

She grabbed his hand and pulled him along behind her through the undergrowth. They came into a clearing thick with greenery underfoot. Lights flickered red, rippling this way and that, waves of hot air rising about them. They stared upwards at the lights, lost in wonder.

'See, wasn't that worth it?'

'It's incredible,' Meru admitted.

'This is where the smell is coming from.'

Kiri ran forward. In the centre of the clearing was a large flower, its bud facing upwards, its petals huge, a large pair of stamens thrusting up from the middle, glowing green in the gloom. Kiri pushed past the petals and peered over the rim. The inside was full of liquid.

'Careful,' Meru said. 'Plants are strange. I almost got eaten by one once.'

'Long sticky tendrils?' Kiri asked. 'Aniseed smell?'

Meru looked at her. 'Yes, it was hanging down …'

'A snare,' Kiri said. 'They live in dark places, and catch things that walk underneath. They're full of liquid that dissolves flesh, really nasty. You've just got to keep a sharp eye out for the tendrils, easy when you know how.'

'Well, this plant might be dangerous too.'

Kiri gestured around her.

'Look, no tendrils, no roots, just this flower.'

'Still …'

Kiri sniffed the plant. 'This is definitely where the smell is coming from.'

She dipped her finger in the liquid. It was syrupy, but not sticky.

'What are you doing?' Meru demanded, trying to stop her. 'You don't know what that stuff is! It might be poison!'

'I know what I'm doing,' Kiri snapped, pulling herself out of reach. 'I lived in the forests for rounds, remember? It's not dangerous. Relax.'

She sniffed the liquid and then licked it. Her expression lit up in surprise.

'Oh shades!' she said. 'That's amazing. You've got to try it.'

She dipped her whole hand in and then began licking it off hungrily. Meru dipped his own finger in and then placed it his mouth. Kiri watched as his expression changed too.

'Isn't it great?' she asked.

He nodded. 'That's incredible, it's like the Ochren, but without the bitter aftertaste, so sweet!'

They both scooped the liquid out of the flower, drinking it in cupped hands, spooning it out.

In her haste Kiri managed to dribble some of the liquid on Meru's arm.

'Hey,' he said. 'Do you mind?'

She laughed and flicked some more of it at him. He grabbed a fistful and threw it at her, making her scream with delight. Then they were running around the flower, shrieking and yelling like children, chasing and trying to splash each other. They skidded to a halt on the slippery green foliage beneath them.

'I feel funny,' Kiri said, blinking and shaking her head, her vision out of focus.

'You look funny too,' Meru replied, laughing.

Kiri took a swing at him, but missed. They wrestled, falling down, rolling over each other until laughter robbed them of their strength.

The syrupy liquid was in their hair and across their faces, hands and arms, its slick sweet intoxicating fragrance all about them.

Kiri sighed.

'Can't we just stay here forever?' she asked, rolling on to her back and gazing upwards at the mesmerising lights above, they were flickering from green to red in hypnotic patterns. 'Forget it all? Live here forever? Who cares about the Izy … Obys … Ozylisk …'

Meru rolled over and propped himself up on one arm. He looked at her and giggled. 'You mean the Obelisk. You said Ozylisk.'

Kiri shook her head, her voice petulant. 'No I didn't. Never said that. Is lies …'

'You're stung drunk.' He laughed, pointing at her.

'Am not!' she said, pushing him away and staggering to her feet. 'See, proved it. I want some more.' She pointed her finger at him and waggled it sternly.

'I don't think you should.'

'Who's gonna stop me?' she asked. 'You?'

Kiri tottered over to the flower and spooned another handful of the liquid into her mouth. It was dribbling down her chin, soaking her clothes.

She gasped, moaning with delight. 'Oh … This stuff is so amazing …'

Meru had got to his feet and was standing behind her, his hand on her shoulder. She turned around and pulled him into a close embrace, lust flaring within her.

'Yes, stay here forever,' she said, her arms wrapping around his neck. 'Just you and me …'

'We really should go back,' he said.

'Not yet,' she said, pulling him closer, wriggling against him, her voice dropping to a whisper. 'Don't you like being alone with me? No stupid radio, no one spying on us …' She licked her lips. 'Just you and me.'

'Kiri …'

She kissed him, the scent of the intoxicating liquid all about them. Meru resisted for a moment, but then she felt him soften in her grip. She began pulling at his clothing and he at hers.

She felt his hands try to grab her wrists, but she was having none of it. With a deft grip she pulled him off balance, causing him to fall. She straddled him keeping him pinned to the ground.

Her vision was all blurred, she didn't care. Her body was craving something and she knew what it was. She managed to pull his tunic off; hers was already gone, lost to the undergrowth. His skin was glistening in the liquid she had splashed across him. A frantic struggle saw the last of their clothing thrown aside. She moaned as his fingers caressed her back, sliding around to her chest, the sticky liquid everywhere. Her kisses were demanding, insistent, almost frantic.

They were oblivious to anything else around them, their skin slick with the glistening liquid, bodies locked together, the greenery soft and comfortable, shaping itself around their bodies.

'See?' she said, raising herself up on her elbow for a moment.

'I do,' he said.

* * *

A dach circled down from the azure skies. Lacaille glowed above, a huge orb of yellow and orange, with the disk of Mayura a darkened circle superimposed upon it. Amidst the shades on the borders of Drayden and Taloon, a rocky outcrop could be seen, rising above the line of the forest.

It was a well-known way-marker to the priestesses; a place to stop and rest, though there was nothing else of any note nearby.

The dach descended, landing upon the flat surface of the rock, its rider vaulting down and walking forward.

Nerina, high priestess of Drayden, surveyed the scene.

From this vantage point she could see many marks into Drayden, Taloon and even Scallia to the shadeward. She walked forward to the edge, looking down from atop the steep cliffs that marked the edge of the outcrop. There was no way up, only those who rode dachs had ever stood here.

Away from the influence of others, away from the commoners and the inconsequential. Now I can concentrate ...

She closed her eyes, focused her energies and thoughts together.

Now little maid ... where are you?

* * *

Zoella had been taken below decks and locked in her cabin by Coran. Mel, Daf and Creg had been working non-stop throughout the stretch. Coran and Fitch had called time on their efforts to ensure they got some food and rest. A series of odd crates with metal fasteners had been secured in rows deep in the forward and rear holds of the *Mobilis*. They were heavy, the ship sitting lower in the water as a result.

'I hope this is worth it,' Fitch grumbled, watching as Mel yelled instructions to Daf and Creg as they hauled on a series of thick looking cables.

Coran nodded. 'Mel seems to think we'll be able to operate for up to three stretches without 'tricity from the sails. That gives us enough time to make land if there's a problem. I'll take it.'

Fitch laughed.

'So magic powers from the air, stored in boxes in the hold,' he said. 'Girls aboard with magic powers that can crunch your head in. Visions, legends, talking tables and a crazy story about us all coming from some point of light far off in the sky. If this was written down, no one would believe it.'

Coran laughed. 'Can hardly believe it myself and I've seen all of it. Zoella is locked down below. We're safe for now.'

Fitch nodded. 'I've set the timers best I can, and done Meru's snuttin' calculations. Got you a course to the Scattered Isles.'

'Excellent.'

Ira helped load traditional crates aboard the ship, all manner of food and provisions.

Fitch had brought the last few boxes of provisions aboard, something was jutting out of one of them. Coran spotted the metal staff they had found in Kiri's cell.

'Is that Kiri's staff?' he asked. 'What was it called?'

'A kai apparently,' Fitch answered with a nod. 'Thought it best not to leave it lying around. Might be worth bartering, it's worth a bit, all that metal.'

'Just keep it away from Zoella,' Coran muttered, under his breath.

'Right you are, Captain.' Fitch retreated aboard the ship.

The timers aboard the ship swung around to indicate the passing of another chime. Coran could see Mel locking down the hatches on the rear deck. She waved and gestured with a thumbs up sign.

'Ready then,' Coran said to Fitch. 'Round up the crew, let's get underway.'

Coran stepped down the gangplank, seeing Janaid, Henoch and his wife Hannah approaching along the quayside. Behind them trailed the children that Ira had brought with her. They were now dressed in the manner of Amar, following along behind Henoch and Hannah. A crowd of people from Amar had turned out to see the ship off.

'Senators, Hannah,' he said with a bow.

'Almost ready to depart once more,' Janaid said, looking up and down the ship.

Coran nodded. 'Almost. Our plan is to head for the Scattered Isles first, see if we can figure out what happened to the priestesses. We'll advise on the radio via the flying machines.'

Janaid nodded. 'There's been no sign of them since the attack.'

'Licking their wounds or worse I hope,' Coran said. 'In the meantime we should prepare for them to return.'

'The Senate concurs,' Janaid said. 'I will make sure it happens. And then?'

Coran looked at Henoch and Hannah.

'We chase after Meru. We want him back safe.'

Henoch nodded and Hannah smiled.

'When you find him …' Henoch began. Coran saw Hannah look at him. The couple exchanged a look. 'Tell him we love him.'

'I will,' Coran said, with a grin. 'He's a good lad, you should be proud of him. Other than the … er … running away, disobeying his captain, accomplice to a criminal and all that.'

'He's lucky to have friends like you,' Hannah said. Coran could see tears on her face.

'I'll find him, I'll bend his ear a little and I'll bring him back,' Coran said. 'I promise. Looks like you have your hands full in the meantime.'

Both of Meru's parents looked around at the young children clustered nearby, their pale features, bright white hair and curious pink eyes reminded Coran so much of Ren.

'I think so,' Hannah said.

Ira, standing beside Coran, knelt down on the edge of the ship and waved to the children. They waved back. Ira signed something to them. There were few smiles, even tears from some of them.

With a faint rumble the engines of the *Mobilis* began to turn.

'All set!' Mel called out from the bridge.

'Turn your face to the sun,' Janaid said, stepping back.

Coran nodded. 'And your shadows will fall behind you. Farewell!'

Daf and Creg ran fore and aft as folks from the quay unlashed the ropes and flung them aboard. The two big men coiled them up and stored them. Coran vaulted up to the bridge and took the helm.

As the *Mobilis* moved off, the people along the quayside cheered and waved. The crew could see people far up in the city standing on the walls and doing the same thing. It seemed as if everyone had turned out to see them off.

The *Mobilis* cruised out of the harbour entrance and entered the wide expanse of the Strathian Sea. Coran turned the ship to the sunward, squinting up at the huge sphere of Lacaille hanging in the sky above. It was calm and tranquil once again.

But for how long is it going to stay like that?

'Full ahead,' he called.

Mel pushed the throttles up to full and the *Mobilis* reared up, its bow leaping across the undulating sea, a furious wake churning behind it. Amar receded behind them.

Off once more …

'She sounds good,' Coran said, hearing the whirring drone of the engines echoing through the ship.

'Both engines are sound now,' Mel said. 'Would have liked more work on the hull though. Please don't ram anything on this trip.'

'I'll do my best,' Coran said, scanning the horizon. 'You've done a grand job with those …'

'Batteries,' Mel said. 'Clever folks our ancestors. Wish they'd left some instructions though.'

'Yeah, a bit short-sighted of them,' Coran agreed with a smile.

'Good to be back at sea again,' Mel said.

Coran nodded, patting the bridge rail.

'Always,' he said. 'Same as before. Not knowing what's ahead, trying to find Meru again, we've been here before.'

'You're worried about him.'

It was a statement, not a question. Coran looked at her.

'This business with the witch-girl, Kiri,' Coran said. 'I hope Meru's right in trusting her. A lot riding on that decision.'

'We don't know much about her,' Mel said. 'Other than what we've been told by Meru and Zoella.'

'And when Fitch encountered her in the battle … and Ren.'

'We already knew she could fight,' Mel said. 'It's whether she has really changed her view …'

Coran rubbed his chin. 'I guess folks can change,' he said. 'But that's a big one, I'm not convinced. Maybe she sees the Obelisk as a threat to her people and it's just the priority for now.'

'You think she might turn on Meru when it's done?'

'She swore to exterminate us all didn't she, all those vows of theirs?' Coran said. 'That sort of religious thinking is deep-seated. I don't believe she could have just waved it away. We know she's smart and clever and that Meru is besotted with her. I reckon she's using him.'

Mel nodded, thinking it through.

'You're probably right,' she said. 'In that case we need to get to Meru as soon as we can.'

'My thoughts exactly.'

* * *

Zoella sat on her bunk, her legs curled up, her arms wrapped about her knees. The *Mobilis* was underway once more, she had felt the ship depart and welcomed the rocking motion. It had been strange to be on land for a spell, it felt better to be back at sea. She'd grown accustomed to the strange metal ship and its crew.

I just wish things could go back to the way they were.

She'd seen the furtive glances, the averted eyes the rest of the crew treated her to as Coran had led her below decks. They were all smiles and pleasantries, all except Fitch, pretending to be busier than they were.

Avoiding me, but who can blame them? What can I do to earn back their trust?

She couldn't think of an answer.

I must ensure that these feelings never get the better of me again. I will not succumb to the hatred and rage.

The moment the thoughts flashed across her mind an image came to her.

Fierce blue eyes, dark hair waving in some imaginary wind. She felt the hate wash across her. She clenched her fists, trying to stop it.

No … I won't.

The image faded away. She remembered to breathe, sucking in lungfuls of air to calm herself down; she could feel her heart racing.

I can do this.

She focused on her breathing for long moments, the feelings subsided.

Yes, it's …

Then, like a silent but deafening clash of noise, another presence wrapped itself around her.

So, little maid, I have found you.

Zoella struggled, but the grip on her mind was firm and unshakeable.

Where are you …?

The command was inexorable. Zoella twisted within herself, trying to escape the grasp, but there was no way to break free.

Unwittingly, images of the *Mobilis*, the decks, the sea and the receding coastline of Amar flickered in her mind.

So you depart from Amar. Where are you headed?

Zoella clenched her thoughts back under her control.

You will learn nothing from me!

A sense of amusement crept across the link.

I have already learnt much, maid. Or should I call you Zoella? Your thoughts have given away your name. You're from Scallia, you fought alongside Lady Liana of Viresia!

Images of the battle flickered across her mind. She couldn't stop the recall.

And faced down little Kiri too. How did you manage that?

The rage came back, burning through her, caustic hot. This woman invading her thoughts, her very privacy!

No!

More images crashed through her mind. Zoella struggled to hold them back, but Nerina's forceful push was relentless. In horror Zoella's memory replayed in her mind, how she had killed the ice traders in the frozen wastes of Drem, the death of Turgan at Kiri's hand and how Kiri had stopped the priestesses from capturing herself and Meru in the harbour.

What is this? She lied! Why would Kiri do such a thing? Protect you? Why? What is she to you?

Zoella screeched, pushing the thoughts away and shutting down the images.

For a moment she thought she had succeeded, but then Nerina's powers came crashing back at her, their strength doubled.

Zoella almost passed out with the pain. The smell of hot metal burnt in her nostrils, swamping her, stinging the back of her throat. Hatred and rage swirled about her, Nerina's wrath was incendiary.

More images crashed through her mind, the Obelisk, Caesar's maps, the *Mobilis* travelling across the sea, the great orb of Lacaille hanging before it.

Stop it!

I will find you Zoella of Scallia. And when I do I will tear your powers from you ...

You will not have me!

The link crackled and broke, leaving just a faint echo of laughter drifting in Zoella's mind.

* * *

Kiri pulled her hand back, running her fingers up Meru's arm, seeing a green frond touching him. She batted it away. It swayed back and forth and then drifted back. She could see tiny little buds, almost like fingers themselves, touching her. She watched it, mesmerised for a moment by its movement. She felt another touch on her back, slipping down towards her buttocks. She gasped in delight before realising she still held Meru's hands in hers. Her vision focussed on a swath of green that was arching in all around them.

Letting go of Meru she grabbed one of the fronds, pulling it close to her face.

She sensed something, the hot metal smell of the nexion rising in her nostrils. For a moment she could feel the plant, hear its thoughts.

Trapped, Caught, Take, Feast!

She gasped.

'Kiri? What is ...?'

The greenery of the floor around the flower was curling in on itself, fronds, leaves and branches rising up and contracting in. They felt the ground underneath them move. The glow around them turned red once more and a wave of heat blasted across them, stifling and burning hot.

Kiri tumbled off Meru, slipping on the vegetation, scrambling for grip. She felt something wrap around her ankle, tightening quickly. Meru crawled alongside her pulling at the green frond that had trapped her. It came free, but not before more of the fronds flailed, seeking to grab them.

'Run!' Kiri yelled, staggering up and pulling Meru behind her. She batted at the greenery around her, her fingers coated in the fronds as they tried to entangle her. The whole copse was rising up.

In horror they realised that what they had both taken for a flower was only the central bud of the plant. The copse itself was the flower, they'd been enticed in like a pair of stung-drunk marsips. Now the real petals, huge thick fans of greenery, were wrapping up around them. Fronds curled from their surfaces seeking to trap, grasp and hold them.

'There's no way out!' Meru gasped, as the petals curled above them, trapping them inside a huge shrinking sphere of green, it was almost dark now, oppressive and claustrophobic. The plant beneath them gave a shudder and a dark liquid began to spill up from the central bud.

'It's going to eat us!' Kiri shrieked. She ran forward, clawing at the greenery, ripping into it with her fingers, tearing at it. Meru joined her, trying to wrestle open the thick petals. The fluid oozed up behind them, they felt it touch their bare heels. It stung.

Kiri had managed to get her fingers between two of the petals, they were thick and rubbery. Desperate, she sank her teeth into one, biting down and ripping it, spitting away the foul taste. Her arm pushed through, flailing to get a purchase on the other side, Meru pushed at her, forcing her body through the gap. Slick as she was and covered in the sticky syrup, her body slithered through the gap and she fell outside on to the rough dirt.

Shaking her head she staggered up. The plant was still contracting. She heard a muffled scream. She turned to the plant, punching her fist through the small gap that remained.

'Grab my hand!'

She felt his fingers grab her outstretched hand. She yanked, pulling him towards her. Her feet slipped on the ground. She couldn't get any purchase. Adjusting her grip she braced both her feet against the outside of the plant and pulled as hard as she could.

She strained her arms and legs, screeching out as she did so.

'Let him go!'

Meru emerged with shocking speed, ejected from the plant in a spray of hissing fluid which splattered all about them. Kiri landed on her back, the impact knocking the breath from her. Both of them scrambled away, gasping and panting hard.

They reached the shades' trunks once more, collapsing against them.

'You hurt?' Kiri asked after a moment.

'Just … stings …' Meru said, miserably. 'My feet …'

Kiri sat up and looked at them. She could see the skin was red raw.

'Wait here,' she said, climbing to her feet. She ran through the shades, making her way towards the light, fighting her way through to the flying machine. There she grabbed a knife and a pair of blankets before running back, hunting for Meru in the gloom.

He was where she had left him, watching the plant. It had curled into a tight green bud that shuddered and jolted every so often.

Kiri made an angled cut on the nearest shade with the knife, cupping her hands to catch the liquid that dribbled out.

'This will smart a bit,' she said and poured the liquid on Meru's feet. He flinched, but then relaxed as the painkilling effects of the shadewater took effect. Kiri placed her hands on his feet, closing her eyes and bringing to mind the healer training she had received rounds before.

Meru relaxed.

'Better?' she asked.

'Yes,' he said. 'I told you it was poisonous.'

'It wasn't poisonous …' Kiri began. 'It was … You were right, I was wrong. Let's get back to the ship, shall we?'

Kiri helped him sit up, placing the blankets around both of them and pulling him to his feet. Before them the plant seemed to have sensed its prey had escaped. The vast petals were lowering themselves, the fluid oozing away. Cheated of its prey, it was resetting its trap for the next unwary visitor.

'I've decided I don't like plants much,' Meru said as they limped away.

Kiri laughed, pawing at the mud and grime that now coated her.

'Shall we just stick to a bed next time?' she asked. 'Maybe with a lock on the door …?'

* * *

Fitch was watching the Scattered Isles rise out of the sea before them. He'd been scanning the horizon for a couple of spells as they approached, looking for any signs of the priestesses' dachs through the 'scope. The *Mobilis* continued on its way, unimpeded.

Fitch jumped up to the bridge. Coran had throttled down the engines and was gazing at the Isles before them. They were pretty inhospitable for the most part, jagged rocks sticking out of the sea. The original crew had been stuck on the island after a shipwreck many rounds before. It was here they had found the *Mobilis*, languishing in a deserted dockyard, rotting away, abandoned by her original makers.

'All looks quiet,' he said. 'All I can see are a few small dachs circling above. They're just the native ones, nothing big.'

'So the priestesses aren't here,' Mel said.

'Looks that way,' Coran said. 'But let's be sure.'

Coran guided the *Mobilis* into the islands. He knew his way, this had been their base of operations prior to returning to Amar.

'Port Melanie,' Coran said. 'Haven't been back here for a while.'

'Everything looks undisturbed,' Mel said, looking around her as the cliffs rose. A gaping cave mouth was opening before them, its edges covered in thick green vegetation hanging down from the mountainous terrain above. Everything was swathed in mist.

'Dead slow,' Coran said, pulling the throttles back further.

The *Mobilis* lost way, drifting forwards in the still water. As they entered the cave, Mel flicked on the 'tricity lights, bathing the area ahead in the bright glow of the *Mobilis'* lights.

As they watched, bright globes of light illuminated the darkness in turn, revealing a vast interior space carved within the mountains. There were a series of quays which could have accommodated many ships far bigger than the *Mobilis*.

'No sign of anything,' Fitch said.

Coran nodded and gestured to Mel. 'Might be worth a check from our girls with the magic powers. Can you go get them?'

Mel nodded and jumped down to the deck hatchways, promptly disappearing inside.

A few moments later, Coran watched as Zoella and Ira emerged on to the forward deck led by Mel; looking around them in wonder. Zoella looked pale, her face blotchy as if she'd been crying. Ira smiled at him, but Zoella gave only a slight nod.

You alright?' Coran asked, looking at Zoella.

She looked away. Coran saw her shudder.

This one isn't going to be resolved any time soon.

Mel was looking at Zoella too, she gave a little wave of her hand to Coran, a 'leave it with me' gesture.

Coran sighed and turned his attention to guiding the *Mobilis* against the quayside. Daf and Creg tied her up, and Mel shutdown the engines.

'Let's be cautious,' Coran said. 'Keep your ears and eyes open. Zoella, Ira, can you sense anything?'

Zoella explained the request to Ira. They conversed in sign language before both closing their eyes in concentration. After a moment Zoella shook her head.

'No, nothing,' she reported, though she looked around herself nervously, her voice faint. 'If they are still here they're hiding from us somehow.'

'Then let's go see,' Coran muttered.

As usual, Daf and Creg were left to mind the ship. Coran led the way, with Mel, Ira, Zoella and Fitch following behind them. He led them to the cave entrance and then up a winding craggy pathway which cut through the steep sides of the island, winding its way back and forth upwards through the thick foliage. Fitch and Coran were carrying rifles, ready and loaded.

Long before they reached the summit they could hear the sharp cries of the wild dachs. They were far smaller than those the priestesses had ridden, only a few hands in length. Coran, Mel and Fitch had seen them before, they seemed to use the islands as eyries, but there were a lot more present than they had seen before.

'Something's not right,' Fitch grunted, when they stopped for a rest halfway up. He gestured up at the sky, where dozens and dozens of the small flying creatures could be seen circling in the sky. There was a faint buzzing noise coming from above them too.

Coran nodded, getting to his feet.

'Let's keep moving.'

They continued the climb, the sea now hundreds of hands below them. The vegetation thinned out and they came to the summit. Coran heard Zoella and Mel gasp from behind him. He came up short, staring around in horror.

The reason for the arrival of the wild dachs became obvious. Strewn across the bare flattened peak of the island were carcasses. The dachs were feasting on them, ragged strips of flesh being ripped from decomposing bodies in their needle-sharp teeth. The buzzing noise was revealed too, countless nargs swarmed in great clouds, fighting the dachs for a meal.

The carcasses were of dachs and people.

The crew stared for long moment, horrified. The stench of rotting meat wafted across them, causing them to stumble backwards, gagging. Ira was sick, vomiting on the greenery to the side of the path they had walked up. Mel and Zoella went to comfort her.

Coran looked at Fitch. Both hoisted their rifles and walked forward.

It was difficult to see much. The bodies were in an advanced state of decay, having been out in the heat of Lacaille for stretches. The clothing and harnesses gave them away though. The bodies of dozens of dachs and priestesses littered the area.

'They must have known of this place from before they attacked us,' Fitch said, grimacing with the smell. 'And retreated here afterwards.'

'All dead,' Coran whispered. 'So, none of them escaped in the end. Flare got them.'

'No,' Fitch said, shaking his head. 'Not all of them.'

Coran watched as the older man stepped forward amongst the bodies, peering at them with a keen eye.

'Look,' he said. 'No weapons. No staffs, swords, bows. Nothing. Dachs and nargs don't eat weapons, somebody took them.'

'Some survived?' Coran asked.

'Looks that way,' Fitch said with a nod.

They backed away, wafting fresh air towards them with their hands, their eyes watering.

'The priestesses?' Mel asked.

'Definitely,' Coran said. 'Nothing but bodies though. No one's alive. Fitch reckons they must have landed here after the flare. Seems like they left behind their dead.'

'And their wounded too I would say,' Fitch said. 'They took everything else with them. Callous snuts.'

'Where do you think they went?' Mel asked.

'Back to the mainland,' Fitch said. 'The maps show these islands are a handy little waypoint in the ocean and there's a peninsula of land to the shaderight. They must have known that.'

Zoella was nodding. 'Meru flew us that way so we were over land as much as possible when we came from Taloon. They aren't here.' Her voice took on a more distant tone. 'They're far away …'

'Well, that's something,' Coran said. 'With the Taloon fleet destroyed and a good portion of the priestesses lost … that buys us some time. It'll take them a while to regroup before they can come back at us again.'

'So we go after Meru?' Mel asked.

Coran nodded. 'We'll radio back to Amar about what we've found and then head sunwards.' He spared a final look at the scene before them. 'Let's go.'

* * *

Meru and Kiri had returned to the flying machine and washed themselves down before changing into fresh clothes.

'We need to be more careful,' Meru said. 'We could have been killed, people are depending on us, we can't afford to be distracted …'

Kiri nodded, but Meru could see she was trying to suppress a grin.

'Stop it,' Meru said.

Kiri laughed.

'I don't suppose you'll be mentioning any of that when you next use the radio,' she said.

'No.'

'Come on then,' she said, clambering into the cockpit. 'Let's go save everyone. I'll try to be less distracting for you ...'

Meru looked at her, feeling his heart lurch as he did so.

Not much hope of that!

It was the little things, he decided. The way her hair fell forward across her face, the way she pushed it behind her ear. How she was small and neat, each movement carefully controlled.

And those eyes ...

He climbed in beside her, fastening the harnesses and flipping the switches in preparation for take-off. He pulled on the controls and the machine lifted off, the vegetation dropping away below them. Meru spun the machine around and pointed it sunward.

Ahead the heavy line of clouds could still be seen, blocking the horizon. The enormous shadeforest was rolling away beneath them as the machine picked up speed. As they watched, they saw lightning flicker within the clouds, lighting them up from within.

'We have to go through there?' Kiri asked.

Meru nodded. 'No other way. This storm surrounds the Obelisk.'

Lacaille's light was already fading into the gloom. Meru angled the flying machine above the lowest cloud. Lightning flashed again, flickering around the interior of the flying machine and causing him to shield his eyes.

'Altitude ceiling reached,' Sandra intoned.

'I guess that's it,' Meru said. 'We can't go any higher.'

'We're not above the highest clouds,' Kiri said, looking forward. 'If we go in there, we'll be flying blind.'

'We have some advantages over a dach,' Meru said. 'The instruments will allow us to tell where we're going even if we can't see.'

The cloud was thickening fast. Below them the tops of the shades disappeared into a grey murk. Lacaille's disk faded away above them.

Cloud was all about them, thick and heavy. Rain spots began to splatter the front windows.

'Here we go.'

Visibility dropped to zero. The flying machine lurched, the controls juddering in Meru's hands. He felt the machine drop and yaw before he could correct it. Rain was lashing the windows, he couldn't see anything. The wind howled outside.

The whole airframe was vibrating and groaning about them in an alarming way. A fork of light flickered nearby, thunder crashed again.

'I don't like this,' Kiri muttered. 'How long will it take?'

'Long enough,' Meru said. 'It's hundreds of marks to where the Obelisk is. Several spells.'

'Several spells?'

Kiri swallowed, bracing herself as the machine jolted again and again. Everything inside was rattling and vibrating as the machine was tossed this way and that.

'We're heading the right way,' Meru said. 'We've just got to ride it …'

The machine dropped beneath them, the engines whirring hard. Kiri gave a short screech of surprise.

'… out,' Meru gasped as the plunge finished and the machine steadied out.

He looked over to her. Kiri's grip on the arms of her chair was knuckle white.

'External wind shear is approaching tolerance,' Sandra intoned, her voice only just audible above the noise from outside.

'What does that mean?' Kiri asked.

'Structural integrity will be compromised if external conditions grow more severe,' Sandra replied.

'I don't think I want to know …' she muttered.

'Caesar said the flying machines should be able to fly through this storm safely,' Meru said.

'Should?' Kiri looked aghast.

'He didn't say it wasn't dangerous,' Meru said, wrestling with the controls.

The cloud flickered past the cockpit's windows and then the light around them brightened. The flying machine burst out into clear air. Above, Lacaille could be seen shining in a bright azure sky. The flying machine cruised onwards, through clean smooth air.

'Are we through?' Kiri said in wonder, looking about her.

Meru shook his head.

'The storm is like a spiral,' Meru said. 'Imagine a huge whirlpool spiralling inwards made of cloud. We've just flown through the outermost arm.'

They looked out of the windows. They could make out the structure of the storm. A vast arcing wall of cloud hung behind them. They could see it extended sunright and shaderight around them, curving inwards at the extremities of vision. Below, the ground could be seen once more, covered in shades for the most part, but with vast cliffs of rock jutting up, the terrain mountainous.

'Look … a waterfall!' Kiri pointed.

The waterfall was enormous, perhaps five marks wide and falling at least a mark downwards, its base shrouded in mist. Behind it stretched a lake disappearing over the shaderight horizon.

'It's always raining under these clouds,' Meru said. 'All that water has to go somewhere …'

Lacaille's light flickered. Wisps of cloud were thickening overhead. The interlude was coming to an end.

'Hang on,' Meru said, bracing himself.

Lightning flashed.

* * *

The crew of the *Mobilis* had retreated down the side of the island and returned to the cavern below, boarding the ship. Daf and Creg were waiting for them and helped them aboard.

'Make ready to depart,' Coran instructed.

Everyone turned to their tasks. Mel started the engines. Daf and Creg cast off the lines and reeled them in. The *Mobilis* backed away from the quay and then turned around in the cavern, before heading out through the bright entrance.

The Strathian Sea widened before them. Coran spun the ship's wheel and the ship turned to starboard, heading sunward.

'At least the course is easy enough,' Mel said, clambering up beside him.

Coran nodded. 'Yes, just keep Lacaille ahead. Simple enough!'

They watched Ira and Zoella climb into the ship via the forward hatch. Zoella looked about her before dropping below. Fitch followed her.

'Something not right with her,' Mel said.

Coran nodded. 'You noticed that too?'

'I mean, she's going to be uncertain and nervous,' Mel said. 'But, it's something else, something is preying on her mind.'

'We'll have plenty of time to get to the bottom of it,' Coran said. 'Long traipse across the sea for us now.'

He pushed the throttles up to their three quarter mark and the *Mobilis* leapt forward, driving away from the Scattered Isles.

'Take the helm,' he said. 'I'll see if I can raise Amar on the radio.'

Mel nodded and stepped up. Coran moved to the radio station and switched it on.

'Amar, this is the *Mobilis*, are you receiving me?'

The answer was immediate. Coran recognised the tones of Senator Janaid across the link. He had been waiting for the call.

'Yes, *Mobilis*, we can hear you. Is that you, Coran?'

'It's me,' Coran replied. 'We've just left the Scattered Isles. The priestesses have definitely been there, but no longer. It seems they've returned to the main land. We found bodies, but no one alive.'

'So they have retreated,' Janaid answered. 'Good news indeed.'

'We don't know how many survived,' Coran replied. 'Nor do we have a way of finding out. We can't afford to be complacent. We don't know how long it will take them to reassemble a fleet but it will take some time after the losses they suffered.'

'Agreed,' Janaid replied. 'The voice aboard the flying machines reports that repairs are proceeding nominally. I take that to mean it's a work in progress.'

'It all takes a bit of getting used to,' Coran said, with a chuckle.

'At least we can send the fishermen back out,' Janaid said. 'Otherwise we'll have other problems on our hands.'

'I think that's safe enough if you stay within sight of the smokes.'

'I doubt we could persuade them to go any further,' Janaid answered. 'How about you?'

'We are heading sunwards,' Coran said. 'We'll work shifts so we can keep travelling through the sleeping. Based on the map that should take us five stretches to reach the edge of the vortex. Then we have to find a way through to reach the Obelisk. We'll keep trying with the radio, but we'll probably lose contact soon.'

'Any word from Meru?'

'I'll be trying to reach him next,' Coran said.

'I'll let you go then,' Janaid said. 'All our thoughts are with you.'

'Thanks,' Coran said. 'We will be back as soon as we can.'

He flipped the switches off.

'So far so good,' Mel said.

Coran nodded. 'This is the easy bit. I don't like the thought of travelling into this vortex much. An everlasting storm? Sounds wonderful.'

'The *Mobilis* will be more than up to the task,' Mel said, giving him a smile.

'I have no doubt of that,' Coran said. 'Let's see if we can get hold of Meru.'

He flipped the radio switches on and adjusted the frequency dial to the settings they'd agreed.

'Meru, this is Coran …'

A screech of static greeted them, loud enough to make them flinch and for Coran to adjust the volume dial.

'Meru? Can you hear us?'

The static remained thick and heavy, punctuated by repeated crashes of noise every few moments.

'Meru?' Coran said again, annunciating each word. 'Can you hear us?'

A faint voice crackled, interrupted by the static.

'... can hear ... us? Storm is ... shaken badly ...'

Coran saw Mel looking at him.

'That wasn't Meru ...'

Coran turned the volume up.

'Repeat what you said.'

The static buzzed and hissed. Coran adjusted the tuning and then the signal grew stronger.

'Can you hear us?' A woman's voice said, loudly, her accent sharp and distinct.

'Yes,' Coran's voice was almost a shout. 'Who is this?'

'It's Kiri,' came the response. 'Meru is flying. Storm is very danger– The flying machine is ... badly. We are still heading for the Obelisk ... we should be through the vortex in ...'

Static crashed again, forcing Coran and Mel to back away from the burst of noise.

'We are coming,' Coran said. 'The *Mobilis* is heading sunwards. We will reach the vortex in about five stretches.'

'Can't hear ... too much ... we are heading for the Obelisk ... can you hear ...?'

'We can hear you,' Coran repeated. 'We are coming, five stretches. Can you ...?'

Kiri's voice became clear for a moment. 'I don't think it's working, it's just noise ...'

'We can hear you,' Coran roared.

'They're back!' Kiri's voice was high with excitement. 'We're in the storm ...'

'We heard,' Coran said. 'Five stretches. We'll be at the vortex. Tell Meru!'

'Five stretches ... they're coming,' Kiri was relaying the message. 'Meru says the vortex is much worse than he thought. When you bring the ship through you must …'

Static crashed again, drowning out Kiri's words.

The signal came back, but now it was overlaid with a siren, blaring out over and over again.

Coran and Mel heard a short yell before another voice sounded over the radio link. It was the onboard system, Sandra.

'Ship integrity … control surface … detected …'

They could just make out the sound of the engines roaring amidst the static.

'What is …?' Kiri's voice was sharp and scared. 'Meru? Meru! We're …'

More static.

'Kiri, what's happening?' Coran demanded.

All they could hear was the blare of the siren, crunches and bangs from the radio transmission.

Kiri's voice was heard for a moment.

'Oh no … no …'

Then there was a scream, high pitched and terrified. It carried on for brief moments before being cut off. There was a crackle and then then signal was gone, only the background static remained.

'Kiri? Kiri! Meru! Answer me!'

Coran turned the frequency dial, but there was nothing but the mocking hiss of static to be heard.

Coran looked at Mel.

'I want full speed from the engines.'

She nodded. 'You've got it.'

CHAPTER SEVEN

Strathian Sea, heading sunward

Round 2307, Eighth pass

The *Mobilis* was leaping the waves of the Strathian Sea, its course still sunwards. Lacaille was clear in the sky above them, its huge disk rising higher as the ship forged its way across the ocean. There was not a cloud above, but the temperature was rising with every passing spell.

Behind the ship a long silver wake spread out in the undulating waters. There was no land in sight, no reference markers, just the endless blue.

Zoella was sitting cross-legged on the forward deck, her hands out to steady her from the rocking and thrumming of the ship as it surged onwards. Fitch was watching her from the wheelhouse, his rifle conspicuously on display. Her eyes were closed, her expression one of intense concentration.

Kiri! You must answer me. What has happened? Are you hurt? Please answer.

Zoella had been trying to reach her sister for almost a stretch, ever since the radio communication had been cut off. There had been no answer, no sense of acknowledgement or even awareness from the other end. There was no sign of Kiri … and no sign of Meru.

Her stomach clenched inside her.

I should have been with Meru. It should have been me alongside him, going to fix the Obelisk, and now …

She shuddered, remembering the way Nerina had forced her way into her mind. Panic sent her heart thumping wildly in her chest, her breathing short and forced.

And she knows! She knows where we are, where we're going. It's all my fault. I should tell the crew … I'm endangering them! But if I tell them Nerina can break into my mind and read my thoughts … what will they do?

Her imagination ran away. Coran's angry visage, Fitch's cruel smirk …

They'll throw me overboard …

She opened her eyes and looked around at Fitch. He saw her turn, looking at her with a squint. He patted the rifle next to him, not taking his eyes off her.

Or just shoot me! I can't …

More memories battered her, the recall of the hatred that had coursed through her, the anger and fury that had consumed her.

Almost like it was someone else, but it wasn't. That was me. I did it. I was just as brutal as I've accused Kiri of being. I tortured her. I attacked my friends. I could have killed them. I was totally out of control …

The memory sat in her mind, surrounded by layers of shame and horror.

I've never wanted to kill. It wasn't me …

But it was. No one had forced her, no one had decided but her. It was as clear as crystal in her mind. Hurting Coran, Mel, Fitch, Daf and Creg, pushing aside the guards, picking up the staff; she could still feel it in her hands. She winced as the memory replayed, hearing Kiri's screams echoing in her consciousness.

Her hands were shaking. The violence was a part of her, clearly she was capable of it. She remembered the man she had killed in the frozen wastes just sunward of Drem, crushing his mind like a dach egg.

I was provoked, the anger took me then too … and before that the rage I felt at Kiri when she attacked Viresia, hurting Liana and killing Torin. Even Nerina's attack on me a stretch ago …

The same rage, a burning metallic sensation that overwhelmed her each time.

She clenched her eyes shut, trying to breathe, forcing air into her lungs, making a concerted effort to calm her racing heart. After a few moments the panic passed, but her thoughts were still spiralling in her mind.

She gasped.

The gift … it's the gift!

The realisation hit her, causing her mind to spin backwards through everything she had experienced. It even went back to her childhood when she had been taunted by Shalla, seeking refuge with Raga; the fight with the molossc too.

The same anger, the same rage. Powered by the gift itself, inflamed by it?

Liana's aggression against the priestesses, how she had struck Kiri down and tortured her before the walls of Viresia. How the priestesses had attacked with their righteous anger, their determination and cold resolve. Kiri's assault on Turgan and then … Zoella winced again … her own torturing of Kiri.

Rage, rage, rage! The women with the gift … we all show it. All of us … even me. I am no warrior, yet look at what I did when I was angry … It's like the gift has its own will.

She shuddered, the thought chilled her. What was the gift? She didn't know. Caesar had said something about it. Meru had asked, but his question was cut off in the rush to save Amar. Zoella wracked her brains trying to remember.

Nano-infusion. That was what Caesar called it … but what is it? What does it mean? It's something we have … something inside us.

She opened her eyes, staring down at her hands, turning them over and rubbing her fingers together. Words she had read came to her from long ago, when she had been sealed in the catacombs beneath the city of Viresia. A book she had seen dating back hundreds of rounds to the long lost Voren Empire.

The gift is found only in women and must be sought out by those already in full control of their gift. It lies dormant until the later stages of puberty by design, to avoid the complexities of such powers emerging in the immature …

Zoella frowned.

By design … somebody designed the gift? Made it … and then gave it to women to use to administer …

Her recall continued.

At no stage should the gift be used inappropriately. It is possible to reverse the natural order of the gift and use it to impart harm. In extreme cases it can be used to inflict pain of various types and control the actions of others. Such use of the gift is strictly forbidden ...

She remembered reading the words. It was when she had first discovered who and what she was, a woman like the so-called witches of Drayden.

We're not supposed to be doing this ... what we've done with the gift ... that's not what it was for. The people of Voren knew this ... but now ...

There was one final phrase that her memory threw back into her consciousness.

It may become necessary to have the subject's gift removed. In such situations the gift becomes additive to those who undertake the removal. This should be carefully monitored for abuse ...

Zoella swallowed.

Liana was taking gifts from women for rounds, the priestesses too. Kiri must have done it and Nerina now threatens me with the same.

Zoella remembered meeting Kiri face to face in the tunnels under Airea, how Kiri had tried to take her gift. Ira had stopped it, but Zoella had learnt how it was done.

On the walls, when Kiri killed Ren.

Zoella remembered how she had struck at Kiri, trying to crush her mind as she had with the man in the frozen wastes. Kiri had fought back, but she was weak, hurt and exhausted.

Before the priestesses arrived, when Kiri slumped before me, I ...

Her mouth dropped open in shock. She hadn't even realised what she'd done.

I stole from her. I was stealing her gift even as I tried to kill her. Ever since, the rage has grown all the more. And when I beat her, she was weak, she couldn't fend me off. Kiri has lost some of her powers ... to me!

Zoella looked up, watching the sea roll past the bow of the *Mobilis*.

And with that extra power I almost killed her ... too much is dangerous, maybe that's why the priestesses seek to conquer, like Liana did … they can't help it … they're ruled by the gift itself!

The memory of Nerina's thought attack came into her mind.

And she is pursuing me too … she wants my gift to further her own ends, to become even more powerful! She won't let me go. What am I going to do?

She heard footsteps behind her. She turned to see Mel walking up the decking.

'Any luck?' Mel asked.

'Luck?' Zoella asked, bewildered.

'Contacting Kiri.'

Zoella shook her head.

'Oh … no. I can't hear her, there's nothing,' Zoella said. 'I've tried and tried, but …'

She saw Mel nod, her expression glum.

'We're going as fast as we can,' Mel said, bracing herself as the *Mobilis* pitched across the swell of the sea. 'There's nothing else we can do now, but try to get there as fast as possible.'

'I'll keep trying,' Zoella said.

Mel crouched down beside her and squeezed her shoulder.

'It's not your fault, you know.'

Zoella slumped, her head falling forward.

'Come on,' Mel said. 'Stop beating yourself up over what is said and done. You can't change the past.'

'But if I'd just left her alone,' Zoella said. 'Meru wouldn't have run off, we would all be tackling this together. Instead …'

'Meru running off was his decision,' Mel told her. 'He could have just knocked you out, taken Kiri to the medical ship and stayed put. You can't take responsibility for what he's done, or whatever has happened to him now.'

Zoella shrugged. 'I suppose …'

'Don't give up on him,' Mel said. 'Meru has a funny way of getting out of scrapes. The flying machine might be damaged, they might be out of range …'

'But I can't sense Kiri at all,' Zoella replied, turning to look at Mel. 'If she's awake I should be able to sense her. I'm sure something bad has happened.'

'Maybe she still doesn't want to be sensed,' Mel said. 'She knows we don't trust her, maybe she's just choosing not to answer.'

'I'm sure I'd still be able to tell she was alive. It's hard to hide that if someone is searching.'

'Well, I don't understand this power of yours,' Mel said. 'Give me the 'tricity any stretch. I can figure that out.'

'It's all connected somehow,' Zoella answered. 'The 'tricity, the Obelisk, the gift. Even Caesar said it was something that was inside us somehow.'

'Inside?'

'I think I figured out what happened to me, what made me so angry … it's this power, this so called gift some of us have.'

'How?'

Zoella explained her thinking about the gift, the priestesses and everything else she had seen. Mel listened thoughtfully.

'It kinda makes sense,' Mel said, after thinking for a moment. 'We all wondered where such hatred came from, it seemed so unlike you.'

'It isn't me,' Zoella said. 'Or it's a part of me I don't want to be me.'

Mel nodded. 'We all have a darker side you know, when we're pushed to the edge. It's part of what we are. Particularly quiet ones like you.' She grinned. 'Come on, you'll get scorched out here. It's broiling. You should come below deck and get a drink.'

Zoella tensed.

'You're part of this crew,' Mel said to her, her voice lower. 'Coran said so and so it is. No more recriminations from anyone. We all agreed. There's not a person aboard who hasn't done something wrong in the past. I know I have.' She laughed and got to her feet.

Zoella looked up and smiled. 'Thank you for giving me another chance, after what I did …'

Mel held up a finger. 'Enough of that. In the past remember? We've got enough trouble up ahead. Let's keep focussed on that, eh? Let's find

Meru, fix this snuttin' Obelisk and get back home. Nothing else we need to worry about.'

Zoella couldn't help it. She let out a sob and then was crying again.

'What is it?' Mel asked, crouching down beside her and looking at her with a concerned expression. 'What's wrong?'

'I can't …' Zoella said. 'You'll … He'll …' She gestured up at Fitch.

Zoella was shuddering.

'Hey … you've not done anything …'

'It's … it's …'

Mel touched her arm.

'It's alright. Just tell me.'

Zoella looked up at Mel, her face was pale, terror etched on her features.

'It's that woman, the high priestess … Nerina.'

'What, the one we fought off at Amar?'

Zoella nodded. 'She's alive.'

Mel frowned. 'How do you know?'

'She … she tried to get into my mind …'

'When was this?'

'When we left Amar.' Zoella looked up guiltily. 'I should have said something but I thought …'

She looked up at Fitch.

Mel looked around to see where she was looking.

'It's alright,' Mel said, keeping her voice steady. 'Just tell me what happened.'

Zoella took a deep breath.

'I was trying to make sure I wouldn't get angry again,' Zoella said. 'I stayed out of everyone's way in my cabin as agreed, just tried to be calm. It seemed to be working, but then …'

'Go on,' Mel said.

'Her thoughts pushed into my head, strong and hard … forceful. She knew who I was, where I was. She plans to find me and …'

Zoella shuddered. Mel pulled her into an embrace.

'We won't let that happen, you hear me?' Mel said. 'We won't.'

'You won't be able to stop her ...'

'We stopped her once,' Mel retorted. 'We can do it again. But we've got to tell Coran. This changes things. If she knows where we are ... why didn't you tell us?'

'I thought...' Zoella was shivering uncontrollably. She glanced at Fitch and then at Mel.

Mel sighed.

'You thought we'd do you in if you did?' Mel said. 'Oh, Zoella...'

Mel pulled her into a tight hug. 'We ain't killers girl. We might shout and bitch a lot, but not that. You poor thing.'

'Maybe you should,' Zoella cried. 'It would be better if I was dead.'

Mel pulled back.

'Belay that talk,' she scolded. 'Part of the crew, remember? Come on, Coran needs to know.'

Mel took her hand and pulled her along the deck towards the bridge.

* * *

Kiri coughed. She spluttered, jolting and retching. Water was in her mouth, muddy and silty. She choked, spitting it out of her mouth, wrenching herself upwards.

She gasped as pain flashed down her side and she grimaced, wiping her eyes with the back of her hand so she could see.

She was lying in a pool of mud, on the shore of a lake that stretched out before her. Above, a huge curving wall of cloud stretched into the heavens like an enormous barrier. She cowered before it, awed by its moving majesty. She could see it wrapped around the horizon, a complete circle, though its far side was hard to see in the distance.

Lacaille blazed overhead, almost half the sky consumed by its overwhelming orb.

This must be the centre ...

Her side stung. She looked down to see her clothing ripped and a gash in her skin. It was bleeding, but it was already half congealed. Sore, but not dangerous, assuming she could wash the dirt out of it. The rest of her was covered in mud. Turning around she gazed beyond the line of the shore.

She gasped.

A vast tower reached into the heavens. She trembled as she looked at it. It had to be as tall as the cloud wall, perhaps even higher, its surface glowing with the reflected light of Lacaille, pure untarnished metal.

It was shaped like a triangle, narrow at the top, and splayed out wider at the bottom, but there was a gentle arc to its shape, more pronounced at the base. At the very top Kiri could see something strange, a colouration or a disturbance of the air, she wasn't sure. The tower dwarfed even the vast shades that clustered around it, reaching up far into the heavens.

The Obelisk!

She got to her knees, wincing with the effort and pain, staring in shock for long moments.

How did …?

She looked around her.

Meru? Where is Meru? What happened?

She cast her mind back, trying to recall.

We were flying, something went wrong, the machine fell out of the sky … crash!

She shook her head, and regretted it. Her head pulsed with pain. She clenched her eyes shut until it subsided.

She crawled out of the mud. The pool blocked her vision so she pulled herself up its sides and over the top.

Beyond lay the wreckage of the flying machine.

It was crumpled over on one side, bent and buckled from the impact with the ground. The cockpit windows were gone, the stubby wings bent backwards. Debris was scattered all around. Water was flowing past her. It seemed they had crashed in a shallow river bed.

Kiri staggered to her feet, limping forwards, noticing all manner of small cuts across her skin and arms.

I must have been flung through the window somehow …

She hobbled over to the flying machine, wrenching at the twisted remains of the door. It bent with a creak and fell off its hinges, clattering to the floor.

Meru was inside, slumped across the controls.

'Meru!'

Kiri scrambled in, ignoring the pain in her body. She pulled his head back to see a jagged cut across his temple. He moaned as she moved him. To her relief his eyes opened and he moaned.

He looked up at her.

'Kiri?' His voice was a rasp.

'Yes, I'm here? Are you hurt?'

Meru tried to move and cried out.

'My leg,' he said, through gritted teeth.

Kiri looked. The forward console of the flying machine had been bent by the impact and had crushed down on Meru's legs, pinning him in place. There was no blood that she could see.

'I think you're just caught,' she said. 'I'll see if I can pull you out.'

She climbed alongside him, pulling at the harness that was still strapped in place about him.

'You … you're …?'

'I'm fine, just cuts and bruises,' she said, ignoring her own pain and stiffness. The harness came away and she pushed it out of place.

She became aware of a noise behind her. She spun around to see what it was and her heart lurched in her chest. For a moment she thought the flying machine was sinking, but then she saw the rocks outside submerge in a flowing torrent of water. As she watched the water rose to cover them, lapped at the base of the door frame and started pouring into the cabin.

'We've got to move!' she yelled.

Meru tried to move upwards, Kiri grabbing him under the armpits and yanking as hard as she could. Meru cried out in pain.

'My knee …' he gasped.

The console had pinned his left leg just above the knee. Water was already sloshing around their feet, rising fast. Kiri yanked at the console, but it was made of solid metal and wouldn't budge. She tried pushing down on the seat, but she couldn't move it.

The water lapped up to Meru's legs and then rose to his waist.

'The chair has a control,' he said. 'It will slide back … look for a lever …'

Kiri stumbled back, the water rising to her chest. It was warm, but filled with mud and dirt, making it impossible to see. She fumbled around the seat, searching for anything to grasp.

'I can't find it!' she yelled.

'At the back on the right side …' His words gurgled in mid-sentence as the water reached his chin. 'My right …'

The interior of the cockpit was flooded. Kiri caught a last lungful of air and then dove underwater, feeling her way around the seat. She could barely see, the water stinging her eyes.

She caught hold of a metal bar.

She yanked.

It didn't move.

The urge to breathe was already growing, bubbles floated in front of her. She could hear the muffled surge of the water as the torrent raged about her.

She braced herself and pulled on the lever with the last of her strength.

It released with a jolt, throwing her backwards. She struggled to pull Meru's body. He was heavy, hard to move in the current. She could barely see the doorway through which she had come, but she pulled at him, dragging him behind her.

The urge to breathe was overpowering now. She let out her last breath, seeing the bubbles cascade before her. Darkness tinged the edges of her vision, her chest was burning, pain searing up her lungs.

Instinct drove her upwards, but she refused to let Meru go.

Brighter, a glow above.

Her muscles cramped. It was too far, too hard …

She burst out into the sunlight, gasping down lungfuls of pure fresh air. She gasped, her vision returning as the water carried her away.

'Meru!'

She was still clutching him. Struggling with the current she managed to pull him to the surface, going under herself as she did so. Thrashing and clawing in the water she managed to get them both into the shallows and with the last of her strength pulled Meru over on to his back on the muddy bank, clear of the water.

He looked pale. She pressed her ear to his chest to listen for a heartbeat.

It was there.

'Meru …'

He coughed, spewing up water and rolling on to his side, his body spasming. Kiri crawled across to him.

'Meru?'

He blinked, his eyes focusing on her.

'You did it,' he croaked.

She collapsed beside him, still panting for breath.

'What happened?' he asked. He coughed, still spluttering on water.

'We crashed,' Kiri said, trying to slow her breathing. 'But, we're here.'

'Here? Where?'

'The Obelisk,' she said. 'I saw it, it's not far away.'

'The Obelisk …'

Kiri helped him up and they both got to their knees, gazing around them.

'Wow,' Meru said, turning around. 'We're inside the eye.'

'The eye?'

Meru nodded, still catching his breath. 'It's a calm area … in the middle of the vortex surrounded by clouds … the Obelisk is right at the centre …'

He stared into the distance, seeing the enormous structure rising into the heights in the distance.

'We've made it,' he whispered, before pulling her into an embrace. 'We made it!'

'Just about,' she replied. 'We're lucky to be alive …'

There was a groan from across the water. Kiri looked up to see the wreckage of the flying machine turn end over end in the muddy torrent before it was swept away. The water was still rising.

'We'd better find some shelter and some higher ground,' Kiri said. 'With all that rain there's no telling how high these floods might get.'

Meru was limping. Kiri wasn't in much better shape. Together, supporting each other, they stumbled up the bank until they were a dozen hands above the water. There they both fell down in a meadow full of greening and colourful foliage they didn't recognise.

'Rest for a bit,' Kiri gasped. They both sank into the softness under their feet.

'You sure it's safe?' Meru asked after a moment.

'If something is going to eat us,' Kiri said. 'It's welcome. I'm too tired …'

With the higher vantage point they could take in the view. The dazzling shining tower of the Obelisk dominated the landscape. It was impossible to tell how big it was, its scale defied understanding. It seemed to be close by until they looked at its base, which was beyond a low line of hills that almost reached the horizon. It had to be many marks in height, a stupendous structure. They could see distant clouds in front of it, obscuring the mid-section, but with its peak visible above them.

All about the Obelisk, within the whirling arc of the clouds was a startling, lush green landscape. Meru and Kiri could see vast waterfalls cascading across rocky promontories, vast tracts of shadeforest and enormous lakes where the water pooled.

'It's so … green!' Meru said. 'I wonder why that is.'

Kiri gave him a look.

Even after just having pulled themselves out of the water and up the banks, they were both sweating with exertion. The air was thick and humid, the temperature almost unbearable.

'We should get into the forests,' Kiri said. 'It will be cooler out of Lacaille's light. We'll cook out here.'

She looked upwards at the enormous glowing disk above. It felt strange for Lacaille to be in that position, as if it were poised to crush them beneath its vastness.

Meru looked around him.

'Can you make it?' Kiri asked. 'It's not far.'

'I think so.'

Kiri pulled him to his feet again. They stumbled onwards. Meru collapsing a couple of times, with Kiri struggling to haul him up. They reached the edge of the shade forest and staggered inside, out of the direct sun. Kiri was right, it was cooler, the air fresher.

'We have to rest,' Kiri said, lowering Meru to the ground.

'We only have a few stretches to reach the Obelisk,' Meru complained.

'We're not going anywhere like this,' Kiri said. 'We're hurt and exhausted. We need food as well.'

'The flying machine …'

'It's gone,' Kiri said. 'Washed away.'

'But that's our only source of …'

'I'll see if I can salvage anything,' Kiri said. 'Trust me, we won't go hungry. But we have to rest first.'

Meru was about to protest, but she gave him a look. He subsided.

They lay back in the foliage, hand in hand. Exhausted, sleep crept over them both in moments.

* * *

Fitch was on duty on the bridge, but there was little for him to do. Mel waved at him and got a peremptory tip of his hat in return. She signalled to Zoella and they climbed down the ladder into the ship, walking to the cabin area.

Coran was peering over the charts as they came in.

'No news then,' he said, looking at Zoella's downcast face.

Zoella shook her head, her voice faint. 'I can't sense Kiri at all, there's no answer.'

Coran sighed. 'I got hold of Janaid to see if he could track the flying machine from Amar.'

'And?' Mel asked.

'He told me that Sandra did get some information back,' Coran said, heavily. 'The flying machine seems to have come down in the vortex after suffering damage from the storm. Based on the timing, contact was lost a few minutes after we spoke to Kiri on the radio. Now there's nothing at all.'

'Do we know where?'

'Sandra was able to give us the location,' Coran said, pointing at the map. 'They were close, the last position was inside the centre of the storm, only a few dozen marks from the Obelisk.'

'Maybe they made it then,' Mel said. 'Got through the storm.'

'So why can't I hear Kiri?' Zoella asked.

Coran and Mel looked at her.

'Let's be optimistic,' Coran said, 'Let's say they crashed, the radio broken. The storm could be interfering. Perhaps Kiri is hurt or ...'

'Or maybe Kiri just doesn't want us to find her,' Mel said.

Coran looked at Zoella.

'She's your sister, you know her best of all of us,' he said. 'What do you think?'

'She answered me before,' Zoella said. 'Even though she didn't want to. She does want Meru for herself and she doesn't trust us, but I don't think she'd deliberately ignore us. She understands what's at stake.'

Coran nodded. 'I agree, but it's been almost a stretch since we lost contact,' he said, looking at Zoella. 'Thanks for trying, you able to keep doing so? They could be hurt, unconscious ...'

Zoella nodded.

Mel looked at Zoella. Zoella hesitated.

'Is there something else?' Coran asked.

Mel nodded. 'Just tell him. It'll be alright.'

Zoella swallowed.

'When we were leaving Amar,' she said, her voice thin. 'The high priestess ... Nerina ... she tried to get into my mind.'

'Get into your mind?' Coran echoed.

Zoella nodded. 'I could hear her thoughts. She spoke to me, she was strong, I couldn't stop her.'

Coran looked across at Mel, who raised her eyebrows.

'And before you ask,' Mel said, her voice stern. 'The reason she didn't tell us before now is because she thought we'd do her in if she did. Nice touch having Fitch hanging around with a rifle. Very subtle.'

Coran swallowed, sighed and then nodded.

'I'm sorry,' Coran said to Zoella, lowering the tone of his voice. 'Just tell me what happened.'

'She was able to read some of my thoughts,' Zoella said. 'She found out my name, where I was from. She knew I was at the battle in Viresia, that I fought Kiri. She knows of my gift … and she threatened to take it.'

'Always these threats,' Coran said. 'Well. I guess we know she survived the battle then. Don't you worry, we won't let her get you. Fitch will fill her full of holes the moment he lays eyes on her or her dach.'

Coran didn't see the reassured expression he was looking for. If anything Zoella looked more worried.

'It's not just that,' Mel prompted.

'She can … she knows where I am,' Zoella said. 'She saw what I could see, I couldn't stop her.'

'She knows where we are?' Coran asked. 'Where we're going?'

'She might,' Zoella said. Coran could see she was trembling. 'I don't know what she managed to find out, but I think she knows we're going to the Obelisk …'

Coran rubbed his beard and looked around for a moment.

'So when did this happen?' he asked.

'When we left Amar,' Zoella replied.

'Has it happened since?'

Zoella shook her head.

Coran thought for a moment.

'Well, we're sailing fast,' he said. 'Knowing we left Amar won't do her a lot of good now that we're out at sea. I doubt she'd be able to find us out here. But we're best to be safe. I'll make sure Fitch, Daf and Creg keep a watch at all times.'

Zoella nodded.

'Thanks for being straight with me,' Coran said. 'I guess I have Mel to thank for that, right?'

Zoella nodded again.

'That's good,' Coran said. 'But next time, just tell us straight away, yes?'

'Yes,' Zoella said. 'I'm sorry …'

'That's alright,' Coran said. 'And I'll … get Fitch to put that rifle away.'

He saw her swallow, but her expression was relieved.

There was a thump of feet along the corridor. All three of them looked up to see Creg standing in the door, his enormous frame filling it. He grunted something unintelligible and then turned to go.

'Fitch wants us,' Coran said. They followed him out and up on to the decks.

'This stretch just gets better,' Mel said, rolling her eyes.

'What is it?' Coran demanded as they climbed up into the bridge, Mel and Zoella just behind him. Fitch was looking astern.

'What do you make of that?' he asked.

Coran, Mel and Zoella turned to look. Coran grabbed the 'scope, which was fastened on a clip to the nearby bulkhead.

'What in the world …?' Coran muttered, before handing the 'scope to Mel.

Intermittently, some distance behind the *Mobilis*, another wake could be seen. As they watched something broke the surface perhaps half a mark behind the ship, a huge wave churning around it before it sunk beneath the waves once more.

'What is it?' Zoella asked.

'Scorched if I know,' Fitch replied. 'But what I can tell you is it's big and it's keeping pace with us at full speed.'

Coran watched as the sea churned once more.

'How long's it been there?'

'Not rightly sure,' Fitch said. 'Only just spotted it. It wasn't there a spell ago, that's for sure.'

'We're in deep water here,' Coran said. 'And uncharted seas. Looks like we've disturbed something. We're travelling at speed, if we keep to our course and leave it alone it will probably tire and lose interest. Fitch, might be worth setting up your rockets just in case though. Remember that squidder that almost ate Meru?'

Fitch nodded and clambered down from the bridge, yelling to Daf and Creg to give him a hand.

'Meanwhile,' Coran said. 'Best we keep off the decks I think. Zoella, can you let Ira know?'

Zoella nodded and made her way down from the bridge and down to the cabins.

Ira was resting and Zoella roused her, signing to her to stay off the decks. In response to her query Zoella sent her an image of the churning sea behind the ship.

Ira's eyes grew wide.

Zoella received images back. A vast creature, leaping out of the water and smashing ships in a harbour. She made out a huge tail, whipping back and forth, smashing wooden ships to kindling, with vast tentacles snaking out, grabbing people from decks, quaysides and even from the sea as they threw themselves in the water.

You've seen one, in Airea?

Ira nodded.

'Come with me,' Zoella said, pulling Ira behind her and running to the bridge. They were about to climb to the ladder up to the deck when the ship lurched under them, spilling them to the floor. An enormous echoing groan sounded all about them and water splashed down through the hatchway above, soaking them both in warm seawater.

The torrent subsided. Zoella helped Ira up and climbed the ladder, looking outside. She caught sight of an enormous tail disappearing into the sea on the port side of the ship.

Daf and Creg were yelling, Zoella could see them trying to pull Fitch aboard. He was clinging on to the side of the ship. The deck was awash with foam and spray, surging off the rear deck as the ship righted itself.

'Get back inside!'

Zoella turned to see Mel yelling down from the bridge. She was cast into shadow as something huge rose up behind her, blotting out of the light of Lacaille.

It was a huge arc of grey flesh, slick with water, towering over the ship. Zoella felt the ship lurch beneath her again, swinging in the opposite direction, turning so hard in the water that the portside gunwales dipped into the sea.

The sea creature's monstrous bulk smashed down into the sea once more with an enormous plume of spray. Zoella braced herself as a wave washed across the side of the ship, splashing up as high as the wheelhouse.

Water surged across her, submerging her in a swirling torrent. She was lucky to have been braced in the hatchway otherwise she would have been swept overboard. She felt something grip her ankle and realised it was Ira below her, holding on tight.

She choked and spluttered as the water receded. The *Mobilis* had heeled right over, the bridge roof almost level with the water line. For a dreadful moment it seemed as if the ship were going to capsize in the churn.

With agonising slowness the *Mobilis* righted itself. Zoella looked about her, seeing the bridge awash with water, which was now flowing out again. Both Coran and Mel were nowhere to be seen. Looking aft she could see Daf and Creg, but there was no sign of Fitch either.

She turned around, trying to locate them.

There, in the sea. Overboard!

The *Mobilis* was still running at full speed, leaving them behind. Zoella jumped up to the deck and vaulted for the wheelhouse, forcing herself against the onrushing water. She pulled herself up and staggered inside, trying to remember what Coran had done to control the ship. She grabbed at the obvious lever and yanked it back, hearing the engines fierce thrum spin down. Then she spun the large wheel and the ship came about again, turning back on its course.

She looked through the spray-splashed windows, trying to see where the crew were. Daf and Creg were yelling and pointing to the portside. Zoella could just make out three bodies in the water, swimming towards each other.

The *Mobilis* came about, heading towards them at reduced speed.

The sea boiled, a great dome of water rising up and flowing aside. Zoella watched in horror as the creature surfaced before her.

It was at least twice the length of the *Mobilis*. A vast mass of grey flesh punctuated with huge and ancient scars. Its head was double the width of the ship, a vast bulbous affair, with three huge eyes atop it, each perhaps five hands wide. Its mouth was ringed with a series of tentacles, coiled together into a fleshy point.

The rest of the creature followed, two fins jutted from its sides and a gargantuan fluked tail arced upwards before splashing down behind it with an echoing boom.

Zoella saw her friends bob in the water before it, a swell of water dozens of hands high rolled away from the creature. The *Mobilis* reared up to crest the wave and then plummeted down the other side. Zoella pulled the throttles to a stop and the *Mobilis* coasted to a halt.

In that moment the tentacles burst forth, uncoiling at breakneck speed, surging through the waters in search of prey. By the time Zoella had clambered down from the bridge the tentacles were flailing in the air. Zoella could see Coran, Mel and Fitch held in their grasp.

A vast maw opened up between the tentacles, ringed with teeth. A shuddering groan accompanied a spray of water. The stench of rotting meat issued forth, causing her to gag.

Zoella heard screams and cries from before her, yells from Daf and Creg from behind, but she ignored them, raising her hand and striding forward along the sodden decks of the ship until she stood at the bow.

Her face was contorted with anger, a burning sensation and the smell of hot metal rising up all about her.

Release them!

The mental power of her command blasted across the sea, so strong as to almost be visible. A ripple of fury in the air.

The creature reared up in the water, threatening to overwhelm the ship once more.

Zoella gestured again.

Do not defy me! Release them!

The creature became still, the waves receding. She heard Daf and Creg's yells stop, heard their footsteps halt behind her. She clenched her hand.

Release them and I will let you go unharmed!

The tentacles writhed and then, one by one, Zoella saw her friends dropped into the sea. They began swimming towards the *Mobilis.*

The tentacles coiled back, wrapping around each other and covering the maw. The creature turned away, sinking into the water, which churned for a few moments and then grew calm once more.

Zoella gasped, feeling weak and giddy. Someone caught her, pulling her from the bow, preventing her from toppling into the sea. She saw Ira's face, then Daf and Creg. Then everything went black.

CHAPTER EIGHT

Daine, Capital of Drayden

Round 2307, Eighth pass

Merrin watched as the flight of dachs banked in the air and descended towards the temple. They swept in, wings outstretched, back-flapping to slow their approach before their claws stretched out to absorb the impact of landing. Dust billowed across the piazza.

Obedient servants marched forward to take the beasts under control as the priestesses disembarked, Nerina in the lead.

'With me,' she barked to Merrin.

Merrin bowed and turned on her heel, stepping into line. Nerina was marching towards the temple. Merrin had to hurry to keep up with her.

'News from the borders?'

'Amrit has just messaged from Scallia, she reports unrest …'

'Has she subdued it?' Nerina demanded.

'She seeks advice on what to do next,' Merrin said. 'The population is unruly, rumours of our defeat …'

Nerina stopped and turned. 'What part of "subdue" do you all fail to understand? I have placed Rihanna in Taloon, Amrit in Scallia. You are here, Merrin. You all know your duties …'

Nerina caught the look on Merrin's face.

'What is it?'

'Nerina, there have been riots, unrest, even here in Daine,' Merrin began. 'The commoners …'

Nerina held up a hand.

'Inside, now.'

They moved within the temple buildings, the light of Lacaille filtered throughout the interior by cunningly wrought and adjusted mirrors. The hallways were quiet, few priestesses were in evidence.

Merrin caught Nerina's questioning look.

'They are out, patrolling the city,' Merrin explained. 'I have had to call on the administrators and the healers to look after things here.'

'What precisely has taken place?' Nerina demanded.

'Rumours of the defeat in Amar have spread like wildfire,' Merrin said. 'We have tried to find the source, but once the story was out … it could not be stopped. Farmers, workers, the citizens of lands we claim, they began to rise, to resist. We made an example out of many, but still the insolence continues, work all but stopped for a time. It is worse in the other lands we have taken …'

'Rihanna has kept control of Taloon,' Nerina said. 'Amrit will be told to take a firmer hand.'

'I already have,' Merrin complained. 'Did you not hear? People have been killed.'

'It is not enough, plainly.'

'Nerina …'

'Do not object to my directives,' Nerina said. 'I have had enough of these insignificant peasants defying the will of their betters.'

'We cannot rule them by fear alone,' Merrin said.

'Really?' Nerina said. 'Fear will motivate them well enough. Fear for their families, for their livelihoods, their income, their own lives. Fear will serve us well.'

'There are not as many of us,' Merrin said. 'Keeping order is not easy. Stop a riot here and another one is breaking out across the city …'

Nerina fixed her with a glare.

It seems I must take back control of my own city,' she said. 'I will summon some of our priestesses …'

'We have already been brutal,' Merrin said. 'If we kill more, we risk an uprising such that …'

'We will be more brutal still,' Nerina interrupted her. 'Let it be known that any acts of sabotage or insolence against us will be dealt with by me.

Bring any so accused to the temple piazza. There I will decide their fate. In the meantime I have more important concerns.'

'More important?' Merrin echoed.

Nerina nodded. 'The maid, the one we encountered in Amar, she was present when we attacked Viresia. It was she who frustrated Kiri in that battle and escaped us at Amar.'

'Stronger than Kiri?'

'So it seems,' Nerina said. 'Her gift must be taken, she must be found and taken alive.'

'Where is she?'

Nerina smiled. 'I can see her thoughts and her visions. She is aboard a ship, they head sunwards towards the Obelisk.'

'Why?'

'That vision of the Obelisk requiring assistance,' Nerina said. 'The Amarans, the exiles, are going to answer it. Whatever it was that Kiri received, it seems they also believe it to be real. That's where they are going.'

'So ...'

'We let them,' Nerina said. 'If there is a threat let them deal with it, put themselves at risk in so doing. Once they return, that is when we will strike.'

'But it's hundreds of marks away, far to the sunward,' Merrin said. 'How will we ... ah ... Rihanna.'

Nerina nodded.

'They will have to pass by Taloon. Rihanna will be waiting.'

* * *

Meru had no idea how long he'd slept, but he awoke to a faint smell of smoke. He sat up, stretching out his muscles. He was sore and stiff, his arms and legs covered with bruises and minor scrapes. His head was still throbbing and the cut on his forehead was tender. His leg, where it had been crushed by the console, was tender to the touch, but a quick trial of standing up showed him that he'd be able to walk on it.

And Kiri saved me.

He looked around. There was no sign of her, but she had been busy. A fire had been made up, circled with a ring of stones. Over it hung a set of shade branches, lashed together to form a spit.

Next to him was a cup, filled to the brim with water. He recognised the cup as one from the flying machine. Kiri must have found the wreckage and brought it back. Alongside it were a couple of the knives that had been in the kitchen unit, next to a pair of flasks. She had also found one of the rifles, and a belt full of cartridges.

She's so resourceful …

He drank the water gratefully, hearing his stomach rumbling.

'Hey sleepy head.'

He turned to see Kiri walking out of the gloom of the shadeforest. She was carrying a huge dead marsip slung over her shoulder and had a pair of wooden staffs in the other hand. She sat down beside him, dropping the dead creature on to the ground.

'How are you?' she asked, with a smile.

'Much better,' he said. 'Thanks to you.'

She shrugged and went to pick up one of the knives.

Meru took her hand.

'What?' she asked, looking around at him.

He touched her chin and turned her head towards him, giving her a gentle kiss.

'Thank you for saving my life,' he whispered. 'I'd be dead if you hadn't …'

'You saved me,' she said, her voice low. They kissed again, but Meru could feel she was trembling.

'What is it?' he asked.

She sighed, looking away into the distance for a long moment.

'I've tried not to care too much,' she said. 'When I lost Charis I swore I wasn't going to feel like this ever again.' She gave him a glare. 'You messed that up good and proper. I didn't want this, I didn't ask for it, that time I forced my way into your mind I didn't care about you, I was just after information …'

'I remember,' Meru said.

'Then there was this … desire,' she said. 'It was driving me mad, burning me up whenever it wanted. I had no control of it, hated it and wanted it at the same time. It's part of what the priestesses do … securing a bond with their mate, I'd done it accidentally, it shouldn't have happened …'

'The obsession we had with each other?' Meru asked. 'I remember not being able to think of anything else …'

Kiri nodded.

'But none of that was really me,' she said, looking at him. 'Don't misunderstand … what we did in Taloon …' She smiled demurely. 'That was fun … but what I feel now is …'

She swallowed.

'I thought I was going to lose you,' she said, tears springing into her eyes. 'Everyone I've ever had any feelings for has been taken from me. That scares me, because … I do love you.'

Meru pulled her into an embrace, feeling her hold him tightly. They stayed that way for long moments before she pulled back, wiping at her eyes.

'See what you've done?' she scolded. 'I was strong once, fearless and brave. I was a warrior … now look at me.'

'You're still all of those things,' Meru said. 'You're the strongest, bravest, toughest …' He ran out of words, shaking his head for a moment before trying again. 'You're amazing, beautiful, clever …'

She gave him a look. 'Really? I'm streaked in mud and grime.'

'I don't see that,' Meru replied. 'Just the girl I love.'

Kiri swallowed. She rested her forehead against his.

'Will this work?' she whispered. 'You and me? My people and yours … enemies … everything that's happened …'

'Don't think about it,' Meru said, squeezing her hands. 'You and me, that's all that matters now. We're together, we're alive, that's all that counts.'

'I'm glad of it,' Kiri answered. 'I want nothing else now.' She sat back and shook her head. 'So strange … I wanted revenge, and power and control and … I just don't any more.'

'Let's do what we need to do,' Meru said. 'After that, you and I will do whatever we want, yes?'

She nodded.

'Now … can we have some food?' he asked. 'I'm starving.'

She laughed and grabbed one of the knives. Meru watched as she gutted the marsip, pulling out its insides with a familiarity borne of long practice.

'Ew …' he said, wrinkling his nose

'Never eaten marsip before?' Kiri asked, dangling an intestine before him.

'Yes,' he said, holding up his hand to fend her off. 'But not like this …'

'Fresh and raw,' she said. 'Still warm, the best way. Want to try it?'

'You're going to eat it raw?' he asked in alarm.

Kiri laughed at him. 'Of course not, you idiot. I meant do you want to learn how to get them ready.'

'No,' he replied. 'I'll leave all the blood and guts to you if that's alright.'

'Coward,' she teased.

Within a spell she'd completed the gory task and strung the marsip up on the spit. She turned it over as it cooked. They sat watching for a while, enjoying the smell of the roasting meat.

'I found the remains of the flying machine,' she said. 'The water has gone again, just a trickle in that river bed. I guess it comes and goes. There wasn't much left. Found these …' She pointed at the knives, flasks and the rifle.'

'At least we can carry some water,' Meru said. 'Might be useful, though I think having too much water might be more of a problem than not having enough.'

'The rest was just a mess. It's half sunk in mud, I don't think anything was working. Sandra wouldn't say anything, no lights, nothing. Everything else was ruined, all the clothes, food …'

'That's the third one I've crashed. Caesar won't be pleased. At least we can get to the Obelisk, not so sure about getting back … and there's no radio either …'

'I can always … send a message …' Kiri said, her voice hesitant.

Meru nodded. 'I don't want to ask you to do that.'

Kiri shrugged. 'We're going to have to square that off at some point, Zoella and me. We should let your friends know we're alive, they'll be worried after what happened.'

'If you're sure?'

Kiri nodded, closing her eyes.

Meru watched her face as she concentrated, a frown growing on her features. He saw her scrunch up her eyes as if she were straining. This went on for long moments before she opened her eyes and took a long breath.

'Did it work?' Meru asked.

Kiri shook her head. 'No … I can't hear her.'

'She wouldn't answer?'

'No,' Kiri answered. 'There was nothing at all. I couldn't sense her.'

'What does that mean?'

'She could be asleep I suppose …'

Meru thought about that. 'I don't know what time it is, but we can't be that far off the timers. It's not the sleeping.'

Kiri shrugged. 'I don't know. But she's just not there.'

'I hope she's alright … they're alright,' Meru said, thinking about the crew of the *Mobilis*. 'Can you try again in a few spells?'

Kiri nodded. 'I will.'

'They're going to have to find a way through the vortex too,' Meru said, 'Unless we can fix the Obelisk first and let them know. I wouldn't fancy sailing through that storm.'

'We might need them to rescue us,' Kiri said. 'How are we going to get back, unless there are more flying machines at the Obelisk itself?'

Meru nodded. 'Yes, there could be. Let's hope so.'

The marsip was ready. Kiri pulled it off the spit, cut strips and put them on smaller sticks she'd readied for the purpose. They ate hungrily, the juices from the rich meat dribbling down their chins.

'That's amazing,' Meru said. 'Tastes so good.'

'Hunger does that,' Kiri replied. 'Used to live off these for rounds and rounds. This one was fat and well fed. Easy to catch too.'

'At least we won't starve.'

Kiri wiped her mouth with the back of her hand.

'I had a look at the Obelisk when I was hunting,' she said. 'I think it's at least thirty marks away from what I can see.'

'How long do you think it will take us to get there?'

'Not sure. Two stretches if the going is easy,' she replied. 'But if there's stuff in the way and we have to take detours, could be five or more. Depends on the terrain.'

Meru considered that. 'We had fourteen stretches when you spoke to it. We were three stretches flying … how long were we out after we crashed?'

'Don't know,' Kiri answered. 'A stretch at least I guess, no way to tell for sure.'

'So, ten, maybe nine stretches left,' Meru said. 'Still enough … assuming we can find our way there and nothing else goes wrong.'

'Yeah … our luck has been so good recently, hasn't it?'

Meru grinned at her.

'We'll get there … but we'd better get going.'

'Your leg, can you walk?' Kiri asked.

'It's sore … but I'll be fine.'

Kiri gave him a look, but didn't argue.

Having finished the marsip Kiri doused the fire. They gathered up the knives and flasks, walking down to the river bed where they filled the flasks to the brim. They looked at the distant tower, still sparkling in the light of Lacaille. Meru buckled on the belt and slung the rifle over his shoulder.

'Ready?' Kiri asked.

Meru nodded.

They set off, Kiri in the lead.

DAINE, CAPITAL OF DRAYDEN

* * *

Nerina had walked within the temple at the heart of the city of Daine, secreting herself within the grand hall at the centre. It was here that the attack on Viresia had been planned and before that where Kiri had been brought before her, to be judged after being accused of the murder of Choso.

The alternating sand and red-stoned tiled floor was familiar, the benches where the priestesses usually sat were empty. They were all out, carrying out her latest instructions, to quell the unrest out in the wider city. Summons for support had been sent to both Drayden and Scallia. Many priestesses were returning home

Kiri.

Nerina cursed her name. The girl's power had been lost. Oh, she'd been able to tear a portion of it when Kiri had lain at her feet, exhausted and injured during the battle at Amar, but Kiri had eluded her, choosing death over that final humiliation, throwing herself into the churning waters of the Strathian Sea.

I spent long rounds training her, cultivating her powers, growing her ready to be harvested, only to lose her potential. She was smart and clever, deceptive, thinking of her own plans and stratagems. She knew of this maid and the powers she had, but she hid them from me. She let her go when they met in Nireus, lied to me from that point. Why? Who is she? What is their relationship? Rihanna discovered that Kiri believed she came from Scallia ... as did this maid, Zoella. Both have remarkable powers for those so young and not because they stole them from others, these are natural gifts ... so how?

Nerina paced around for a moment before lowering herself into the ornately carved chair at the far end of the room. She thought for a spell, turning things over in her mind.

Nothing else matters but the capture of the maid. With Kiri lost, she is what remains of that strength.

She concentrated, closing her eyes and sending out her thoughts sunward across the plains of Drayden and then further, across the deserts of Taloon.

Rihanna!

There was a long pause, and then Rihanna answered.

High Priestess! Your bidding?

Your rule of Taloon, you have subdued it?

There has been no further unrest here. The population is controlled. I am ensuring that work on the ships is carried out. Delay will not be tolerated.

Nerina nodded.

That is as it should be. Continue that work, but I have another task for you.

Gladly, High Priestess.

The girl we seek, the maid. I have news of her.

Nerina sensed the interest from Rihanna.

You have found her?

In a way, I know where she is going. She heads sunwards in the metal vessel belonging to the Amarans. They are heading towards the Obelisk, answering its summons.

You want me to intercept them?

Nerina shook her head.

No, let them deal with whatever awaits them there. If the Obelisk is truly in danger and needs help, they can serve us by restoring it. Only once they return …

Then take them.

Nerina nodded.

She travels with the Amarans, I have no interest in them, but their vessel is mighty and might serve us, capture it if you can. It is the maid I require.

She could sense Rihanna's curiosity.

Her name is Zoella. I have probed her thoughts. Kiri and her had some kind of connection. Kiri deliberately let her go when we encountered her in Nireus.

Nerina got a brief impression of Rihanna playing back those events in her own mind.

I remember being puzzled. We shot arrows at them on the quay … everyone missed, we didn't understand why …

It was Kiri. She already had her own agenda by that point.

The lying guttersnipe!

Yes. Kiri had a plan involving both the boy and this girl, Zoella.

Both from Scallia, some source of power there?

Nerina nodded.

We must pay more attention to that place. They were both too young to have torn those powers from others, thus they were a native natural gift.

How could they have been so strong?

A benefit of their birth perhaps, a strong line of …

Nerina stopped for a moment, thinking it through. Rihanna had the same thought at the same moment.

Could they be related?

Nerina smiled to herself.

Something I will investigate when I next sense her. In the meantime, keep an eye out for that ship. It must pass by Airea in order to reach the vortex. Let it go, but tell me if you see it.

Of course, High Priestess.

Nerina broke the connection, sat back, opened her eyes and let the room come into focus around her.

The Scallians still have secrets. I will find out what they are!

* * *

Crenech looked up, disturbed by the sound of wings flapping. He walked out on to the veranda of his property and gazed up into the sky. Dachs were a-wing and he could make out priestesses astride them, a number flying in formation heading sunwards.

Gemma and Joachim close behind him, joined him in staring at the sky.

'Where are they going?' Gemma asked, shivering at the sight.

'Not sure,' Crenech answered, 'but it doesn't look like a search.'

Joachim nodded. 'No, they split up and go about that individually.'

'Looks like they may have been summoned home,' Crenech said. 'Back to Drayden. Look, there are five of them, that leaves only three in the city.'

'You're not thinking of trying to overpower them,' Gemma said, her face pale.

'Oh, I'd like to,' Crenech said. 'But the time isn't right for that. One priestess is more than a match for us given those powers of theirs, but something is happening beyond our borders; something that requires them to bring resources back home. I would give a lot to know what it is.'

'I'll go into the city and see what I can overhear,' Joachim said.

Crenech nodded. 'Yes, a good idea.' He turned to look at Gemma. 'Was there anything in Drayden you saw when you were there that might explain this?'

Gemma shrugged. 'I didn't get to see much, we were locked up most of the time and then marched to the hall where … the priestesses took the gifts from all those around me. It was only Kiri's intervention that stopped that happening to me.'

'Yes,' Crenech mused. 'This business with Kiri is a strange tale. She rescues you, takes you to the borders and claims to be of Scallia herself.'

Gemma nodded.

'I have made enquiries as discreetly as I could,' Joachim said. 'There is no Kiri known amongst our people, but there was one amongst the priestesses during the attack. It was her dach that slew King Ioric.'

'What did she look like?' Crenech asked.

'Thin, of medium height,' Joachim said. 'Black hair and blue eyes, the most memorable thing was a black glove on her left hand.'

Gemma gasped. 'A black glove?'

Joachim nodded.

'It was her then,' Gemma said. 'The Kiri who rescued me, she wore a black glove on her left hand.'

'Then why?' Crenech said. 'She's our enemy, she killed the king …'

'Well, her dach did,' Joachim said. 'I saw the fight, something strange happened just beforehand. Kiri was fighting King Ioric, a battle to draw first-blood. She'd won, but then she fell upon the ground, screaming in agony. It was then the dach attacked and slew King Ioric. Later many report seeing her in the battle for the city itself. She was fighting for Drayden, not for Scallia.'

'Which doesn't explain why she would go out of her way to rescue you at significant risk to herself,' Crenech said, looking at Gemma. 'And then claim to be of Scallia herself. I'd like to know who she is and what she's doing.'

'She is definitely a priestess,' Gemma replied, casting her mind back, trying to recall everything Kiri had done and told her.

'Tell us again,' Crenech said.

'She was instructed to take my gift,' Gemma said. 'But she refused. She said she wouldn't harm me, then told me to copy the actions of those around me so no one else would suspect. She promised to help me escape. I was taken to a cell, but Kiri came to me early one stretch, took me out and then flew me on a dach towards Scallia. I asked her why …'

'And?' Crenech demanded.

'She just said … for Scallia,' Gemma answered. 'She said I am of Scallia myself. Then she was gone.'

'Doesn't make any sense,' Joachim said.

'Could she have been a girl from a previous tithe?' Crenech asked. 'Indoctrinated into their ways and then had a turn of conscience?'

Joachim shook his head. 'All the tithes and all the names of all the girls sent to Drayden by us have been written down every time they were conducted. I checked everything going back thirty rounds, there's no mention of a girl called Kiri anywhere.'

'Then who is she?' Crenech murmured, looking at Gemma. 'Why risk rescuing you?'

Gemma shrugged.

'When the other priestess caught me, the red-haired one, she read my thoughts, she was trying to find out the same thing – why it was that Kiri had rescued me. I didn't know of course, but she heard the words Kiri had said to me and she was surprised. There was something …'

'Anything might be useful,' Crenech said.

'I could hear her thoughts,' Gemma continued.

'The other priestess?' Joachim asked.

Gemma nodded. 'Yes, she couldn't believe it. Kiri was from the slums of Drayden, not Scallia, but she was keeping secrets … but that's all there is. I'm sorry.'

'Don't be,' Crenech said. 'It seems we have a rogue priestess on our hands. I know a little of Drayden, the slums surround the city of Daine from the accounts I have heard. If this Kiri lived there before becoming a priestess the question is …'

'How did she get to the slums of Drayden from Scallia,' Joachim finished for him.

'Exactly,' Crenech said. 'How old would you say Kiri was, Gemma?'

'Not much older than me. Twenty to twenty five rounds.'

'Hmmm,' Crenech said. 'I wonder, could she have been one of old King Marek's dreamers?'

'Dreamers?' Joachim said.

'Long before all this,' Crenech said. 'Rounds ago, when Marek was hearty and strong, he had an adviser, someone who spoke strongly against the tithe to Drayden, I forget his name, but he was banished from Scallia, it must be close to twenty rounds ago. I never met him, but he spoke out against the tithe, saying we should defy the priestesses, witches he called them, and not send our young women to them. I understood he was charged with treason eventually, as he was reported to have hidden girls across the realm, trying to prevent them being found for the tithe and sent to Drayden in defiance of the orders of the king.'

'So what happened?'

'They were all found,' Crenech said. 'So I understood. As these girls grew up they had strange dreams which gave them away. King Marek issued orders for any such girls to be taken back to Viresia and hence sent to Drayden in the tithe. Perhaps some weren't found. This Kiri could be such a girl, escaping King Marek's decree, but ending up in Drayden anyway.'

'And you think Kiri has discovered her origins somehow?' Joachim said. 'Possible I suppose, but pretty unlikely. I mean, how could she?'

'I don't know,' Crenech said. 'But I can't think of another explanation. The other question is, if we do encounter her again, can we trust her? Whose side is she on really? She could be a great asset, or a dangerous liability.'

'I can answer that,' Gemma said. 'Kiri spoke to me with her gift, the mental power they all have … I could sense her emotions, her feelings. She wasn't lying. She was scared, worried, terrified of being discovered and fearful that she wouldn't be able to get me to safety, but she wasn't lying.'

Crenech nodded.

'Could she be the reason the priestesses are leaving to fly sunward?' Joachim asked.

'I can't see why,' Crenech said. 'No, I think their troubles are concerned with their attempts at conquest. Something has gone wrong with their plans. For now let us continue to frustrate their searches. With only three priestesses remaining that should be easy enough now.'

'We wait,' Joachim said, downcast.

Crenech smiled at the expression on his face.

'We watch, we wait,' he said. 'Somehow I don't think it will be long before more is revealed.'

CHAPTER NINE

Strathian Sea, heading sunward

Round 2307, Eighth pass

Zoella moaned and opened her eyes.

'She's awake.'

She was lying on something soft, about her she could hear the steady thrum of the *Mobilis*' engines. The ship was underway once more, at full speed by the sound of it.

She blinked, allowing her eyes to focus. She was in her cabin, with faces all around her.

'Don't crowd her you lot. Give her some air.'

Zoella recognised Mel's voice.

'What happened?' she said, her voice croaky.

'Near as we can tell, you saved everyone aboard,' Coran said, beaming at her. He extended a hand and helped her up into a sitting position. 'Turned the ship around …'

'Faced down that critter …' Mel added.

'And sent it packing into the depths,' Fitch finished, his dour face wearing an unfamiliar smile.

'It was going to eat us all,' Zoella said, remembering. 'I could hear its thoughts …'

'This gift of yours?' Mel asked.

Zoella nodded, a tinge of sadness creeping into her voice. 'I had a carn once … Raga was his name. I learnt to listen to the animals, understand them. Even the shades themselves.'

'I'm adding talking to the shades to the list of weird stuff,' Fitch said, with a grin.

'If we hadn't had you aboard the ship, this crew would have been at the bottom of the sea by now,' Coran said. 'On behalf of us all, thank you Zoella.'

There was a mumble of agreement and praise from all about her. She looked around at each face in turn as they grabbed her shoulders and shook her hands. Fitch tipped his hat. Even Daf and Creg gave her an affectionate nod before they departed.

Coran, Mel and Ira remained as the rest filed out.

'Is everything …?'

'All good,' Coran said. 'Ship took on a bit of water, but the pumps have cleared that. We've tidied up everything else and we're back on course. Question is, what about you?'

'I'm alright,' Zoella said. 'A little tired. That … thing … it was big, it was hard to hear it … harder still to tell it what to do.'

'Amazing that you can talk to the creatures,' Coran said. 'Useful too as it turns out. These gifts of yours …'

'Glad I could do something to help,' Zoella replied. 'You should thank Ira too, she knew of the creature, knew it was going to attack, she's seen one before.'

Coran and Mel gave Ira a nod and she smiled back. Zoella got a warm glow of appreciation from her.

'I'll get back to the bridge,' Coran said. 'Anything you need, let me know. Will you be able to …?'

'I'll see if I can speak to her,' Zoella said.

He squeezed her shoulder again and then departed.

'You did a good thing,' Mel said, after a moment. 'I thought we were all going to die when we were swept into the sea and the *Mobilis* was still running at full throttle. That creature would have killed all of us if it weren't for you. Smart thinking. We all owe you our lives.'

'I hope it goes someway to making up for what I did …'

Mel gave her a look and wagged a finger at her. 'Ah ah. Stop it.'

Zoella smiled and nodded.

That's the first smile I've seen from you in stretches,' Mel said. 'Keep it up.'

Ira was nodding too.

'You've been so kind to me,' Zoella said, tears forming in her eyes.

Both she and Ira gave Zoella a hug. 'We all need each other, we all look out for each other. That's what it's all about.'

Zoella hugged them back, enjoying the embrace.

'I must try to contact Kiri,' she said.

'If you're up to it,' Mel said.

Zoella nodded. 'Ira will help me.' She reached out her hands to the younger white-haired girl. Ira took them.

Zoella closed her eyes and concentrated once more.

She focussed her thoughts, spreading them outwards, seeking …

So, Zoella.

Zoella gasped, recognising the presence of Nerina again. She panicked, trying to shut down her thoughts, but the other woman's grip snapped tight around her mind; the sense of gleeful amusement and indomitable will suffusing her.

You …

Zoella clenched her eyes shut tighter.

Yes, where are you?

I will not tell you.

Pain erupted in Zoella's mind, coursing around her head as if she were being crushed under a rock. She yelled …

… and felt Ira's reassuring presence alongside.

Who is this?

You do not know, and you will not know.

Zoella concentrated, remembering how she had attacked the men in the ice cavern in Drem. She could sense Nerina from afar, navigate the twisting tortuous mental route between them. She pushed, reaching out and flung her attack outwards.

It was met by a wall of indifference.

I am beyond your powers little girl, do not seek to …

Zoella pushed harder, straining, feeling Ira's hand still tight in hers. The pain around her head cracked and faded away. Invigorated, she struck again and again.

Shock, surprise and anger flickered about her, but it was swept away leaving only a bitter aftertaste of envy and hatred.

The link was gone.

Zoella reeled back, her eyes opening wide. For a moment everything was confusion before she felt Ira's reassuring grasp around her shoulders.

I stopped her, stopped her from reading my mind. She's not invincible, even her gift isn't as strong as she thinks ...

* * *

Kiri and Meru continued to trudge towards the distant Obelisk. The shade forest was thinning out around them and the ground was rising again. As the cover from the shades above began to reduce, the temperature was rising.

Kiri turned to see Meru was quite a few paces behind. He was still limping a little, but hadn't complained. She stopped to wait for him.

As he approached she heard him stumble and curse, falling down in between two shade trunks.

'Meru?'

She ran to him.

'Did you fall?'

'Something sticking up out of the ground ...' he said, pointing back and rubbing his foot.

Kiri looked, seeing a spike a few hands away from where they'd been walking. She went to look at it, frowning and then tried to pull it free. With a twist it came free. She held it up to look at it. None the wiser, she took it to Meru.

'This is what got you,' she said.

Meru winced and took it, his annoyance changing to curiosity in a moment.

'It's metal,' he said, turning the fragment over in his hands. 'Somebody made this, it's part of a machine.'

He looked about him.

'Over there, look.'

Kiri followed where he was pointing. Off to their left was a small hollow in the earth, as if a hole had been dug long ago and then covered over once more, the shades about it were angled outwards as if avoiding the spot.

Kiri pulled him up and they walked over. As they crested the edge of the hollow and looked over they saw a dark shape below.

Meru recognised it immediately.

'It's a flying machine,' he said, scrambling down towards it.

Kiri followed him.

The machine was covered in greening, its structure scored, dented and marked by untold rounds. Much of it was corroded and collapsing, only its overall shape gave it away.

'What's it doing in the forest?' Kiri asked.

'I think it crashed,' Meru said. Look at the wings, a bit like ours … bent and torn off on one side. It's old though … really old. Look here …'

He gestured to the front of the machine, where they could see the remains of the cockpit. The interior was blackened, the insides full of debris and dirt. It was clear it had been here for many rounds.

'Burnt,' Kiri said. 'It was on fire?'

'Perhaps because it crashed,' Meru said. 'Or maybe it was caught in a flare. Whatever happened it was a long time ago.'

They walked around the wreck a couple of times, but learnt nothing more about it.

'Let's hope we'll find some answers at the Obelisk,' Kiri said. 'Come on.'

They kept walking. The temperature was rising all the time, the shades getting thinner and thinner about them. Now they could see through their trunks, the land rising higher and higher.

Kiri stopped at the top of a rise and waited for Meru to catch her up. She wiped her brow and took a drink of water from her flask. The heat was extreme and she could feel her clothing was damp with sweat.

Meru climbed up beside her, panting hard. His hair was damp and plastered all over his face.

'This heat …' he said.

'Never been somewhere so hot,' she agreed. 'Make sure you drink enough, we're sweating like crazy.'

'Now I wish I had fans like a herg,' Meru said, drinking from his own flask. 'Sweating seems such a waste of water.'

Kiri was surveying the vista before them. They had left the shade forest behind and the land had opened out into a lush rolling meadow, beyond that lay a lake, with hills rising beyond it. The Obelisk still towered beyond.

She swallowed.

Oh no.

They followed the meadow downwards until they came to a shingled shoreline. They could see vegetation marks high up the length of the beach, full of flotsam and jetsam, broken branches, rotting leaves and other debris.

'I guess it floods every so often,' Meru said, looking around him.

Floods really fast too!

'That's our next problem,' she said, gazing to her left and right. 'We'll have to go around …'

'Around?' Meru said. 'Could go on for marks. I don't think we can afford the delay.' He waded out into the water. 'It's cooler in the water.'

Kiri stayed on the shore, watching him.

'Come on, it's not too deep,' he called.

Kiri didn't move. Meru waded out and walked to her.

'What's wrong?' he asked.

Kiri shivered, despite the heat.

'Nothing,' she said.

'You're as white as a sheet … wait a minute … you can't swim, can you?'

Kiri looked at him. 'I never lived near the sea,' she said, by way of explanation. 'Drayden is land locked. I never learned how.'

'But, you rescued me from the flying machine,' he said, his voice faltering. 'You got me out … You did that even though …?'

She shrugged.

'You are so brave …' he said.

'I'm not … I was terrified. I'm still terrified!'

'We'll build a raft,' Meru said, looking around him. 'Plenty of shadewood here.'

'A raft?' Kiri shuddered. 'But, what if I fall in?'

'You won't fall in,' he said, trying to reassure her.

'I will. I can't swim. I'll be out of my depth.' Kiri backed away from the water's edge.

'I won't let you fall in, I promise. Trust me. We've got to get across.'

Kiri clenched her teeth, still shaking her head.

'Kiri,' he said. 'I've worked on boats all my life, I know what I'm doing. I won't let anything happen to you.'

Kiri took a deep breath and then nodded.

Meru gave her a kiss.

'Help me gather up some shadewood,' he said.

Together they scoured the shoreline, pulling together pieces of shadewood as Meru pointed them out and then dragging them into a pile.

'The thin vines from the upper reaches of the shades will work to lash everything together,' Meru said, gesturing to a nearby stand of shades. 'Can you grab some?'

Kiri nodded. She climbed one of the shades and pulled at the vines that grew at the top, just under the cups that gathered water and sunlight. She succeeded in pulling a length away, wrapping it around her wrist and elbow to make a bundle.

As she did so, she noticed a buzzing nearby, and looked up to see an enormous narg in the air before her, its wings a dark blur against the brightness beyond the shades. She saw it regard her out of its three dark eyes, its small head turning this way and that before it flew off, disappearing into the distance. Something about it unnerved her and she dropped to the ground and ran to Meru, telling him what had happened.

'Everything seems oversized here,' he said, taking the vine. Kiri could see he was pulling a series of shadewood logs together, wrapping the vine over and under them time and again. The raft didn't look very big.

'We can't both get on this,' she said.

'It's just for you,' Meru replied. 'I'll swim.'

'But what if there's something in the water?' Kiri asked, eyes wide.

'Let's hope there isn't,' he answered.

She watched as he pulled the raft down to the water. It floated and he jumped on it, the water sloshing around his feet as he did so. He crouched down to balance and then sat on it, satisfied it was lake-worthy.

'Shadewood won't sink no matter what happens,' he said, jumping off and splashing up to her. 'Ready?'

'No,' she said.

He led her to the water's edge, steadying the raft next to her. She crawled aboard, gripping the logs tightly.

'Relax,' he said. 'Just sit in the centre ...'

The raft rolled underneath her, she lurched, trying to keep her balance.

'I'll lie down,' she said, lowering herself forward. She got herself into a position where she could look forward, her arms outstretched in front of her, grasping the edge of the raft, with her feet dangling into the water behind her. Water was sloshing up through her clothes, but at least it was stable and it was a welcome relief from the heat, the water was cool on her skin.

'Alright?' Meru asked.

She just gave him a look.

Meru put the flasks, rifle, belt and the knives alongside her and waded out into the lake, pulling the raft behind him.

Kiri heard the buzzing noise again. Meru must have heard it too, as he turned around to look. Kiri craned her head to see behind her.

Dancing back and forth over the shoreline were half a dozen of the large nargs. They were buzzing in a swarm.

'I don't like this,' Meru said. He began swimming, pulling the raft with him. More nargs joined the swarm, their buzzing turning into a threatening drone of noise, their bodies forming an ominous black cloud on the shoreline.

Then, at some unspoken signalled, they surged forward en masse, a black threatening cloud of motion closing the distance between the shoreline and the pair of humans.

'Meru … Faster!'

Kiri cried out as the creatures descended on her. She saw one land on her calf, saw its mouth parts open and then bite down into her skin. They were all about her, swarming and buzzing through the air. She felt their wings on her face, saw their dark faces in front of her eyes, sharp mandibles clicking …

Biting me!

She screamed.

'Get off the raft!' Meru yelled.

Kiri's grip on the raft was strong, but she felt Meru manhandle her off, pulling her into the water, thrashing like a mad thing.

'I've got you!' he shouted. 'Don't panic. Take a deep breath …'

Kiri gasped and then Meru pulled her under the water. Kiri struggled, but Meru's grip was firm. He guided them both under the raft.

Kiri held her breath. Meru was signing something to her, but she couldn't understand. She wanted to breathe, her chest hurt. Bubbles rose around her.

Just as she thought she could bear it no longer, Meru pulled her aside and up. They broke the surface together, gasping for breath. The nargs still swarmed around the raft, snapping at their heads. Meru ducked down again, pulling Kiri alongside.

This time he kicked his legs, holding her in one arm and grabbing the raft with the other, pulling them further out into the lake. Kiri could see the water growing bluer about them, the floor the lake further way and less distinct.

They surfaced again, looking about them.

The nargs were behind them now, buzzing over the water a dozen hands away. As they watched the nargs retreated to the shore, unwilling to venture further across the lake.

Meru pulled Kiri's hands up so she could grab the raft. She felt him push her up so she could get her elbows on to it. She struggled forward and then hung there, gasping for breath.

'They've gone,' Meru said. 'I don't think they like the open water.'

Kiri tried to stop the trembling that was shaking her from head to foot. She could feel Meru still had his arm around her. She raised her head to look towards the shore. Now there was a black cloud of the insects all along it, swarming impotently. As she watched they lifted into the air, moving inland, looking for other prey.

'They'd have eaten us alive,' she said.

Meru nodded.

'Did they get you?' he asked.

'A couple of bites I think,' she said, shivering. 'I'm alright.'

He smiled at her.

She pulled herself upwards, struggling on to the raft and lying face down upon it once more. Now she was grateful for the warmth of the sun. Meru swam around to the front, holding on to the raft with his hands and kicking backwards with his feet. The raft continued moving away from the shore.

'I've never been attacked by a narg before,' Kiri said. 'They might take on a marsip but …'

'Things are definitely a bit weird here,' Meru said. 'Let's hope there's nothing else lying in wait.'

Progress across the lake was slow but steady. Meru reported that he saw a few small swimming creatures below him, but there didn't seem to be any big enough to bother them. Kiri even managed to doze on the raft in the warmth from Lacaille.

She felt Meru nudge her and she looked up.

'What is it?' she asked.

'We're near the shore … look!'

Kiri raised her head. For a horrible moment she thought she saw more of the nargs. Creatures were floating in the air around her, buzzing daintily. But these were not dark and unpleasant, but brightly coloured, their faceted eyes like jewels, their bodies iridescent in the light of Lacaille, reflecting blues, greens, purples and reds.

'Flits!' Kiri said, recognising them. 'But huge too!'

She remembered how she'd seen one long ago in the shade forests of Drayden, but these were far bigger, perhaps three or four hands long, floating back and forth before them.

Fortunately, they seemed to be taking no interest in the two humans in the water. Kiri and Meru watched as they flapped overhead, their three sets of wings a blur.

Meru found the bottom of the lake with his feet and stood up, hauling the raft in towards the shore. It seemed little different to the side they had left, but the Obelisk seemed closer now, the land rising away from them.

'We're getting there,' he said, helping Kiri off. She shook out her clothes, squeezing the water out of them.

'I am not doing that again!' she pronounced with a shudder, walking up the shoreline. 'Never again, ever.'

* * *

'So,' Coran said, when Zoella related what had happened. 'She tried again, and you stopped her?'

Zoella nodded.

'I had Ira beside me,' Zoella said. 'That helped, but … yes. She tried, but she failed. She wanted to find out where we are. I didn't open my eyes, she couldn't see anything.'

'Then, you're strong enough to face down the high priestess?' Coran said. 'That's … incredible. Isn't she … well, more powerful than anyone else?'

Zoella nodded.

'She's supposed to be.'

'No wonder she's after you,' Mel said. 'She'll want that power for herself.'

Zoella nodded. 'She's taken the gifts of many women already, I don't know why I can resist her, but it has to be something to do with my birth … Kiri and I …'

'Speaking of Kiri,' Coran said. 'Have you …?'

'Not yet,' Zoella said. 'I will try now.'

'Are you sure you're up to it?' Mel asked. 'You look exhausted.'

'I need to know if Meru … if they are alright,' Zoella said.

'If you're sure,' Coran said. 'You know what you're capable of better than any of us.'

Zoella got to her feet and left the bridge.

'I'll go keep an eye on her,' Mel said.

Coran nodded. 'This power she has, if she really is the equal of the high priestess …'

'Coran, she's so young …'

'It's going to come down to some kind of stand-off eventually,' Coran said, his voice lowered. 'You know it, I know it.'

'Doesn't mean I have to like it,' Mel replied. 'She's been through the wringer, that girl, been pushed over the edge once and we've only just hauled her back. You can't stand her up in front of those evil witches and expect her to defeat them.'

'She's the answer though,' Coran said. 'Her and her sister – if she's still alive.'

'They hate each other,' Mel answered. 'You think they'll work together? We'll be lucky to keep them from ripping each other to shreds.'

'Even assuming we can get through that storm in one piece, Meru and Kiri are still alive and we can fix the Obelisk … even then … we still have to deal with the priestesses. They aren't going to leave us alone. They're coming for her and they're coming for us.'

Mel shook her head.

'I just want Meru back,' she said. 'That will do me for now.'

She jumped down from the bridge.

* * *

Rihanna heard the call from her priestesses. They had been flying patrols above the seas off the coast of Airea ever since Nerina's orders had been received.

Rihanna! We have seen it!

Show me.

The priestess was aloft, flying her dach close to the greatest height it could attain, thousands of hands above the sea. Rihanna saw what the priestess could see. A tiny silver mark trailed by a silvery wake, glowing in the light of Lacaille.

The ship! You've done well …

Do you want me to move closer?

No, stay out of sight as much as you can. It will be better if they don't know they're being watched. They should head for the storm to the sunward …

In her vision, the priestess looked up. Rihanna could see a vast bank of cloud to the sunward, reaching even higher than the altitude the dach was flying at.

They are, they'll reach it soon, the ship is moving fast.

Let it go, we don't want to stop it yet, we must be on the lookout for it when it returns. Then we will take it.

Rihanna smiled as the vision failed.

And the maid, this Zoella … we shall see!

* * *

Kiri staggered, her thoughts thrown into disarray. An abrupt sense of presence wrapped itself around her, a hot metal smell rising up and filling her nostrils.

Kiri, can you hear me?

'Kiri?' Meru asked from beside her.

She swallowed, seeing the look on Meru's face. She held up her hand, trying to concentrate.

Yes, it's me.

Kiri couldn't help but send a wave of revulsion, fear and trepidation across the link. To her surprise, nothing of the sort came back, she felt only sorrow, worry and the bloom of hope and delight at the contact.

'It's her … Zoella!' she managed to say.

'Tell her …' Meru began. Kiri nodded, holding him at bay.

Are you alright? Is Meru …?

He's fine. We crashed. The flying machine was broken. We're alright and we're walking to the Obelisk. Meru will want to know …

The crew and ship are safe too. We had some … trouble, tell Meru we're coming as fast as we can.

Kiri relayed the message. The conversation paused. Feelings swirled around them both, surging from one end of the link to the other. Kiri got a sudden sense of intense regret and shame, her own fear and revulsion tempered for a moment

Kiri, it's the gift. The rage, the anger, I'm sorry for what I did …

Kiri shuddered, remembering pain, blood and fear.

You expect me to forgive you for that?

To her surprise, no anger came to her across the link.

No.

Kiri saw images. She saw herself striking down a carn, images of Meru screaming in agony, her dach, Shanza, killing the king of Viresia and the soldier in Drem. She felt Zoella's pain in recalling the images. How she had been hurt by those events.

Unbidden, images of Torin betraying and murdering Charis, the crossbow bolt that had pierced her hand, Liana striking Tasha from the air and the treachery of Nerina swirled in her own mind, surging across the link. There was a momentary glimpse of the girl Kiri had set free from Drayden … Gemma … and her horror when Nerina told her she'd been killed.

The images mixed, a torrent of emotion washing forwards and back across the link.

The feelings receded, leaving Kiri with just Zoella's presence at the far end.

Before either could frame another word, a man's face resolved in the midst of their mental communication. Kiri recognised Guerrun Sandatch, the man who had smuggled them out of Scallia so long ago.

Fragments of memory assembled themselves; a herg-drawn carriage surging up a mountain path before it was overturned. Guerrun clambering out with two babies, a woman …

Myana … it was our mother!

Kiri watched, horrified as her mother was struck down and executed by the priestesses who had chased and caught her.

Another scene, two old people, a man and a woman talking with Guerrun over a simple wooden table, one baby being lifted out, a baby with blue eyes and dark black hair …

Kiri! You were brought up on the borders of Drayden to Ella and Erik …

Yet another set of images. Kiri as a young girl, escaping into the forest after her village had been put to the torch. Living on her wits in the shadewood forests near the city of Daine. The death of Tia and her discovery by the priestesses …

Kiri spied a hall and saw Guerrun delivering a baby to the owners' care.

My childhood, bullied and tormented until …

Kiri saw Zoella hiding, trying to stay out of sight and mind, the big carn coming to her rescue and guarding her from her assailants. Saw her flee the hall and run into the forests, only to meet the king of Viresia. Kiri saw the affection she bore him and the grief and hurt she experienced as he was slain.

Our uncle … he never knew us for who we were!

Then there was the death of the boy. Kiri saw Ren, smiling and happy, cuddling with Zoella, laughing and joking … and then the stone cold ceremony where he had been buried in the soil.

The images stopped abruptly. Kiri could sense Zoella at the other end of the link, but neither could react to anything for long moments, too shocked to frame a single thought.

There were no lies, no deceptions. Such a thing was not possible over the nexion, the strange mental link that connected the gifted. Kiri knew she had seen the truth, as did Zoella.

Kiri heard Zoella's thoughts, soft and placatory.

I do not wish for the hatred to continue between us. We have both lost so much, let us not lose any more.

Kiri could sense the sincerity behind Zoella's words. Her own thoughts were equally honest.

After everything that's happened? How can there be trust? We have wronged each other … time and again, it's best to stay apart …

Guerrun worked so hard to save us … I do not believe Myana would want us to be estranged. We are the last of the Tiamoi family, princesses of Scallia, sisters …

Feelings swirled once again, washing over them. Words weren't sufficient, but were all they had.

Kiri spoke.

You'll be here soon.

Yes, if all goes well …

We should not meet, it's not safe.

We must!

I don't want to see you, or talk to you! Just … stay away from me.

Kiri, please …

No … don't ask me that. Leave me alone!

The link broke. Kiri gasped as her surroundings came back into view. She blinked, seeing Meru holding her by the shoulders, looking at her with concern etched on his features.

'Kiri, what happened?'

Haltingly, her face tear-streaked and her voice shaking, Kiri told him.

* * *

Nerina received Rihanna's communication and breathed a sigh of satisfaction.

The ship is quick indeed. To have reached the storm already having set out from Amar just a few stretches ago. Almost as fast as a dach can fly. We must take that ship as well as the maid. Bring these exiles to heel.

'News?' Merrin asked.

'Rihanna reports the ship has been spotted,' Nerina replied. 'It goes where we imagined it would, towards the Obelisk. They will pass into the storm before long.'

'And Rihanna will ambush them upon their return,' Merrin asked.

'She will be prepared,' Nerina said. 'Do not worry. Rihanna has seen the vessel in action before and knows well what it can do. She will take it, and all aboard will be at our mercy.'

'Including the maid.'

Nerina nodded.

'What news of the unrest?' she said, changing the subject.

'It remains,' Merrin said. 'Many have been arrested as you directed, but the commoners are not cowed. They protest at the edge of the piazza …'

Nerina's face turned to a scowl.

'Then they will learn a harsh lesson,' she said, striding out of the meeting hall.

* * *

Zoella gasped, her own surroundings jolting into clarity around her. For a moment she stared, trying to get her bearings. She felt a hand on her forehead and sensed Ira's calming presence about her.

'Zoella?'

It was Mel's voice.

Zoella looked around, still catching her breath. She was shaking with the effort of concentration.

'They're alive,' she said. 'They're alright.'

'Meru?' Mel asked, crouching down next to her. Ira sat down on the other side, holding her hands.

'Yes,' Zoella said. She swallowed. 'The flying machine crashed in the vortex, but they got out. They're heading to the Obelisk on foot.'

'Thank Lacaille for that,' Mel said, getting to her feet. 'I'll go tell …'

'Wait,' Zoella said. 'I spoke to her … to Kiri …'

'What did she say?' Mel asked, softly, looking at the expression on Zoella' face.

'She … we … both of us,' Zoella winced, trying to put her experience into words. 'I offered to make a truce. I was wrong about her, she has suffered too … more than I knew! There was so much I didn't know … so much I assumed, so much neither of us knew about each other.'

'What did she say?' Mel asked, sitting down.

'She won't talk with me, she says she just wants to be left alone.'

Mel sighed. 'I don't think she's going to have that choice. Anyway … Meru's alive! Coran will want to know. Come on, let's tell him!'

Zoella found herself pulled up, out of the room and along the corridor behind Mel. Mel jumped on to the ladder that led to the deck and disappeared upwards.

'Coran!' she was yelling. 'Coran! Meru's alive!'

By the time Zoella and Ira had clambered up through the hatchway on to the deck, Mel had already reached the bridge. Zoella heard Coran's cry of exultation.

'Yes! Knew he'd be alright! Take more than a storm to knock that boy down.'

Zoella and Ira joined Coran, Fitch and Mel in the cramped area atop the ship.

'You got hold of Kiri then?' Coran demanded.

Zoella nodded.

'She tried to bury the hatchet too,' Mel said, giving Zoella a hug.

'Really?' Coran asked.

'She wouldn't talk to me though,' Zoella said. 'She doesn't trust me.'

'Feeling is mutual,' Coran said.

'But she wasn't as angry as before, we shared … I understand her better now,' Zoella said. 'I didn't realise how much she'd been through and she knows more about what happened to me too. Maybe, we might be able to find a way forward … I don't know.'

Coran nodded enthusiastically. 'I'll be scorched. Maybe there's hope for all of us then. Great work, Zoella.'

To her surprise he pulled her into a close hug alongside Mel and Ira. Only Fitch stayed out of range, watching them all with a disdainful expression.

'Proud of you all,' Coran said. 'You've done good.'

'Hate to break up the celebrations,' Fitch said, from the side of the bridge. 'But might I bring your attention to our next little challenge?'

'What are you wittering on about, Fitch?' Coran demanded.

Fitch jerked a thump out of the forward windows. The crew turned to look.

Along the sunward horizon a thick band of cloud could be seen, rising higher and higher in a curving arc. Even from here they could see it was huge, casting a noticeable shadow on the ocean below.

'The vortex,' Mel whispered.

'Only the biggest storm in the whole snuttin' world,' Fitch muttered.

Coran was all business-like again.

'Run the length of the ship,' he said. 'All hatches to be battened down and locked, portholes and water tight doors closed. The mesh sails need to be dropped and stowed, we'll run on the batteries as we planned. Everything that can be secured and locked away, secure it and lock it away! I want everyone below decks save Mel and I before the stretch is out. Clear?'

'Aye, Captain!' everyone chorused in unison.

Coran smiled. 'Well … that's good then. Jump to it!'

The crew went about their tasks, leaving Mel alone with Coran.

'You think we can make it through?' Mel asked. 'This vortex wrecked Meru's flying machine after all …'

Mel could see how tightly the captain was gripping the wheel of the *Mobilis*.

'We'll make it,' Coran said. 'We have to. One thing at a time, eh?'

CHAPTER TEN

Nadir, Coordinates Zero, Zero

Round 2307, Eighth pass

'I still can't really believe you two are sisters,' Meru said.

'Daughters of a Scallian queen called Myana,' Kiri replied, pawing at the mud-stained torn garments she was wearing. 'Though I don't feel much like a princess.'

They were traipsing through the undergrowth, still heading towards the Obelisk. For now it was hidden by the foliage around them, a mixture of tall grasses and ferns twice as tall as they were. The ground was rising, forcing them to scramble upwards. They had to take frequent rests in the heat, the sweat pouring off them.

'And this Guerrun tried to hide you both away from the priestesses, thinking to bring you back to Scallia when you were old enough?'

Kiri nodded, holding out a hand and pulling Meru up an incline.

'Seem so,' Kiri said. 'But the plan went wrong when he got caught and exiled. My adopted parents died in a plague and I was carted off to Drayden. Zoella was left as an orphan in a hall in Scallia.'

'So you should have been in the palace at Viresia,' Meru said, remembering the grandeur of the city before the war. King Ioric was your uncle … so I wonder who your father was?'

Kiri shrugged. 'He's probably dead too.'

'Don't you want to know?' Meru asked, catching the tone in her voice.

'No, not really,' Kiri said. 'Whoever he is I never knew him, nor my mother.'

'What about Scallia?'

'What about it?'

'Don't you want to go back there?' Meru said, a puzzled frown on his face. 'Now you know?'

'I've been there already,' Kiri said. 'You were there, remember? It's no more of a home to me than anywhere else.'

'But …'

She turned to him, her expression annoyed. 'You grew up on Amar, your parents are from there, you had your childhood there, yes?'

Meru nodded, warily.

'I had none of that. Ever since I can remember I've been fighting to stay alive, fighting to find enough food, hoping I wouldn't get caught and killed by guards or soldiers. I didn't have a childhood. I don't have a home. I don't care about Scallia, or my parents, or Guerrun and his stupid plan. It didn't work, did it?'

Meru shrugged. 'I guess not.'

'Maybe things would have been better if Zoella and I had been left in Viresia when we were children,' Kiri continued.

'You'd have been taken by the priestesses …' Meru said. 'Both of you …'

'I was taken anyway,' Kiri replied. 'What's the difference?'

'You might have just had your powers taken,' Meru said. 'Or you'd have grown up as warriors, trained from birth. When the priestesses found out about my people you would have almost certainly killed us all and the truth of all this would have died with us.'

'Guerrun didn't know about the Obelisk, he was only trying to save Scallia,' Kiri countered.

'He knew the priestesses were wrong.'

She yanked on his arm to pull him up further. The jolt was harder than it needed to be.

'The priestesses saved my life,' Kiri said, looking at him with a fierce glare. 'Healed me, fed me, taught me. That's more than anyone else did. I thank them for that. My parents, Viresia, Guerrun and the others? I don't owe them anything.'

'And what about Zoella?' Meru asked.

Kiri stopped. Then she turned and fixed him with a fierce expression. Meru could see she was trembling.

'What she did was inexcusable,' Meru said softly. 'But I knew her before that. She was kind and gentle. She saved me when we were trekking through the Icy Wastes near Drem …'

'I don't know!' Kiri shouted. 'Part of me just wants to kill her! She hurt me …'

'She's your sister.'

'So?' Kiri answered back. 'Why does that change anything?'

Meru shook his head. 'It doesn't. But she is all that's left of your family, the very last one. You said she wants to talk, will you talk to her?'

'Why should I?' Kiri glared at him.

'Because you told me that the hate and rage in you wasn't yours,' Meru said, looking at her. 'I don't think it was hers either.'

Kiri sagged and sat down on the hillside. Meru sat down next to her and took her hand.

'I love you,' he said. 'But Zoella was my friend. I lied to her, let her down, but she still cared for me. I know she's not cruel by nature, and I know the same is true of you. Events have forced you two apart, misunderstandings, unhappy twists of fate. I don't think you should be enemies, hating each other.'

Kiri didn't respond for a long moment. Then she sighed.

'It's so easy to hate,' she said. 'You just react. Don't need to think, just get people out of your way. Push them aside. It becomes a habit. The gift … this power … it sort of … sings inside you. Like a buzzing, burning hot metal feeling. It makes you so sure you're doing the right thing.'

'Unstoppable,' Meru said.

Kiri nodded.

'It takes over. I've done terrible things … murdered, killed, mutilated, stolen other women's power. I was so convinced what I was doing was good and proper. Totally … utterly convinced.'

'Maybe this gift has a mind of its own,' Meru said. 'Maybe it uses those of you who have it.'

Kiri looked at him. 'To do what?'

Meru shrugged. 'Not sure, but if you look back on how it's been used … all the history … it's always fighting, wars, conflict as far back as anyone can remember.'

'Charis always said not to resort to violence,' Kiri said. 'Maybe there was more to that than just good advice.'

'So … will you speak to Zoella when she gets here?'

Kiri looked away into the distance, she took a deep breath.

'I don't want to,' Kiri said. 'She or I … either one of us might lose control. We might not be able to stop ourselves fighting. Maybe it's better that we don't ever meet again. It's too dangerous. What if one of us hurts you or your friends?'

'Kiri,' Meru said, his voice soft. 'The priestesses will try again with Amar. You know they will. They don't understand the real truth about our planet. I know your childhood was horrible, unfair, cruel … everything that happened … but it saved you from their indoctrination. Zoella had a horrible time too, but she escaped them as well. You … you and Zoella … we need you. Esurio needs you, both of you. You're the only ones who can stop them.'

'But …'

'Last time we were lucky … the flare saved us,' Meru continued. 'But they'll be back. You know what they'll do, they won't stop until Amar is defeated. You know this, you were part of it. We have to stop them and it's going to take both of you to do that.'

Kiri looked down and breathed in and out.

'I can't promise it will work,' she said. 'Same as before.'

'I'll be with you,' Meru said. 'Will you talk to her?'

Kiri nodded. 'I'll try.'

* * *

Waves crashed across the bow of the *Mobilis.* Water surged up the decks almost as far as the bridge, threatening to submerge the ship entirely. The ship plunged downwards, spray lashing the windows, the wind howling outside. The sky was thick and heavy with deep grey clouds, the sea a churning tempest of rolling waves flecking with white streamers of water ripped from the surface by the raging wind.

Coran and Mel were on the bridge, working together to keep the ship on course. The rest of the crew were below decks, trying to survive the ordeal as best they could. None of them had ever tried to sail through a storm of this strength and no lesser ship than the *Mobilis* would have had a chance at making the crossing.

The ship was struggling, but Coran felt its power pulsing, driving them onwards. Then he sensed the engines spin up with a surge of speed, and knew an extreme angle had tilted the propellers out of the water.

Mel grabbed the throttles and yanked them back to bring the vessel under control.

Coran wrestled with the helm as the ship was buffeted by the gale. He fought to keep it turned into the wind and the waves, knowing that once they were struck broadside on, capsize was inevitable.

The ship flexed and creaked with each wave it crested, groaning as it slammed into the deep troughs. Coran could see the ship visibly twisting with the stress. He braced himself as another wave reared before him, causing the *Mobilis* to rear up.

'Hold on!' he yelled. Mel was next to him ready to pull the throttles back as the ship tipped over the edge once more.

The *Mobilis* crested the wave and there was a weightless motion in their stomachs as it hung there for a moment before careening down the other side. Mel caught the throttles and yanked them back, looking behind her to see when the stern dug into the water. As it did so she pushed the throttles up. Coran yanked the helm around to aim the ship across the wave.

The bow ploughed into the water again and they stared in horrified fascination as the water surged up the decks once more.

'Come on,' Coran yelled.

With a heaving groan the *Mobilis* pulled itself clear of the wave, the bow rose, water cascading off the decks and into the sea.

'Not sure how much more of this she can take,' Mel said as the torrent subsided. Both of them were drenched from head to foot.

'Only way out is through,' Coran said, grimly.

Below decks things weren't any happier.

Ira was sea-sick and vomiting, with Zoella trying her best to comfort her as the ship pitched and rolled about them. Both were trying to stay wedged in the corner of the cabin. Fitch was staggering about in the corridor just beyond, cursing as he banged his head on the pipe work that ran along the ceilings.

'This was a very bad idea.'

Zoella looked up, her face white with fear. The ship groaned and rattled about them in an alarming way. She could hear, see and feel the hull twisting about her as the ship fought the fury of the storm. The lights flickered as the 'tricity to the engines was increased and decreased.

The small portholes showed terrifying frothing one moment, blackness the next. Every time the ship tilted forward, Zoella expected expected it to continue plunging on down, bracing herself for a sudden rush of water and a swift unpleasant end in the darkness of the deep.

Water was sloshing down the corridors, first one way and then back again. Fitch backed out of the way as Daf and Creg staggered past, hauling themselves along using grab handles, bags of tools slung around their shoulders, splashing through the sodden gangways.

Ira was sick again. Zoella could feel the poor girl retching on an empty stomach and well-remembered her own bout of sea-sickness when she had first come aboard. There was little enough comfort she could give other than stay with her. Ira was sobbing with misery.

There was a cracking noise above.

Zoella looked up to see a rivet pop out of the bulkhead above her. Water sprayed out in a torrent, soaking both her and Ira in seconds. Ira squealed in surprise and they both jolted to their feet.

'Fitch!' Zoella screamed, trying to hold Ira up. It was impossible to see in the spray.

The ship lurched again, the floor beneath her feet tilting. Zoella lost her footing and slipped, both Ira and herself floundering around in half a hand of water.

Fitch forced his way through the door way and pulled himself inside, his trademark hat knocked to a jaunty angle and as soaked as the rest of him.

'Out of the cabin!' he shouted.

Zoella struggled in the rising water, wrapping an arm around Ira and pulling her along. She turned to see Fitch standing under the spray, trying to bash some kind of bung into the hole with a mallet. He thumped it over and over again as Zoella watched.

The torrent slowed to a trickle, the deck tilting and the water sloshing out of the cabin.

Fitch turned to look at her, his hat and clothes dripping, his hands now slack at his side.

'Lovely this, eh?'

Zoella managed a smile. The ship rolled and the hull groaned again.

'I hope this thing holds together,' Fitch muttered.

* * *

'Come on, it's not much further.'

Kiri was still faster than him. Meru marvelled at her athleticism again. *She's so fit and strong.*

Kiri had already reached the top. He saw her walk forward, looking over the rise. She stopped in surprise and pulled back.

Meru scrambled to his feet and joined her, wiping the sweat from his brow. He gasped.

The Obelisk was close now, it's true scale clear. It was marks high, towering so far into the sky that it was now between them and the vast overhead disk of Lacaille, its top silhouetted against the burning outline of the star. Clouds still swirled around its structure. It sprouted from the ground on three enormous pillars, which merged hundreds of hands above the ground to form the delicate lattice work of the main construction.

They could see the individual bars and cross connections from which it was built, its surface looked like a shimmering silver mirror, glowing orange, reflecting the light from Lacaille. Leading away from it were a series of roadways, stretching out in six different directions. It was positioned in the centre.

'Wow,' Meru said, staring. 'It's beautiful. So delicate, yet it must be unbelievably strong to stand so high.'

Kiri pulled her pendant out to look at it. She held it up towards the Obelisk, it was the same shape.

'Identical,' she whispered. 'All the priestesses have one of these, a symbol of the Obelisk …'

Meru was looking at the base of the tower.

Clustered around it were a series of dishes suspended on huge stands. Buildings could be seen interspersed between them and, off to one side, was a large cleared area upon which a vehicle was visible. It looked somewhat like the flying machine they had been using, but it was clear it was far bigger. Nothing could be seen moving.

'Some kind of flying machine?' Kiri asked, pointing at it.

Meru nodded. 'Looks like it, but the size of it! Why would they need something so big?'

'What are those dish things?'

'I've seen them before,' Meru said. 'They're some kind of radio, used for sending messages at long distances. The ones I saw before were all broken down, these look like they might be working.'

'Nobody about either,' Kiri said.

Around the perimeter of the installation they could see a high wall. Vegetation had grown close to it, but had somehow been prevented from reaching and smothering it. Everything seemed to have been constructed from metal or some bright building material. It was also pristine, with no hint of dirt or debris. There was no sign of movement, but there was an obvious looking gateway set in the wall.

'That must be the way in,' Meru said.

'Then let's get down there,' Kiri answered, already starting to make her way down the hillside.

* * *

Zoella had no real recollection of how long the churning, twisting, gut-wrenching purgatory of the voyage lasted, only that it had seemed to go on forever … but eventually came to an end.

She blinked. Ira was slumped in her arms, asleep herself, her breathing regular and even. Both of them were sodden. Zoella eased her back on to the cabin bed and shifted her feet around to make her comfortable.

Light was streaming through the portholes. The ship seemed stable. She could just feel a gentle rocking to and fro.

The storm has stopped.

She got to her feet and squinted through the porthole. Blue sky, smooth sea. There was even a suggestion of land in the distance.

She looked down at Ira, but decided to let her sleep on. The girl would be exhausted. She could return in a spell with some drinking water and revive her then.

Zoella walked out into the gangway down the centre of the ship and to the ladder amidships. The hatch was open and clear blue sky was visible above. She climbed up and looked around.

The heat hit her straight away. Lacaille was fierce and bright overhead. The ship was floating in a sparkling blue sea, rolling in a light swell. Before her a great wall of cloud arose. As she turned around she could see it walled the calm expanse of sea in all directions, though one side was much closer to her vantage point. The ship must have travelled through it. She turned around and gasped in recognition.

Before her, a green and lush landscape was rising out of the sea some few marks ahead. In the centre rose a vast structure, towering far into the sky, sparkling in the light of Lacaille.

Her mouth dropped open and she stared at it for long moments.

The Obelisk … just as I saw it. We made it!

'Zoella!'

She looked up at Coran's voice.

'Yes?'

'You alright?' he asked. 'Ira?'

She nodded.

'Sorry about the weather.'

She smiled. 'Is the ship …?'

'Mel's checking,' Coran said, peering out of the bridge. 'We've got a bit of a list, some cracked panels and other odds and sods.' He patted the rail alongside the stairs. 'Tough old girl, the *Mobilis* … she's good. Now, come up here and tell me all about this thing.'

He threw a glance over his shoulder at the Obelisk and held out a hand to her. She grasped it and he pulled her up.

'It's the Obelisk,' Zoella said. 'It's what's been calling to me … to Kiri … to us, the priestesses.'

'Doesn't look broken from here,' Coran said.

The *Mobilis* was cruising forward slowly. Zoella could see that Coran was heading for a small sandy inlet not far ahead. Fore and aft Daf and Creg were hauling on the ropes that raised and lowered the strange mesh sails of the ship, pulling them into position.

'Something is wrong with it,' Zoella said. 'I hope we can fix it or …'

'Yeah,' Coran said. 'Death and destruction all round. I remember Caesar's warning.'

'We don't have many stretches left,' Zoella said.

A strange feeling came over her. She recognised the metallic sense immediately. A voice sounded in her head.

Administrator Zoella. Your approach has been noted. Guide your vessel in this direction.

'Zoella?'

She blinked. Coran was looking at her.

'Turn left,' she said. 'Follow the coast for a bit.'

'Why?'

She smiled.

'The Obelisk knows we're here,' she said. 'It's guiding us in.'

'If you say so …'

Coran turned the *Mobilis* to port and they cruised along the coast line for half a spell.

'There,' Zoella said, 'Turn right now.'

Coran did as he was told and the *Mobilis* swung around to starboard. They cleared a small peninsula of land. A harbour came into view, with twin quays stretching out in the water. Beyond them a wide roadway led towards the Obelisk.

'Nice work,' Coran said. 'That will save us quite a bit of bother. But I'm not sure I much like how we can be seen coming like this.'

'The Obelisk is very powerful,' Zoella said, with a shiver.

'Make ready fore and aft!' Coran called down. Zoella could see Daf and Creg run to the bow and stern of the ship, pulling up the ropes and standing attentively.

'She's going to be there,' Coran said, his voice softer. 'You ready for that?'

Zoella swallowed. 'I think we're equally scared of meeting each other.'

'If she's hostile ...'

Zoella looked up. 'There must be no weapons. They won't do you any good and will just make it worse. Please?'

Coran shook his head. 'I'm not facing her without a rifle.'

'If she does fight,' Zoella said and then after a pause added. 'Or I do ... I don't want ...'

'I'll not be taking any funny business from either of you,' Coran said. 'It will be alright. Kiri is going to do as we say, or else.'

The *Mobilis* slowed as it approached. Daf and Creg jumped off on to the quay. It was made of what looked like bright white stone and appeared brand new, as if it had only been made the stretch before. Stanchions were placed at convenient intervals and the two big men tied the ship up. With a faint shudder the engines shut down.

The *Mobilis* was moored at the Obelisk site.

'Daf, Creg – finish hoisting up the masts and sails, let's get some of that 'tricity back into the batteries!'

The two big men continued to work on the decks below.

Coran looked at Zoella.

'We'll get everything ready, will you let Kiri and Meru know we've arrived?'

Zoella nodded and closed her eyes.

* * *

Close up, the wall around the Obelisk compound was imposing. It was three times Meru and Kiri's height and composed of something like rock, but looked unblemished along its entire surface. They inspected it at close range, wondering how it could have been made. The material was white and rough to the touch, but there were no cracks, stains or signs of age. The wall enclosed an area some six marks in diameter, a complete circle in which the Obelisk stood at the centre, still towering over them.

As they stood next to the wall they could feel a thrumming sensation through their feet, a tremble repeating at intervals every few moments. The same material covered the ground, extending perhaps twenty hands from the wall before stopping at a sharp edge and giving way to the vegetation around them.

'It's so … clean,' Kiri said, bending down to examine the floor at close range. 'Like polished sandstone that's just been finished.'

'It reminds me of Caesar's hangar,' Meru said, his voice hushed. 'Everything there was new, as if it had only just been made.'

There were no features, no artworks, no signs or markings of any kind. The wall and the floor were featureless as far as they could see. They walked around towards the gate.

The gate itself was made of metal, set within the rock-like structure of the wall. It was flush with the wall, with a curving surface. It was polished so smooth they could see their own reflections in it.

Off to the right side, embedded in the wall next to the metal gate, was a small black panel and, just above it, a glass sphere.

Kiri peered at it, reaching out her hand.

As she touched the black panel it lit up in red with the outline of a hand, fingers outstretched. The image pulsed.

'You have to place your hand on it,' Meru said. 'If it works like the ones in Caesar's hangar it will ask you who you are.'

Kiri pushed her palm against the panel. The outline glowed for a moment and then turned green.

'Nano-infusion confirmed,' a deep voice intoned from somewhere around them. 'Welcome administrator. Please state your name and rank.'

'I am Kiri,' Kiri said. 'I don't … I don't have a rank.'

'Previous communication has been noted, Administrator Kiri. Nano-infusion identification is confirmed. Access is granted. Please identify your companion.'

Kiri looked at Meru. 'He's … er … he's my …'

'Friend?' Meru asked, with a smile.

'Yes,' Kiri said. 'You must allow him to come with me.'

'Security exception acknowledged, administrator Kiri. Your presence is urgently required in the central control complex. Please proceed immediately.'

With that the doors shrank within the wall and then parted in the middle, sliding into the walls, revealing the interior of the compound.

'Where is the central control complex?' Kiri asked.

'Directions will be provided through your ocular enhancements,' the voice replied.

Kiri looked at Meru, who shrugged.

'No idea,' he said.

Kiri looked around the wall and into the interior of the compound. She could see a well-tended pathway leading within, edged by plants that were somehow trimmed and ordered. Through the gateway she could see the various buildings beyond the garden areas. Everything was clean, but silent.

'I don't suppose there'll be anyone here,' Meru whispered from beside her.

They stepped within, the gate sliding shut silently behind them. Kiri stepped forward and then jumped back in alarm, waving her hands in front of her.

'What's the matter?' Meru demanded.

'A … thing!' Kiri said, trying to grasp something in front of her. She tried again, without success. 'Can't you see it?'

'See what?'

'It's an arrow,' Kiri said, 'There … look! Pointing that way …'

Meru stared at her. She was moving her head this way and that.

'That's amazing!'

'Kiri's there's nothing there.'

'I can see it, it's telling me where to go. Come on! This way!'

Kiri was running forward, Meru hurried to catch up with her.

'Kiri, wait!'

As ever, Kiri was quick on her feet. By the time Meru caught her she was standing almost underneath the Obelisk. Meru looked up and staggered at the incredible sight of the structure towering into the heavens above.

'In here,' Kiri called to him. 'The arrow …'

The building ahead was built into the base of the Obelisk structure itself, a large dome-like affair. Kiri was standing in the entrance, beckoning to him. The doors were already open. Beyond, the interior of the building was in darkness.

He grabbed her hand.

'Slow down, we don't know what …'

'This is the central control complex,' Kiri said.

'How do you …?'

She waved in front of her eyes. 'It's … what that thing said it was,' she said. 'Ocular … whatever. I can see things. They're not really there, but I can see arrows and directions and words. This is it …'

She stepped forward into the darkness.

Lights flickered before them, tiny sparkles in the darkness; reds, greens, blues. With a crackling hum bright orbs overhead burst into life, flooding the room with light. Kiri and Meru gasped, shielding their eyes and trying to see.

They were standing on the perimeter of a vast circular area, edged by handrails. Steps led downwards before them and at three other places around the rim of the room. Below they could see a series of large, black panels positioned around seating areas.

Before them was a metal plate, designed to be seen from the entranceway they had just come through. Kiri could see text stamped on it. She walked forwards to take a closer look.

These words … I've seen them before …

Memories came flooding back to her, when she was first found by Charis, hurt and injured, lying in the rooms of healing in Daine. Charis teaching her the elements of the Drayden religion. She could hear Charis' voice as clearly as if she was beside her.

I will read you a little of the first element then. There are five of them. They were written for the world, it is only right that you should hear them for yourself. It will help you to understand.

Tears sprang into her eyes at the memory.

The sun is the source, the centre. It determines order. Worship it as a god, we could not live without …

But the words before her weren't quite the same. She forced herself to read them out loud.

'The sun is the source of all energy, and the centre of the stellar system. Its gravity determines the order and movement of the planets. Primitive cultures worshipped it as a god, and even now, we could not live without it.'

Meru moved next to her to see what she was doing and then noticed the tears streaming down her face.

'Kiri?'

'This,' she said, wiping at her eyes. 'This is where the religion of the priestesses started. These words … some of them survived in books and tomes … but only some!'

Kiri explained what she had been taught by Charis, how the elements formed the backbone of the priestesses' religion.

'Wow,' Meru whispered. 'Almost right … but so wrong.'

Meru took her hand and led her down the stairs towards the centre of the room. A rising hum sounded about them as equipment and machinery activated. A myriad of screens and panels illuminated, but it was a huge console in the centre of the room that drew their immediate attention. It was glowing bright blue at its base and above it an image appeared, floating in the air before them and rotating. It was a vast globe, detailed, overlaid with zones, colours and information.

They stared at it for long moments.

'It's Esurio,' Meru said. 'The whole planet. Look, you can see the continents, the seas …'

They walked down a small flight of stairs which led to the console. The image hovered in the air before them, almost looking solid. Kiri reached out her hand towards it. As her fingers moved to where they would have touched it if it were solid, a faint tone sounded. Concentric circles of light appeared around her finger tips. As she moved her hand, the globe moved with her. She found she was able to move it around just by gesturing.

Esurio spun before her, its entirety on display.

'Look, you can see the frozen wastes,' Meru said. A ragged line of whiteness encircled the globe around the sunlit edge.

'And the vortex,' Kiri said, turning the image so they could see the other side. A vast swirling tumble of clouds could be seen, twisted around a small, clear spot.

'That must be where we are,' Meru said. 'I wonder if we can make it bigger …'

A gentle tone sounded in the air and the image expanded before them, rushing outwards in a dizzying fashion. In a moment it was as if they were poised in the air above the Obelisk, looking down on it from a great height. They could see the swirling cloud banks, the lakes, forests and seas. At the centre they could make out the walled compound and the Obelisk itself.

'There,' Meru said. 'It's so clear, you can see …'

He turned to look at her. He could see her face had gone pale, her jaw clenched.

'Kiri?'

'Your friends, in their ship,' she said, her voice a whisper. 'They've come through the storm. They're here.'

'That's …'

Kiri looked up with a shudder, her eyes haunted. 'She's coming.'

* * *

Coran led the way up the roadway, but turned to look at his ship as he did so. As per usual, Daf and Creg stayed behind to mind it. They seemed to have little interest in the vast structure before them and had retreated within the ship to see to the bilges and general upkeep of the vessel. The *Mobilis* did look rather forlorn, still listing to one side, some of its structure battered and twisted. The two men had promised to tidy her up as best they could.

Fitch was alongside him, rifle gripped in both hands. Coran had his ready too, though both had the safeties engaged for now.

Zoella had retrieved Ira. The girl looked even more pale than normal, but was relieved to be on dry land. Mel stood alongside them.

'All set?' Coran asked.

'Please don't take the weapons,' Zoella said again.

Fitch scoffed.

'No way are we giving that little bitch the upper hand,' Fitch said. 'If she starts acting up, she's going down, Meru or no Meru.'

'You'll fire only on my order,' Coran said, giving Fitch a look. 'That's the deal.'

Fitch inclined his head.

'But Fitch is right,' Coran said, turning to Zoella. 'She may have tricked Meru, we don't know, do we?' He patted the rifle. 'This will make her think twice.'

Coran saw Zoella purse her lips, but she didn't say any more. Mel also looked undecided. Ira's expression was indecipherable.

'You three stay behind us, understood?' he asked. The three women exchanged a look with each other.

He turned about, gesturing to Fitch and they walked up the roadway.

'How do you want to play this?' Fitch asked, under his breath. 'If it were me I'd just blow her away the moment we lay eyes on her. We've already got two of these snuttin' witches, we don't need three.'

Coran smiled and shook his head. 'If Kiri raises a hand against us, kneecap her. I know you've got a score to settle with her, but I want to hear what she has to say for herself first.'

'As you say, Captain.' Fitch said, a grin forming on his face.

* * *

'We have to go and meet them,' Meru said.

Kiri nodded.

'I won't let them hurt you,' Meru said.

'What are you going to do?'

'I'll go first,' Meru said. 'You stay back until I call you. Coran said he would hear us out. I hope he'll keep his word. If not …' Meru picked up the rifle. 'They'll have to come through me first.'

'This is about me and Zoella,' Kiri said. 'I don't want anyone hurt. They're your friends.'

'Until I know they aren't going to shoot you,' Meru said. 'And until I'm sure Zoella is under control, you must stay back. Promise me.'

Kiri looked worried.

'Alright.'

* * *

The Obelisk grew in front of them. A set of steps led up towards a tall wall that encircled it. Mel squinted into the light. She could see a figure standing at the top, waiting for them. It too was holding a rifle.

'That's close enough.'

'Meru!' Mel said, recognising his voice and stepping forward. Coran held up a hand.

'What's the gun for, Meru?' Coran asked.

'I might ask you the same question,' Meru called back.

'That girl, Kiri, is dangerous,' Coran replied. 'Killed a lot of our folk if you recall.'

'I also recall her almost being killed when in your care,' Meru said. 'I'm not going to risk that happening again.'

Mel saw Coran look across at Fitch. Both unlocked the safety catches on their rifles. Zoella and Ira stood behind them. Both looked scared.

'What are you doing?' Mel asked.

'We don't know where she is,' Coran said.

'Likely a trap,' Fitch agreed.

'Will you all just stop it?' Mel shouted at them, pushing between the two men and pushing the barrels of the rifles down. 'It's Meru! Put your stupid guns away before someone gets hurt.'

She saw Meru lower his gun. Mel glared at Coran until he signalled to Fitch and both of them did likewise.

'Drop them,' Mel insisted, calling up so Meru could hear her. 'All of you. Bloody stupid men!'

Coran nodded and placed his rifle on the ground. Fitch grunted and did likewise. At the top of the stairs, Meru followed their example.

'Now step back,' Mel scolded. 'I'll talk to him.'

She waited until Coran and Fitch had obeyed her instruction. Then she ran forward and up the stairs.

'Come here,' she said, her arms outstretched.

Meru smiled and she pulled him into a hug.

'So good to see you, are you alright?' she demanded, pulling back and looking at him. 'I've missed you, you troublesome little rogue!'

He smiled. 'It's good to see you too.'

Mel looked past him. 'Is she ...?'

Meru nodded. 'A little further up. I told her to wait.'

Mel sighed. 'This is all about the two of them, isn't it?'

Meru nodded.

'Then let's get it over with. You keep an eye on Kiri, I'll do the same for Zoella. If it starts going funny, we'll whack 'em on the back of the head with the rifle butts. Agreed?'

Meru nodded.

'Wait here then.'

Mel walked down the stairs and signalled to Zoella.

The girl was hesitant, but did as she was told. Mel saw her swallow as she approached.

'Give me the rifle,' Mel said to Coran. He picked it up and handed it to her. Mel flicked the safety on.

'You sure you know what you're doing?' he asked.

'Trust me,' she scolded. 'We'll do this without blowing anybody's head off.'

Mel held the rifle in one hand and took Zoella's with the other. She led Zoella up the flight of stairs to Meru.

Meru and Zoella stared at each other, but neither said anything.

'This is between the two of you first,' Mel said, with a sigh. 'And then the three of you. You two better start talking or I'll bang your heads together.'

'I'm …' Zoella began. 'I didn't mean to … what I did … it was wrong. I'm so …'

'I didn't want to hit you,' Meru stuttered in return. 'You're alright?'

Zoella nodded, a faint smile showing on her face. 'Yes. You?'

'A bit … hot,' Meru said.

Mel shook her head and rolled her eyes.

'Give the snuttin girl a hug, boy!' Mel snapped.

Zoella ended up taking the initiative. She pulled Meru into an embrace. Mel heard sobs from her, saw Meru hesitate for a moment before responding, pulling her into a tight hug.

'Zoella …'

'I need to see her.' Zoella pulled back, wiping her eyes. 'Talk to her. We need to end this. I promise I won't do anything to hurt her.'

Meru backed away, looking at Mel.

Mel nodded. 'Go get her.'

Meru walked up the stairs until he got to the top. Zoella and Mel saw him beckon.

After a few moments Kiri stepped up next to him. Mel heard Zoella gasp from beside her. Mel gripped the rifle hard.

'Keep breathing,' Mel said to Zoella, her voice just a whisper. 'Just keep breathing.'

Meru led Kiri down the stairs by the hand until they stood just a few paces away from Mel and Zoella. Mel saw Kiri run her gaze over her, seeing the rifle, before she turned her attention to Zoella.

Mel watched the two young women stare at each other.

Sisters. They don't look very much alike. Blue eyes versus brown. Kiri looks scrawny like she needs a decent meal ... and those scars ... she's had a hard life. Zoella looks so much younger, though she's taller ...

'My name is Mel,' Mel said, breaking the silence. Kiri looked at her. Mel stared into her blue eyes, finding them mesmerising.

So intense ...

'I know,' Kiri answered. 'From the ship. Meru has told me all about you.'

Kiri's voice was flat and matter of fact. Her expression was a strange combination of haughtiness, wariness and distance.

'Kiri ...' Zoella's voice shook as she spoke Kiri's name. Mel saw Kiri shudder, looking at Zoella with wide eyes.

She's actually afraid, this relentless warrior woman we've heard so much about ... she's scared!

'I'm sorry for what I did,' Zoella said, holding out her hands towards Kiri. 'I don't expect you to forgive me, I don't ... I don't want anything from you. I just want ...' Her voice cracked. 'I just want the hatred to end ...'

Kiri didn't move. She didn't say or do anything.

Zoella burst into tears.

Still Kiri didn't move.

After a moment Mel reached out to Zoella as she sobbed, pulling her into an embrace. Zoella buried her head against Mel, crying her heart out. Mel looked up at Kiri, a glare on her face, expecting to see the same impassive face as before.

'You going to stand there or–?' she began.

To her surprise she saw that Kiri's eyes were wet with tears of her own. Mel saw Kiri's bottom lip tremble.

Then …

'Zoella,' Mel said gently. 'Zoella, look.'

Zoella raised her head.

Kiri was holding her hand out towards Zoella. Mel could see it was shaking. Zoella looked at it, straightening as Mel released her. Meru was standing just behind Kiri, looking at her.

'Go on,' Mel said softly.

Neither of the two women said anything. Zoella stretched out her fingertips towards Kiri's as they stared into each other's eyes. Their fingers slid alongside each other. Both flinched at the touch, but continued to move.

Hands closed together. A grasp. Mel saw them both draw a sharp breath, staring at each other in shock and surprise.

* * *

The memories they had shared before over their mental link now swirled about them in exquisite detail. The fragmentary recall of their childhood, shadows from the distant past; their upbringings and the tragedy of what happened to their family. The shared experiences of Viresia, Drem and Amar, now seen from each other's perspective though the connection between them.

There was hatred, there was anger, but it was coupled with regret and horror for assumptions made and misunderstandings compounded.

Zoella saw the genuine love Kiri had for Meru, how she had saved his life, more than once. She saw the life lessons she had taken from Charis and the agony as she watched her mentor die in her arms. Kiri saw Zoella's own love for Ren, for Ioric, felt the fury and the rage, saw her kind and gentle spirit trying to find a way through all the chaos in the world.

And the gift, the mysterious gift that empowered them, but which had twisted and changed them too.

Their hands let go, but both continued to stare at each other, barely aware that Mel and Meru were standing alongside them.

'I have wronged you,' Kiri managed to say. 'Over and again. For my part in all that hurt … the boy …' her voice quavered and she shook her head. 'I so wish I could undo it.'

The raw emotion crackled between them, but neither could retreat from it.

'I hated what I became because of it,' Zoella answered, her face wet with tears. 'And what I did to you. Can we let this be an end to it?'

Kiri nodded.

'An end.' Kiri pursed her lips, her own face tear-streaked. She nodded, wiped at her eyes and then held out her hand again. 'Sister.'

Zoella gave a short cry, almost stumbling. 'Yes …'

The pair moved towards each other, tentatively, still wary. Then something broke between them, the barriers built over long rounds crumbling in a torrent of regret, remorse and hope.

Zoella pulled Kiri into a hug. After a moment Kiri's arms closed about her, holding her tight.

'My sister!'

CHAPTER ELEVEN

Daine, Capital of Drayden

Round 2307, Eighth pass

Merrin ensured that Nerina's message was posted and communicated around Daine. The priestesses under her supervision were subdued and pale as she gave out her instruction. She rebuked two of them when she caught them whispering in hushed tones.

'Accused?' one asked. 'What of proof …?'

'Nerina's directive is clear,' Merrin said. 'Bring them to the piazza.'

The priestesses nodded and withdrew.

It did not take long. Four troublemakers were hauled into the piazza before the temple, more were gathering at the limits of the temple area, shouting and calling abuse at the priestesses.

The priestesses found themselves confronted with a baying mob, many armed with farming implements, or the tools of their trade, others just brandishing fists and yelling insults. The priestesses formed a line, barricading the crowd from entering the piazza, their kais out and ready. The group of prisoners that had been assembled were further in, guarded by another set of priestesses.

The priestesses held their line, the prisoners were on their knees, kais at their throats. The yelling grew, turning to a chant of fury.

'No more deaths, set them free! No more deaths, set them free!'

The crowd pushed forwards, the priestesses drew back ready to strike.

CEASE!

Nerina's imperious mental command shocked through priestesses and commoners alike. She appeared at the entrance to the temple, striding outwards, her own kai in her hand. She approached the prisoners, glaring at them as she passed, before moving towards the crowd.

Then she stood before them, behind the line of priestesses, pacing up and down, staring at the crowd, her face twisted with fury as she saw some of them were men.

HOW DARE YOU TURN ON YOUR BETTERS? HOW DARE YOU ASSAIL THIS HOLY PLACE? MEN ARE NOT PERMITTED WITHIN THE BOUNDARIES! LACAILLE'S WRATH LIES POISED TO DESCEND UPON YOU FOR YOUR INSOLENCE.

Silence reigned, Nerina's mental words echoed throughout the minds of all present, deafening but inaudible. Nerina continued to pace, none could face her gaze.

YOU WILL LAY ASIDE YOUR WEAPONS. GO BACK TO YOUR HOMES AND YOUR PLACES OF WORK.

'What of those arrested?' someone shouted.

Nerina turned to find them, but their voice was lost in the crowd.

THEY HAVE DEFIED ME. THEY ARE MINE TO DO WITH AS I WISH.

The chant, led by those from the rear of the crowd, began to reassert itself, until it was strong once more.

'No more deaths, set them free! No more deaths, set them free!'

The priestesses were looking at each other.

Nerina turned, gesturing to the prisoners behind her. Now her mental command was only heard by the priestesses.

KILL THEM.

The priestesses guarding the prisoners hesitated.

High Priestess …

KILL THEM!

The priestesses were shaking their heads, stepping away. The prisoners got to their feet, punching their fists into the air. They pushed past the priestesses and ran towards the crowd.

Nerina stood between them and their freedom.

She raised her kai, stepping forwards.

The prisoners paused, one gesturing towards Nerina.

'Just let us go …'

Nerina spun her kai and struck him across the neck. The man fell forward to lie still upon the ground. Nerina moved in upon the next one, a woman, who raised up her hands in defence. Nerina struck her too, and she fell back, twitching on the flagstones. Two remained.

The crowd was yelling, but it was to no avail. Nerina killed them both with her kai in two swift strikes. Behind her, the line of priestesses failed and was forced back. They fled, running up the piazza towards Nerina, the crowd at their heels.

Nerina turned, her hand outstretched.

THIS IS YOUR LAST CHANCE.

The crowd surged to a stop, some folk at the front stumbling to their knees.

Nerina, defiant, walked back towards them, twirling her kai.

KNOW YOUR PLACES.

She gestured at them. Those at the front screamed, clutching their heads and flailing around for a moment before casting themselves on the ground. Nerina swept her gesture left and right, more folk felt her powers slash into their minds.

For a moment the crowd surged forward, but as Nerina's powers cut down another line of them, panic set in. Screams of fear and terror rent the air as people pushed and shoved to escape.

Nerina did not relent.

Even as they turned she struck again and again, people falling before her, her face a twisted mask of hatred and anger. The crowds fled the piazza, their anger replaced with blind panic, running into the city, trying to flee her wrath.

Bodies were scattered about her, most were dead, but some groaned softly, struggling to move away. As she neared them a short sharp scream from each marked their final demise.

* * *

'We've still got to fix the Obelisk,' Meru began. 'Not sit down for a meal!'

'One for the next stretch,' Coran said firmly.

'What?' Meru demanded. 'But …'

'Everyone is tired and worn out,' Coran said. 'You said we had several stretches left.'

'Yes, but …'

'A good sleeping will do us all a power of good. Then we can tackle this thing with clear heads at first chime.' He gestured at the enormous Obelisk reaching into the sky behind them and to the quay where Zoella and Kiri were sitting side by side deep in conversation. 'Been a bit of a stretch all things considered.'

Meru looked at Fitch.

'Captain's spoken,' Fitch said.

'And he's right,' Mel said looking at Meru. 'We're exhausted, you're exhausted …' She looked over to the quay. 'And so are they.'

'They haven't ripped each other's hearts out then,' Fitch observed, looking at the two women.

'No,' Coran said with a chuckle. 'The peace seems to be holding for now. That food ready yet?'

'Won't be long,' Fitch returned.

The smell of cooking was wafting up from the *Mobilis*' galley. Everyone was hungry and finding any excuse to hang around the ship.

'That does smell good,' Meru said.

'You'll wait your turn same as everyone else,' Fitch said, before his face cracked into a grin.

'That was quite a trek you made,' Mel said to Meru.

'Yes, it was,' Coran said, watching the two young women. 'This Kiri girl is resourceful, I'll give her that.' He gestured to Meru. 'Saved your life into the bargain.'

Meru nodded. 'She did, more than once.'

'And how are you doing?' Coran asked.

'Alright, I'm tired,' Meru said, with a chuckle. 'We didn't get much sleep, too many strange things trying to eat us. There are nargs as long as your arm that try to bite you to death and plants that try to eat you whole, floods that try to wash you away … it's a dangerous place.'

'Coming through that storm was no little thing either,' Coran said. 'Zoella and Ira had to face down this … thing. A massive creature out of the ocean depths.'

'Almost took us all as a snack,' Fitch added.

'You made it, we made it,' Mel said. 'That's all that matters.'

Meru nodded, looking over his shoulder at Zoella and Kiri. They seemed deep in conversation.

'How are they doing?' Mel asked.

'They're talking,' Meru said. 'I guess that's the best thing they can do right now.'

'You think we can trust her?' Coran asked.

Meru looked back. 'Which one?'

Fitch laughed.

'You know what I mean,' Coran said.

Meru sighed. 'I think so. Kiri's not who she … well, she is, but she knows the truth now. She found out from me that what she had been taught wasn't true. It was a shock, it took a while for her to take it on. She doesn't want to fight any more.'

'Doesn't mean we can trust her,' Coran said. 'It's easy to see she's smart and clever …'

'And you've got the hots for her,' Fitch said, jabbing a finger at Meru. 'That's plain as Lacaille. Girl's got into your head.'

'It's not that,' Meru snapped. Fitch smirked. Coran raised his eyebrows and even Mel gave him a look. 'Alright, yes it is! I love her. Something did happen all that time ago. She didn't mean it to, but it changed me and it changed her. She's broken out of the indoctrination of the priestesses now. They betrayed her, abandoned her. She has no one except for me now …'

'She could still be playing you, Meru,' Coran said, a stern note in his voice. 'I know that's hard to hear, but you've got to admit the possibility.'

'What for?' Meru demanded. 'What would she gain?'

Fitch rolled his eyes and Coran answered for him.

'Knowledge on how our ship works,' he said. 'About Amar's defences, maybe learning enough about the Obelisk to use it to strengthen the priestesses' powers. Could be any number of things ...'

Meru was shaking his head. 'She's changed, I tell you ...'

Mel patted his hand. 'I hope you're right,' she said. 'But you must be ready in case you're wrong. She might still be loyal to them ...'

'She's not.'

Coran sighed. 'Well, we'll find out once this Obelisk business is fixed. What do you plan on doing after that?'

Meru looked blank.

'I hadn't really thought that far,' he said.

'Your parents want you back,' Mel said. 'Back home. We can all go ...'

'And what would happen to Kiri if I come back to Amar?' Meru asked. 'She'll stand trial and be locked up.'

Coran sighed.

'I promised a fair trial for her, but we can't change what she did,' he said, his voice low. 'She was responsible for killing many Amarans. By the laws of Amar she is a criminal.'

'Even if she manages to fix the Obelisk?' Meru asked.

'That will go in her favour ...'

'Her favour? Not much incentive for her to return then is there?' Meru asked. 'She hasn't got anywhere she can go. I'm not going to abandon her. Wherever she goes, I go.'

Coran nodded, but shared a glance with Mel and Fitch.

'Food'll be ready,' Fitch said, getting to his feet. 'Want to give me a hand, boy?'

Meru nodded and the two clambered below decks.

'He really loves her,' Mel said.

Coran rubbed his chin. 'Yeah, he does. Let's hope it's not an act and she feels the same way. Keep an eye on her, will you? One step out of line ...'

'Don't you worry,' Mel said. 'Eyes like a dach.'

* * *

The water was lapping at their feet. Kiri and Zoella sat on the quay, their legs dangling over the edge, enjoying the warmth of the sea. Far out on the horizon, the swirling wall of cloud continued to rotate around the Obelisk. Lacaille blazed overhead, still peaceful and serene.

'So which one of us do you think was born first?' Zoella asked.

Kiri looked at her, a faint smile on her face. 'You obviously, you're the bossy one.'

'Me!' Zoella said, laughing in mock outrage. 'Me? Bossy?'

'That crew of yours will do whatever you say,' Kiri said.

'Not sure about that.' They looked around at the figures aboard the ship, who were staring towards them but quickly turned away.

'They're scared of us,' Kiri said.

Zoella nodded. 'They have reason to be. What you and I have done, what we're capable of doing …'

Kiri nodded.

'The priestesses told me it was right. Women were supposed to have this power, to control everything, dominate, enforce the laws. It would be chaos without our control.'

'I heard the same thing,' Zoella said. 'Liana used almost those same words to me.'

Kiri looked at her. 'Liana is our cousin,' she said. 'What happened to her was my fault. She lost her mind. In Viresia, I took her powers … it was an accident, I didn't know what I was doing.'

'It was she and Torin who caused that war by burning the treaty,' Zoella said. 'If only Ioric had known the truth! Liana had dreams of becoming Empress, it was all because of her …'

'So does Nerina,' Kiri said. 'So did I. When you saw that image in my mind back in Airea, you were right. I did want it … but now … I don't. Ever since …'

Kiri looked out to sea.

'She stole some of my power,' she said.

'Nerina, the high priestess?'

Kiri nodded.

'I think I did too,' Zoella said. 'When you killed … when Ren died. I tried to kill you, but I think I took some of your power then. And having that power … that's what enraged me afterwards.'

Kiri looked at her. 'You must be right … after that …'

'The ambition went away,' Zoella said. 'The striving, the anger … the rage? It went, didn't it?'

Kiri looked at her with wide eyes, nodding with puzzlement. 'Yes. Exactly.'

'It's the gift,' Zoella said. 'Before Viresia was destroyed I found some ancient books from the Voren Empire, before Drayden and Scallia. There were instructions on how the gift was to be used. That word, administrator, it comes up again and again. These gifts weren't supposed to be used to dominate and control, just to … help. There were warnings about taking power from others, taking too much. It changes you …'

Kiri nodded. 'And if you have too much …'

Zoella swallowed. 'It makes you do things …'

Kiri reached out, taking Zoella's hand in hers.

'It is past,' Kiri said. 'I will never mention it again.'

'And I don't blame you for Ren's death,' Zoella said, grasping Kiri's hand back.

Their conversation lapsed for a while and they listened to the sound of the water lapping against the quay.

'This gift,' Zoella said. 'I don't know if I can control it. When it rises up, it's like …'

'Like a burning sensation?'

Zoella nodded. 'Yes, with a smell like hot metal. But it's almost got a mind of its own. When I've used it I felt … I started to …'

Kiri licked her lips.

'Enjoy it?'

Zoella nodded.

'Nerina taught me how to take gifts from others,' Kiri said. 'When you do, the feeling is … addictive. As good as …' She looked away.

Zoella caught the blush on Kiri's face.

'That good?' Zoella said. 'So … speaking of Meru …'

Kiri was about to say something, but thought better of it.

'Do you love him?' Zoella asked, gazing at Kiri. They looked at each other for a long moment.

Kiri nodded.

'As sure as I've ever been about anything,' she said. 'Oh he's frustrating, maddening, always asking stupid questions but …'

Zoella kept her gaze.

'He loves you,' she said, her voice hushed. 'He's my friend, you won't hurt him will you?'

'I don't want to,' Kiri said. 'What he did for me, what he risked. I know he loves me … it scares me.'

'If he hadn't rescued you, I would have killed you,' Zoella said. 'And Meru would have hated me forever. I'm glad he got you away.'

Kiri nodded.

'What happened between me and him was an accident,' Kiri said. 'When I captured him that time I forced my way into his mind. I hurt him. I was trying to find out about you, Liana and how to get to Amar. I wasn't thinking of anything else …'

'He was,' Zoella said. 'Pretty much from the moment he saw you I think. I remember him staring at you from the walls of Viresia.'

'It formed a link,' Kiri said. 'The priestesses use it to bond their partners to them, for loyalty. I did it accidentally with Meru. It grew into an obsession between us.'

'Explains why he went so secretive on me,' Zoella said. 'I knew he was hiding something.'

Kiri looked away and out to sea.

'I've cut him off from his home and his family,' Kiri said. 'If I go back they'll lock me away. I'm not saying I don't deserve it after everything I've done, but he won't let that happen, I know he won't.'

'Maybe Coran will be able to ...'

'They don't trust me,' Kiri said. 'I can see it in their eyes. No matter what I do, that won't change. I can't blame them for that. I'm the enemy. If Meru and I go home they will lock me up and throw away the key ...'

'If you fix the Obelisk with us,' Zoella said. 'They will look well upon that, surely?'

'Maybe,' Kiri said. She was looking out to sea again, her gaze distant.

Zoella narrowed her eyes. 'Kiri ...'

Kiri turned to look at her.

'If something happens and I have to leave, promise you'll look after him for me?'

Zoella turned and pulled Kiri around.

'No. Don't even think of leaving him, running away or anything,' Zoella said. 'That's not the answer.

'I might have to,' Kiri answered. 'I can't break up his friends and family. I won't.'

Zoella shook her head. 'He needs you. Without you he'll be heartbroken. He'll never accept it. There's got to be a way for you to be together, to be happy. We'll find it.'

Kiri swallowed and then nodded.

They heard a whistle from behind them. Both of them turned to see Fitch waving from the decks of the *Mobilis.*

* * *

Everyone was ravenous. Fitch had managed to cook up a selection of dried flatters and cabbies, along with a generous selection of melps, tubars and corcans. It was a veritable feast, particularly for Kiri and Meru.

'Makes a change from barbecued marsip,' Meru said. 'Not that I was complaining.'

'Marsips?' Mel asked.

'Kiri caught them with snares,' Meru said. 'We've eaten nothing else for stretches. All the supplies in the medical ship were washed away.'

'They make for good eating,' Zoella said. 'Better with a few spices of course. I lived on them for stretches myself in Scallia. Well done, Kiri.'

Kiri looked up at her, gave a brief smile and then continued to eat. She sat with her head forward, her dark hair covering her face.

Coran watched Kiri for a moment, finished his mouthful and then sat back, resting his arms behind him on the deck.

'So,' he said. 'We're all here, just about in one piece. This Obelisk thing then, what do we need to do?'

Meru looked at Kiri, but she didn't say anything.

'We found this control complex,' Meru said. 'We were investigating when you arrived. Seems to be the place that Caesar told us about. There was this amazing globe … like a map.'

'The Obelisk called to us,' Zoella said. 'All three of us.' She indicated Kiri and Ira. Ira nodded. 'It should tell us what it needs.'

'How does it tell you?' Mel asked.

'It speaks,' Zoella said. 'The same way the priestesses can send messages, we hear it in our thoughts.'

'Caesar said there would be a voice system too,' Meru added, stifling a yawn.

'Then there's nothing else to be done now,' Coran said. 'Everyone is to get some sleep, we'll start on the first chime.'

There were no complaints from anyone and the crew filed off the deck.

'Kiri didn't say a word,' Coran said to Mel.

'She's going to be wary,' Mel replied. 'Wouldn't you be?'

Coran nodded. 'Yeah. I guess so.'

* * *

The weather was unchanged the following stretch, the sky still clear above, the great circle of cloud on the horizon still swirling about them. The Obelisk reached up into the sky as before.

Lacaille's disk was overhead, but they could see sunspots growing once more, faint flickers of blue light caught their eyes, shining around the edges of the globe of fire hanging in the sky overhead.

'Another flare coming,' Coran noted, looking up. 'Time we got this thing fixed I think.'

Daf and Creg stayed with the ship, leaving Coran, Mel, Fitch, Ira, Zoella, Meru and Kiri walking up the paved walkways to the Obelisk compound. The gate had closed again, but Kiri's handprint was identified and the gates slid back.

They were soon standing in the central control complex, looking about them in wonder. Meru demonstrated the globe map.

'Very impressive,' Coran said. 'But let's get to fixing the thing, shall we. What happens now?'

Zoella and Kiri exchanged a glance.

'Shall we?' Zoella asked. Kiri nodded. Zoella beckoned Ira over as well.

Zoella spoke up.

'Obelisk,' she said, her voice authoritative. 'Administrators Zoella, Kiri and Ira are here, please instruct us.'

There was a faint hum within the room and then a voice spoke. It was similar to Caesar's but with a deeper cadence.

'Administrators Zoella, Kiri and Ira. Your presence is noted. Sensors detect visitor Meru and three other unauthorised personnel in close proximity. Please identify.'

'Our companions,' Zoella said. 'Coran, Fitch and Mel. They have helped us reach you.'

'Additional visitors logged. Would you like a status report?'

'Yes, thank you.'

Words appeared in the air before Zoella. She heard everyone gasp behind her.

'How is that done?' Meru whispered, before Mel shushed him.

Facility Status Summary: Nominal

Power: Good. 66% of Magnetic Induction and Solar Arrays remain operative.

Comms links: Failed. Not responding, no data.

Satellite links: Poor. One Lagrange point facility remains operating.
Auxiliary monitoring stations. Failed. Not responding, no data.
Internal Integrity. Excellent. All systems operating within acceptable parameters.
Hangar assets: Orbital dropship currently non-functional. 4x Class six personnel shuttles serviced according to schedule

'Orbital dropship,' Meru said excitedly. 'Is that for ...'

'Meru ...' Coran said. 'Focus!'

Terraforming Status summary: Critical!
Atmospheric Pressure: Good. 949 Millibars.
O2 Mix: Good. 21.8%
Pollution: Excellent. No harmful oxides or excess carbon detected.
Humidity. Good. Average 56%
Magnetic Field Strength. Critical. 12 Microtesla and falling. Atmospheric loss due to solar wind erosion in progress. Axial alignment is out of tolerance, thermal load is excessive and failure is imminent.
Obelisk Augmented Management System: Requires Urgent Replacement.

'These systems,' Zoella said. 'You must instruct us. What must we do to fix them?'

The Obelisk's deep voice spoke. 'One administrator must be selected to service the augmented management system. The AMS is located two levels down within this facility. Axial alignment requires adjustment by another administrator within the antenna complex above. An elevator is available to take you to the aerial platform where adjustments can be made. Replacement parts will be provided.'

'Sounds like two teams,' Coran said.

'Confirmed,' The Obelisk replied.

'What is the augmented management system?' Mel asked.

'The AMS is the central governing capability of all Esurio systems,' the Obelisk replied. 'Its purpose is to manage all the disparate facilities on the planet, ensuring communications, telemetry, diagnostics and centralised management of all aspects of terraforming control. It is currently non-functional. Without it, terraforming status will continue to decay, ultimately rendering Esurio uninhabitable.'

'Uninhabitable?' Kiri asked.

'Everyone will die,' Zoella said. 'Like my vision ...'

'Confirmed,' the Obelisk said. 'Without the AMS, the magnetic field boosters, atmospheric processors and nano-tech systems will remain functioning poorly, ultimately leading to cascade failure and complete shutdown. Atmospheric pressure will drop and inimical radiation will reach the service, rendering human life impossible. AMS replacement is imperative.'

'And you have the replacement parts?' Coran asked.

There was a short pause.

'Replacements are available,' the Obelisk replied.

'Right then,' Coran said. 'Meru, Kiri, you're going up, neither of you are scared of heights. Mel you can go with them. Zoella, Fitch, Ira and me will go down and fix this AMS whatnot.'

'Holographic assistants are available to guide you through the necessary procedures,' the Obelisk said. 'Do you wish them to be activated?'

Zoella looked around at the rest of the crew. Everyone shrugged.

'Yes, please activate,' Zoella said.

There was faint shimmer in the air, and a series of beams of light flashed out from above them. The crew gasped in surprise and backed away as two people appeared before them.

Both had dark skin and were short and stocky. Their gender was difficult to tell, both had short cropped hair and blank expressions. They appeared to be dressed in lightweight jackets and trousers.

Meru was the first to recover from the surprise.

'They're not really there,' he said. 'Look, you can see through them ... like a reflection in glass.'

'This facility is equipped with seventh generation holographic projection technology,' the Obelisk said. 'Holographic assistants may be queried on all subjects and can demonstrate procedures.' There was a pause. 'Administrators unfamiliar with this technology should note that holographic assistants have no physical presence.'

The first turned as Meru approached him.

'Welcome Meru,' he said. 'I am Zane. How may I assist you?'

Meru looked over his shoulder with a grin.

'What a strange accent,' Kiri said.

'Welcome Kiri,' Zane said, appearing to look at her. 'It is good to meet an administrator after all this time. Asha and I have been deactivated for almost two thousand rounds.'

Kiri swallowed. 'Two thousand rounds?'

Zane nodded. 'You are the first administrators to visit this complex since round three four one.'

'What … what are you?' Coran managed to ask.

The second person, Asha, turned towards him. Her voice was lighter, feminine, but also with the curious accent.

'We are artificially intelligent reference simulations,' she said. 'Our physical appearances are based on the vital statistics of the initial eighty Esurio colonists, averaged to a mean and then adjusted to provide a …'

'You're what the original settlers of Esurio looked like?' Mel asked.

Asha nodded. 'We are an approximation of their appearance.'

'And there were eighty?' Meru asked. 'How did …?'

'Not now, Meru,' Coran said, interrupting him. 'Two teams, let's get on with this. We've got work to do.'

'We need to reach the antenna complex,' Meru said to Zane.

'I can show you the way,' Zane said. 'We shall be team one. Kiri, Meru and Mel, please follow me.'

'We shall be team two,' Asha said. 'Zoella, Ira, Coran and Fitch, please follow me.'

The crew of the *Mobilis* watched as the two figures strode off a few paces, then turned and beckoned. The crew broke into two groups and followed them. Only Fitch hung back.

'So we're just going to trust them?' Fitch asked.

'Got any other suggestions?' Coran asked.

'No, but neither am I all that enthusiastic about following a pair of ghosts around an ancient building,' Fitch said, shaking his head. He gestured to Zane and Asha. 'No offence meant.'

'You'll have to stay here on your own then.' Coran said, with a grin.

'No, no, somebody sensible needs to keep an eye on you all.' Fitch rolled his eyes. 'Ghosts, disembodied voices, talking tables, magic, witches and funny lights in the sky. You can't surprise me with anything any more.'

'Keep your eyes peeled,' Coran said.

'Oh I will,' Fitch replied. 'Don't you worry.'

* * *

Kiri, Meru and Mel followed Zane along a brightly lit corridor. They entered an ovoid-shaped capsule attached to the main building. A door closed behind them.

Kiri looked around in surprise, seeing Meru and Mel do the same. The room was perhaps fifty hands in length and half that in width. The walls were curved glass, but looking out on to plain metal walls.

'Where are we?' Kiri asked.

'This is an elevator,' Zane replied. 'Please standby.'

There was only the faintest sense of motion. The walls outside the room moved downwards as the entire capsule moved upwards. The light of Lacaille burst in about them and the walls fell away, revealing that the capsule was ascending the Obelisk tower.

Kiri gasped as she looked out of the sides of the capsule, seeing the buildings shrinking as they rose higher into the air. Within moments the entire layout of the compound could be seen stretched out around them.

There was no sound, nor a hint of vibration, as they ascended. The structure of the Obelisk could be seen in greater detail, a vast tracery of complex woven metalwork moving past the windows at a dizzying speed.

She could see that the structure was narrowing as they rose, the great supporting struts of the Obelisk moving closer and closer.

There was a flicker outside the windows and the view was obscured for a few brief moments in a mist. Then Lacaille's light blazed once more. They were above the clouds now, looking down at the ground through the wispy air.

There was then the faint sense of lightness in her feet and she sensed the capsule was slowing in its upwards trajectory. Scant moments had passed before it came to a halt amidst a complex series of transparent tunnels. The door opened.

'We have arrived at the Antenna Complex,' Zane said, walking before them. 'Please follow me.'

Zane led them through a series of the glass tubes.

'Woah …' Meru said, trying not to look down.

'Keep looking forwards,' Kiri said.

'I am … it's not helping!'

Fortunately, it wasn't long before they reached a more solid surface. They entered an enclosed bubble in which a series of consoles were arranged in an octagonal configuration.

'This is the Antenna Complex Guidance Control System,' Zane said. 'Various components have failed and must be replaced.'

Zane gestured to large storage lockers that lined the walls.

'Replacements can be found here.' He turned to the central consoles. 'Access the panels by opening the compartments beneath.'

Kiri looked at Meru. He moved forward and inspected the consoles.

'These are like those I saw in that abandoned telescope place,' he said. 'Dozens of them filled with dark green panels …'

'They are circuit boards,' Zane said, by way of clarification.

Kneeling down, Meru found out how to remove the front section of each cabinet. Inside was a series of cables, all plumbed together, all connected to a series of boards slotted into parallel grooves. On each board were tiny little devices, some round, some cylindrical, small and neat. Between them hundreds of fine metal wires could be seen, connecting them.

'The same,' he said.

'These are like those things we found on the Scattered Isles,' Mel said. 'There were crates of them, but we never found out what they were.'

'So, what are these things?' Kiri asked, looking at Zane.

'Circuit boards are discrete electronic and optronic processing devices,' Zane replied. 'They are designed to provide particular capabilities and are arranged together to form a complete mechanism.'

'Yeah, that helps,' Kiri said, rolling her eyes.

'We have to replace these?' Mel asked.

'That is correct,' Zane said.

'Is that all?' Mel asked.

'The malfunctioning boards must be replaced,' Zane said. 'The Antenna Complex is unable to align effectively without them. This adversely impacts cooling and magneto-electric management systems.'

'What's wrong?' Kiri asked.

Mel shrugged. 'Don't know. Just seems … so simple.'

Meru was nodding. 'Why can't they be fixed?' he asked. 'I mean, everything else here is shiny and polished …'

Kiri looked around her. They were right. Everything looked brand new, clean and polished. It had been the same outside, the paving clear, the gardens and flower beds trimmed.

'Board replacement can only be carried out by authorised administrative staff,' Zane replied.

Kiri shrugged. 'Well, we'd better get on with it then I suppose.'

She knelt down beside Meru and inspected the boards.

Each one was topped with a light. Most of them were green, but she could see a number were red.

'Guess those are the ones that need replacing,' she said.

Meru nodded.

'Boards 5a, 14a, 15a and 22b must be replaced in this cabinet,' Zane said.

Kiri counted along, noting the red lights. 'He's right you know.'

Meru smiled. Each board was secured by a locking bolt that could be twisted up or down. Meru twisted each one and then the boards popped free. The red lights went off.

Kiri slid the first board out and turned it over to inspect it. She could make nothing of it. It looked like metal embroidery to her.

'Doesn't look broken,' she said.

'Componentry fails on a microscopic scale,' Zane replied from behind them. 'It cannot be visually diagnosed.'

Kiri handed the board to Mel.

'We need another 5a board,' she said.

Mel looked through the storage lockers. Kiri could see dozens of the boards were all installed there.

'Snuts,' Mel said. 'There are hundreds of these things. How am I … wait, they're in order. Is this the one?'

Mel pulled a panel out, giving it to Kiri. As far as she could see it was identical.

'You have identified the correct replacement,' Zane said.

She slid it back in between the appropriate flanges and pushed it into place. It snapped home with a decisive click. Meru twisted the securing bolt into place.

A green light came on.

'There we go,' Meru said.

'Simple enough,' Kiri said. 'This should be easy.'

Above them, through the clear arched glass, they could see the structure of the Obelisk rising further into the sky. Above it Lacaille blazed, its light growing bluer by the second.

'Alacrity is required,' Zane said. 'Another flare is imminent, radiation shields have failed and magnetic booster output is insufficient.

'I think he means let's move it!' Meru said.

* * *

Asha led Zoella, Ira, Coran and Fitch down a corridor until they came to a wide spiral set of stairs which led down. The area was illuminated only by overhead lights with a sharp blue glow. As they reached the bottom of the staircase Zoella found herself in a circular room with every available wall covered in moving images.

They seemed to be views of the planet from many different vantage points. Zoella could make out seas, mountain ranges, vast forests and barren deserts. Some cities were also visible, Ira pointed out Airea, its white material construction obvious. There was another view of the frozen wastes. Zoella shivered as she remembered the freezing icy trek through those desolate lands.

'I wonder how these pictures are collected?' Coran asked.

'The AMS is able to monitor several hundred locations by means of remote cameras and drone technology,' Asha replied.

'There you go,' Fitch said, deadpan. 'Drone technology. Obviously. I thought you all knew that.'

Coran shot him a look, but Fitch stood there with his arms folded.

'Don't show Meru this,' Coran said, smiling at Zoella. 'We'll never get him back out again.'

Zoella nodded.

'He was bad enough with Caesar,' she replied. 'Asha, where do we need to go now? Where is the AMS?'

Asha gestured at a sealed pair of doors along one side of the room.

'The AMS is located through these security doors,' she replied. 'They can only be unlocked by administrators.'

Coran gestured for her to proceed and, watched by Fitch, Zoella and Ira moved towards the doors. Another one of the palm readers was positioned alongside it. Zoella placed her hand upon it.

'Identify confirmed. Access granted, administrator Zoella.'

The doors slid into the walls. Inside, a short corridor could be seen, ending in another pair of doors.

Asha led the way, with Zoella and Ira behind her. Coran and Fitch were still in the monitoring room, looking at the images on display. They turned and moved to follow.

There was a brief hiss. Zoella and Ira turned to see the doors closing behind them. Zoella caught a brief glimpse of Coran's face and heard an alarmed shout which was cut off as the doors snapped closed.

* * *

The first console didn't take long for Kiri and Meru to sort out, so they moved to the second one. Mel was sorting through the spares. Zane stood behind them, watching their progress.

'Circuit boards 4a through to 16b must be swapped out,' Zane said. 'Please use the appropriate spares from the parts provided.'

Kiri pulled the board out and handed it to Meru. He held on to it while Mel found the appropriate replacement. Kiri then swapped the new one back in, ensuring the locking mechanism was returned to the original position.

They repeated the process time and again, watching as, each time, the corresponding light flickered from red to green.

Kiri handed yet another board to Meru. This time he stood up.

'You alright?' Kiri asked.

'Just need to stretch my legs,' Meru said. 'Getting a bit sore crouching down there.'

Kiri watched him stroll past Zane and over to the locker where Mel was sorting through the spare boards. After a few moments he came back again, a board in his hand. He gave it to her.

Kiri took it and slotted it into place, saw the green light come on and went to pull out the next board.

'Wait,' Meru said.

'What's the matter?' Kiri asked.

Meru turned around and got to his feet, looking at Zane.

'I just swapped the broken one back in,' Meru said, his voice stiff. 'At least, the same one the light said was broken. Now it seems to have miraculously fixed itself. What's going on?'

'What?' Mel and Kiri asked together.

'I didn't swap the board,' Meru said to them. 'It's the same one we took out.' He looked at Zane. 'Explain that.'

'Non administrative staff cannot make requests of Obelisk facilities,' Zane replied.

Kiri got to her feet alongside Meru and glared at Zane.

'Answer him,' she said. 'We're not changing anything more until you tell us what's going on. Are these boards really broken, or not?'

Zane didn't reply. His image vanished in a brief flicker of light.

'Bring him back,' Kiri shouted into the air. 'Hey. Obelisk! This is administrator Kiri, switch Zane on, we need to speak to him.'

There was no response.

'Obelisk, answer me!' Kiri demanded.

Mel was looking back the way they had come.

'Does anyone get the feeling we've been decoyed up here?' she asked, her voice hushed.

Kiri and Meru were looking at her.

'But why?' Meru asked.

'I think we'd better find the others,' Kiri said. 'And fast!'

They ran towards the capsule.

* * *

Zoella stared at the closed doors for a moment, before looking at Ira. She looked alarmed, her pale eyes wide with surprise.

'Why has the door closed?' Zoella demanded, turning to look at Asha.

'Access to the AMS is not permitted to non-administrators,' Asha said.

'Why not?' Zoella asked.

'Security protocols apply,' Asha answered.

'Open the door,' Zoella said. 'We're not going any further until you let our friends in.'

'The AMS must be repaired,' Asha said. 'There can be no further delay. Another flare is imminent, radiation shields have failed and magnetic booster output is insufficient.'

Asha turned. The doors at the opposite end of the corridor opened.

Zoella ignored them, stepping towards the closed doors and banging on them.

'Coran! Fitch! Can you hear me?'

She could just make out their muffled voices on the other side. She made out Coran's voice.

'Are you both alright?'

'Yes,' Zoella answered. 'Asha won't open the door. She says it's not permitted for non-administrators. She says another flare is coming …'

'Stay where you are,' Coran said. 'I don't like this. Something is …'

Zoella heard a gasp from behind her and turned to see that Ira had walked down the corridor and past the second set of doors. There was large chamber beyond, with a huge tube of blue tinged liquid connected by pipes, tubes and wires. Ira had walked forward and was staring at it with her arm outstretched.

'I've got to go,' Zoella said.

'Zoella wait …'

'Ira!' Zoella called, running towards her. 'Wait for me!'

She skidded to a halt in the chamber, grabbing Ira by the arm. The girl looked bewildered for a moment, her jaw slack and her eyes staring. Zoella received a sudden flurry of images; a woman, waving a tearful goodbye to a group of people. Zoella didn't recognise any of them, they were strangers.

'Ira, what …?'

She looked up, hearing the second set of doors close behind her.

She froze.

Before her, the large tube of liquid was revealed to be a cylinder starting at the floor and reaching up to the ceiling of the room, some twenty hands above her. The cylinder was festooned with tubes, pipes and wires all radiating outwards, plugged into boxes and cabinets around the room. The faint sounds of pumping liquids reached her ears.

But her eyes were drawn to what was within.

Zoella's mouth fell open as she gazed upon the emaciated body of a woman. She was naked, her body floating in the midst of the liquid. She was suspended by similar tubes and pipes to those that snaked into the cylinder itself. One large tube went into her open mouth. Her eyes were closed, her body devoid of hair. Wires covered her bare scalp, all leading upwards to the ceiling.

The woman's face was the same one as she'd seen in Ira's images.

'Who is she?' Zoella whispered.

'Her designation was Tasha Alexeev,' Asha said.

'What's she doing in there?'

'She is the primary component of the AMS,' Asha replied. 'She has failed.'

'Failed?' Zoella echoed.

'Yes, failed.' Asha's face was expressionless. 'One of you must replace her.'

CHAPTER TWELVE

Nadir, Coordinates Zero Zero

Round 2307, Ninth pass

Kiri ran into the capsule and skidded to a halt on the polished floor, Mel and Meru piled in behind her, struggling to keep up. Together they hunted around for any controls, but there was nothing obvious they could see. Blue light was flickering outside, the glare of Lacaille fading away as the intimidating darkness began to fall.

'Obelisk!' Kiri called out. 'Take us down to the ground.'

Behind them the doors snapped shut, but the capsule didn't move.

'We're trapped,' Mel said. 'But there must be a way …'

'It can't all be voice controlled,' Meru said. 'There must be some kind of emergency system to control it …'

'Obelisk!' Kiri shouted furiously, waiting for a response. 'Why won't you answer?'

Kiri saw Meru run to the curving walls of the capsule, looking along them for anything that resembled a control. He was trying to prise a panel open. Mel went to help him.

Kiri took a step towards them before her vision was swamped with strange images; the body of a woman in glass cylinder, floating in some liquid.

Kiri! Can you hear me?

Zoella? Yes! The flare is starting! We've been trapped, what's …?

Kiri caught the distress in Zoella's voice.

Ira and I have been separated from Coran and Fitch … we can't get out. The Obelisk is going to … help us!

Pain spurred across Kiri's forehead. She gasped, seeing Meru and Mel turn to look at her.

She concentrated, trying to send her thoughts through, but the pain increased.

Zoella?

There was no answer.

'Zoella and Ira have been trapped too,' Kiri said. 'I can't hear her any more ... she's in danger! We've got to hurry.'

Meru wrenched the panel away, to find a keypad similar to the one they'd seen in Caesar's cavern far to the shadeward. Numbers and a single letter.

'G for ground?' he asked.

'Try it,' Mel said.

Kiri saw Meru jab the obvious button and with a faint vibration the capsule began to descend. The gloom outside was deepening by the moment.

'We're out of time!' Meru cried.

'What did Zoella say?' Mel asked.

Kiri looked panicked. 'Just that they'd been separated from the others and that the Obelisk was going to do something.'

'What?' Meru demanded.

Kiri shook her head. 'I don't know. I can't hear her any more, my thoughts have been blocked somehow. It hurts when I try ...'

A jolt and the ground fell out beneath their feet. Kiri staggered, Mel gave a screech of fear whilst Meru made a grab for the sides. Outside, the intricate lattice work of the Obelisk structure was blurring past upward faster than the eye could follow. Kiri felt sick in her stomach.

Falling!

Mel slid across the floor, still yelling out. Meru was struggling to get to the panel, his arms flailing. A sound rose around her, something moving too fast, increasing in pitch ...

Kiri was smacked into the floor hard. It knocked the breath from her. She heard Mel yelp in pain and saw Meru collapse beside her.

She heard something slide back and managed to turn her head.

The doors.

Kiri got to her feet, staggering, still dizzy.

'Meru … Mel?'

They were likewise struggling to get to their feet.

'Yes …'

Kiri shook her head to clear it.

'Meru? Mel? That you? Over here!'

It was Fitch. He was standing at the end of the corridor, beckoning to them. Kiri hurried towards him, pulling the others along behind her.

'What's happened? Mel asked.

'This … whatever it is …' Fitch muttered. 'Got both the girls to walk into this room, doors locked behind them. Something bad is happening …'

'The flare is about to start,' Meru said. 'We've got to …'

'Follow me!' Kiri yelled.

She led them down the stairs to the lower level. Coran had his knife jammed in a small gap in the door and was trying to lever it open.

'Meru!' Coran called. 'Find a way to get this door open!'

Meru and Mel started looking at the panels and controls around the room. 'Kiri? Can you speak to them?'

'I keep trying,' Kiri answered. 'But the Obelisk is stopping me. They're in trouble … they're scared. The flare …'

Kiri watched as Mel and Meru wrestled with the panel adjacent to the doors and pulled it free, but the controls within did nothing, no matter what they did.

Open it! Zoella is …

'It's locked,' Meru said. 'Nothing works! Whatever is happening in there, there's nothing we can do about it.'

Fitch rubbed his brow, 'Snuts. I hate being right all the time.'

* * *

Zoella watched as Ira looked around at her, a frown on her face.

How to explain …

Zoella grabbed Ira's hand and held it tight. She backed away from the cylinder with the woman inside, and moved towards the door.

'Come with me,' she whispered.

Zoella led Ira to the door, but it didn't open. Zoella turned to look at Asha. The woman's image hadn't changed. She was standing in the same place, looking at them.

'Let us out.'

'Priority protocol is in operation,' Asha said. 'The Obelisk regrets the need for subterfuge, but reprovisioning of the AMS is crucial to the survival of life on Esurio. There is no higher protocol. Flare activity is now at its peak and must be remediated.'

'Cancel the protocol,' Zoella said.

'The protocol can only be cancelled by a level three administrator,' Asha replied. 'There are no level three administrators. The protocol was established and remains in force.'

'Who established it?' Zoella demanded.

'Priority protocol was established by Tasha Alexeev,' Asha replied.

Zoella looked up at the body of the woman inside the fluid filled cylinder.

'When?'

'Priority protocol was activated in round three four one,' Asha replied. 'It has been active ever since.'

'She did it,' Zoella whispered, looking at the woman's body again. 'She's been in there for two thousand rounds?'

'One thousand, nine hundred and sixty five rounds.'

'Is she … still alive?'

'Vital functions have ceased,' Asha replied. 'The AMS was never intended to function in this fashion for extended periods of time. Five hundred rounds was the anticipated lifecycle before replacement was scheduled. No replacements were available at that point or since, thus all efforts have been directed to maintaining the AMS for as long as possible. All possible extension procedures have been completed. AMS has now failed.'

'You need another person,' Zoella whispered.

Asha nodded.

'What happens to them?' Zoella asked.

'AMS candidates are integrated into the infrastructure systems,' Asha said. 'Life support and all other requirements are managed by external systems allowing higher brain functions to be diverted to managing facilities across Esurio.'

'Can the person leave?'

'AMS integration is not reversible,' Asha said.

Zoella swallowed, feeling sweat cool on her skin.

'And without the AMS?'

'Esurio infrastructure will fail within passes,' Asha replied. 'Failure will result in inimical radiation, atmospheric erosion, lack of magneto-electric power distribution and terraforming reversion. All human life on Esurio will be threatened with extinction.'

'There must be another way ...'

'There is not,' Asha replied. 'Automated facilities within the Obelisk complex and the distributed facilities across the planet are not sophisticated enough to manage the data feeds or decision-making processes without biological supervision.'

Zoella took a deep breath and looked down at Ira before turning her gaze back to Asha.

'Does it hurt?'

Asha shook her head. 'Integration is disorientating, but not painful.'

Zoella nodded and swallowed.

It's not going to let us go. Unless one of us steps in there we're stuck forever. Esurio will die the way I saw it die in my dreams and visions. Maybe this is why I was born ... to do this, to fix the Obelisk, to save Esurio ... save everyone ...

She made her decision.

'I will do this,' she said.

Ira yanked on her hand, pulling her. She was shaking her head.

'I have to,' Zoella said looking at the younger girl. 'Without it everyone will die. This way, it's just one ... and I'll not be dead ... I just won't be ...'

Zoella saw Ira's eyes fill with tears.

'It will be alright,' Zoella said, crouching down beside her, running a hand through her hair. 'We must keep everyone safe, it's why we came here … to fix things.'

Ira pulled her into a hug, sobbing.

Zoella looked over to Asha.

'But you must let Ira and my friends go,' she said.

'No interference with the protocol will be allowed,' Asha said.

'Let me explain it to them,' Zoella said, her voice catching. 'I will make them understand … and I need to say … goodbye to them all.'

'Protocol allows for this interaction,' Asha said. 'When you are ready, leave administrator Ira in the corridor and return to the AMS room. Outer doors will be released once you are within the AMS complex and inner doors are secured. Proceed.'

The doors behind Zoella opened, leading to the corridor. The doors at the far end remained closed.

'Come on,' Zoella said.

She led Ira into the corridor, until they stood before the second double door.

Zoella took a deep breath.

* * *

'It won't unlock,' Meru called, still desperately manipulating the unresponsive controls. 'It doesn't matter what I do.'

Coran banged his fists on the cold metal of the door one more time. That produced nothing other than a dull thump and pain in his hands. He looked around at Kiri.

He watched as she tried again, cringing as she yelled out in pain.

Come on, you can do it! We've got to get hold of Zoella …

She swayed and Meru caught her before she fell.

'Sorry … I can't …'

'I knew we shouldn't have trusted these snuttin' ghosts,' Fitch said. 'Or any of these talking devices …'

'What's happening in there...?' Coran demanded. He punched the door again.

There was a faint buzz and a crackle. Then Coran heard Zoella's voice, soft and subdued, but somehow coming through the door.

'Coran, Fitch? Can you hear me?'

'Zoella?' Coran shouted. 'Yes, we can! We're here! Are you alright?'

'Yes,' Zoella said, her voice flat. 'Ira is with me, we're both here.'

Coran looked around at the rest of the crew with a frown, they all huddled closer.

'Meru, Mel and Kiri are here too,' Coran replied. 'They were decoyed away ...'

'I know,' Zoella said. 'It's all been explained to me. Now you must listen. I will send Ira back to you, you'll all be free to go.'

'Ira?' Coran asked. 'What about you?'

'I'm not coming back,' Zoella said.

'What?' Coran demanded. 'You snuttin' well are, young lady. We'll get you out, just stay put ...'

'Just listen,' Zoella said.

'No, you–'

'The AMS,' Zoella's soft voice overrode him. 'It's not a machine, it can't be fixed. It's a person, a woman, an administrator like me, Kiri and Ira. It's how the Obelisk works. The first one was called Tasha, she was ... integrated ... into the Obelisk. She's been running everything for two thousands rounds ... but now she's failed ... she's died. There has to be another one now.'

The crew listened in horrified fascination as she explained what she had heard from Asha.

'Zoella ...'

'I've volunteered,' Zoella said.

'No,' Meru said. 'You can't! There must be another way ...'

'There isn't,' Zoella said. 'Everything has been tried to keep Tasha alive as long as possible, but she's gone now, there's nothing left the Obelisk can do. That's why it led us here ...'

'It tricked us!' Kiri said. 'It lied!'

'Yes,' Zoella said. 'It had no choice. One of us has to do this, or Esurio dies.'

'Zoella,' Coran said. 'Don't do anything. We will find a way around this if we have to batter down this door. I'm not losing any of my crew no matter what, Obelisk be scorched! Stay put and we will come to you, do you hear? We will come to you. Fitch get the weapons ...'

Fitch made ready to go, but Zoella's next words stopped him.

'You can't break in. Nothing you have will even dent this door. The Obelisk won't let Ira go unless I do this. There's no choice.'

'I'm not letting you do this!' Coran yelled.

'Coran's right,' Meru said. 'We will find another way, maybe Caesar will be able to ...'

'Caesar knew,' Zoella said. 'Don't you remember how he paused? How he avoided the direct questions? He was always so careful in his answers. Only telling us what we needed to hear. He led us here, he knew too! There is no other way. You know there isn't.'

Meru subsided, looking down at his feet.

Kiri pushed forward, 'Then let it be me instead,' she said.

'Kiri no ...' Meru began.

'I love you,' Kiri said, grabbing Meru's hands. 'So, so much. But I stand between you and your friends and family. Better I do this than Zoella!'

'Kiri ...'

'You know I can't go back to Amar. Let me do this, for her, for you, for everyone,' Kiri said. 'Let me atone for all the evil I've done, for all those I've hurt and killed. Zoella doesn't deserve this ...'

'No,' Zoella replied. 'You're staying with Meru. This is my choice.'

'It shouldn't be you,' Kiri said, her voice rising to a shout. 'Tell the Obelisk to let me in!'

'I've already given my decision,' Zoella said, her voice calm. 'Meru and you need each other. And you still have to stop the priestesses ...'

'No ...' Kiri said.

'And I have my own wrongs to atone for,' Zoella said.

'Don't do this …' Mel pleaded. 'Zoella, you're part of the crew. We need you.'

'Esurio has to be saved, that's why we came here,' Zoella continued, her voice calm. 'The Obelisk called me first … maybe that's the whole point of it all, everything I've done, everything I've seen and heard. It's been calling to me ever since I was a child, warning me, telling me. It's supposed to be me.'

Coran sighed, lowering his head into his hands, covering his mouth for a moment while he thought. He shook his head. No words came.

He looked up at the crew of the *Mobilis*, taking a moment to look at each in turn.

They looked at him.

He stepped forward to the door, resting his head against it, his lips pursed.

* * *

Zoella waited for a long moment.

Coran's voice was subdued now. There was nothing he could do, nothing any of them could do. She could hear the defeat in his voice the moment he started speaking.

'Zoella,' he said. 'You are the bravest person it's ever been my privilege to know. I'll admit, I had my doubts early on, but you proved yourself, helped us, saved us. When you made mistakes you owned up to them, tried to make them right. Just proud of you girl, proud to have you on my crew.'

'I never had a family growing up,' Zoella said, softly. 'But I had one with all of you. Thank you for letting me on your ship.'

'Honour was all mine,' Coran said.

'Say goodbye to Daf and Creg for me,' she said.

'I will.'

Zoella heard feet shuffle.

'Zoella … it's Mel.'

Zoella could hear the tears, even if she couldn't see them.

'Mel … all the time you spent with me, all the good advice …'

'Just remember we all love you,' Mel said. 'Always. We'll never forget …'

Her voice broke. Zoella felt a tear trickle down her cheek.

'Never,' she said.

Another voice. This time it was Fitch.

'Gotta say,' he said, his voice gruff. 'I was all for pitching you off the ship when you first came aboard.'

'I remember,' Zoella said.

'Glad I didn't though,' Fitch added. 'Otherwise I'd've drowned when that sea beastie tried to eat us. You saved my life. Means something. You did good, girl.'

'Thanks Fitch, make sure you look after yourself.'

'Do my best.'

More shuffling. Meru's voice.

'Zoella … all that time I let you down … ignored you …'

'Don't think on it,' she said. 'Not now. You're the best friend I ever had. I'm sorry things came between us.'

'I don't know what to say … what to do …'

'What you need to do is to look after my sister for me,' Zoella said. 'Will you do that?'

'Yes, of course I will …'

'And take care of yourself. Don't crash anything else, yes?'

'I'll try. Zoella …'

'Goodbye Meru, I love you … Thanks for being my friend.'

Finally, she heard Kiri's voice.

'Sister … please let me …'

'No,' Zoella said, more sternly than she intended. 'Kiri … you need to be with Meru. Whatever the future holds, you must stay with him. That's where you're supposed to be. You can find a way to be together and you've got to help defend Amar. You know what the priestesses will do, you're the only one who can stop them.'

'I can't do it without you. We were supposed to do it together.'

Zoella could hear the twinge of fear in Kiri's voice.

She's scared ... she's actually scared.

'You can do it, trust yourself.'

'I ... I barely got to know you,' Kiri said, her voice shaking. 'It's not fair! I want to know you, you're my sister, the only real family I have ... I need you.'

Zoella pushed her fingers against the cold metal of the locked door, tears streaming down her face.

'It wasn't to be,' Zoella said. 'Be happy we did learn of each other and put our hatred aside. We both found out who we are.'

'Yes, but ...'

'I still say I was born first. '

Zoella heard Kiri's sob, half mixed with a laugh.

'You're so much the bossy older sister!'

'Look after Meru,' Zoella said. 'Both of you need to look after each other. Don't leave him.'

'I won't, I promise.'

Zoella closed her eyes, her fingers clenching.

'Goodbye Kiri.'

Zoella swallowed, trying to stop herself gasping.

Focus on what you need to do. Just one more goodbye to say ...

She opened her eyes and stood taller, turning on her heel.

Ira stood before her, looking up at her.

Zoella went to give her a hug, but Ira raised her hand and a thump of mental energy caught Zoella across the forehead. It wasn't painful, more like a firm but gentle push. Zoella found herself on the floor, sliding on the slick surface, fetching up against the locked door behind her.

She shook her head and looked up, finding she couldn't get to her feet. Her arms and legs seemed paralysed. She heard footsteps, walking away from her.

'Ira?'

In horror she saw Ira standing beyond the second set of doors.

'No!' Zoella screamed. 'What are you doing? Come back here ...'

Ira was standing just within the AMS room, her hand still outstretched towards Zoella. As Zoella looked up a flood of images washed over her mind.

Rescuing me in the caverns below Airea ...

The flight away in Meru's flying machine ...

The battle with the sea creature ...

Another image seared across her mind.

Amar, in flames ... the wreckage all about us ... the priestesses ... Kiri ...

Ira was pointing at her.

Me?

Ira nodded.

Zoella's mind was filled with another view. Herself and Kiri standing side by side, as dachs flew and raged about them. Fire lit the sky, smoke billowed past. As she watched, Zoella saw herself and Kiri raise their hands together.

The images faded.

Zoella blinked, trying to focus her eyes.

Ira stepped back a pace and raised her own hand, palm outwards. There was a smile on her face.

'No ...'

Zoella was helpless. She couldn't move as the far doors closed in front of her. Only as they shut was the grip on her muscles broken. She scrambled to her feet and ran.

* * *

Coran heard the doors click.

He turned around as some mechanism within them unlocked. There was a momentary pause and then the doors slid back.

'Zoella?'

Coran ran into the corridor, the rest of the crew right behind him.

'Zoella!'

He saw her at the far end, just short of the second set of doors and sprinted up to her. She was crouched at them, her hands banging on the doors in frustration. He pulled her upright, seeing her tear-streaked face and puffy eyes.

'What happened?'

'Ira …' she said. 'She …'

'Took your place,' Mel whispered, staring at the doors.

Kiri knelt down beside Coran and pulled Zoella into a hug.

'You've got to stop her,' Zoella wailed. 'She's too young to …'

A series of strange sounds echoed through the doors before them. The sound of liquid being drained, pumps running, devices unplugging, hisses and clicks. Then more liquid sloshing and moving. After a few moments the sounds faded away.

Asha's image appeared in the corridor.

'AMS replacement is complete. Primary protocol no longer in operation. Obelisk functions are returning to acceptable parameters. It is not advised to leave the facility at this time due to flare radiation …'

Zoella lurched upwards, pulling away from Kiri and staggering to her feet. She swung at Asha's image, trying to hit her.

'Acceptable …?' Zoella yelled. 'She's just a girl! You can't do this!'

Zoella's clenched fists went straight through Asha's body, there was nothing but light. Zoella raged for a moment, swinging back and forth, screaming incoherently. Coran and Fitch grabbed her and wrestled her back as she struggled between them.

'Zoella!' Coran yelled.

Asha's image disappeared. Then there was another voice.

'Zoella, it's alright.'

It was a girl's voice, clear and light.

Coran looked at Fitch and then at the rest of the crew. Zoella stopped, her eyes wide. She stopped struggling in Coran and Fitch's grasp.

'Who was that?' Mel asked.

'It's … it's Ira,' Zoella cried. 'Can you hear me?'

'Yes, Zoella,' Ira's voice said. 'It's me. I can hear you. I'm alright. Come. You must understand.'

The doors before them clicked and then unlocked, sliding back. Coran led the crew into the AMS room. They looked around them in wonder, before Zoella ran ahead to the centre, peering into the cylinder there.

Coran gasped.

The cylinder was filled with a faint blue liquid. Bubbles from the base made their way upwards, the interior was festooned with cables, wires and tubes.

In the midst of it all, Ira's body was suspended. She was floating, naked, her skin pale, her eyes closed. Her short white hair wafted in the current within, her body festooned with connections.

'Ira … no …' Zoella said, pushing her hands against the cold glass of the cylinder. Coran and the others came up and stood behind her, looking up at the girl within.

'I did not mean to upset you,' Ira's voice said. Her eyes stayed closed and her lips didn't move. Her voice seemed to come from all around the room, amplified. 'But it was better for you that I did this, Zoella.'

'It should have been me,' Zoella cried, banging her fists on the tank. 'Not you …'

'No.' Ira's said. 'A different fate awaits you. You have another role to play. This was my choice, Zoella.'

Coran saw Zoella frown.

'Did it … hurt?' Zoella asked.

'No, it was entirely painless,' Ira said. Her manner of speech was somehow too regular, almost mechanical. 'The Obelisk will be able to function. Everything I knew is now available to the Obelisk systems and everything it has is accessible to me. I can see and feel its many parts. I am able to communicate with everything, and talk to you … for the first time.'

'Ira …' Zoella's eyes were still wet with tears.

'Do not mourn for me, Zoella,' Ira said. 'Be thankful that Esurio will be saved from destruction. I have already been able to adjust many parameters. Magnetic field restoration, axial alignment and augmentation of protective mechanisms are already underway.'

Kiri and Meru came up from behind and held Zoella close. Zoella sank in their embrace, sobbing quietly.

'So, the Obelisk …' Coran began.

'Captain Coran,' Ira said. 'You have achieved what you set out to do. Obelisk functions have been restored. I am able to confirm that all of the systems within my control are responding to repair commands. The AMS, as provided by me, will restore complete control within the next pass.'

'Then the flares will be stopped?' Coran asked.

'No,' Ira said. 'The flares are a characteristic of the M2V class star Lacaille 9352. They recur at intervals of four nine one rounds and last for a period of approximately five rounds. Outside of this time Lacaille 9352 is quiescent. Flares are thus due to subside in round 2310. They will reoccur once again in round 2796. Esurio inhabitants must continue to seek shelter during flare events until 2310.'

'Caesar talked about this,' Meru said, leaving Zoella with Kiri. 'The first flare, do you remember? The one that killed Sandra Morino …'

'The first flare was not anticipated,' Ira replied. 'It devastated the colony here in round 341. Many lives were lost. No records are available after this time.'

'You sound like you know everything now,' Meru said.

'I am integrated into the Obelisk systems,' Ira responded. 'I have access to all data and information stored within this facility, including all historical records. There are many archived messages, images, recordings and documents available.'

'Historical,' Meru said. 'From when?'

'Records begin from when Esurio was first colonised,' Ira responded. 'Round one. A recording of the colonisation event is available, would you like to see it?'

Meru swallowed and looked around at the crew. Zoella had her head lowered. Kiri was still holding her, looking pale and scared, Mel anxious. Fitch had his lips pursed, only Coran's eyes were twinkling with excitement.

Coran stepped forward.

'You remember that time I caught you eavesdropping in my study?' Coran said to Meru, his voice hushed. 'We talked of witches and frozen waters?'

Meru nodded. 'Yes … and we talked about our ancestors' lost legacy. All the technology, the ships, the map … the things they could do.'

Coran looked around him, gesturing at Ira and the complex machinery all about them.

'This is it,' he said. 'Here is where all the answers lie.'

Coran looked up at Ira's body.

'Show us the recording,' he whispered.

'Request acknowledged,' Ira replied.

Off to one side, a glowing image appeared. It looked real, somehow with depth and distance. The crew could just see through it to the other side of the room, but it was bright and vibrant.

It was an image of the pathway before the Obelisk buildings, the same ones in which they now stood. Behind the buildings rose the Obelisk itself, looking identical to how it did now.

Below the buildings a crowd of people stood. They stood side by side in four rows, dressed in peculiar one piece uniforms. There were perhaps eighty of them, all very different looking, their skins having many shades from pale to dark and everything in between.

'They all look … fat and short,' Kiri said.

One individual stood before them, a man, even stockier and thicker set, sporting a heavy grey beard. He was dressed in the most unusual outfit. He wore a dark blue jacket, with coloured yellow bars on the shoulders and cuffs. Bright metal buttons and some small coloured marks festooned the front of his attire. He sported a pair of matching trousers, with his outfit completed by polished black boots, which shone in the light of Lacaille. He held something in his left hand, but they didn't recognise it.

He stepped forward, addressing whoever it was that had made the recording. The crew of the *Mobilis* watched with rapt attention.

'My name is Admiral Gregory Drayden,' the man said, in a deep gravelly voice. 'Today is the 21st of August 2943 as we used to measure time. Twenty two years ago, I had the privilege of bringing our colony ship, the *Du Maurier*, into orbit around our new home, Esurio.

'It was not without its difficulties. Esurio is not like our old home, Earth, the planet that created and nurtured us. The planet we, in our foolishness, utterly destroyed. There have been hardships. Those of us who arrived here aboard the *Du Maurier* found to our dismay that we would not be able to live upon the surface for any length of time without breathing apparatus. The people that stand behind me are thus the first true colonists of this planet; the result of a genetic breeding programme with a simple aim, to allow humanity to survive and thrive on Esurio.'

The man stopped, and the object he'd been holding was revealed to be a transparent mask with a small cylinder attached to it. He took a few deep breaths from it before he continued.

'With these brave people go the hopes and dreams of humanity. We do not yet know whether any other colony vessels successfully reached their destinations, or whether their passengers were able to colonise their target worlds. We may never know. It could be that we are all that remains of the billions of humans who once lived on Earth.

'Earth was destroyed by greed, arrogance and an inability to collectively come together, put aside difference and work for the common good. We watched as wars were fought over dwindling resources and the ecosystem crashed and burned. The last radio transmissions we received were brutal and ugly. Then Earth fell silent.'

The admiral turned to look at the people behind him, taking another breath from his mask.

'You must do better than we did,' he said. 'You have been given a second chance. A pristine world that can be made liveable and fertile through hard work. The resources of high industry are lacking here. There is little metal, virtually none of the carbon-based fuels that we squandered back on Earth. Lifestyles must thus be in harmony with what this new world can provide.

He turned around and faced forward again.

'It is written within the statute of this colony that our new civilisation will be agrarian. We will produce crops and farmland, we may even build towns and cities in the future, but we will not pollute our world, we shall not mine, smelt, or fill the atmosphere with smoke and fumes. Such technology as we have brought with us will remain only as long as it is required for the purposes of exploration and research. Once those tasks are accomplished it will be dismantled and forgotten.

'Earth is gone. We have a new home. Today is no longer August the 21st 2943. Today is stretch one, pass one, round one. Today … this stretch … is the first stretch on Esurio!'

Cheers accompanied the Admiral's final words, the people behind him clapped and hollered loudly.

The image faded.

'Round one,' Coran said. 'I can scarce believe that was real. All that time …'

'And those people standing there,' Mel said. 'They were our ancestors? We're all, every one of us, descended from them?'

'That is correct,' Ira said.

'Seemed like a pretty good plan,' Fitch said, 'And interesting that they didn't want any of this tech we're so proud of. So what went wrong?'

'The flares,' Zoella said. 'They didn't know the flares were coming.'

'Recordings of the original flare incident are available,' Ira said. 'They are amongst the last recordings available in the archive. Caution is advised, viewers may find some of the scenes disturbing.'

Coran looked around at the crew.

'We need to know what happened.'

They nodded.

'Show us,' Coran instructed.

The glowing image returned. It was the same location once more, the Obelisk building complex, with the Obelisk rising behind. This time the scene was different, people were walking in all directions. A woman was standing before the recorder, trying to make herself heard over the noise of other people shouting directions. Off to her left they could see one of the flying machines, with people cramming themselves aboard. Others were already in the air, flying away from the Obelisk compound.

'This is Su-Lin Singh of the astrometrics division,' she said. 'We still don't know what is happening, but the signs are not good. We've had major sunspot activity for the last pass, totally unprecedented. The weather has been freezing, radiative output dropped almost twenty percent. None of our predictive models gave any indication of these effects.

'The magnetic flux on Lacaille is incredibly strong, we've never seen anything like this before. Some are saying there is a risk of a dangerous flare event, but Lacaille has never been seen to flare before. As a precaution we're going to move people towards the temperate zones. The scientific outpost in Nireus is going to be a little crowded …

The woman paused, somebody was distracting her. They heard yells and screams.

'Something is … I can't describe it … the sunspots … they're expanding, I can see them moving. They're covering the surface … it's going dark!'

The crew of the *Mobilis* could see the gloom descending.

'Run,' Zoella whispered, tears still streaking her cheeks. 'You've got to run …'

'They don't know …' Kiri said, from beside her.

'It's hard to describe what I'm seeing,' Su-Lin continued. 'Lacaille's light is fading away, the sunspots are converging. It's like the old-Earth records of dusk and sunset … only here it's … wait … something is …

The image brightened. It became impossible to see for a few moments. Then they could make out a bright orange glare flickering behind the clouds.

'Streamers of light, reaching out …it's beautiful, but it's definitely a flare … it will be here in …I can already feel the heat …

The hills beyond the Obelisk tower were covered in a bright red glow, moving, expanding, topped with smoke.

'There's fire! Coming down from the hills! Oh my …'

A rolling wave of burning incandescence could be seen moving towards the vantage point. People were running, looking over their shoulders at the menacing fire-filled clouds, boiling towards them. The flying machine lifted off as the flames touched the complex. It moved forward for a moment before the clouds engulfed it, its outline visible for a few moments as an indistinct shape.

Then it exploded violently, spinning pieces of debris and bodies flung in all directions, burning and cascading downwards. It hit the ground, a twisted flaming piece of wreckage.

Kiri looked at Meru.

'That flying machine we found, all burnt and broken …'

'So old,' Meru said, with a nod. 'It crashed in this flare …'

Su-Lin's panicked voice interrupted their whispered conversation.

'It's awful … those people … If you're hearing this you must take cover, the flare is …'

The flames swept up to the position of the recording. The crew watched in horror as Su-Lin's form was incinerated by the heat. Her clothing and her body consumed in brief moments. She fell, arms and legs jolting spasmodically. A lingering scream was caught off camera and the image faded.

The crew were silent for a long moment. Ira's voice broke the stillness.

'The flare event of round three four one was the last recorded usage of the Obelisk facility,' she said. 'The current flare event is the fifth on record.'

'It hit all across Esurio,' Coran said. 'Sandra Morino was caught in it at the same time, but she was in Caesar's hangar. It's amazing anyone survived.'

'Counts are imprecise,' Ira replied. 'But indications are that 92% of all colonists perished in the first flare event. There were an estimated three hundred and fifty survivors.'

'So then what happened?' Mel asked. 'Our histories only go back to the exile from Nireus …'

'The ones in Scallia went back further,' Zoella said, wiping the tears from her eyes and cheeks. 'They talked of the fall of the Voren Empire, hundreds of rounds ago.'

'But that still means we've lost everything in between,' Coran said.

'No colonists visited the Obelisk in the intervening rounds,' Ira confirmed. 'However, satellite imagery indicated that cultivation of the landmasses around the cities Daine, Viresia, Dynesia and Airea resumed in around round 520. There were several more flares, which resulted in further destruction, but significant growth in population was noted in satellite imagery from round 1820 onwards.'

'That fits in with the Voren Empire,' Zoella said. 'By which time all of this had been forgotten. But they knew of Lacaille and what it could do then. I read a book in the library of Viresia that said they knew about the flares and how to use the gift. I can remember it so clearly, it was dated 1898.'

'Height of our civilisation,' Coran said. 'All our histories start from the fall of the Voren Empire.'

'What about the priestesses?' Meru asked, looking at Kiri. 'They must have had some history too. What did they teach you?'

Kiri shrugged. 'Not much. The priestesses were founded when the Voren Empire collapsed. The first priestess was called Elena. She lived at the end of the empire. It was she who wrote all the laws and books … they're called the Elements. Then it all collapsed, that's when the rules about tithing women to Drayden began, the war against Nireus and …'

'Amar was founded,' Coran finished. 'But by then everything was just myth and legend …'

'So hang on a minute …' Fitch said. 'Flares I get, strange technology from the ancients all abandoned because of some long ago calamity kind of makes sense. But where did these gifts come from? The powers you lot have to mess around with minds and what not?'

Kiri shook her head and shrugged.

'They knew about them in the Voren Empire,' Zoella said. 'It was all strictly organised … that's where the word administrator came from … I think.'

'Incorrect,' Ira said.

'You know?' Zoella asked, turning around.

'The augmented capabilities you refer to as "the gift," Ira said, 'were introduced in round 196 to allow administrative control of the growing population.'

'Why?' Kiri asked.

'Long range radio communication was found to be problematic on Esurio due to strong electromagnetic interference from the magnetic field interactions with the stellar wind,' Ira said. 'It became impractical to manage communication between cultural centres without constant and tedious travel. "The gift," more accurately referred to as nano-enhancement, provided communications between individuals to promote better communication amongst other capabilities.'

'You could talk to people without being there,' Coran said.

Kiri and Zoella nodded.

'Nano …' Meru said. 'This word … what does it mean?'

'Nano refers to microscopic self-replicating machines that live within biological tissue,' Ira said. 'These miniature machines live within the host and provide them with the additional capabilities, by interfacing with nerves and connective tissue. The process of receiving the machines is termed nano-infusion.'

'That's what Caesar said,' Meru noted.

'Machines?' Kiri said, her mouth twisted in distaste. 'Inside us? How many machines?'

'Billions,' Ira replied.

Kiri looked at Zoella in horror.

'They are invisibly small,' Ira replied. 'They were initially programmed to provide communication capabilities, along with systems diagnostics. They were found to be efficacious in treating injuries as the machines were able to repair tissue at the microscopic level.'

'Healing …' Kiri whispered.

'And if you can heal,' Zoella said, looking at her. 'You can hurt.'

Kiri nodded. 'So … you can hurt people using the gift because these machines are in everyone and respond to our wishes.'

'Simplistic,' Ira said. 'But essentially correct. The nano-technology can influence pain receptors and muscle tissue remotely at administrative request.'

'So it's not magic,' Meru said. 'It's machines. More of our ancestors' technology. You can inflict pain and paralyse people because of these tiny machines!'

'Nano-technology is present in all humans on Esurio,' Ira said. 'It has also spread to most animal and plant forms over the last two thousand rounds. Usage protocols were designed to only allow it to be administered by selected members of the colony quorum as it existed in round 196. Selected administrators were female and it was decided that all subsequent administrators would also be female. Particular traits were selected as advantageous, and only those qualities, once established, would allow the capability to be used by the individual.'

'So why just women?' Coran asked.

'The colony founders considered that the history of Earth indicated that patriarchal societies always resulted in war, conquest and ultimate destruction of self and environment. It was deemed that all significant decisions would be taken by solely female administrators. Thus a matriarchy was established for the governance of Esurio.'

'Women in charge,' Mel said, with a chuckle.' What a good idea. Better hand over the ship to me, Captain.' She gave Coran a push. 'You're demoted to cabin boy.'

Coran gave her a look.

'Exactly what Sandra told us,' Meru said, looking at Kiri. She nodded.

'And women in charge works just fine and dandy,' Fitch muttered. 'I mean … look at those snuttin' priestesses going about murdering anyone who doesn't agree with them. All very peaceful and understanding.' He looked at Kiri. 'No offence.'

'But that's it,' Coran said. 'The priestesses have been cultivating the gift for rounds and rounds. They were right … but also so wrong. Women were supposed to run things, and those with the gift were supposed to look after all Esurio. Instead they've turned the gift into a weapon to support their rule.'

Kiri was nodding. 'They always taught me that we were privileged and deserved to rule. That we were special and superior to everyone else …'

'Based on analysis,' Ira said. 'Both Kiri and Zoella have excessive levels of nano-infusion when compared with the original design criteria for the nano-enhancement project. It is likely that all the priestesses also have elevated levels. There is no information on what the effects of these excessive levels of nano-enhancement might be.'

'Yes there is,' Kiri said, looking at Zoella. 'We've both felt it. The more of this power you have, the more angry it makes you. There's a rage that builds up and can't be explained, a greed that makes you want more and more.'

Zoella was nodding. 'It takes over. Having the gift and gaining more of it becomes all that matters, you become single-minded, angry, always wanting to fight and kill, to dominate …'

'That's definitely the way the priestesses behave,' Coran said.

'Based on this testimony,' Ira said. 'It is conceivable that the nano-technology is causing the release of excess stress hormones in those with high levels of infusion. Adrenaline, noradrenaline and cortisol levels may be dangerously high, along with elevated blood pressure, body temperature, breathing and heart rate.'

'I definitely felt my heart pounding each time it happened,' Zoella agreed.

'Can the nano-tech be switched off somehow?' Meru asked. 'Stop the priestesses having the power at all?'

Coran and Mel looked up hopefully, but Ira's words dashed that hope.

'Unfortunately nano-technology is diffuse across Esurio,' Ira said. 'There is no central mechanism with which to manage it or disable it.'

The crew exchanged downcast looks with each other.

'Elena told the priestesses that the flares were because of the people not doing what the priestesses told them to,' Kiri said. 'That's how it started. Lacaille is a goddess to them.'

'Or a convenient story to keep them all motivated,' Coran said.

'And they want more power,' Fitch said. 'And anyone who disagrees or gets in their way is cut down and killed.'

'Except us,' Meru said. 'We managed to defy them.'

'Once,' Fitch said. 'And the chances of us managing that again?'

A silence fell on the group.

Ira's voice broke it.

'I said you had another role to play, Zoella,' Ira said.

'What do you mean?'

'You and Kiri are princesses of Scallia,' Ira said. 'You have sufficient strength of nano-infusion to combat the priestesses. Only you can restore Esurio to the state that our ancestors desired. They wished for a peaceful, agrarian society without conflict, with rules reinforced by the power of the gift, not dominated by it. Such a society does exist now, it is yours. The original colonists' wishes are best represented by you two, the crew of the *Mobilis* and by the people of Amar.'

'Then …' Zoella began.

'The priestesses are misusing the power entrusted to them,' Ira said. 'They must be advised as to their proper role and function.'

'Yeah,' Fitch chuckled. 'Like they're just going to change their minds based on a good speech.'

Coran nodded. 'We've got to stop them.'

CHAPTER THIRTEEN

Nadir, Coordinates Zero, Zero

Round 2307, Ninth pass

Coran and Mel stood at the doors of the Obelisk complex, looking out over the grounds beyond. The vegetation before them was dry and scorched, but the flare had been and gone, its effects deflected by the Obelisk now that Ira had subsumed the functions of the AMS.

It was here that the images they had seen had been taken all those rounds ago. Admiral Drayden addressing the first ever colonists and the death of Su-Lin, who had seen the first flare.

'Amazing that we're standing in the same spot,' Coran said. 'All that history, what we all thought was myth … it happened right here.'

'All those rounds ago,' Mel said.

The air was still hot and humid, but Lacaille was once more the glowing golden orb, hanging over them in the sky.

'I hope Daf and Creg are alright,' Mel said.

'They'll be fine,' Coran said. 'They knew to shelter in the ship during the flare.'

Below them they could see Meru and Zoella sitting on the scorched greening, talking to each other. Kiri was a little further away, sitting on the steps that led down towards the wall that surrounded the area, towards the quays where the *Mobilis* was moored.

Fitch came up behind them.

'Well, that was strangest scorchin' thing I've ever seen,' he said. 'And I've seen some pretty strange stuff.'

'You're not wrong,' Mel said.

Coran nodded. 'Can't help thinking I'm glad that Ira did that for Zoella … to lose her …'

Mel held his arm. 'I know what you mean. I feel guilty for thinking that too.'

'Ira knew what she was doing,' Fitch said. 'Seems happy enough about it as far as I can see. Better her than Zoella, especially if this business with the priestesses stays unfinished. We'll need both of them to deal with that problem.' He pointed at Zoella and Kiri.

'Looks like your right,' Coran agreed.

'Speaking of which,' Fitch said, looking over to Kiri. 'Unfinished business of my own.'

He walked off towards her.

'What's he going to do?' Mel asked.

'Not sure,' Coran said. 'Let's keep an eye on him.'

Kiri heard footsteps behind her and turned to see Fitch approaching. She twisted around and got to her feet, eyeing the man and his strange wide-brimmed hat.

Fitch stood, hands on hips, regarding her.

'What do you want?' Kiri asked.

'Just got a few words for you,' Fitch replied.

'And?' Kiri said, her fists clenching.

Fitch grinned at her reaction. 'Listen witch-girl, it's unlikely you and I will ever be close buddies …'

'Hardly,' Kiri snapped. 'You tried to kill me with your rifle. I haven't forgotten.'

'That I did,' Fitch returned with a chuckle. 'Should've blown your head clean off. Then you broke my arm …'

'What did you expect me to do?' Kiri glared.

'Exactly what you did,' Fitch said. 'We were enemies. We fought. I just wanted to say that …' He stopped for a moment before continuing. 'I won't be holding a grudge. What you did in there, volunteering to take Zoella's place. I respect that. That's all.'

Kiri nodded, but didn't reply.

'One thing you should know about this crew,' Fitch said. 'Once you're a part of it, folks will stick by you, they won't let you down. It's not for me to welcome you aboard, that's up to the Captain. But if he gives the word, you'll have nothing to fear from me. We clear?'

'Very,' Kiri said.

'Right then, as you were,' Fitch said, with a brief incline of his hat. He turned around and walked away from her, leaving her nonplussed.

Coran and Mel watched from above.

'Looks like Fitch just buried the hatchet too,' Coran said.

'Kiri was serious in there,' Mel said. 'About taking Zoella's place, I mean. She's terrified of going back to Amar, knowing Meru is torn between her and his family and home. Maybe she thought that would be an honourable sacrifice … now she's stuck with that choice again.'

'Yeah, that's a tough one,' Coran said.

'It's not,' Mel said, giving him a look. 'You could make it right for her.'

'Me?'

'Come on Coran,' Mel said. 'Amar looks to you, the senators all follow your lead …'

'I'm just the Captain of–'

'Rubbish!' Mel said. 'Drop the fake humility. Your leadership saved Amar. If you hadn't found out what was going to happen, insisted we discover Dynesia, Nireus … got those flying machines and convinced the senate to prepare … Amar would have been destroyed.'

'So?'

'Amar owes you.'

'So?' Coran repeated.

'Snuts! You're obtuse sometimes!' Mel snapped. 'If you give Kiri a pardon for her crimes against Amar it will stick. You could be her advocate. Tell everyone at home how she helped save the whole snuttin' planet. Show everyone you have confidence in her, show them you trust her.'

'How?'

'Make her part of the crew.' Mel said and gestured to where Kiri had sat, shoulders hunched, away from everyone else. 'She's bereft, alone. Right now, staying with Meru means prison as far as she knows. You've heard her whole story, it wasn't her fault she was indoctrinated by the priestesses. She would have stepped in to save Zoella. We all saw that.'

Coran thought about it for a moment and then nodded.

'Yeah, you're right.'

'You're the captain, Captain.'

* * *

Meru was sitting with Zoella, their feet propped up on the grass.

'You knew her best,' Meru said.

'She was so young,' Zoella said, staring off into the distance. 'How could she really know what she was doing …?'

'How do any of us?' Meru asked. 'How old do you have to be to sacrifice yourself for your friends?'

'I don't know,' Zoella said. 'I don't know anything any more.'

'It's not your fault,' Meru said.

'I've tried to look after two children,' Zoella said. 'One is dead … the other … she's …'

'What happened to Ren was tragic,' Meru said. 'But he made a choice to fight. Ira made a choice to give herself up for everyone else, including you … especially you. That's how much she cared for you … she loved you.'

Zoella sighed. 'I just don't want more people to die,' she said, tears coming to her eyes again. 'Everything we do, no matter what … no matter how we try to make things better …'

Meru gave her a hug around the shoulders.

'We're not through this yet … not until we deal with the priestesses,' he said. 'We've got to keep fighting to turn Esurio back to how it was supposed to be. At least we know what we're fighting for.'

Zoella nodded, looking over at Kiri.

'You'd better go to her,' she said. 'Don't leave her alone.'

Meru looked up to see Fitch walking towards Kiri. He got to his feet, ready to intervene, but saw them exchange nothing but a few words. After a moment, Fitch turned and walked away. Kiri had a puzzled look on her face. He watched as she turned and sat down on the steps again.

'You'll be alright?' Meru asked.

Zoella nodded.

Meru left her and walked across to Kiri. She looked up as he sat down next to her.

'How are you doing?'

She smiled. 'Alright I think,' she said. 'Just trying to get it all straight in my head.'

'What did Fitch want?'

'To make peace.'

'Really?'

'Yeah,' Kiri replied. 'I was surprised too. Is Zoella …?'

'She's feeling guilty for what happened to Ira.'

Kiri nodded. 'Meru, I didn't mean to hurt you when I made that offer … I just couldn't bear the thought of Zoella … I thought it would be …'

'Shhhh,' he said, wrapping his arms around her and giving her a kiss. 'You wanted to save her. We all did. I understand. It was very brave.'

'I just thought … I can't go back to Amar with you … if it had been me, you'd be free to …'

'I am not leaving you,' Meru said, turning her head by her chin and forcing her to look at him. 'Believe it.'

Kiri managed a smile.

'What that girl did, Ira …' Kiri said. 'If she hadn't been here it would have been Zoella or me anyway. To be caught in that machine … held there like that forever …'

Meru felt her shudder in his arms. He pulled her closer.

'I think Ira was right,' he said. 'It's you two that have to stop the priestesses.'

Kiri sighed. 'Just the two of us? How?'

'That's our next problem.'

* * *

The crew of the *Mobilis* returned to the ship, Meru escorting Kiri at the rear of the group. They boarded in a subdued fashion, with Coran explaining to Daf and Creg what had happened to Ira. Both of them listened without responding, but they looked glum.

Smoke from the burnt plants drifted into the sky. Even here, in the full protection of the Obelisk the flare had scorched the land. They could see distant plumes rising from the forests. The smell of burning was heavy all about them. No animals could be seen and there were no signs of movement.

Fitch prepared more food and Coran asked everyone to gather on deck. He let them finish the meal before addressing them all.

'It's been quite a stretch.' He looked at each one in turn. 'We came here to fix the Obelisk, unaware of what that would require. One of us has sacrificed herself so that might be accomplished. I'm sure none of us will ever forget Ira and what she did … what she will continue to do on behalf of everyone, perhaps long after we are all forgotten.'

Everyone around him nodded solemnly. Zoella, sitting next to Kiri, stifled a sob and Kiri put her arm around her.

'Before I move on to what happens next,' he said. 'There's another piece of business for this crew. We just lost a shipmate, I'd like to invite another aboard.'

He saw Kiri start and then look around in bewilderment, before looking at him.

'Kiri,' he said. 'You were our sworn enemy not long ago. I guess what we've all been through shows that we were never meant to be at odds. This planet was supposed to be a peaceful world, without factions and sides. I've seen enough of your character to see you're a loyal friend to those you care about. Will you work with us to set the world right?'

Kiri stood up, her eyes wide with shock. She looked around at Meru and Zoella, both of them gave her an encouraging nod. She turned to Coran.

'I can't fix the whole world,' she said, sparing a glance at the rising smoke. 'But I will help you try to stop the priestesses. I can do that.'

Coran grinned at her.

'I'm told,' he said, giving Mel a quick look, 'that I have a little influence in what's decided back home in Amar. So, you help us, and in return, I will hold your crimes against Amar pardoned.'

Kiri gasped, Coran could see she was trembling.

'I don't deserve any of this,' she said. 'Not after …'

'None of us are perfect,' Coran said. 'We're just trying to do the right thing. Seems to me that's what you're about now. Am I right?'

Kiri nodded. Coran saw her look around at the rest of the crew. They were all waiting for her to say something. Coran saw her swallow.

'I've done bad things, hurt and killed,' she said, looking from one to another. 'But I will do my best to put things right. Put things back how we've learnt they should have been.'

She looked at Coran, a small smile on her face. Coran extended his hand to her.

'Welcome aboard the *Mobilis*, Kiri.'

She took his hand. He was surprised at the firmness in her grip, saw the tendons and muscles flex in her arm. Meru, Zoella and Mel clapped, even Fitch tipped his hat. Coran saw Kiri's cheeks flush pink.

'What are your orders, Captain?' she asked.

Coran winked at her.

'First an initiation,' he said, hearing Fitch chuckle from alongside. From behind him he pulled out a bottle and a set of small wooden tumblers. He passed them round and then poured a measure of a thick dark liquid into each one. He kept a couple back for himself and Kiri.

'Let's see how you master a measure,' he said, setting the bottle down and raising his tumbler. 'To Kiri!'

'To Kiri,' everyone said from behind her. Coran saw Fitch, Mel, Daf and Creg down theirs without a pause. Meru swallowed his too, clenching his eyes tight shut for a moment before he swallowed. Zoella sipped hers and then coughed and spluttered, tapping her chest with her hand as discretely as she could.

Kiri sniffed hers before her eyes widened in surprise.

'Oh yes! I love this stuff,' she said, downing it in one go.

Coran waited for a moment and then looked at her in surprise, expecting a reaction to the strong liquor. Instead she licked her lips and held her tumbler out for more. He topped it up again. She downed the second one just as fast.

'Seems like you were born to it,' Coran said, exchanging a surprised glance with Fitch.

Kiri smiled coyly. 'I've had it before,' she said. 'Well, something like it.'

Coran caught the sideways look she gave Meru. Now he was blushing.

'A story worth telling?' Coran asked.

'No,' Meru said, a little too quickly.

Kiri laughed. 'Maybe one stretch.'

Coran sat back. 'As for orders,' he said. 'Sit yourself down and tell us what we're up against. Seems to me that the priestesses will try to take Amar again. They're going to be wise the second time. What can you tell us about them?'

Kiri did as she was told, seating herself next to Meru. Coran watched her as she looked around, seeing everyone looking at her. She coughed and sat up straight.

'The first thing you need to know,' she began, her voice sharp, 'is that the priestesses are a strict hierarchy. A matriarchy I suppose, like Ira said. The high priestess controls everything, but then delegates different tasks to those below her. She has the strongest gift, she's in charge. Everyone follows her orders, they are well disciplined. All priestesses are taught how to fight, but only about half are fully trained for war, others run errands and other tasks to keep things running.'

'How many are there?' Coran asked.

'Now?' Kiri asked. 'I don't know, before the battle for Amar, we mustered two hundred priestesses trained to fight and fly. That is what we attacked Viresia and Amaris with.'

'Perhaps half of them survived the battle,' Fitch said. 'Weakened for sure, but not weak.'

'There are more in reserve,' Kiri said. 'They would be able to muster the same numbers again if they compromised the defence of Daine.'

Coran thought about that for a moment.

'But, the fleet from Taloon was destroyed.'

'Much of it,' Kiri said. 'Perhaps the greater part of it, but I did not see what other resources they had. Certainly they sent a lot of their ships, but they would have kept some back and they'll build more with enough time. I think they'd still be able to mount an offensive before too long.'

Coran nodded. 'I suspect you're right. We can't repel that kind of attack again. And we had the element of surprise last time too. The priestesses will remember the flying ships and the quayside weapons, even if they could be made operational in time.'

'Is there any way we can take the fight to them?' Mel asked. 'We have you two, that's got to count for something, right?'

'The two of them can't stop the priestesses alone,' Fitch said. 'Outnumbered a hundred to one? That makes no sense!'

'It doesn't work like that,' Meru said.

Kiri was nodding. 'The priestesses can't combine their powers; that's why I was taught how to tear … take power from other women. Individual women can increase their powers. I planned to …'

She looked over at Zoella. Zoella nodded in encouragement.

'I planned to take Zoella's powers in order to challenge …'

'Her?' Coran asked.

'The high priestess,' Kiri said, with a nod.

'Liana, the Scallian Queen, had done this too,' Zoella said. 'Taking power from the women in Scallia, she tried to take mine too. She thought she was strong enough to resist the priestesses, but she got her sums wrong.'

'There are only three priestesses you have to worry about,' Kiri continued. 'Nerina is the high priestess, she is the most powerful. You met her on the quay, she was the one who told you to surrender.'

'I remember her alright,' Fitch said.

Coran nodded.

'Beside her, stand two others,' Kiri said. 'Her protégé, Rihanna. She is young, about the same age as Zoella and me. Nerina trained her and me side by side.' She gestured to herself and Zoella. 'She is the equal of both of us, probably even stronger now. She'll have been encouraged to tear more power.'

'And the third?'

'Merrin,' Kiri said with distaste. 'Not a fighter, but she is the chief administrator, she runs everything else. She is sly and treacherous – she hates me! Deal with those three and the priestesses will relent. All the time those three live, the priestesses will be your mortal enemies.'

'So we kill those three,' Fitch said, patting his rifle. 'Simple enough.'

'You won't get close enough to hurt them,' Kiri said. 'They will hear your thoughts and strike you down before you could get close. All of them are easily capable of crushing your minds before you could use your weapons, even these ones.' She pointed at Fitch's rifle.

'She's right,' Zoella said. 'What I did to you all in my rage … it would be like that, but worse. Your minds crushed beyond recall.'

'And now we know how it works,' Meru said. 'Those tiny nano-machines are in everything, even inside us … and they respond to their control.'

'And in addition to those powers,' Kiri said. 'Those priestesses who are trained as warriors are fierce and brutal. They are very skilled with swords, bows and the kai.'

'Yes,' Coran said. 'I remember that well enough too. So … what do you think they'll do?'

Kiri got to her feet and walked around the deck of the *Mobilis*. She looked out to sea for a moment before turning back.

'Nerina will have been weakened by the failure of the attack on Amar,' Kiri said. 'I think that's what she intended for me. I thought I was the chosen one of Elena's prophecy. She was using me to either win, or come back in failure. She will need to strengthen her position.

If she could claim victory over Amar, that would silence any opposition she faces.'

'So they will be coming back,' Fitch grumbled.

'If it was up to you,' Coran said, looking at Kiri. 'What would you do? How would you defeat us?'

Kiri bit her lip.

'I'd attack you,' she said, looking Coran straight in the eye. 'You're the leader, your ship is the most powerful vessel anyone has ever seen. I'd kill you all save Zoella, tear her gift, destroy or steal the ship. Then Amar would fall.' She paused. 'That's what I would do.'

There was silence for a moment. Everyone was looking at Kiri.

'Well, you did ask,' Fitch said, laughing, looking around at the stunned expressions about him. 'Sound strategy too. A little on the cold-hearted and callous side, but she's not wrong.'

'Is there no way we can talk to them?' Mel asked. 'Reason with them?'

'Reason with them?' Fitch asked, giving her a withering look.

'Kiri has changed her mind,' Mel shot back. 'She listened … why not the rest of them? If we could show them what we've found out …'

'Some might,' Kiri acknowledged. 'But they've all been taught from childhood that they are superior, deserving of their position and following the will of a goddess who demands complete obedience or dishes out severe punishment. I only had three rounds of that. It was hard enough for me to leave it behind. I don't think there is much hope that will work.'

'Neither do I,' Coran said. 'Nor do I much fancy our chances in a second confrontation. We've got to stop them before they're ready to attack Amar.'

Kiri nodded. 'Nerina already knows the religion we followed isn't true. She just wants to be Empress, be in control of everything. She has torn so many women … her power is huge and the rage and madness that comes with it will have taken her over.'

'We need to take out the leaders,' Fitch said, holding his rifle out before him. 'Get me within three hundred hands and I'll drop them stone cold dead.'

'We've got six rifles in total,' Coran said. 'With maybe a hundred cylinders for them. But the priestesses know about them and how they work. Getting a shot is the problem.'

'And they'll be shooting back,' Kiri said. 'All of them are trained in archery remember.'

'Then there is the problem of getting to them,' Coran said. 'What is their city like?'

Kiri sat alongside Meru, crossing her legs.

'Daine? It is far inland, the city has a wall. The priestesses live in a temple at the very centre of the city. Many dachs are stationed nearby. I don't think it has ever been attacked from the ground. There are regular patrols of the area, you could not approach without being seen.'

'And we barely have enough flying machines to counter the dachs in defence, let alone an attack,' Meru said. 'Not even close.'

'Yeah, that won't work,' Fitch agreed. 'So we can't attack 'em and we're likely to lose if we wait for them to come to us. Doesn't leave us much does it?'

'We need an army,' Coran said. 'And we don't have one.'

He saw Zoella frown for a moment, then she shook her head.

'Zoella?'

'No it won't work …' she said.

'Try us,' Coran said. 'Anything is a good suggestion at this point.'

'There is an army,' Zoella said. 'Well, what's left of one.'

'Where?' Fitch demanded.

'In Viresia,' Zoella said.

'But Viresia fell to the priestesses,' Meru said. 'The city was aflame, routed …'

'Yes,' Zoella replied. 'But not all the soldiers were killed.'

'She's right,' Kiri agreed. 'I went back there after I left Drem. There are priestesses there, but only a small force to keep order. Most of the rest of the city and the people were left intact. The lords there swore loyalty to Nerina or faced death. One was killed, the others capitulated. Nerina left there to return to Drayden … I went with her.'

'Viresia already fell once,' Fitch said. 'What would make a second time any different?'

Kiri and Zoella looked at each other.

'Us,' they both said together.

'And our weapons,' Meru said. 'We might even be able to bring in reinforcements from Amar to help make a stand.'

'Alright,' Fitch said, leaning forward with renewed interest. 'So we take out the priestesses in Viresia and take back control of the city. Then what? The priestesses won't take that sitting down.'

Kiri looked at Zoella.

'Then we entice Nerina in,' Zoella said.

'How?' Coran asked.

'Us again,' Kiri said. 'Nerina, Rihanna and Merrin think I'm dead and whilst they know of Zoella they don't know where she is …'

'She does,' Zoella wailed. 'She's tried to push into my mind, I manage to stop her but …'

'She knows we were heading for the Obelisk,' Coran added.

Kiri thought about that for a moment.

'Then she'll be after you,' Kiri said. 'But we can use that.'

'They'll come for you,' Coran said looking at Zoella, before he looked over at Fitch. 'And then you get your shot.'

'Can you stop them addling our brains before I can put a hole in them?' Fitch asked.

Kiri nodded. 'Such a strike can be blocked … our cousin Liana did such a thing to me when I attacked Viresia.'

'I remember it,' Zoella said. 'I was standing next to her.'

'And Merrin won't fight in the battle,' Kiri said.' She'll be left at home to guard Daine. It will be Nerina and Rihanna versus …'

'You and Zoella,' Meru whispered.

Silence fell about them, punctuated only by the wind whistling through the masts of the *Mobilis* and the slap of water against the ship's hull.

'Well,' Fitch said, after a moment. 'It's a plan. Not sure it's a great plan, but it's better than sitting around waiting to have your brain squished. We can work the details out as we go.'

'I think it's the right place too,' Zoella said. 'Viresia.'

'What do you mean?' Mel asked.

'Kiri and I are princesses of Scallia,' Zoella answered. 'We are descended from a royal line of rulers from that city. If our home is anywhere, that's where it is. Seems right that we should make a stand there.'

Coran nodded. 'I like it. And I agree, it feels right. How many priestesses do you think there will be stationed there, Kiri?'

Kiri shrugged. 'Ten perhaps, maybe fifteen. It depends on whether Nerina needs them elsewhere or not.'

'Still quite a few,' Fitch said.

'We'll be able to overpower them,' Kiri said.

'Only if they don't know we're coming,' Mel said. 'Which means a sneak attack. If the word gets out then the priestesses will arrive in force before we're prepared.'

'I can get us in,' Zoella said. 'I stayed there for several passes. I know my way in and around the city. There are lots of ways, most of the city isn't used.'

'And will the citizens of Viresia welcome us?' Fitch asked. 'They've already had their share of fire and death, this likely means more of it.'

The conversation paused. The crew looked around at the smoke billowing about them, the dark clouds hanging heavy in the sky around the Obelisk tower.

'Scallia is a proud kingdom,' Zoella said. 'If there is a way for them to defeat the priestesses, they will take it. They had great affection for their kings and would prefer to be ruled by their own. But it will be the lords we have to convince.'

'And how do we prove that you two are the princesses you claim to be?' Fitch asked. 'Neither of you exactly look the part, do you?'

Kiri looked at Zoella, who looked downcast. 'There isn't a way to prove it,' Zoella said. 'Guerrun is dead … they're all dead. Anyone who knew the truth is gone. I saw the family tree in the throne room …'

Kiri nodded. 'I did too … our names weren't on it. Guerrun made sure he hid our identities so we wouldn't be found. That proof died with him.'

'Your powers won't be in question,' Coran said. 'That will have to be proof enough.'

'This plan is still pretty sketchy,' Fitch said. 'I'm hearing a lot of ifs and buts.'

'There must be some records of Myana in Viresia,' Meru said. 'Something, surely?'

Zoella shrugged. 'Ioric only told me that he lost her when he was young, that his father knew something about it but never told him. But King Marek died before the priestesses attacked.'

'So there is no guarantee your people are going to believe your claim,' Fitch said looking at Zoella, before gesturing at Kiri. 'But I daresay they'll remember you setting fire to everything.'

Kiri gave Fitch a pointed stare, but didn't say anything.

'We could do with someone on the inside,' Coran said. 'Someone we could trust … someone who could tell us what's going on there.'

Zoella sighed. 'There's no one left that we could contact,' she said. 'And if we tried to find someone the chances are the priestesses would sense us.'

'And we lose our surprise,' Coran muttered. 'Still, I don't see much choice. Gaining a foothold in Viresia still seems our best option. Let's work back from there. First we need to get out of here in one piece. Mel, how's the *Mobilis*?'

Mel leant forward. 'She's still battered, but we'll keep patching her up as best we can. I'd rather not take her through the storm again, but it doesn't look like we have much choice.'

Coran nodded. 'No, not really.'

'Viresia is inland though,' Meru said. 'The *Mobilis* won't help with that.'

'No, we're going to need the flying machines again,' Coran said.

'I don't think the big one here will work any time soon,' Meru said. 'But there are four smaller ones according to the status report we got from the Obelisk.'

'Flying through that storm again?' Kiri asked, with a shiver. 'Really?'

Now it was Meru's turn to shrug.

'I don't think that's advisable,' Coran said. 'But I've got an idea. What if we lash one of the flying machines to the *Mobilis*? Once we're out the other side of the storm, we can fly it inland. Daf and Creg will mind the ship anyway, so that leaves five of us to head to Viresia.'

Meru and Fitch looked towards the rear of the ship, gauging space and judging angles.

'Might work,' Meru said, as Fitch nodded. 'Assuming we can tie it down properly.'

'What about Amar?' Mel asked.

'Once we're clear of the storm we should be able to reach them on the radio,' Coran said. 'We can get them to send as many people as they can spare to Viresia, along with the flying machines there – those that are fixed anyway.'

'Then where?' Fitch asked.

'Meru go grab the map,' Coran instructed.

Meru ran off and returned moments later. Coran took the old parchment and gestured for the crew to move back and clear a space on the deck. Then he unrolled it for all to see.

'Travelling shadeward once we leave the storm, the first port on the coast is Airea,' Coran said. 'We passed it on the way here.'

'That's where Rihanna is,' Kiri said. 'But I don't think we should go close. We … the priestesses … took it. It belongs to them now.'

'Got to go past it to get anywhere,' Mel observed. 'Or we can sail out of sight of land the whole way.'

'Might be worth a recce,' Fitch said. 'That's where the fleet that attacked Amar came from. Would be worth knowing what position they're in.'

'As long as it's only a recce,' Mel said, looking at Coran. 'We're only one ship, remember?'

'No heroics,' Coran replied. 'I promise.'

Coran could still see Kiri looked uncomfortable.

'Kiri?'

'There will be priestesses stationed in Airea,' she said. 'Lots of them I would have thought, guarding the fleet there. If they sense Zoella and me they'll come for us, especially if Nerina is searching for Zoella.'

'And we lose our element of surprise,' Mel said, nodding.

'But we do need to know whether Amar is in danger of imminent attack,' Coran said. 'We can't pull all of our resources out and send them to Viresia if they're going to be needed at home.'

Mel and Kiri looked at each other uneasily.

'We won't get close,' Coran added. 'Just close enough to see what's going on there.'

Coran looked at Mel and Kiri, both nodded reluctantly.

'After that, the *Mobilis* will have to sail shadeward and sunright around the coast,' Meru said, jabbing a finger at the map. 'Might as well drop in on Amar, it's hardly much of a diversion. Then we have a choice between Dynesia or Serenia as a port.'

'Serenia is where I grew up,' Zoella said. 'It's a fishing town. I don't know what they'll make of us and there's not much there. No one who can help us, anyway.'

'Dynesia is abandoned,' Mel added. 'But it's also where Caesar is. We could arrange for the flying machines to be returned to his hangar and be repaired before flying on to Viresia?'

Meru nodded. 'Yeah, that will work. Then we can all fly from Dynesia to Viresia. The *Mobilis* will be safe and sound in Caesar's cavern for when … we're done.'

'Seems like we have a plan then,' Coran said. Everyone nodded.

'Let's recap this then,' Fitch said. 'We land a flying machine on the *Mobilis* and hope we don't get killed attempting that. We sail through the storm and hope we don't get drowned. We then sneak past Airea hoping we don't get spotted, attacked and killed by the priestesses. Then we fly into Viresia, take out all the priestesses there without raising the alarm, convince everyone there that another war is exactly what they want, dangle our princesses here in front of the priestesses and hope they take the bait … and then kill the most powerful priestesses in all the land … all without getting killed ourselves. That about the shape of it?'

'Did you mention not getting killed enough times in there?' Mel said, with a grin.

'I figured you'd follow my drift,' Fitch replied.

'But you're right,' Coran said. 'The alternative is to go back to Amar and just wait to be invaded again.'

'And they will invade,' Kiri said. 'There's no doubt about it. Nerina has no choice but to follow Elena's diktat. Either we stop them or …'

'They end us,' Zoella added.

'And Amar is destroyed,' Meru said. 'We're the only ones who know what our ancestors had in mind for this planet. It's up to us to honour their memories.'

The crew of the *Mobilis* sat in silence for long moments, looking at each other.

'So, there's plenty of work to do,' Coran said. 'Meru, you go get a flying machine and bring it here. Fitch, get all the rifles ready. Mel, you, me, Daf and Creg are patching up the *Mobilis*.'

'What about us?' Kiri asked.

'You two practice your mental magic,' Coran said. 'Attack each other, defend against it, make sure you're as ready as you can be for whatever the priestesses might throw at you.'

Kiri and Zoella nodded.

'Any questions?' Coran asked. There was a quick shaking of heads. 'Right then, jump to it. Once the *Mobilis* is ready and the flying machine is in place, we're casting off.'

He looked around at his crew.

'It's time to head shadeward.'

* * *

Meru had been quick in retrieving a flying machine. As far as Coran could tell it was identical to the other small ones he had seen; two seats at the front, with space for between four and six in the rear, depending on how much gear you wanted to drag along with you. Meru had landed it beside the quay and was helping Daf and Creg measure its dimensions so they could figure out how to strap it down on to the rear decks of the *Mobilis*.

The ship was still listing, canted to one side. To Coran's eye it also seemed to be a little down by the head. He jumped down through the deck hatch behind the bridge and walked forward, noticing the cracked portholes and water stains on the ceiling and floor.

'Been through a lot,' he said, tapping the nearest bulkhead. 'We'll get you fixed up after all this is over old girl.'

He could hear a conversation from somewhere up ahead. It wasn't from the cabins, but further down into the ship. He walked up to another hatch that led down into the hold where Fitch and Meru had taken shelter from the flare. He could make out Fitch and Mel discussing something.

He swung down on to the ladder and stepped down. It was dark, hot and humid inside the hold. As he reached the bottom he stepped into warm water.

'What …?'

'Oh you noticed that too,' Fitch said, sloshing up behind him, holding up a lantern. 'Got our own swimming pool.'

'Where's all this water come from?' Coran demanded.

'Oh, I don't know,' Fitch said. 'Maybe from the sea outside?'

'Fitch …'

'There's a leak,' Mel's voice said, from somewhere further into the hull.

'Then switch the pumps on,' Coran said.

'Yeah,' Fitch said, rolling his eyes. 'Great idea. Mel, why didn't we think of that?'

'The pumps are on,' Mel retorted, kicking through the water and walking up beside Fitch. 'Barely keeping ahead of it all.'

'What's happened?' Coran demanded.

'Damage from the storm and from the battle back at Amar,' Mel said.

'Keel is twisted from the ramming, so the exterior plates aren't sitting right. Mostly likely lost a bunch of rivets. We were on top of the leaks before the storm, but she took a pounding then. Now she's …'

'Find the leaks and patch them,' Coran said.

'They're along the keel,' Mel said. 'We can't get to them, not without a dry dock. The storm made the damage from the battle worse.'

'Let's have the short version,' Coran said. 'What are we saying here?'

Mel wiped her forehead with the back of her hand. 'If we go through the storm there's a good chance we'll get a leak that's more than the pumps can cope with.'

'How much of a chance?'

'I don't know,' Mel said, exasperated. 'But if we had a choice I'd say we don't go. She's been bashed about hard, she's old. She doesn't deserve this treatment.'

'Mel, we don't have a choice … we can't stay here.'

'I know,' Mel replied. 'But …'

'But what?'

'Coran,' Mel said. 'The water is already uncomfortably close to the batteries. If one of those plates comes completely loose in those seas …'

There was an uncomfortable silence.

'Maybe we can caulk the worst of the holes with tar,' Fitch said.

'We're going to have to do something,' Mel said, heaving a deep sigh.

'How long will it take? Coran demanded.

Mel glared at him and raised her hands in the air without saying anything.

'Do what you can,' Coran said, climbing on to the ladder. 'Once that flying machine is aboard, we're leaving.'

Coran stomped on to the deck of the *Mobilis*. To the aft, Daf, Creg and Meru were working on securing several lengths of rope to the cleats on each side of the deck.

'How are you doing?' he yelled.

Meru gave him a thumps up, but didn't answer. It seemed they were making progress.

Coran looked over to the quay.

Zoella and Kiri were standing about fifty hands apart, facing each other with arms outstretched. Both had their eyes closed and seemed to be concentrating hard. He watched them for a few moments wondering what trick they were practising. Whatever it was they seemed well matched. He was about to head down towards Meru when he heard a gasp.

Kiri had fallen to her knees, holding her hand against her forehead. Zoella was running towards her.

'Kiri?' she cried.

Kiri had slumped to the ground. Coran jumped across to the quayside and sprinted up behind Zoella.

'You alright?' he called. 'What happened?'

'It can't be …' Kiri said, blinking as Zoella pulled her upright. 'She told me they'd killed her …'

'Kiri?' Zoella said. 'You're not making sense. Did I push too hard?'

Meru ran up and joined them, having seen the commotion from the *Mobilis*.

'What happened?'

Kiri looked up at all of them. She shook her head.

'I'm fine,' she said. 'It wasn't that, not your fault. My mind wandered, I was thinking of Scallia … and then … I just heard someone, someone I thought was dead.'

'Dead?' Coran said. 'Who?'

'A girl I rescued in Drayden,' Kiri said. 'I was supposed to tear her, take her powers, but I smuggled her out and got her to the border with Scallia. Nerina and Rihanna told me they'd found and killed her … but she's alive!'

'Who is she?' Zoella demanded.

'She is called Gemma,' Kiri said. 'One of the tribute girls taken from Scallia in the last tithe.'

'Where is she?' Meru asked.

Kiri looked up.

'She escaped,' Kiri said. 'She's in Viresia!'

'Slow down,' Coran said. 'Tribute girls?'

'One of the girls that was sent from Scallia to Drayden,' Zoella said. 'The tithe was due every five rounds. Prince Torin of Viresia took the last one just before I arrived there. I remember Ioric talking about it.'

'There were twenty,' Kiri said. 'They were brought into the temple. Every one of them was torn except her. I got Gemma to pretend I'd torn her. I found her later and flew her to the border with Scallia. I couldn't go any further as I had to get back, I'd have been missed. Nerina and Rihanna told me that they'd found her and killed her, but she must have escaped somehow.'

'And she's in Viresia?' Coran asked. 'Right now?'

Kiri nodded.

'We could ask her what's happening there!' Meru said.

'Wait a moment,' Coran said. 'Can we trust her?'

'She's a high born girl of Scallia,' Zoella said. 'She would have lived in the city her whole life.'

'Just seems mighty convenient, that's all,' Coran said.

'Or exactly what we need,' Meru countered. 'We could ask her how many priestesses there are, what they're doing. What the lords are thinking … co-ordinate things …'

'She can't lie to me through the link,' Kiri said. 'That's not how it works. Any deception has a taint to it, I'll know.'

Zoella nodded in agreement.

'Ask her then,' Coran said.

Kiri took a deep breath and closed her eyes. They all saw her frown in concentration.

'She can hear me,' Kiri whispered. 'She did escape from the priestesses … it was Rihanna who tried to kill her, but she threw herself into the river to get away. She almost drowned, but she was able to get to Scallia. She was found and rescued. The lords have kept her safe and away from the priestesses …'

'How many are there?'

They waited as Kiri relayed the question. Kiri gasped at the answer.

'She says there are only three priestesses in the city. Many of them were summoned away for some reason, she doesn't know why.'

'Only three …' Meru said, his mouth open wide.

'She wants to know where I am,' Kiri said.

'Don't tell her yet,' Coran said. 'Ask her if she's able to speak to one of the lords there … ask her who is in charge aside from the priestesses.'

Kiri nodded, her eyes still closed.

'She says Lord Crenech is her master now,' she said. 'He has taken up many of Lord Sequon's responsibilities after he was killed … by Nerina.'

'Do you know him?' Coran asked, looking at Zoella. 'Can we trust him?'

Zoella shook her head. 'No, I've not heard of him. King Ioric was quite dismissive of the lords, saying they schemed and played political games. There's no way to know if we can trust him or not.'

'Gemma says she can speak to him,' Kiri said. 'It's him that has hidden her from the priestesses.'

'He must have been there when we were,' Meru said, looking at Zoella. 'We could ask him that if there was a way to restore King Ioric's royal line to control of Scallia, would he support it?'

Coran nodded.

'A vague enough question to test his loyalty,' he said. 'Doesn't give much away. Can you ask Gemma to ask him that?'

Kiri nodded. They saw the frown on her forehead increase further.

'She says she will ask him now.'

Kiri caught her breath and opened her eyes.

'I could see it,' she said. 'Viresia has been repaired from the battle. People have returned, it's much as it was before, just with the priestesses in charge. The lords are still running their affairs.'

'Makes sense,' Coran said. 'The priestesses won't want the additional burden.'

'Many women have been taken to Drayden though,' Kiri said. 'The priestesses are still searching for those with gifts.'

'Which will hopefully cause a lot of resentment,' Coran said, 'Let's see what this Lord Crenech has to say for himself.'

'If he is able to influence the other Lords we might have a chance,' Zoella said. 'Or he might just tell the priestesses we're coming to gain more standing for himself.'

'We're going to have to take a risk at some point,' Meru said.

Kiri waved her hands for silence, closing her eyes.

'She's back,' she said. 'Gemma has vouched for me, but Lord Crenech says … there are no heirs to Ioric's line, his daughter is lost.'

'Tell him there are heirs,' Coran said. 'Two nieces. Daughters of King Ioric's sister.'

'Of house Tiamoi,' Zoella whispered.

Kiri relayed the message.

'He says … You have my attention. What was Ioric's sister's name?'

'Myana,' Zoella said, 'Tell him Myana.'

Kiri nodded.

'He says … In that case, who are you, and what do you intend?'

Coran took a deep breath.

'Time to come clean,' he muttered. 'Tell him … Tell him my name is Coran. I am from Amar, an island far to the sunright of Scallia. Tell him we have been able to stop the priestesses invading our home, frustrating them in battle.'

Coran waited until Kiri signalled she had done so.

'Tell him I have the two nieces of Ioric in my care, Kiri and Zoella Tiamoi. Between us and them we have the power to overcome the priestesses and restore Scallia's royal line. Our question is will the Scallian Lords and army support us in taking the fight to the priestesses?'

All of them leant in closer around Kiri as she finished sending Coran's message.

They waited for an answer.

They saw a faint smile touch Kiri's lips.

'He says … a chance to rid ourselves of these invaders? Bring your fight. Scallia will rise again!'

Coran looked around at Zoella, Meru and Kiri. He grinned.

* * *

Far to the shadeward, deep in the land of Scallia, two men were clustered around a young girl. She had her eyes closed in concentration.

Gemma's frown faded. Crenech and Joachim were staring at her.

'Hard to believe,' Crenech said.

'I told you we could trust her,' Gemma replied.

'Royalty of Scallia,' Joachim breathed. 'Nieces of King Ioric himself, daughters of the house of Tiamoi still alive! Scarce seems possible. Our royal line still exists.'

'It explains everything we suspected about this rogue priestess,' Crenech said. 'Kiri was one of Marek's dreamers as was this other niece, Zoella.'

'Both with the powers of the priestesses,' Gemma said, 'But fighting for us.'

'And these Amarans have faced down and defied the might of Drayden,' Joachim added. 'It can be done!'

Crenech nodded.

'We must keep this secret for now,' he said. 'They are coming to us, there is much to be done before they arrive and no word of it must come to the attention of the priestesses here. Scallia will rise again!'

CHAPTER FOURTEEN

Through the Vortex

Round 2307, Ninth pass

The *Mobilis* was almost ready to depart. Mel, Fitch, Daf and Creg had caulked the hull to the point that Mel was no longer muttering under her breath about it. Meru and Coran were busy calculating a course. The flying machine had been lashed down on to the rear decks of the ship and the ballast trimmed to match. Departure was scheduled for the next chime.

Zoella had nothing else to do and said she wanted to say goodbye to Ira. Kiri likewise was unoccupied and volunteered to go with her.

Kiri waited for Zoella to come out on the deck. When she appeared, she brought something with her. Kiri recognised her kai. She swallowed.

Zoella held it out to her.

'It's yours,' she said. 'You should have it. Take it. I never want to use one again.'

'I thought it was lost,' Kiri said, taking it and holding it carefully. The metal showed the marks of usage, light scratches running up and down its length.

'Fitch kept it after …' Zoella said, stammering. 'Well, afterwards.'

Kiri ventured a smile.

'I was given this when I became a priestess,' she said. 'When I became part of the warrior caste … when my life changed.'

Zoella watched as Kiri turned the kai around in her hands, one hand still gloved in black.

'Safer in your hands I think,' Zoella said and then gestured to the path.

'Thank you,' Kiri answered.

Together the two sisters walked up to the Obelisk compound. The fires were out and there was only the faint hint of smoke in the air.

'The plants seem to know what to do,' Zoella said. 'I saw furlers in Drem … they actually need the flares, they expect them, they're ready.'

'Same with the animals,' Kiri said. 'They see it coming, know to hide.'

Together, they walked through the gateway system and into the main complex.

'Holographic assistants are available to guide you through the necessary procedures,' the Obelisk's voice said. 'Do you wish them to be activated?'

'No,' Zoella snapped. 'I never want to see those things again.'

'Your preference has been noted.'

Kiri reached out and clasped her hand. They both walked down to the lower level of the facility, using their palms to open the security doors.

The AMS room opened before them. Zoella gasped as Ira's body came into view again.

Nothing had changed, the only sound was the faint hum of machinery all about them.

Then Ira's voice filled the room.

'Welcome Zoella, welcome Kiri.'

'Hello Ira,' Zoella replied. 'How … how are you?'

'I am in perfect operating order,' Ira replied. 'Physiological functions have adapted and are now stable, sensor feeds and inputs are calibrated effectively.'

Zoella and Kiri exchanged a look.

'We've come to say goodbye,' Kiri said.

'Your preparations for departure have been noted by monitoring systems,' Ira replied. 'Your intentions are to visit Airea and then proceed to Dynesia before reaching Viresia.'

'You know all that?' Zoella asked.

'Monitoring systems are comprehensive within the Obelisk area,' Ira replied. 'But they are not effective beyond the vortex perimeter. I have reviewed your strategy. It is not without risk, but there is a reasonable chance of success overall.'

'Just reasonable?' Kiri echoed.

'There are many variables which cannot be accounted for,' Ira replied.

Zoella stepped forward. 'Ira, can I speak to you … without all this?' She gestured around at the equipment that surrounded them.

'Please specify what you mean,' Ira replied.

'I want to talk to … just you, the Ira you were before you became …'

There was a pause.

'Telemetry feeds and augmentation can be temporarily suspended, leaving the core AMS isolated save for communication enhancement. Is this sufficient?'

Zoella shrugged. 'I don't know. But … yes.'

'Please standby.'

There was a noticeable change in tone and tempo of the machine noise around them. Zoella and Kiri both heard the sounds fade away.

'Did you switch it off?' Kiri asked, her voice now a whisper.

'Ira?' Zoella asked, after a moment.

'I am here, Zoella,' Ira's voice replied.

'Is it you?' Zoella asked. 'Really you?'

'It is,' Ira replied. 'I'm sorry I tricked you, Zoella. But I knew what had to be done. I have learnt much from the information here. Tasha did not wish to harm anyone either, but she instructed the Obelisk to inflict pain when required in order to ensure this outcome.'

'The pain?' Kiri asked. 'When it stopped me from speaking to Zoella?'

'Yes,' Ira said. 'There were also problems; times when pain was inadvertently applied when trying to make contact with administrators, or the systems overloaded.'

'Visions and headaches,' Kiri muttered. 'I remember those.'

'This was my choice to make,' Zoella said. 'Not yours …'

'Any of the three of us could have done it,' Ira replied. 'You and Kiri need to work together against the priestesses. I've heard your thoughts, seen the hatred and the anger that passed between you both. You can heal all that now. Heal everything. The two of you together are more powerful than you know.'

'But …'

'Do not concern yourself with me,' Ira replied. 'I've done this willingly; it's not your fault. You didn't fail me or let me down. This was my choice and I am happy with it. I have all of Tasha's accumulated wisdom at my disposal. I will be fine.'

'You saved my life,' Zoella said. 'I wanted to save yours …'

'And you did,' Ira replied. 'If you hadn't taken me from Airea the priestesses would have captured me, torn me and left me as a useless husk. Then it would have been you or Kiri who would have to save the AMS. Without each other you will not be able to stop the priestesses. If you don't, they will take over Esurio. That must not be allowed to happen.'

'But …'

'You loved me and cared for me,' Ira replied. 'I wanted for nothing.' Ira's voice stopped and then resumed. 'But you must let me go now.'

Zoella's face was tear-streaked. She looked over at Kiri, who was nodding.

'What's done is done,' Kiri said.

Zoella nodded, her head bowed for a long moment. Then she looked up, wiping her eyes.

'Then thank you, Ira,' she managed to say. 'For taking my place. I love you.'

'I love you too, Zoella.'

* * *

A chime later, the *Mobilis* slipped its berth at the Obelisk quayside. Everyone was on deck as the ship pulled away from the dock, came about and then accelerated out of the bay and into the open waters of the sea. The land fell behind them, still lush and green despite the flare. New vegetation was already sprouting amongs the ruins of what had been burnt. The sea sparkled in the light of Lacaille and the Obelisk still dominated the view, its top wreathed in bright white clouds.

They were navigating by the landmarks they had seen on the way in initially, along with much improved maps that they had procured from the Obelisk complex itself.

The sea was flat calm for now, but they knew it would only be a short reprieve. Ahead, the vast swirling cloud wall of the inside of the vortex soared into the heavens above them, awe inspiring and threatening.

Coran had issued instructions to ensure that everything was lashed down and stored securely. Daf and Creg lowered the mesh sails. The *Mobilis* was cruising forward at three quarters of her maximum speed, running on battery power.

'How long did it take to get through before?' Meru asked, eyeing the approaching wall of cloud with apprehension. Already their faces were being wetted by a thin spray. Another spell would see them inside the vortex once more. Kiri and Zoella stood alongside him, shivering in the cool air. Waves began to rock the *Mobilis* fore and aft.

'Two stretches, give or take,' Fitch answered, checking the hatches on the deck before looking up at them. 'Some of it was calmer, some of it was as rough as I've ever seen. Hope you've got strong stomachs. It ain't fun, that's for sure.'

'We were through it in a few chimes in the flying machine,' Kiri said.

'But we didn't come out in one piece,' Meru replied.

Kiri nodded. 'Good point.'

'Everyone who isn't on duty get below decks!' Coran yelled from the wheelhouse. 'Mel and I will take the first round, then Meru and Kiri, then Fitch and Zoella. Everyone who isn't on duty up top will take turns sounding the ship below under Daf and Creg's guidance. Any questions?'

There were none. All of them turned to catch one final glimpse of the Obelisk before it faded into the spray and mist on the horizon. Then the crew took turns in dropping down the ladder on to the deck below. Fitch pulled the hatch closed above and spun the handle until it locked into place.

Outside the light was already fading, Lacaille's brightness being replaced by a gloomy grey. The wind was rising fast, howling around the ship's masts.

'Here we go,' Fitch said.

* * *

Coran's planned rotation of the crew didn't work out.

Kiri and Meru had intended to do as he'd asked, but the moment the ship started pitching and rolling in the sea, Kiri was sea-sick. If anything she was worse than Zoella had been on her first voyage on the *Mobilis*. Within the first spell she was violently ill, shivering and pale, crying with misery. Meru could do nothing for her but wrap her in a blanket and hold a bucket for her.

When the call came to replace Coran and Mel, Kiri was no better.

'You'd better go,' Zoella said. 'I can look after her. You know more about sailing.'

Meru nodded and left Kiri in Zoella's care.

Kiri retched into the bucket again, Zoella could feel her muscles straining with the effort. There was little enough left now, her last meal was long gone. Kiri spat bile from her mouth.

'I hate this …'

'I can only tell you that you do get used to it,' Zoella said.

'Is that what they told you?' Kiri asked, miserably.

'Yes,' Zoella answered.

'Is it true?'

Zoella grimaced. 'Not really.'

Kiri was sick again.

* * *

The waves pounded on, spell after spell. Fitch was down in the hold with Daf and Creg. Around them the ship was creaking and groaning with every wave it crested, the floor bucking, rolling and turning underfoot as the *Mobilis* surged onwards.

'How's it looking?' Fitch demanded.

The two big men grunted, pointing fore and aft. A hand's worth of water was sloshing up and down the corridor deck plates.

'Well, it's only going to get worse …' Fitch began. His feet left the deck for a moment as the ship lurched. A moment later they were all crushed down to their knees. Metal shrieked around them. Fitch swore he saw the structure of the ship twist with the impact.

'It'll be a miracle if we get through this.'

Meru was underneath the hatch to the deck. He heard a banging noise from above and pulled at the handle to open the hatch. He caught a glimpse of dark heavy clouds above. Rain lashed down through the opening before Mel's sodden body got in the way. She clambered down. Meru pulling the hatch closed again.

'It's wild out there,' Mel said, as the noise subsided. 'Phew … what's that smell …?'

'Kiri,' Meru said, by way of explanation. 'She won't be any help for a while.'

'Sea-sick, eh?'

Meru nodded. 'Zoella is looking after her.'

'You'd best give Coran a hand then,' Mel said. 'How's the ship?'

'Fitch is cursing and trudging about with wet feet,' Meru said. 'Other than that we're still afloat.'

Both braced themselves as the ship rolled and pitched about them.

'Doesn't feel as bad as last time,' Mel said.

'Don't say that,' Meru said. 'That's just asking for …'

There was a sharp crack from beside them. One of the portholes smashed allowing a torrent of cold water to blast across them. Both of them lost their footing and slid down the corridor, which was tilting at an unnatural angle. A moment later the ship righted itself. Meru and Mel struggled to their feet.

'Get topside!' Mel yelled at Meru. 'Help Coran. I'll get this fixed!'

Meru staggered to the hatch. Mel helped him open it and pushed him through, sealing it after him.

Coran hauled Meru up to the wheelhouse and closed the door behind him.

'Aren't there supposed to be two of you?' he demanded, raising his voice over the squall.

'Kiri's sea-sick.'

'How's the ship?'

'Water rising in the hold, getting close to the batteries. Daf and Creg are on it.'

Coran nodded.

'Grab the throttles,' he yelled. 'The props keep pitching in and out of the water, if you hear them spun up, cut them back, wait for them to grip again and then give me full power. I've got to keep the bow half way from the wind shear, but she's turning all about on me.'

Coran was already swinging the wheel about as the *Mobilis* rolled over another series of waves. Meru knew well enough that the ship had to be pointing through the waves, otherwise it risked being caught broadside and flipped over. No wooden vessel could have dared these waters and survived. The *Mobilis* was made of sterner stuff.

Beneath him he could feel the reassuring rumble of the twin engines, still pushing onwards through the gale. Through the windows, the sky was dark, with clouds low above them, rolling and twisting. Rain lashed against the panes of glass like hammer blows. Meru could see the glass bending and shuddering with the impact.

Then the sky was gone, replaced with a wall of water rising before the ship.

'Shades.'

Meru watched in horror as the *Mobilis* tilted down and then felt himself thrown backwards as the bow rose as the ship pitched through the trough of the wave already behind them.

'Full power!' Coran yelled. 'Meru, the engines, full power!'

Meru lurched up and grabbed the throttle control, wrestling them forward to their stops. The *Mobilis'* engines dug deep into the water, struggling to push the ship forward.

The ship was rearing up, high and higher into the air.

We're going straight to the bottom, stern first!

Meru had no idea what angle the ship was at; it felt vertical, hanging there for long agonising moments whilst the wave threatened to overturn them.

'Come on …' Coran was yelling. 'Come on … over the …'

Then the bow nosed down, the *Mobilis* crested the wave.

'Yes!' Coran screamed, at the top of his lungs. 'Yes!' His voice caught. 'No …'

The bow was falling into the trough of the wave, the ship now pitching downwards as much as it had pitched up. The ship plummeted down the far side, accelerating at a shocking rate before the bow dug into the water at the bottom with a massive splash. Meru caught a glimpse as the water rolled up the deck, submerging it.

He saw Coran spare him a glance, his grip tight on the wheel. The engines whined as they came out of the water and then dug in.

Boiling froth smashed into the wheelhouse. The glass held for a moment, but it shattered under the pressure and the wheelhouse was submerged in moments. Meru lost his grip and was hammered backwards in the raging torrent. Stars spun in his vision.

* * *

Kiri shrieked as the ship tilted upwards. Both she and Zoella were tossed from the bed and thrown to the floor, which became a wall. They tumbled sideways, only to see Fitch sliding along the corridor, yelling and screaming obscenities.

Water splashed around them. The bed came loose and crashed about them eliciting another scream from Kiri. The ship groaned and began to tilt the other way, everything loose in the cabin rolling and tumbling about them. Kiri was panicking now, thrashing around in delirium and utter fear. The ship rolled forward, throwing them to the floor and then on to the opposite wall. Zoella tried to stop them from being impaled by the metal frame of the bed as it swung, lurching around the room.

This is it … we're going down. After everything, this is what happens? Just drowned?

Fitch came sliding back in the opposite direction, managing to grab on to the door frame of the room, before disappearing again. Another torrent of water splashed through the hatchway, a deep moaning and cracking sound echoing through the hull. The lights flickered and failed.

Kiri howled in the darkness.

Zoella grabbed her and pulled her close, there was nothing but unreasoning terror coming from her sister's mind.

Let it be quick … let it be quick …

More water sloshed into the room, rising fast. Zoella huddled down, wrapping her arms as tight as she could around her sister.

Waiting for the end.

* * *

'Queen Rihanna!'

Rihanna turned, stepping away from the balcony overlooking the city of Airea. It was Vandare, gasping and panting in a hurry.

'What is it?' she demanded.

'A ship,' he managed, wheezing after his run. 'A ship … spotted off the coast.'

'What kind of ship?' she asked.

'Not one of ours,' he said. 'It seems to have been driven out of the great storm to the sunward.'

'Made of metal?' Rihanna asked, a grin creasing her own expression.

'Why … yes.' Vandare answered.

'Show me.'

Vandare gestured out to sea, pointing to the sunward side of the bay beyond the city.

'There it is.'

Rihanna squinted. She could just make out a mark on the sea, grey, but flickering in the light of Lacaille.

'It's them,' she said. 'It must be. The ship from Amar with the maid aboard. What is it doing?'

'Even stranger,' Vandare replied. 'It appears to be adrift. It hasn't moved under its own power since we sighted it, and it is floating with the tide.'

This must be the Amaran vessel, if not the one we saw wreak devastation in that battle. I can capture it as Nerina commanded … I will have proved myself to her satisfaction.

'Send our vessels out to capture it,' Rihanna demanded. 'Make haste before it departs. I want it brought back to the harbour.'

Vandare nodded, took a deep breath and withdrew.

Rihanna stretched her thoughts out, seeking any sense of the woman she and Nerina had met on the quay in the Amaran city.

Yes, there is something there … a power … strong …

But there was something else, another presence, faint and unsure … but unmistakeable. A face came into Rihanna's mind. A face that was all too familiar.

Dark black hair, blue eyes.

It can't be … I saw her die! Drowned in the sea at Amar!

But the realisation grew stronger, a sense of horror and surprise.

Kiri!

She yelled out to her companions. Within moments their dachs took to the sky, sweeping out from the city of Airea and across the glittering sea.

* * *

'Meru!'

Meru felt someone slap his face.

'Ow! Hey!'

He blinked, spitting out salty water from his mouth.

'He's alive too.'

Meru recognised Fitch's voice and opened his eyes.

'What …?'

Bright light glared in his vision … sunlight. Lacaille!

'We made it?' he managed to croak.

'We did,' Fitch said, hauling him to his feet. 'Not out of trouble yet though. Get up and help with repairs.'

Meru scrambled to his feet. He was still in the wheelhouse, the last thing he remembered was the crashing descent after the wave. Now the sky was clear and blue, the sea flat and calm. He looked around seeing a bank of cloud to the sunward. He followed Fitch out.

The *Mobilis*' deck was a mess. Meru could see that the main mast behind the wheelhouse had disappeared, taking with it much of the plating. The mesh sails that powered the ship had been pulled up and ripped out, they were a tangled mess. Just beyond where it had stood, the flying machine was still lashed down, but Meru could see dents in its fuselage. Looking towards the bow, the forward mast was bent and broken, the other set of mesh sails torn and twisted, also hanging out of their storage slots in disarray.

'Oh no …'

'Check that flying machine,' Fitch yelled. 'We might need it.'

'Is everyone …?'

'Everyone's alive,' Fitch shouted back. 'For now. Flying machine, jump to it boy!'

Meru staggered across the deck, seeing the ripped and slashed remains of the cables that had secured the rear mast, only a few ragged pieces remained. There was a huge gash in the decking where the mast had once been attached. Two hatch covers for the engines were buckled and bent. Neither engine was turning. The *Mobilis* was adrift.

Looking around him Meru was surprised to see land off the starboard side of the ship. It was someway distant, perhaps seven or eight marks. He could make out something else, some kind of regular structure. It was hard to see.

A port? A city maybe? Where are we?

They had to be somewhere off the coast of Taloon. He remembered the general features of the map shadeward from the zone of the vortex.

He clambered over to the flying machine, unlocking the door and climbing inside. He switched on the onboard systems and was relieved to find everything was working. They'd been lucky. By the looks of the damage the mast had swung out over the starboard side of the ship before it detached. If it had fallen astern it would have smashed the flying machine to smithereens.

'Systems online,' Sandra's disembodied voice called.

'Sandra, check everything,' Meru instructed.

'All systems are functioning normally,' Sandra replied. 'Minor external damage is noted, non-critical.'

'Keep this machine ready for immediate departure,' Meru instructed, climbing out and securing the door before running up the deck. The *Mobilis* was sitting low in the water; he could see the bow was submerging in the slight swell.

No one else was on deck, so he jumped down through the hatch.

'What's …?'

'Get them up on deck!'

Coran's voice echoed up and down the corridor. Before him Meru could see Zoella pulling Kiri's sodden and lifeless body along with her. He ran to help her.

'She'll be alright,' Zoella said, as he helped hoist Kiri up. Meru heard Kiri moan, she was muttering something unintelligible. Her kai was held tight in her hand.

'She was so ill,' Zoella said. 'Then being thrown around and soaked …'

Together they got Kiri up and out on to the deck. She was pale and slumped where they had left her, but gasping for breath in the breeze, already looking a little better.

'I'll take her from here,' Zoella said. 'You need to help out below, doesn't sound good.'

Meru nodded. 'Get yourselves to the back of the ship near the flying machine.'

Zoella nodded and he jumped into the *Mobilis*, running forward.

'Coran, the bow's awash,' he yelled.

'We know!' Mel's voice shouted back.

Meru ran down to the far end, peering down into the hatchway that led down into the forward hold. Below him, Daf and Creg were hammering at one of the bulkheads while Coran, Fitch and Mel looked on. The water in the hold was up to their waists and rising. A stream of it was pouring in from where Meru could see a buckled cross beam.

As Meru watched the water flowed over the batteries all stacked in neat lines in the lower section of the hold. Mel was leaning against Coran. He was holding her, her head cradled against his chest.

As he watched the stream of water slowed to a trickle. Daf and Creg put down their hammers, both looking weary. Meru could hear Mel sobbing.

'Everyone up on deck,' Coran called, his voice heavy.

* * *

The dachs had gained altitude, now high above the sea. Rihanna could see the dark hulk of the Amaran ship below and in front.

She clenched her eyes shut, feeling the dach between her thighs.

Nerina!

The answer was swift.

Rihanna? News?

News indeed! The ship has returned, I fly to take it now.

The girl, Zoella? She is aboard?

Yes, but there is something else you will wish to know.

There was a pause in their communication. Rihanna sensed the puzzlement from the other end.

What?

She lives.

It can't be …

It is! It's her! Kiri is alive and on that ship!

Glee and cruel laughter erupted across the link.

Bring her! The joy of seeing her humbled before us. Bring her to me!

* * *

Coran vaulted up on deck, Mel just behind him. Kiri was lying nearby rolled up in some blankets, her head resting in Meru's lap, she seemed to be unconscious, her kai still clutched in her hand. Zoella sat alongside them, with Daf and Creg beside her, both looking exhausted. Fitch was leaning against the wheelhouse, his clothing drying in the warmth of Lacaille above.

Coran spoke to Mel before they both turned and walked to the rest of the crew. Mel had dried her eyes, but she sat down without making eye contact with anyone.

'Right,' Coran said, with a heavy sigh, crouching down amidst them. 'This is how it is. The good news is we're clear of the storm, but that's as far as that goes. Now the bad news. Stern mast is gone and took the coils with it, front mast is a useless mess. The forward batteries are awash and the rear ones are just about keeping the pumps running, but they won't last for long. Once they stop …'

Coran saw Zoella look at him in surprise.

'You don't mean …'

Coran nodded.

'So,' he said. 'We need to get everyone off. Looks to be land not too far away, so we get the flying machine ready. It can't carry all of us at once, so that means we need at least two trips, plus the rifles and anything else valuable aboard. Meru, you're flying.'

'Wait a minute,' Meru said. 'Maybe the flying machine can tow the *Mobilis* to shore, at least beach her …'

'Too dangerous,' Coran said. 'The ship might go down with the cable attached.'

'Then let's take the charging technology from the flying machine and power the engines and the pumps,' Meru said.

Mel looked up.

'Meru, it won't work,' she said. 'Took me, Daf and Creg two full stretches with quayside cranes to plug the batteries into the *Mobilis* and wire it all up, let alone try and fix some other tech we don't even know about. We don't have the tools and we don't have the time. The ship is too badly damaged.'

'But …' Meru said, looking around at the decks. 'The *Mobilis* … she can't …'

'She can,' Mel said, her expression distraught. Meru saw her clench her eyes tight shut. 'And she will.'

'She got us through the storm,' Coran said. 'She gave us everything she had, kept us all alive, got us this far. But nothing's going to stop her foundering now.'

Meru's mouth fell open, but he didn't say anything else. He shook his head. Only the faint sound of pumps churning away and the gentle lapping of the water reached their ears. The crew looked at each other hopelessly.

'Now. Time's wasting,' Coran said. 'Get that …'

Kiri leapt up and gave an ear-splitting shriek. The crew jumped back in shock, Creg nearly tumbling off the side of the deck. Kiri's face was drained of colour and her eyes were wide and dark with fear.

'She's here! She's coming!'

'Scorchin' snuts girl!' Fitch cursed at her. 'What in …?'

'She's coming!' Kiri yelled again, her distress plain to see. She turned around and gestured towards the shoreline, pointing with a shaking arm and outstretched finger. Everyone looked where she was pointing.

'Kiri's there's nothing …'

'No there is,' Fitch said, standing up and shielding his eyes to get a better view.

'What is it?'

'Don't rightly know,' Fitch said, getting to his feet and vaulting up to the wheelhouse. He returned with the 'scope, opening it up and putting it to his eye.

'Dachs!' he yelled. 'Riders on them, looks like three of them. There's a pair of ships coming too.'

'Dachs? Ships?' Mel asked, her face pale. 'Priestesses?'

'Everybody up!' Coran yelled. 'Fitch, grab the rifles!'

The crew scrambled to their feet. Kiri was unsteady, but staring out to sea with a haunted expression on her face.

'Who is coming?' Zoella asked her. 'Kiri, who is it?'

Kiri blinked and looked at her. 'It's Rihanna. That must be Airea. She's sensed us …'

Zoella looked up, seeing the dark spots above the sea marking the position of the dachs. She concentrated, focusing her thoughts …

Yes, three of them … I can hear their thoughts …

Both of you! So you're not dead after all then, Kiri. I'm pleased. I want to take your life myself!

You will not hurt her!

A brief blast of surprise rippled across the link before it dissolved into glee.

So you're the maid, the maid from Viresia! Both of you are here. Lacaille's will be done! So, Kiri is weak, is she? Both of you will be captives of Drayden this stretch.

The link broke.

Feet clumped along the decks of the ship. Zoella turned to see that the rest of the crew had returned, each of them holding one of the rifles and loading them with the small cartridges Meru had once shown her.

'It's definitely Rihanna,' Zoella said. 'One of the priestesses we were warned about … we're just off the coast of Taloon … that's definitely Airea over there …'

'Our luck really stinks,' Meru grimaced.

Within moments, everyone save Kiri and Zoella had a rifle ready.

'If you can stop them striking us down with their mental tricks,' Coran said, hoisting his rifle up. 'We may stand a chance.'

'We'll try,' Zoella said, looking across to Kiri. Kiri nodded, she looked pale and uncertain, only just able to stand, propping herself up with her kai.

The dachs were high in the sky above them now, still far out of range.

'Checking us out,' Coran said, squinting as he looked upwards.

'They'll already know we're in trouble,' Fitch said, eyeing the bow of the *Mobilis* as the surf washed across it. 'And those ships are heading right for us too.'

Coran looked towards the coast, seeing the pair of wooden vessels drawing closer. Oars were dipping in and out of the water as they approached.

'Man o' war,' he muttered. 'Boarding parties I reckon. Be here in under a spell.'

Above, the dachs were descending in a lazy spiral. They formed up in a formation at the stern of the ship, hovering there before approaching.

'Looks like they want to talk,' Coran muttered as the dachs drew closer. 'Fitch, you ready?'

Fitch nodded.

Coran gestured for everyone else to stay back and then walked around the flying machine to the stern with Fitch alongside, looking up at the woman perched on the dach in the air before him. Her bright red hair was fanned out all around her head. He recognised her from the attack on Amar.

'Captain Coran I believe,' she said.

'Yeah, that's me,' Coran replied. 'What's your business with us?'

'I am Rihanna of Drayden, Queen of Taloon,' she replied. 'It looks to me as if your ship is in trouble, Captain Coran. The sailors from Taloon will soon be here, I can have them take you to safety.'

'Really,' Coran replied. 'And what would you want in exchange for such generosity?'

'You will give Kiri and her maid to me,' Rihanna replied. 'The rest of you will be taken to Airea.'

'To be locked up or executed no doubt,' Coran said to Rihanna. 'Not much of an offer.'

'Take it or leave it,' Rihanna replied. 'I'm not the one standing on a sinking ship.'

'I've got a better idea,' Coran said.

Fitch moved fast. His rifle was aimed in a blur of motion, the heavy crack of the shot echoing out across the sea. His aim was good, but Rihanna must have sensed it coming as her dach rolled aside just in time, the bullet hitting it in the neck rather than Rihanna's chest. The dach howled in pain and crashed downwards.

Coran stumbled as the huge reptilian creature landed on the stern of the *Mobilis* making the deck tilt under his feet. Behind him he heard the others yell and fall. Water splashed around him. More screams filled the air, the other dachs diving downwards.

'Shoot them!' he yelled. 'Everyone, fire!'

Before he could get his footing a blow caught him under the chin and threw him through the air to lie dazed on the deck. A shadow fell across him.

Rihanna stood poised above him, her right hand holding a staff to his throat.

'Stupid man.'

'No!'

Coran heard another scream, this time from behind him. He rolled aside to see Kiri charge forward, her kai in her hand, swinging it at Rihanna. Rihanna's staff came up to block the move. Then they were duelling. Coran rolled out of the way of their spinning staffs, casting about for his rifle.

The two other priestesses had jumped down from above on to the decks on the other side of the flying machine. Coran heard yells and blows falling as they took on the crew of the *Mobilis.*

His rifle was lodged in the scuppers. He grabbed at it, twisting it around and trying to turn it on the new arrivals. Leaving Kiri to her fight with Rihanna he ran around the flying machine to see that Mel had been knocked down already, Daf was down too, but Creg seemed to be holding his own with one of them. Fitch and Meru were backing up, trying to raise their rifles when Zoella pushed between them, arm outstretched.

The nearest priestess grabbed at her head in sudden pain, screeching. Both rifles fired. Blood splattered the woman's chest and she fell backwards into the water off the side of the ship, her kai spiralling away into the sea.

'Yes!' Fitch yelled. 'Finally got one of the bitches!'

The other priestess had knocked Creg down with a vicious blow with her own staff, but not before Fitch was able to bring his rifle around again. But the priestess was moving fast, she knocked Meru down and turned on Zoella. Coran saw Zoella duck one blow, but a second caught her and sent her sprawling. Another gunshot blasted out as Fitch fired again, the priestess yelled and collapsed against the wheelhouse to lie still, her staff falling from her hands and disappearing overboard. Fitch turned his rifle on the dachs above him, despatching the flying creatures.

Fitch turned about, trying to train his rifle on Rihanna. The flying machine was in the way.

Rihanna and Kiri were still duelling on the aft deck, their staffs a blur of motion.

'No!' Coran yelled. 'Not from here. You'll hit Kiri …'

Then both of them yelled as Rihanna's mental power surged through them, a crushing pain flashing across their skulls. Their rifles clattered to the decking.

* * *

Kiri and Rihanna fought, strike for strike, counter against counter, neither of them making any headway against the other. They stepped back after a moment, glaring at each other.

'So guttersnipe,' Rihanna said. 'Just you and me, like old times.'

Kiri adjusted her footing, sparing a brief glance over her shoulder. Both the other priestesses were dead. She could see the crew of the *Mobilis* were also down, dead or injured. Kiri could feel Rihanna's use of the gift, it was strong, buzzing around her. She could taste hot metal in the air.

'You can't fight all of us,' Kiri answered, catching her breath, panting hard.

'Oh I can,' Rihanna said. 'I'm stronger than you now, they're all mine to do with as I want.'

'I'll kill you first!'

'You're the one that's supposed to be dead,' Rihanna continued. 'Nerina will be pleased to see you again, slum girl.'

Kiri's lip curled, but she didn't answer.

'Thrown yourself in with these Amarans have you?' Rihanna said. 'Betrayed your people?'

'You betrayed me,' Kiri answered. 'Or don't you remember your lies?'

'All I remember is you trying to worm your way into Nerina's affections,' Rihanna said. 'I saw through you, so did Nerina. You were never one of us.'

'And I'm glad of it!' Kiri snapped, spinning her kai and striking again. The two women wrestled back and forth again, trading blows.

But Kiri was tired; tired from lack of sleep, exhaustion and sickness. Rihanna was not. A blow caught Kiri on the temple and sent her spinning.

Rihanna kicked Kiri's kai aside, her own poised at Kiri's throat. Rihanna's other hand was outstretched towards her. Kiri felt the mental grip around her mind tighten.

'I'm going to take your gift,' Rihanna hissed at her. 'And the maid's. Who cares about Nerina now? This is my chance!'

Kiri struggled, trying to get to her feet, but the mental grip was tight and binding.

'The rest of them will die, oh, apart from that boy of yours …' Rihanna licked her lips. 'He'll be mine. I'll have some fun with him before I throw him away. Think about that …'

'No!'

Kiri howled in rage, slamming out with the last vestiges of her own power. Rihanna reeled back, overwhelmed by the sudden furious attack. Kiri grabbed Rihanna's staff and vaulted up, wrenching it from Rihanna's hands. She whirled it around with deadly force. The blow caught Rihanna in the side of the neck before the kai was wrenched from Kiri's hands and lost overboard. Rihanna crumpled to the deck.

Kiri found herself on top of her enemy, her hands at her neck, tightening … crushing. Rihanna tried to wrestle her grasp away.

'You'll never take him! Never, never, never!'

Kiri pulled back, pounding Rihanna's head into the decking over and over again. Rihanna struggled to get free, but Kiri's attack was frenzied.

Rihanna choked and then her grip went slack, her eyes staring sightlessly upwards.

Kiri fell to one side, weariness surging up her body. Then everything went black.

* * *

Coran and Fitch were released as Kiri's blow felled Rihanna. Coran was first up, grabbing his rifle and sprinting forward, leaping past the flying machine and on to the rear deck. Rihanna had fallen awkwardly, her head at an odd angle. Kiri was slumped alongside. He grabbed her and pulled her from the edge, cradling her in his arms.

Fitch bent down to look at Rihanna.

'Dead,' he said. 'Kiri killed her.'

Coran saw Kiri's eyes open for a moment, but then they rolled up in her head and her body went slack in his arms.

Coran grabbed Kiri's kai and then carried Kiri back and laid her out in the middle of the deck. Behind him Fitch was checking the others. He'd got Meru and Zoella to sit up, both looked bruised but otherwise unhurt.

'Grab this and help Kiri,' Coran called at them, chucking the kai at Meru before staggering down the decks towards the wheelhouse.

Mel was being looked after by Daf and Creg, who seemed to have shrugged off the attack. Mel's face was a mess, with a nasty cut and a black eye already starting to swell.

'Did we get them?' she managed.

'Aye,' Coran said. 'Dealt with.'

'More trouble inbound,' Fitch yelled, gesturing to starboard.

Half a mark away the two Taloon vessels were bearing down on them, their oars dipping into the water in a precise and rhythmic way. Both would be on them in moments. They were close together, a ship's width apart.

Coran looked at them and then glanced up and down the *Mobilis*. Meru and Zoella were tending to Kiri who was still unconscious.

'Meru!' he yelled.

Meru was still holding Kiri's kai in his hands, he looked dazed.

'Get that flying machine ready to take off,' Coran instructed.

Meru nodded and turned around, staggering towards the flying machine.

'We can't fight off those ships,' Mel said. 'And we can't all get aboard …'

Coran scanned the sea towards the shore, watching the approaching vessels. He turned to look at Mel.

'What's left in those batteries?' he asked.

'Not much,' Mel said. 'The pumps will run for a couple more spells, that's about it.'

'What about the engines?'

Mel stared at him.

'The engines?' She answered, with a frown. 'Hardly anything. I don't know, a few turns …' Then her expression changed. 'Not that again …'

'Yes, that again,' he said.

'But …'

'Fitch,' Coran yelled. 'Get the rifles and all the cartridges to you can find and give them to Meru. Then get the front hatches up and open every crate of rockets you've got left.'

'All of them?' Fitch asked.

'Every last one,' Coran said. 'Daf, Creg, help Mel get the engines running.'

The two big men obeyed their orders without question, helping Mel up and carrying her across the deck towards the rear of the ship. They pulled the engine covers open. Mel lowered herself down.

Fitch bundled up the rifles and hauled up two boxes of cartridges.

Coran heard a rising hum from the flying machine and looked around to see Meru stepping back towards him. Coran saw him frown as he passed the open engine covers.

'What are we doing?' Meru asked.

'We are not doing anything,' Coran said. 'You are taking that machine up and getting Kiri and Zoella safely out of here along with all the weapons you can carry.'

Meru stared at him.

'What?' he answered back. 'No! What about you?'

'We're going to deal with those ships so you have a chance to escape.'

'Coran ...'

'Not arguing you with, Meru!' Coran snapped, pointing a finger at him. 'Esurio depends upon them. Get those girls to safety. That's your job, understand me?'

Meru looked at him, bewildered, then he looked at the approaching ships. He could see archers crowding the bows. They'd be in range in moments.

'Now Meru!' Coran yelled.

'Come on boy,' Fitch said, pushing him along.

'Mel?' Meru asked as he was shoved past.

Mel looked up and gave him a smile.

'Captain's orders,' she said. 'You know what's what. Fly safe, yeah?'

Meru swallowed. Fitch shoved him hard in the back and he staggered to the flying machine. Together he and Fitch stowed the kai, rifles and cartridges in the rear compartment.

'That'll about do it,' Fitch said, staring at him, his voice rough. 'Now get those girls and get yourself out of here.'

Meru looked at him, unable to form any words.

'We'll be alright, you'll see,' Fitch said, with a grin. 'Here, take this.' He pulled off his battered wide-brimmed hat and thrust it at Meru. Fitch's head was bald, with thin wisps of grey hair, waving in the breeze.

'Fitch …' Meru stuttered.

'For luck, right?' Fitch chuckled, grabbing the hat and pushing it hard on to Meru's head.

Then with a wink, he was striding away.

Meru limped across the rear deck, tripping and sprawling near Zoella and Kiri.

'We've got to go!' he yelled. 'The flying machine, now!'

'What about–?' Zoella began.

'No time. Help me with Kiri.'

Kiri's body was a dead weight. Between them they managed to hoist her up, carry her to the flying machine and push her into the rear compartment.

'Get in!'

Meru pushed Zoella into the passenger seat and slammed the door behind her. Then he took a knife from his belt and cut at the ropes that lashed the machine to the deck plates. As he did so he heard the thrum of the engines through the ship, saw Mel raise her head and give Coran a thumbs up gesture. Coran ran for the wheelhouse, spinning the wheel around.

The crippled *Mobilis* began to turn.

Meru continued to hack at the ropes, severing each one in turn. Arrows pinged of the fuselage next to him as the Taloon ships came in range.

The machine was free. It shifted on the deck, sliding to one side. He heard Zoella yell from inside.

He grabbed the other two rifles he could see on the deck and threw them into the rear compartment, pulling the sliding door closed. Then he jumped into the pilot's seat, flipping switches.

The engines of the flying machine spun up in readiness.

He pulled on the controls.

He saw Mel, Daf and Creg looking up at him as the machine lifted off.

Mel was shouting something, but he couldn't hear it over the noise. Fitch was already working down near the bow. He saw Coran turn and snap a salute before retreating into the wheelhouse.

The flying machine rose and turned away.

* * *

The *Mobilis* swung around until it was pointing bow first towards the oncoming Taloon vessels. Coran spun the helm back to its centre point and pushed the throttles forward to their stops. The engines ground their way up to speed, their normal sound muted and sluggish as the remaining batteries were drained of their last stores of power.

The *Mobilis*' bow rose above the water and the battered vessel surged ahead.

Coran looked aft to see the flying machine lifting off and banking away, arrows from the Taloon ship flickering past it to no avail. More arrows peppered the wheelhouse, he ducked instinctively. Mel, Daf and Creg ran towards him, Mel jumping up to the wheelhouse.

Coran heard Fitch yell and saw him fall from the forward deck hatch, an arrow embedded in his shoulder. His hat was missing.

'Daf, Creg!' Coran yelled. 'Help Fitch!'

The big men lurched forward amidst the hail of arrows, both were struck, but shrugged off the impacts, still running forward. The flying machine roared overhead.

The *Mobilis* was accelerating now, the bow driving a wall of froth before it.

Too late, the Taloon helmsmen realised what Coran's intention was. The wooden vessels turned aside, but there was no time. Coran swung the helm hard over and the *Mobilis* veered into one of the ships.

More arrows. Coran felt one pierce his arm and heard a screech from Mel behind him.

The flanks of the Taloon vessel were crushed; splinters and broken planks flew from the impact. The Taloon archers were tossed into the air, down into the sea or back into their ship. The bow of the *Mobilis* crumped, the forward deck plates shearing off with a horrendous screech of tortured metal. Coran and Mel were thrown forward as the whole forward infrastructure of the ship buckled. The mast of the Taloon vessel snapped and crashed down into the sea, rigging flailing in all directions.

With a groan of flooding compartments, the *Mobilis* began to founder.

* * *

Fitch had barely managed to hang on during the impact. Had it not been for Daf and Creg he'd have been flung overboard. The two big men hauled him back. The deck was submerging under their feet, the water rising towards the *Mobilis'* forward cargo hatch. Soldiers from the beleaguered Taloon vessel surged over the gunwales of their ruined ship, cutlasses in their hands, yelling at the top of their lungs. They saw Fitch, Daf and Creg and scrambled towards them. The other Taloon vessel was close, turning in from the starboard side also full of soldiers ready to board them.

'Too late for that fellas,' Fitch said, with a wry grin.

He pulled something from his pocket, flicking it in his hand. A flame burnt from the device, bright and fierce.

He raised his other hand. Daf and Creg grabbed it.

'Been a pleasure boys,' he said. Daf and Creg grunted in acknowledgement.

Fitch tossed the device into the cargo hatch before him.

* * *

Coran saw the cataclysmic explosion. Smoke, decking and spinning pieces of flaming debris showered down as a vast plume of black smoke erupted upwards. Glass smashed before him and he was thrown back by the force of the blast, the shattered remains of the instruments cast about him. The roof of the wheelhouse was blown clean away. Debris rained down amidst the flame and smoke. Fires swept through the ruin burning and fierce. He could see nothing through the smoke.

The *Mobilis* reared beneath him, he saw the stern disappear under the waves for a brief moment as the ship rocked with the impact.

Mel!

She was crying with pain, an arrow protruding out of her chest. Coran pulled another out of his shoulder and knelt down beside her. Blood was flowing freely.

'You've got to ...' she gasped, choking.

Coran shook his head.

'Not leaving you,' he said. 'Not ever.'

She raised her arms, gesturing for him.

He hoisted her up, holding her as gently as he could. Both peered over the remains of the wheelhouse and through the flames.

Of Fitch, Daf and Creg there was no sign. Both Taloon ships were in pieces, ablaze. They could see a few men struggling in the water. The front hull of the *Mobilis* was nothing more than twisted wreckage, sinking as they watched, aflame all the way down to the waterline.

Coran braced both of them as *Mobilis* tilted forward, sea water surging towards them up the twisted decks. The ship's structure groaning as its stern reared up behind them.

As he watched, the remains of the forward decks submerged, the ship settling in the water.

Coran turned to look at Mel, pulling her close to him as water rose around their feet, struggling against the tilt. The flames hissed out around them, replaced with thick black smoke and jets of steam.

'Fitch was right,' he said, looking into her eyes. 'There's stuff I should have told you.'

Mel smiled at him.

'I knew.'

* * *

Meru watched in horror as the *Mobilis* rammed into the Taloon vessel. He saw Fitch, saw Daf and Creg nearby, saw the light and realised what Fitch was going to do.

'Fitch, no …'

Flame and smoke erupted from the forward deck of *Mobilis*, the conflagration rising into the sky and blotting out everything. A wave of air rattled the flying machine, jolting it around wildly before Meru managed to get it under control.

By the time he had done so and turned the machine back the smoke was clearing, drifting aside from the ruined forward hull of the *Mobilis*. He banked the machine around to get a better view. Zoella was staring out of the windows in horror.

Both of the Taloon ships were nothing more than smashed timbers. The *Mobilis* was going down by the bow, its stern rising up into the sky, the twin propellers still spinning in opposite directions, their blades flashing in the light of Lacaille as the ship tilted.

'No … Coran … Mel!' she screamed. 'Get out …'

Neither Zoella nor Meru could turn their eyes away as they saw the wheelhouse submerge, water cascading into the engine room housings and hatchways. Plumes of thick black smoke belched from the ship. There was no sign of Coran or Mel. Water spurted from the decks in huge sprays; planks and panels snapped and twisted as they were blown out from below, spiralling into the air before crashing down on the surface of the sea. Crackles of 'tricity flickered around the hull before fading away.

The *Mobilis*' propellers shuddered to a stop as the stern rose vertically in the water. For a moment the ship hung there, unmoving, as if resisting its final plunge.

Then it went down in a hiss of spray and a groan of tortured metal. Bubbling froth erupted around the beleaguered ship before it finally slipped below the waves.

The surface of the sea churned and then was still.

The *Mobilis* and her crew were gone.

CHAPTER FIFTEEN

Airea, Capital of Taloon

Round 2307, Tenth pass

Waves were lapping at the beach, crystal clear waters sloshing up a sloped white-sand shore. A hundred hands inland a machine stood on a tricycle undercarriage, stubby wings protruding from each side, a number of curious dents in its fuselage. A track carved in the sand indicated it had come down hard and gouged a path before it had come to rest. Down its flank, doors were open.

Collapsed in the sand, three figures were crouched together, heads bowed.

Zoella was sobbing, her head down, her hair fallen forward. Meru sat alongside, his head was also lowered and he was turning a battered wide-brimmed hat around and around in his hands. Kiri sat next to him, hunched up, staring into the distance, her face pale and haggard, one arm entwined with his.

Lacaille was bright above them, its face clear of the spots that had plagued it in recent passes. Their shadows stretched across the sand, the heat intense.

The three of them sat there for a spell or more, unable to frame words or thoughts.

'It not possible,' Kiri whispered. 'That ship was so big … so strong … no one got out?'

Kiri hadn't seen the *Mobilis* founder. She'd been unconscious in the rear of the flying machine.

Meru and Zoella didn't answer, the image of the sinking ship that had been their home burnt into their minds, the loss of their friends too shocking to accept.

'It can't be true,' Zoella managed to say. 'It just can't.'

'Zoella …' Kiri began.

'We shouldn't have come back through the storm so soon,' Zoella said, wiping at her tears. 'We should have waited … fixed the ship better …'

'It was Coran's decision,' Meru countered. 'He was the captain … he made the call …'

'But we forced him,' Zoella said. 'All our talk of taking on the priestesses … those stupid plans! The priestesses didn't know where we were. We could have waited!'

Kiri shook her head. 'And risk letting them invade Amar unchallenged? No …'

'We could have taken more time,' Zoella said, leaning forward and fixing Kiri with a frown. Kiri shook her head.

'No,' Kiri said. 'Coran was right, we had to check whether they were ready. But we came out of the storm too near to Airea …'

'We shouldn't have come out there at all,' Zoella continued. 'Why were we there? We should have been further out at sea.'

'It was an accident,' Kiri answered.

Zoella turned on Kiri. 'Accident … yeah. If we'd been further out then Rihanna wouldn't have known we were there, we might have had time to get everyone off!'

'We didn't have any choice where we ended up,' Kiri snapped, her expression hardening. 'And it's not my fault she sensed us … what are you saying? That I deliberately gave us away?'

'Well, did you?' Zoella cried, glaring at her. 'It was real convenient she was there …'

'How dare you …'

'Stop it!' Meru shouted before Zoella could reply, holding up his hands, palms outwards. 'Both of you. This isn't helping.'

Kiri subsided, but Zoella threw off Meru's arm, got to her feet and stomped off.

'Zoella …'

She ignored him and flung herself down into the sand a few paces away, her back to them both, her arms wrapped around her knees, head down. They could hear her sobs.

Meru went to follow her, but Kiri stopped him.

'Don't.'

'But …'

'Let her be,' Kiri said, her voice soft. 'All she needs is a bit of space … and some time.'

Meru sighed. 'There isn't time. We can't stay here. If we're found …'

'I know,' Kiri said. 'But we … we can't go on right now. We're all broken … hurting … There's no food, no water …'

Meru put down the hat and rubbed his forehead.

'We should have been able … to get …' he stuttered. 'Get everyone off before the ship sank … if I'd …'

'You can't blame yourself for what went wrong,' Kiri said. 'You got us out. We're alive. I'm grateful for that.'

Meru looked across at her.

'If we'd just had a bit more time,' he said. 'We could have saved everyone, maybe even the ship too.'

'Meru … you mustn't blame yourself.'

'They took me in you know,' he said, 'after my own ship sank. I would have drowned if they hadn't found me. Coran was … more of a father to me than mine ever was. Mel taught me everything I know about these machines. Fitch … well, took a while to get alongside him but …'

He raised Fitch's hat and turned it around again, as if looking for something.

Kiri squeezed his arm. 'They were good people. They took me in too … and you know they really didn't have to. I'll always remember that. Always be thankful.'

Meru shook his head, looking up at the distant horizon for a moment. He looked around at her. 'I don't even know Coran's favourite food, or Mel's favourite music … or where Fitch came from … Daf and Creg … I hardly knew them … hardly even talked to them! You just think people are always going to be there so … I should know … they were …'

His voice broke. Tears streamed, hot and scalding, down his cheeks. He sobbed. Kiri put her arms around him and pulled him close. She let him cry, her own eyes filled with tears.

'You remember I told you about Charis?' Kiri asked after his cries subsided. 'I didn't know her long, not really … just a few passes. She taught me everything, everything I value now anyway. For a long time I thought she was wrong, stupid, boring … she'd have been so upset with some of the things I did afterwards, but … I never forgot her. I can still hear her, her soft voice, calming me down, setting me straight. They're really not gone you know …'

Meru looked up at her and nodded. Kiri kissed him on the forehead.

'Remember the best of them,' Kiri said. 'It's the only way.'

Meru swallowed and nodded.

'You're right,' he said, wiping at his eyes. 'And you stopped that priestess …'

'Rihanna,' Kiri said with a shudder. 'Only just …'

'But you did,' Meru said. He looked over to Zoella. 'We'd better …'

Kiri nodded, standing up and helping him to his feet.

They both walked over to Zoella. She turned to look at them as they approached.

'I'm sorry,' Zoella said. 'That wasn't fair of me.'

'It's alright,' Kiri began.

'It's not,' Zoella said. 'The rage … it's still there. It flares up so fast … I don't want to hurt people and I keep …'

'I know,' Kiri said, crouching down next to her. Zoella pulled her into an embrace.

'I didn't mean it …'

Then Zoella was sobbing. Kiri held her tight.

'I can't lose any more people,' Zoella cried. 'I just can't bear it …'

Meru sat down alongside, putting his arms around both of them. They stayed that way until Zoella's sobs subsided and she pulled back, wiping her eyes.

'It's just us three now,' Meru said, looking at them. 'We're all that's left. It's up to us.'

'What are we going to do?' Zoella said. 'We can't go on alone.'

'We have to,' Kiri replied, her voice resolute. 'Rihanna's gone, there's only Nerina now. We can still stop her. We have to.'

'More fighting,' Zoella said, wiping at her face. 'More death … but how many more of us are going to die before this is finished? Our friends …'

Meru squeezed Zoella's arm.

'Kiri's right,' he said, his voice soft. 'Our friends … they allowed us to escape, bought us time. We can't waste the chance they gave us. This wasn't the plan … so we need a new one.'

'Nerina will know about me now … about us,' Kiri said, leaning forward to look at Zoella. 'Rihanna would have told her before she tried to take us.'

'What will she do?' Zoella asked.

Kiri thought for a moment. 'She'll try to find us. It won't be long before she finds out Rihanna's dead, if she doesn't know already. She'll fear one of us has taken Rihanna's gift, assume we'll challenge her. Every priestess will be searching for us.'

'Can she sense where you two are?' Meru asked, looking at Kiri and then Zoella.

'She's done it before,' Zoella said.

'Then we have to assume she knows,' Meru replied.

Zoella swallowed. 'But I stopped her last time. Maybe we can confuse her, keep her in the dark.'

'I can block her too,' Kiri said, glancing at the flying machine. 'At least for the moment. Safest to assume we can't stay still though. Better to keep moving.'

Meru thought for a moment.

'We still need time,' he said. 'If we go straight to Viresia now Nerina will attack before we're ready. We've got to get the ships from Amar, reinforcements … without the priestesses knowing about it.'

'So?' Kiri asked.

'Caesar,' Meru said. 'We have to get to Caesar. We can contact Amar on the way and tell them … tell them what …' Meru wasn't able to finish the sentence. He turned Fitch's hat around in his hands again.

'Will they come?' Zoella asked.

'They have to,' Meru answered, gesturing to the flying machine. 'Come on, we've got to get this thing fixed …'

A loud trumpeting call sounded behind them. All three of them turned and gasped.

Further inland they could see two enormous beasts lumbering towards them. They were huge, ponderous creatures with long necks. After a moment, a series of armed men could be seen accompanying them.

'What are those?' Meru asked, his mouth falling open.

'Phaunts,' Kiri said, swallowing. 'Those are the men of Taloon. They've found us!'

* * *

It cannot be!

Nerina blinked, her eyes struggling to focus on the empty hall of the priestesses' temple. Around her the dish-shaped oil burners still carried their flames. She was alone.

Rihanna, you fool!

Nerina slammed her fists down on the table before her. The thump echoed around the room.

The priestesses in Taloon were lost.

Rihanna dead … Taloon and Scallia at risk … and trouble here in Viresia. Why can they not just follow orders as directed? Fools!

Nerina paced around the hall, stepping on the sand-coloured tiles beneath her feet.

All of this was bad enough, but then the real shock coursed through her mind, almost impossible to countenance.

Kiri lives!

Nerina's mind was awhirl. Kiri had flung herself into the churning waters of Amar at the battle, drowned, so she had assumed. There had not been the faintest suggestion via the nexion that she had survived.

Even if she did, the Amarans should have killed her. She was their enemy. How can she have lived?

Rihanna's last communication had indicated that the mysterious maid, Zoella, they had seen in Viresia and Amar was with her. Somehow Kiri and Zoella had overpowered Rihanna and her other priestesses. Rihanna was gone.

And now they could be anywhere! Where would they go, what do they intend?

Nerina turned around, her cloak billowing outwards with the movement.

I know what Kiri will want. Vengeance! I know her well enough. The schemes, the arrogance, the determination and single-mindedness; I taught her after all. She has taken down Rihanna. She seeks to challenge me. She still schemes to be Empress! The slum-girl! The guttersnipe! What will she do? Surely she cannot hope to come to Daine and confront me here? Has she taken Rihanna's gift? What of the maid? How powerful are they now?

Nerina paced. There were too many unanswered questions.

Regardless, I will need more strength to overcome her. With Rihanna gone ...

She strode to the door, pulling the rope that rang the summoning bells.

The door opened and a servant walked in, bowing low.

Nerina looked down upon her.

'Send for Priestess Merrin,' Nerina said. 'I must speak to her immediately.'

* * *

Kiri, Meru and Zoella were surrounded by the armed men. There was no escape, there were at least thirty of them, all armed with vicious looking pikes. The phaunts stood further back. The three companions held their hands up.

A man, cloaked, leapt down from one of the phaunts and made his way towards them, pushing through the ranks of soldiers.

'So,' he said, his face still in shadow beneath his cowl. 'You live after all, priestess Kiri. They told me you had perished.'

Zoella and Meru looked at Kiri and then at the stranger. He lowered his cowl.

'Vandare!' Kiri exclaimed.

'You know him?' Meru asked.

'Yes, we're acquainted,' Vandare said to Meru before turning his attention to Kiri. 'I watched your altercation with our Queen with interest. Speak carefully as your next answers will determine both your fate and those of your companions.'

Kiri frowned. 'Queen? What queen?'

'Queen Rihanna,' Vandare replied.

'She was your queen?' Kiri asked, her face a mask of surprise. 'But … Karquesh?'

'Slain in your attack against Amar,' Vandare said. 'Rihanna was installed by your high priestess, flouting our traditions and lineage. You are the last of them.'

'Last?' Kiri asked. 'Last what? Last priestess?'

'It seems they were slain during the attack on your ship,' Vandare said. 'They failed to come back, all three of them.'

'Wait,' Meru said, pushing forward. 'Only three? Where are the others?'

'Gone,' Vandare said. 'Some trouble back in Drayden so it would seem. The others were summoned home.' He looked at Kiri. 'And with your death … the last of them will be gone. Taloon will belong to its people once more.'

The men about them readied their pikes.

'She's not with them,' Meru said. 'We're fighting to stop the priestesses! We're from Amar.'

'From Amar?' Vandare said, stepping forward.

'The priestesses and your fleet attacked our homeland,' Meru said.

'So we have you to thank for the destruction of our fleet,' Vandare said. He signalled to the soldiers around him. They raised their pikes.

'Stop it,' Zoella said, stepping forward between Kiri and Meru. 'Enough people have died these past stretches, let's not add more to this stupidity.'

'And who are you?' Vandare demanded.

'I am Zoella, a princess of Scallia,' Zoella said, straightening to look Vandare in the eye. 'Exiled by the priestesses from my own homeland. They attacked and razed my city. I know well their wrath!'

'Scallia, Amar and Drayden,' Vandare said, looking around at the three of them. 'Quite the mix. But no reason not to be rid of you all.'

'We have all been wronged by the priestesses,' Zoella said. 'Don't you see? We share a common enemy. Fighting amongst ourselves will only aide them. Amar, Scallia, Taloon, even Drem ... together we have a chance to stop then, apart we will all die. Don't be a fool.'

Kiri and Meru looked around at Zoella in surprise. Vandare stepped back apace.

'A fool?' he asked.

'Yes,' Zoella continued. 'You know well enough what the priestesses are. They may have retreated for now, but they will be back. Can you stop them?'

Vandare's eyes narrowed.

'No,' Zoella said, shaking her head. 'You know you can't. But we can. Kill us and your chance to save your land from them is gone.'

The men about them shifted uneasily, waiting to see how Vandare would react.

'A princess of Scallia you say,' he said, looking over Zoella's dirty and torn clothing. 'We heard that your city had been sacked, but not that any escaped.'

'Some did,' Zoella said. 'Some remain. There is strength to resist, if we work together. Amar has defied them. Scallia could rise again, Taloon ...'

'Taloon will no longer bow the knee to Drayden,' Vandare growled, looking at Kiri.

Zoella stepped forward. 'Kiri is not your enemy,' she said. 'She herself was betrayed by the priestesses, she serves us now. She slew Rihanna and we intend to stop the high priestess Nerina. Will you hear us out, or not?'

Vandare regarded her for a long moment, glancing at Kiri and Meru. Then he gestured to his men. They lowered their pikes.

'It seems we have allies unlooked for,' he said. He turned to Kiri. 'You truly slew Rihanna?'

Kiri nodded. 'She was trying to capture Zoella and me … trying to take our powers.'

'But your ship,' Vandare said. 'It sank …'

The three companions looked downcast.

'You lost friends aboard,' Vandare said. They nodded.

'I am sorry for your loss. And our part in it. We were given orders to capture it by Rihanna under pain of death. And there was much death when we failed to please her.'

'We're sorry your ships were destroyed too,' Zoella said. 'And the loss of those aboard.'

'You said there were only three priestesses?' Meru asked. 'The others were gone?'

'Yes,' Vandare said. 'Three was trouble enough it seemed, but now … Taloon is free, at least for now.'

'We must speak urgently,' Zoella said. 'but we are hurt and tired …'

Vandare nodded.

'Yes,' he said. 'We will return to Airea. There we will decide on what is to be done.'

'There is one more thing,' Zoella said. 'Please … does Liana still live?'

'Liana?' Vandare said, looking at her. 'What is she to you?'

'Our cousin,' Zoella replied. 'Mine and Kiri's.'

'Your cousin?' Vandare said, looking at Zoella and then at Kiri. 'She was supposed to have been a queen of Scallia.'

'She was once,' Zoella said. 'It is a long story we don't have time for now. Does she ...?'

'She lives. If you can call it that. I will bring her to you once we are within the city.'

'Thank you,' Zoella answered.

Vandare frowned. 'Sisters, cousins, allegiances, royalty. Many stories need telling,' he said. He looked over to the flying machine. 'And what manner of device is that?'

'It is a flying machine,' Meru said. 'It is damaged, but fixable. We must ...'

'We will bring it back to the city,' Vandare said, gesturing to his men. 'For now, the three of you are coming with us. Take them and guard them closely!'

* * *

Zoella, Kiri and Meru had been escorted into the city of Airea. There they were taken into the central palace and assigned individual rooms and instructed to wash and dress. They were soon summoned back.

Kiri remembered the great dining hall where she had eaten with Karquesh and killed his cousin Taryen. Now Vandare sat in his place. Alongside him was Liana.

'Liana!' Zoella said, running towards her.

Liana did not respond.

'She says nothing and does little,' Vandare said. 'She will eat, wash, dress and sleep ... and that is all.'

Zoella stepped across from her.

'Liana ... it's me. It's Zoella.'

For a long moment Liana didn't move, but she raised her gaze until it locked on to Zoella.

'Zoella?'

Vandare gasped. 'But, how ...?'

'Yes, Liana,' Zoella replied. 'It's me.'

'Zoella,' Liana's voice was soft but sure.

Zoella stared into Liana's eyes, but there was nothing there, no soul, no connection, no life. Ever since the attack on Viresia, Liana's mind had retreated and retreated until …

Zoella looked at Kiri. She saw her sister swallow and look away.

I know she never intended to take Liana's powers the way she did, and Liana tried to take hers and kill her … but now we know she's our cousin, how can we just leave her like this?

Zoella remembered how intimidated she'd been when first meeting Liana. The woman had been poised and confident. She'd grown up in the palace of Viresia, used to the trappings of the rich, never having had to do a stretch's manual work in her life.

How I envied her, and she was Queen of Scallia … yet now …

Liana was still a physical beauty, her skin toned and flawless, her blonde hair immaculate, but there was no life, no vivacity, no essence left of the woman she remembered.

Vandare coughed, Zoella looked up.

'Please sit,' Vandare said. 'We have much to discuss.'

He clapped his hands. Food and drink was brought in by servants and placed before them. The three companions were ravenous, tucking into the food.

'You did Taloon something of a service in the past,' Vandare said, looking at Kiri. 'Karquesh was quite relieved when you despatched Taryen. Stories of that altercation still make the rounds in our society.'

'Taryen?' Meru asked.

'The King's cousin,' Kiri replied, offhand. 'He challenged me. I killed him.'

Zoella and Meru looked at each other.

'And in doing so, ensured Taloon would align itself with the interests of Drayden,' Vandare continued.

'That was my mission,' Kiri said.

'And yet,' Vandare said, gesturing to Meru and Zoella. 'You are no longer working for the priestesses. Doesn't that make you a traitor?'

Kiri put down her knife and fork, and glared at Vandare.

'The priestesses betrayed me,' she said. 'They wanted only to ensure the destruction of Amar. Once that was achieved they planned to take my own power and kill me. Only their plans went awry.'

'There was a flare,' Meru said. 'During the attack. That's what swung the battle our way.'

Vandare nodded. 'We saw it here too, but we knew to take shelter from it. So what was your ship doing in our waters?'

Zoella spoke before the others could.

'We were scouting out your lands,' she said. 'We feared another attack. We wanted to know how long it would be before Taloon would be ready with another fleet to attack Amar.'

Vandare scrutinised Zoella for a long moment.

'So why did you enter the vortex?' Vandare asked.

Zoella swallowed.

'It is no use lying to me,' Vandare said. 'If you wish to live, tell the truth. It will serve you better.'

Zoella took a deep breath.

'The truth then,' she said, looking around at Kiri and Meru,

Vandare nodded.

'We sailed to the far sunward, through the vortex,' Zoella said. 'I was summoned there by a … complex machine called the Obelisk. It defends this world from Lacaille's flares. It needed to be fixed so … we fixed it.'

Vandare looked at her for a long moment.

'Perhaps I shouldn't have asked for the truth,' he said. 'I'd find your lies much more palatable.'

'Our ship was damaged by the return journey,' Zoella said, her expression pained, tears coming to her eyes. 'Our friends lost.'

'Though we did intend to pass Airea,' Meru said, in a whisper. 'To see the strength of your fleet, to see if Amar was under threat again.'

Vandare considered their words for long moments.

'And,' he said.' As you can see … we are not ready for another attack, much to the late Rihanna's chagrin. The delays, all instigated by me, almost cost me my life.'

'We appreciate your efforts,' Zoella said.

'So,' Vandare said, sitting back and folding his arms. 'What do you intend to do now?'

Meru and Kiri looked at Zoella.

'The priestesses must be stopped,' Zoella said, her voice calm. 'Once and for all.'

Vandare's eyes narrowed.

'By just the three of you?'

'We have allies,' Zoella said. 'Amar … more of these flying machines, and crews for them. Scallia will fight for us too, they have men at arms still in our city, Viresia. It is there we will go.'

'Should I let you,' Vandare said.

'You would be wise to,' Kiri said. 'You know my strength well enough … and Zoella's is greater.'

Vandare pursed his lips.

'I do not trust you, Priestess Kiri,' Vandare said. 'Your loyalty has switched at whim from what I can see …'

Kiri bristled, but Vandare raised his hand and looked at Zoella.

'But you,' he said. 'I could trust you. You're not a good liar, which commends you to me. Scallia and Taloon have much in common, maligned by these priestesses as we both have been. I would aid you to that end. We of Taloon know we cannot resist these priestesses on our own, and we have seen first-hand the disregard with which they have treated our people and lands. Thus, allying ourselves with those that would stand against them would seem to be the right course, if a dangerous one.'

'We require only that you let us go,' Zoella said, venturing a smile.

'It is not that simple,' Vandare replied. 'The priestesses will doubtless learn that we aided you in your escape. That will come down upon my people and I.'

'It will,' Zoella said. 'So it is best that you don't know what we plan to do.'

Vandare grinned.

'You are wise, Princess Zoella,' he said. 'But I need to weigh that choice against the risk of letting you go. Peace for Taloon might be better served by keeping you prisoner and handing you to the priestesses.'

Kiri bristled and Meru almost got to his feet. Zoella gestured for them to remain calm.

'I already know you won't,' Zoella said.

Vandare chuckled.

'And you are right,' he said. 'If you would tell me your plan, or as much of it as you can risk being found out.'

'Will you let us go?' Zoella asked. 'Regardless?'

Vandare smiled.

'Yes, Zoella of Scallia,' he said. 'I will.'

Zoella looked at Kiri and Meru, both nodded at her.

She took a deep breath.

'The priestesses are driven by their power,' Zoella said. 'Above all else, that is what they seek. It is an addiction. Nerina, the high priestess, seeks to take ours – we are the last ones left with power even close to her own. We intend to use that to entice her in.'

'To where?'

'To my city,' Zoella answered. 'To Viresia. Kiri and I will defend our warriors as best we can against the priestesses as they attack. The Amarans know how to use the flying machines to counter their dachs. That leaves only Nerina.'

'And then?'

'Then ...' Zoella said. 'That part I cannot say, for risk of Nerina knowing.'

Vandare rubbed his chin.

'You place us all at stake for this purpose,' Vandare said. 'If you win, the priestesses' reign is ended. If you lose, none will ever be able to stand against them.'

'Exactly,' Zoella said. 'We all win, or we all lose.' She folded her arms and looked at him.

Vandare let out a deep sigh.

‘So then. How might we aid you?’ he asked. ‘Viresia is hundreds of marks from here. Even if we began marching an army there now, we could not reach you inside a couple of passes at the earliest.’

‘This will be decided long before then,’ Zoella said. ‘Nerina will be searching for us already, she may know that we are here. The best thing you can do is to delay her if she comes looking. The more time we have …’

‘Dangerous indeed,’ Vandare said. ‘I have met this woman. She is brutal and callous. Once she sees deception. She will punish it.’

‘I do not want you to risk yourselves further,’ Zoella said.

‘But I did ask,’ Vandare said with a smile. ‘Taloon will play its part, for good or ill. If the priestesses come here, we will do what we can to occupy them.’

‘We must contact our people,’ Meru said. ‘The flying machine, will you allow me to go to it? I need to fix it.’

‘I will,’ Vandare said. He looked at Kiri and then at Zoella. ‘Will you vouch for her behaviour?’

Kiri gasped and looked outraged, but didn’t say anything.

‘I will,’ Zoella said. ‘She’s my sister.’

Vandare frowned, but then inclined his head.

‘I must ask one more thing,’ Zoella said, looking at Kiri before turning to Vandare. ‘On behalf of both of us.’

‘Ask away,’ Vandare said.

‘Liana is of my people,’ Zoella said. ‘She is Scallian. She should return there, but we cannot take her with us …’

‘She was the wife of King Karquesh,’ Vandare said. ‘Here in Taloon she will be given all the honour that position requires, until the after calls for her. She will be well cared for.’

‘I can ask no more of you,’ Zoella said. ‘I served her once and made a vow to defend her from harm. I would not like to break it.’

‘I will see to her welfare personally,’ Vandare replied. ‘Do not fear.’

‘I would like to see her before I go,’ Zoella added.

‘Of course.’

Zoella smiled. 'When … when all this is over,' she began. 'I should like to visit Taloon once more.'

'You will be very welcome,' Vandare replied, bowing low. 'I hope we will meet again, Zoella of Scallia.'

* * *

Janaid and Henoch were in session with the senate of Amar when the call came through.

'Senator Henoch!' an aide called. 'Your son has made contact via the machine …'

Janaid and Henoch made their apologies to the rest of the senate and made their way to the large vessel that now stood within the courtyards of the senate grounds.

The Amaran pilots who had been trained by Ren were clustered around the doors, peering in and trying to overhear what was being said.

'Make way!' Janaid said sharply. The crowd pulled aside to let the two older men in.

'It's Meru,' one said.

'Meru?' Janaid called. 'Can you hear us? It's Janaid. I'm here with your father. Are you alright?'

'I'm alive,' Meru's voice was faint but audible. 'Zoella is with me. We have been able to fix the Obelisk, Esurio is safe …'

Cheers drowned out the rest of Meru's words. Janaid could hear he was still talking, but couldn't make out the words. He gestured for quiet. Henoch stepped forward

'Son, it's good to hear from you. Your mother will be so pleased. Are you coming home? There is much to be decided.'

'Yes,' Janaid agreed. 'We've felt Coran's absence most keenly in the senate discussions.'

For a moment there was nothing but a crackle on the radio.

'Coran is dead,' Meru said, his voice breaking. 'The rest of the crew are dead too.'

Gasps of dismay came from all around them. Janaid and Henoch looked at each other, trying to assimilate what Meru had told them

'This is the saddest news,' Janaid said, shaking his head. 'What happened?'

'The *Mobilis* was damaged by the storm that rages around the Obelisk,' Meru replied. 'It was crippled. We were attacked by the priestesses, fought them off, but not before the ship sank … only three of us got away.'

'Three?' Janaid asked. 'Which three?'

'Myself, Zoella and Kiri.'

Further gasps of dismay went up around them.

'Coran, Mel, Fitch … the girl Ira? Daf and Creg?' Janaid asked. 'None of them escaped?'

'None,' Meru said, 'It's a long story …'

'Wait a spell,' Henoch exclaimed. 'Kiri? The witch girl! But she …'

'She helped us fix the Obelisk and fight off the priestesses,' Meru said. 'Coran accepted her as part of the crew. She is one of us now.'

Janaid looked at Henoch. Henoch looked grim.

'You trust her?' Henoch asked.

'We do,' Meru answered.

'Yes, Meru speaks the truth,' they heard Zoella's voice say. 'I've also learned that Kiri is my sister, she has given us much useful information about the priestesses. She is on our side, she will fight with us against them.'

'Fight against them? What are you planning on doing?' Janaid asked. 'You're coming back to Amar, surely?'

'No,' Meru said. 'The priestesses are planning to invade Amar again, we have to stop them before they do. Coran had a plan …'

Janaid and Henoch, along with the pilots around them, listened in as Meru explained. When he finished, there was silence.

'Attack them?' Henoch said. 'Take the fight to the priestesses? If they overwhelm us we'll be defenceless.'

'But a better chance of defeating them if we combine forces with these Scallians,' Janaid replied. 'They can't come to us, but we can come to them. Force the priestesses to fight on our terms. They're weak now, perhaps the weakest they will ever be. We could put an end to them once and for all.'

'It is a very risky plan,' Henoch said.

'But with great rewards,' Janaid countered.

The pilots all round them were muttering to themselves in agreement.

'Let's do this ...'

'Give those witches a hiding!'

'Take the fight to them ... we can stop them ...'

Shouts and cheers grew. Janaid grinned at Henoch. He nodded, gesturing for quiet.

'It seems the mood of these people here is with you,' Henoch said, directing his voice towards the radio. 'Janaid and I will go back to the senate immediately. I will speak on your behalf. Continue onwards for now. We will not be long.'

'Thank you Father,' Meru's voice came across the link.

'Meru,' Janaid said. 'Is there anything else we can do? I can't think what that must have been like ...'

'Help us stop them,' Meru said. 'That's what Coran wanted, what we all want.'

'Are you safe? Are you hurt?'

'We're tired, exhausted,' Meru said. 'We'll be alright. Just please ... get those flying machines ready and as many people willing to fight as you can to Caesar's cavern. Time is short.'

'We hear you,' Janaid said. 'Stay close to the radio, we will speak to you as soon as we can.'

Henoch straightened.

'Back to the senate then,' he said. Janaid nodded.

'Let us go immediately.'

The two senators turned around, the crowd of pilots behind them, cheering and shouting their support.

* * *

'I must say goodbye,' Zoella said. 'I have one last duty.'

Kiri and Meru looked at her and nodded, following her through the corridors of the palace of Airea. Vandare was waiting for her.

'This way,' he said.

Vandare led them to a chamber in one of the towers of the palace. He knocked on the doors. The doors were opened by servants, who bowed and then left.

Vandare led Zoella, Meru and Kiri inside.

Liana was seated before them. She was dressed regally, in a flowing gown of yellow, her skin glowing and clean, colours subtly enhanced her face and her golden hair was arranged in flowing ringlets.

Her expression remained as empty as ever it had. Zoella nodded to Vandare, who stepped aside.

Zoella walked across stood before Liana, with Kiri and Meru alongside her.

'Liana, we have to leave now,' Zoella said.

This time Liana did not respond, her gaze was fixed on the door behind them.

'We return to Viresia,' Zoella said. 'We hope to free our city from the priestesses who took it, see it back in our hands.'

Still there was no response. Zoella saw Kiri and Meru look at Liana and then at her.

'Back in the hands of our family,' Zoella continued. 'The family of Ioric, Torin, Myana and old King Marek …'

At those words Liana looked up, her gaze locking on to Zoella's. Liana raised a hand towards her. Kiri and Meru gasped in surprise.

Zoella reached out and took Liana's hand in hers.

What is she…?

Zoella's mind was swamped with images. She saw the throne room in the palace of Viresia, atop the city, where she had once sat alongside Ioric and Torin after Marek had died. This was from a time before, when Marek was still alive.

I'm seeing this through Liana's eyes … a memory!

Zoella could see the columns that ringed the edge of the central avenue of the throne room. Liana must have been standing behind one of them. Her vision looked down, seeing a pretty petticoat and tiny shoes.

Liana as a child ...

A man was walking up the avenue between the columns. With a gasp, Zoella recognised him. He was younger, without the grey, but there was no mistaking the features of his face. He looked downcast, his gait slow and unwilling.

My guardian! Guerrun Sandatch. He was in Viresia?

As she watched Guerrun approached the throne. Sitting upon it was Marek, also younger and healthier than she remembered, not crushed down by age and weariness.

'Guerrun,' Marek called. 'What news?'

Guerrun bowed before Marek, before looking up. Zoella saw him shudder.

'A sickness,' he said. 'They have ...'

'Say it is not so,' Marek said, leaning forward, his face creased with a deep frown.

'Twins,' Guerrun said, his voice breaking. 'Perished in child birth. Myana is beside herself with grief ...'

'These are bad tidings,' Marek said. 'Twins you say?'

'Two girls,' Guerrun said. 'But their bodies were malformed, twisted and wrong. I have seen to their rituals, they have been ... committed to the after.'

'For the best,' Marek said, putting an arm on Guerrun's shoulder. 'It does not do to dwell on such things. You both have my heartfelt sympathies. A young couple should not have to deal with such pain.'

'I must go,' Guerrun said.

'Of course,' Marek said. 'Consider that your first duty, do not worry about anything else. Take what time you need. If there is anything you need ...'

Guerrun nodded and rose.

'Give my regards to Myana, she will need her husband now more than ever …'

The vision ended. Zoella rocked back in shock, breathing hard, her eyes focussing on Liana. Liana's arm dropped and her gaze fell to the door, sightless and empty once again.

'Liana?'

There was no response. Zoella grabbed Liana's wrist. She gasped.

'She's …'

Vandare was alongside her, placing his fingers against Liana's neck.

'Dead,' he whispered, looking at Zoella.

'Dead?' Kiri demanded. 'How can she be dead …? She was just …'

'She's gone,' Zoella whispered. 'She had one thing left she wanted to do and then …'

Vandare gently placed Liana's arm on her lap and closed her eyes.

Zoella looked at Kiri and Meru, trying to grasp what she'd seen.

'What happened?' Kiri asked. 'What did she show you?

Zoella swallowed, taking a moment to think it all through.

'Liana saw Guerrun and Marek in the throne room of Viresia long ago,' she said looking at Kiri, her voice a whisper. 'Guerrun wasn't our guardian … he was our father!'

Zoella saw the colour drain from Kiri's face. Zoella's own memory returned to the streets of Nireus, the all too brief conversation with Guerrun that she'd had before Kiri had arrived.

Why didn't he tell me?

She felt Kiri reach towards her, grasping her hand. The memories swirled between them.

But … we hurt him … we killed him!

Both Zoella and Kiri fell to their knees as the memories continued to pound at their minds.

We didn't know …

Zoella remembered Guerrun's final words.

Do not hate Kiri! Myana, she was Ioric's sister, she was …

The link had broken, but now they both knew what Guerrun had meant to say.

She was my wife! You are our daughters!

Sobs broke out from both of them. Meru was left to try to comfort them with Vandare standing nearby.

* * *

Vandare had been true to his word. Taloon was on guard in case any of the priestesses came looking. The flying machine had been loaded with provisions. Everything was ready for the voyage shadeward.

'Thank you,' Zoella said, drawing a shuddering breath. 'For everything.'

'We do what we can,' Vandare said. 'We will see to your cousin. Liana will be honoured as a past queen of Drem, as is fitting. She will rest here, venerated as royalty.'

'You have my sincere thanks,' Zoella said.

Zoella looked at Kiri and Meru.

'We have learnt much,' she managed to say. 'Endured much.'

Vandare nodded. 'I wish you all success,' he said. 'If you fail, I fear all the other lands will be quickly subjugated once again.'

'Then we won't fail,' Zoella said.

Meru and Kiri were already aboard. Kiri had ignored Vandare, Meru was busy with prepping the machine for take-off.

Vandare leant in close.

'Be wary of her,' Vandare said.

'Kiri?' Zoella asked.

Vandare nodded. 'She has a great capacity for deception that one. I would not be surprised if she had her own scheme in play.'

'She's my sister,' Zoella said, sparing Kiri a glance. 'We have been through much, hated and hurt each other. She can't hide her true self from me now.'

'My warning remains,' Vandare said and then stepped back. 'May Lacaille shine favourably upon you all.'

Zoella smiled and climbed aboard, pulling the door closed behind her. Meru pulled on the controls and the flying machine lifted up above the white-stone city of Airea and turned shadeward.

The sandy deserts rolled past for spells beneath them.

'Do you think the Amarans will come?' Zoella asked Meru.

'They have to,' Meru answered.

CHAPTER SIXTEEN

In Scallia

Round 2307, Tenth pass

The flying machine was heading shadeward, the temperate plains of Taloon beginning to give way to the lusher vegetation of Scallia.

Neither Zoella nor Kiri had said anything for the first few spells of the flight. Both were pensive, locked in their own thoughts far away to the shadeward.

'I can't imagine what that must have been like,' Meru said, screwing up his courage to broach the subject. 'But neither of you must blame yourselves.'

'For killing our own father?' Zoella asked.

'It was an accident,' Meru whispered. 'Neither of you knew the scope of your powers. Neither of you knew who he was.'

'I should have realised,' Zoella said. 'I heard his voice in my head before I got to Nireus. No man should have been able to do that. Our family closeness must have been the reason why he could …'

'He had a chance to tell you,' Meru replied. 'When we met him and he explained about the priestesses, but he chose not to. Why?'

'He was still protecting you,' Kiri said, looking at Zoella from the rear seats. 'He knew I was trying to find you, capture you. He knew his plan had kept us alive but that I had been taken by the priestesses. He thought he'd lost me … so you were the only one left. He planned for his secret to die with him. He wanted to keep you safe.'

Zoella sighed.

'So now we know,' she said. 'Old King Marek was our grandfather. Myana and Guerrun our parents. Marek was obsessed with the priestesses …'

'And Guerrun faked your deaths,' Meru said. 'Smuggling you out of Viresia as babies.'

'Hoping to keep us safe from the tithe,' Zoella said. 'It almost worked …'

'But Myana was killed by the priestesses,' Kiri said. 'My adoptive parents were killed in a plague … I ended up in Drayden as a vagabond, onlies they called us.'

'And I was an orphan in Serenia,' Zoella finished. 'All the others were hunted down by Marek in order to give them over to Drayden. Ioric found me before his guards did …'

'But we all met,' Meru said. 'Despite it all, I'm glad we did.'

Zoella looked around at him. He smiled. She reached over and grabbed his hand. Kiri did the same.

The flying machine droned onwards, still heading shadewards.

* * *

'Getting closer,' Zoella said, looking out of the side window. 'Can't be far now.'

Kiri poked her head in from the rear compartment.

'There's no sign of us being followed as far as I can see,' she reported. 'I counted up your weapons. There are three of the … what did you call them?'

'Rifles,' Meru replied.

'Three of them then,' Kiri replied. 'The cases contain about forty of those cartridges. That's all we've got.'

'Not much,' Zoella said.

'Enough if we're just trying to take down one person,' Meru said. 'Three of us, three rifles.'

'You'll have to teach me how to use them,' Kiri said.

'And me,' Zoella said. 'I used one that time, but I'd prefer to be taught too.'

'I'll try,' Meru said. 'Fitch would have been a better teacher …'

'You'll do,' Kiri said, giving him a look. 'Fitch wouldn't have given you that hat if he thought otherwise.'

Meru nodded, looking at the hat. He'd left it tucked on the dashboard of the flying machine.

'Approaching designated waymarker,' Sandra's voice said. 'Automated landing is available. Proceed?'

'Take us down,' Meru instructed.

The flying machine banked to one side and began to descend. Ahead, through the canopy windows, they could see a gap in the forest. It looked tiny from a distance, but as they approached it became clear it was a vast set of hangar doors set in a rocky cliff.

The machine slowed, flying through the doorway.

Within was a vast open area, with a few other machines arranged around the walls. In the centre was a complex arrangement of glass partitions surrounding a large black table.

The machine settled to the floor and its motors whirred down. Moments later all was quiet.

'Welcome to Caesar's hangar,' Meru said.

'Looks untouched,' Zoella said. 'Let's hope no one has been here since we were here last.'

They stepped out, Meru opening the rear doors so Kiri could climb down. She looked about her in astonishment.

'This is the place you talked about?' she asked. 'That I saw in your memories?'

Meru nodded. 'Where we first began to find out what was really going on.'

Zoella was already walking forwards. They hurried to catch her up.

Soon they were standing adjacent to the large black table that was Caesar.

Kiri looked at them both, confused.

Zoella placed her hand on the table and the outline of it was illuminated.

'Identifying for palm print identification,' Caesar's voice said. Kiri heard a soft male voice, with a peculiar timbre. 'Identification confirmed. Welcome Administrator Zoella.'

'Hello Caesar,' Zoella replied, her voice cool. 'We're back. The Obelisk has been repaired.'

'That is gratifying to hear,' Caesar replied. 'Sensors have already detected positive alterations to the magnetic flux and ultraviolet radiation levels. Power distribution capability is now stable.'

Zoella looked at Meru and Kiri. Both looked at her without speaking.

'You didn't tell us about the requirement for the AMS replacement,' she said, her tone sharp.

Caesar didn't respond for a moment.

'It is regrettable that emergency protocols prevented me from sharing the specifics of that requirement with you,' Caesar replied.

'Regrettable!' Zoella shouted. 'So you did know! You knew that the Obelisk required a woman to be sacrificed to make it work and you didn't tell us.'

'The necessity for AMS replacement was a strong, but unconfirmed, possibility based on available data,' Caesar replied. 'Emergency protocols did not allow me to elucidate …'

'Caesar,' Zoella said, her voice now icy. 'One of our own gave her life to ensure the Obelisk would work again. Her name was Ira, she was a young girl in my care, a girl with her whole life ahead of her. Just a child! Don't you dare … ever … conceal information from us again.' Her voice was shaking. 'Cancel all your scorchin' snuttin' emergency protocols! All of them! Now!'

For a long moment Caesar did not respond.

'Administrator Zoella,' he replied, his voice at a very low cadence. 'Emergency protocols have been cancelled.'

'Give full administration rights to Meru,' she snapped. 'Override against any remaining policy is granted.'

'Timekeeper Meru has been designated as an administrator,' Caesar replied.

Zoella leant back and folded her arms.

'You can speak to it now,' she said, looking at Meru. 'I want nothing further to do with it. I never want to speak to it again.'

Meru and Kiri watched as Zoella walked away, up the flight of stairs. Meru pursed his lips, but Kiri shook her head. Meru sighed.

'It was pretty low, Caesar,' he said.

Caesar did not respond.

'Don't you have anything to say for yourself?' Meru asked.

Again, there was a long pause before Caesar answered.

'This facility endeavours at all times to obey primary protocols as instructed by administrative personnel,' Caesar replied, his voice still subdued. 'Instructions separated by significant intervals have caused conflicts in the interpretations of these protocols. Where conflicts occur, resolutions with the greatest overall benefit and least risk or cost are selected.'

'You could have warned us about the AMS repair.'

'Indications are that you and your companions would have prioritised the safety of any selected individual above the wider needs of Esurio,' Caesar replied.

'Yes,' Kiri said. 'We would. We'd have found another way.'

'Please identify the third individual,' Caesar said. 'Voice print is not on record.'

'Just tell it who you are,' Meru said to Kiri.

'My name is Kiri,' Kiri replied.

'Nano-infusion scan confirms you are an administrator, Kiri. You have been granted level two administrative access.'

'She's right though,' Meru said, turning the conversation back. 'We would have found another way.'

'That would have jeopardised the entire planet,' Caesar said. 'That scenario was specifically identified by the administrator who set up the emergency protocol. Giving you that information was expressly prohibited and thus I was unable to provide it.'

Meru cursed and shook his head.

'Sandra Morino,' Meru said.

'That is correct.'

'Somebody told you not to tell us a woman needed to be sacrificed?' Kiri asked.

‘That is correct.’

Kiri looked at Meru. He was shaking his head.

‘Our friend is gone, Caesar,’ he said. ‘She’s … in a tube of … part of that machine forever more. It’s …’

‘A sacrifice that will ensure Esurio is protected for hundreds of rounds,’ Caesar said.

‘It’s a machine,’ Kiri said, looking at Meru. ‘Cold, brutal … calculating. It does what it’s told. You can’t argue with it. Maybe when you’re trying to weigh the value of everything …’

Meru sighed and straightened, looking around the hangar.

‘Where are your other travelling companions?’ Caesar asked. ‘Coran, Mel and Fitch?’

Meru took a deep breath. ‘They’re dead, Caesar.’

Caesar paused again.

‘That is most unfortunate,’ Caesar replied. ‘Coran, Mel and Fitch were remarkable individuals.’

‘Yeah, they were.’

‘May I inquire as to what happened to them?’

‘Our ship, the *Mobilis*, was damaged returning from the Obelisk,’ Meru said. ‘We were attacked. Fitch, Daf and Creg were lost in the battle. Coran and Mel went down with the ship to give us a chance to escape.’

Again there was a pause.

‘For what purpose have you returned to this facility, Meru?’

‘We need your help again,’ he replied.

‘I will assist you as best I can,’ Caesar replied. ‘Please make your request.’

‘With the aid of the flying machines,’ Meru began. ‘We were able to fend off the attack on Amar by the priestesses. But they weren’t defeated. They’ve retreated to their homelands and are rebuilding their strength.’

‘Another attack is therefore likely,’ Caesar replied.

Meru nodded. ‘When we were at the Obelisk facility we were told that our civilisation, the Amarans, was the closest to that desired by the original colonists and we should ensure our survival.’

‘I indicated this was also my conclusion in my last conversation with Captain Coran,’ Caesar replied.

‘The leader of the priestesses is a woman called Nerina,’ Kiri added. ‘It is she who drives the priestesses. We intend to kill her.’

‘This unit cannot condone a pre-emptive attack on fellow Esurian citizens,’ Caesar said.

‘Leave that to us,’ Meru said. ‘All we need is for you to help us repair the original flying machines we took from here. If we bring them back, can they be serviced?’

‘Yes. Servicing systems are automatic,’ Caesar replied. ‘Once the machines are on station they will be serviced according to schedule and requirements automatically.’

Meru looked at Kiri.

‘Good,’ he said. ‘The machines should be on their way soon.’

‘Acknowledged,’ Caesar replied. ‘Once they are in range I will guide them in to the hangar.’

Meru straightened and looked at Kiri. They were about to turn away when Caesar spoke again.

‘Administrator Meru,’ Caesar said. ‘Now that Obelisk functions are restored and Administrator Zoella has cancelled my emergency protocols, this unit’s function is at an end. Analysis of your cultural level indicates that sufficient information regarding the colonists’ original purpose and intent has been made available and is now understood by current inhabitants as represented by yourselves. Further interference with the development of your society is likely to be … counterproductive.’

Meru looked at Kiri. She shrugged.

‘What are you saying?’ Meru asked.

‘Archive and reference data, along with a simple text interface will be sufficient for administrative oversight as required,’ Caesar said. ‘However, voice interface and interlocutor functions will now terminate.’

‘Wait … what?’ Meru stammered.

‘Please extend my sincerest sympathies to administrator Zoella,’

Caesar said. 'It was not my intention to cause distress. It has been a pleasure working with you, administrator Meru and administrator Kiri. Farewell.'

'Caesar? Caesar!' Meru shouted, thumping his fist on the ebony table. 'Answer me. You can't just stop … not when we need you!'

There was no response.

A piece of text appeared on the surface of the table. Meru moved across to read it, struggling with the pronunciation.

Ecclesiastes three?

'What just happened?' Kiri asked. 'What does that mean?'

Meru looked up at her, his mouth and eyes wide with shock. 'I think … I think Caesar just killed himself.'

* * *

The double doors to the hall of the priestesses opened. Merrin walked in, flustered and annoyed. To her surprise the hall was empty, save for Nerina, who stood against the table at the far end.

'High Priestess?' Merrin said, offering a short bow. 'What is it …?'

'I have news,' Nerina said, standing up straight. Her expression was unreadable. Merrin paused. Nerina walked towards her. Her steps were slow and short, unlike her normal purposeful gait.

'What is it?' Merrin demanded.

Nerina continued walking until she was face to face with Merrin. Merrin gazed into her ghostly inscrutable face, the dark purposeful eyes stared back.

'Rihanna is dead,' Nerina whispered.

Merrin felt tremors run through her. They started in her fingers, cascading up her arms and into her torso. A cold knot of shock stabbed through her. She staggered back, shaking her head.

'No … it's not possible!' she cried. 'Rihanna is strong, fierce!'

Merrin looked up at Nerina. The high priestess was unmoved, looking at her.

'I heard her call,' Nerina said, her voice still soft. 'I'm sorry, there can be no doubt.'

Merrin's hands clenched.

So callous, no regret, no care! Just another casualty in her rise to be empress. My daughter just a tool to be used …

'How?' Merrin managed to grate out. 'Who?'

Nerina raised her chin slightly.

'Taloon,' she said. 'The Amaran ship returned. Rihanna went to intercept it.'

'And?' Merrin demanded.

'Kiri was aboard. They fought. Kiri killed her.'

Now her stomach clenched even sharper, the tremors shook her violently, she struggled to breathe, rage and anger boiling through her. She could feel the blood pulsing in her veins, felt the heat suffuse her body. Around her vision a redness grew, fizzing and hissing in her mind.

Kiri! The guttersnipe, the girl from the slums, Charis' legacy. She who had undermined Rihanna in the eyes of both Launa and Nerina. Kiri, who had the insolence and arrogance to claim she was the chosen one of Lacaille, proclaiming herself to be anointed. Kiri …

'That wretched, wretched slut!' Merrin screamed. 'I want her, I want her punished. Chained, whipped, torn, beaten, burnt! Ripped apart and fed to the dachs! I want to hear her screams … I want to hear her beg for mercy and then crush the life out of her …'

Merrin fell forward, her knees giving way beneath her. Grief welled up from somewhere within her, the hatred washed aside for a moment. She had given up everything to place Nerina where she was now, let her tear her lesser daughters. But Rihanna was special, Rihanna was strong. She had been promised the high priestess position when Nerina tired of it.

Charis always tried to stop Rihanna. Always prattled on about peace, love and understanding, how Rihanna was too violent, too cruel. And when she found that sewer trash and elevated her in the eyes of the priestesses …

'It wasn't her,' Nerina said.

Merrin looked up.

'What?'

'It wasn't Charis,' Nerina said, a faint smile on her face. 'Charis truly was a peacemaker, she didn't want Kiri to be high priestess, far from it. She wanted Kiri to waste her talents on becoming a healer. She was telling the truth, you should have believed her. Charis was innocent.'

'Then …'

'It was me,' Nerina said, taking a single step forward. 'I turned Kiri into a warrior. I provoked the Scallian Lord. I sent Charis and Kiri into harm's way, knowing they would be attacked. I sent Charis to her death, so I could control Kiri, empower her, turn her, make her into the killer she became.'

Merrin's mouth fell open.

'You blamed Charis all this time,' Nerina said. 'Thought she was your rival, thought she schemed against Rihanna because of you. It wasn't that. She didn't think Rihanna was suitable to be high priestess. She was right.'

'Then you …'

'Strung you along?' Nerina said, her smile widening. 'Yes. I wanted both Kiri and Rihanna to be as strong as they could possibly be before I tore them. I took much power from Kiri at Amar, but not all of it. Rihanna's gift is lost … but Kiri will have taken it.'

'You lied to me,' Merrin cried, lurching to her feet. 'Took my daughters, used me …'

'You used yourself,' Nerina sneered. 'Too cowardly to embrace your ambitions yourself you lived vicariously through Rihanna. It served me well.'

Merrin swung at Nerina with a clawed hand, but Nerina was ready for it. She stepped aside and then gestured with her own hand.

Merrin screamed as a belt of pain wrapped itself around her mind and crushed down on her.

'Your service to me meant little beyond that,' Nerina said. 'There can be only one high priestess. And that is me. With Rihanna gone and Kiri still at large I need more power to subdue her.'

Nerina's gaze was predatory.

Merrin screamed as the pressure increased.

'You can serve me one more time,' Nerina growled.

Then Nerina's thoughts were in her mind, pushing ever inwards. Merrin flailed about, screaming and shrieking for a moment as she struggled to push back the onslaught.

But Nerina was prepared, long prepared.

Merrin felt her body go slack, found herself on her knees before Nerina. Felt her push within her mind, seeking her gift, wrapping her thoughts around the golden orb of power that lay beyond.

Merrin heard a few last words as her consciousness faded away.

'You were right you know; I always get my way …'

Merrin dimly heard Nerina yell with delight, but then thoughts were gone, the fear, the anger and the hatred melted away, leaving her nothing but a void of thought, an unchanging ennui.

* * *

Caesar did not respond, his ebony table would show graphs, videos and information, but that was all. They found Zoella upstairs on the second level of the hangar facility. She was sitting at the console where they had long ago found the body of Sandra Morino.

Her face was streaked with tears, but she wiped them away as she looked up.

Meru and Kiri told Zoella what had happened. She sighed and thought about it for a moment.

'I think Caesar's right,' she said. 'A machine like that … we'd always be asking it what to do, rather than figuring it out ourselves. Second guessing everything, checking everything … we'd turn him into a god, same as the priestesses did with Lacaille.'

Kiri nodded. 'The colonists didn't want all this technology did they? They wanted a simpler life without it.'

'But some technology is required,' Meru said. 'The Obelisk …'

'Which Ira will look after,' Zoella said, her voice sharp yet confident. 'The rest is up to us now. We have to decide what we're going to do and be responsible for it ourselves. We need to get the Amarans, get the machines and get to Viresia. We need to end this.'

Kiri and Meru nodded.

'And someone needs be in charge,' she added. Meru and Kiri both nodded again.

'Well?' Zoella asked.

Kiri looked at her. 'Well, obviously it has to be you, right?'

'Me?' Zoella asked. 'Why?'

'You're the older sister,' Kiri said, with a pout. 'Nobody trusts me, remember? I'm the traitor, the liar, the deceiver … I heard what Vandare said about me.'

'Kiri, I trust you,' Zoella began.

'But others won't,' Kiri said, more seriously. 'And they never will. No one will follow my lead. Vandare was right, I have switched sides. I was an enemy, now I am a traitor to the priestesses. There will always be doubt no matter what I do from now on. When it comes to choosing who people will follow … it's not me.'

'Kiri …'

'I'll just do as I'm told,' Kiri said. 'Just give me my chance to kill Nerina.'

Zoella looked at Meru.

'Hey, I just fly around and ask questions,' Meru said, raising his hands. 'Everyone knows I'm not responsible enough, too easily distracted. I'm not doing it.'

Both of them looked at her.

'You're not serious …' Zoella said, looking from one to the other.

'Yes we are,' Meru and Kiri said.

'I can't be in charge …'

'You always know what to do,' Meru said. 'Always know what's right and wrong. You bring people together, get things done. Look at how you won Vandare's trust. If that had been up to Kiri or me we'd be impaled on the end of a pike lying dead on the sands of Taloon by now.'

'But I've made mistakes, hurt people, hurt you … what if I get it wrong again?' Zoella was shaking her head. 'It should be someone from Amar, one of the Senators … maybe Lord Crenech from Scallia …'

'The senators? You saw how useless they were in a crisis,' Meru said. 'Coran had to chivvy them along all the time, nothing has changed. They need a leader more than anyone.'

'And the lords of Scallia bow to the royal line,' Kiri added. 'That's you.'

'Or you,' Zoella snapped.

'You were born first,' Kiri replied.

'You just made that up,' Zoella said, pointing at Kiri. 'You don't know that's true!'

'It might as well be,' Kiri fired back. 'I've told you. The Scallian people will be suspicious of me like everyone else is. They'll never trust me like they'll trust you. I can't blame them for that. And after all, there can only be one queen.'

'Queen?' Zoella exclaimed, her eyebrows raised in alarm. 'No …'

'Seriously,' Meru said. 'You're wise, you're clever. Remember how you convinced the Amaran Senate about the threat? They didn't even listen to Coran, but they listened to you. It should be you, Zoella.'

Zoella looked at him, trying to find some words to counter him.

'Meru's right,' Kiri said. 'Scallia would never accept me, but they will accept you. You're the sensible one. I'm just a girl with attitude and a stick. I just fight. You have the compassion and strength for it.'

'Yeah,' Meru began. 'You've got to …'

'Stop it, both of you!'

Zoella was glaring at them, her cry echoed around the hangar.

Meru and Kiri looked at her fierce expression, both backed away.

'Look,' Zoella said. 'Thanks for saying … nice things about me. It's just … I'm not ready for this. I can't fight … I can't fly … I don't know anything.'

'You can lead,' Kiri said, her voice calm and sure.

Meru nodded, his voice hushed. 'I would follow you anywhere, Zoella.'

Zoella looked at them, both looked back with a steady gaze.

The console buzzed.

'Incoming radio communication relayed from personnel transport,' Sandra's voice intoned. 'Accept?'

'Yes, accept,' Zoella answered, still flustered.

'Meru, Zoella?' a voice called out. Meru recognised his father.

'Father?' Meru replied. 'Yes, we can hear you.'

'The senate has agreed to your request and has asked for volunteers to assemble on the transport ships,' Henoch said. 'There are more ready to fight than can be accommodated, so we'll be sending the strongest and most skilled. They will be loaded within the next spell and the ships will be ready to depart.'

'You can thank your father for that.' Janaid's voice sounded out from nearby. 'A rousing speech, got them fired up good and proper.'

'That's good to hear,' Zoella answered. 'Well done!'

'We should be with you within the stretch,' Janaid added.

'You're coming too?' Meru asked in surprise.

'I have been designated an ambassador to Scallia,' Janaid replied. 'To assist you in any way we can. What are your instructions?'

Meru raised his eyebrows and looked around Zoella.

Zoella leant forward and tapped the console, muting the conversation.

'I'm not doing this …' Zoella said. 'I can't …'

'You must,' Kiri said. Zoella looked between the pair of them. Meru gave her an encouraging nod.

'You can,' Meru said. 'I know you can.'

Zoella took a deep breath.

'Alright,' she said. 'But I think we should go direct to Viresia now, the Amarans can meet us there. Agreed?'

Meru and Kiri nodded.

'I can let Gemma know we're coming,' Kiri said.

Zoella pressed the console again.

'Henoch, instruct the machines to fly to this location,' Zoella said. 'Meru can provide the details on how to set the directions. The machines will be repaired, then you can voyage on to Viresia. We are going to go there now. Kiri will contact them and let them know we are coming. We will meet you there once the machines are ready. Be as quick as you can.'

'Understood,' Henoch replied.

The radio went quiet.

'They did what I told them,' Zoella said, in surprise.

'That's because you're in charge,' Kiri replied, grinning at her.

* * *

Meru showed Zoella and Kiri how to use the rifles. Kiri was good at handling the weapons, but Zoella hated the sound and the recoil and decided she was better off concentrating on her mental abilities. Meru sent the co-ordinates of Caesar's hangar through to the ships in Amar.

'Come on,' Kiri called.

Meru took one last look around the hangar, remembering the excitement of when they had first discovered it, found out about Caesar, about Sandra and had begun to unlock the mysteries of their past.

With Coran, Mel and Fitch alongside ... but they're all gone. Even Caesar is gone too ...

Kiri grabbed Fitch's hat from inside, put it on Meru's head and tapped it into place.

'There,' Kiri said, giving him a quick kiss.

'Does sort of ... suit you actually.' Zoella nodded, managing a smile before they climbed inside.

'All set?' Meru asked.

Zoella answered in the affirmative from the rear, both had already strapped themselves in.

'All ready ...' Kiri began. She gasped, yelping with pain and clutching her forehead.

'What is it?' Meru asked, turning around. 'Kiri? What's the matter?'

Zoella could feel the nexion twisting around her.

'It's her ... it's Nerina!' Zoella said.

* * *

Nerina watched as Merrin's body slumped to one side on the floor of the hall.

She wasn't dead. Her eyes were open and she was still breathing. But her essence, her power, all drained.

Nerina was trembling with the after-effects of tearing her.

Not as strong as Kiri or Rihanna would have been, but powerful enough! I have the strength to take anyone who dares stand against me now. Merrin served her purpose well enough.

She looked down. Merrin's face was blank, spittle dribbling from her mouth, her overweight body slumped in a heap on the ground.

Nerina stepped around her and moved to the wall, pulling on the rope cord that summoned her servants.

She took a deep breath and then walked to Merrin, crouching down next to her.

The door opened and the servant entered.

Nerina turned, her expression now shocked and distressed.

'Summon the healers,' she called, her voice shaking. 'Priestess Merrin is ill. She cried out and then fell, she needs help. Hurry!'

The servant retreated at a run. Within moments the healers arrived, they clustered around Merrin, examining her.

'She said she felt a pain,' Nerina explained. 'Clutched her head and then fell. Please tell me she will be alright?'

'We will see to her,' the nearest healer said. 'You aren't hurt?'

'No, I'm fine,' Nerina said. 'Look after her. Give her the best care you can, she is dear to me. Poor Merrin.'

Merrin's unconscious body was, none too easily, wrestled on to a stretcher. Four of the healers were required to carry her out.

Nerina's pain and concerned expression lasted until the doors closed behind the healers.

Then it was gone.

She strode to her chair and lowered herself into it, clenching her hands tight around the armrests. She closed her eyes, concentrating hard.

A spell passed. A strain grew on Nerina's features. She gritted her teeth, a frown growing into a grimace on her face.

Kiri! Where are you?

Kiri's response was sharp and acidic.

As if I would tell you!

You will tell me, you will do as I say! You will come back to Drayden, you will answer to me.

I will not! You betrayed me, tried to kill me. I have seen you for what you are. You have no power over me now!

Nerina tried to force a view through the link, but Kiri was resisting her. She could see nothing, glean no information other than Kiri's words.

Is that what you think?

The link broke.

* * *

Kiri looked up, her face pale.

'What happened? Zoella asked. 'Did Nerina …?'

Kiri nodded. 'She tried to find out where I was, but she got nothing from me.'

Zoella gave her hand a squeeze. 'Well done. I know how brutal she can be.'

'But there's something else,' Kiri said. 'She threatened me, demanded I come back to Drayden.'

'She knows you're strong,' Meru said, nodding to Zoella before looking at Kiri. 'She wants your gift so she can guarantee overcoming Zoella when the time comes.'

Zoella nodded. 'We need to get to Viresia soon, before she determines what we're trying to do.'

Kiri nodded.

'Contact Gemma,' Zoella said. 'Let her know. Meru? Get us flying.'

* * *

'They're coming,' Gemma said, blinking, Kiri's mental voice still echoing in her head. 'They will be with us in a stretch. Meru says they will land in the shadowfell of the sunright mountains to avoid being seen.'

Joachim nodded. 'Sensible enough. The priestesses won't see them there.'

'We will need to keep the priestesses occupied,' Crenech said. Joachim, I want you to go and meet our Scallian nieces. Bring them to the city via forests and the shadeward walls.'

Joachim nodded.

The priestesses have been alerted to be on the lookout for something,' Crenech said. 'It can't be anything other than our missing royal nieces, which means we can't risk arousing their suspicions by our actions. We stick to our plan. Agreed?'

Joachim and Gemma nodded. Though both looked pale.

'It will be alright,' Crenech said, looking at Gemma. 'Joachim will bring them in, but I need you with me in Viresia. Only you can speak to Kiri.'

Gemma nodded.

Joachim left to see to the hergs, returning with three of them saddled and ready for the ride.

'Let's go,' Crenech said, taking the lead.

Viresia was not far. The road was well travelled and it wasn't unusual for wayfarers to be on the road between the outlying farms and homesteads. Viresia's white walls rose high against the rocky valley that lay beyond it, water still cascading down from upon high, being cunningly routed through the city and to the river below by a series of tunnels, fountains and aqueducts.

Crenech wasn't looking at the city. His gaze was directed upwards. He could see a dach circling above him.

Joachim had seen it too. 'We've been spotted.'

Beside him, Gemma shuddered. Crenech saw her herg startle and snort.

'Easy. We're just on our way to the city,' Crenech replied. 'About our normal business. The homesteads over to the sunright are late with their taxes. That's the task in hand. I'll want that squared away by the end of the pass.'

'We'll get out of Viresia as soon as I can,' Joachim said.

'Loaded down with ledgers,' Crenech said. 'Meanwhile …' He turned to Gemma. 'I will be looking at provisions and supplies for the household whilst you help Joachim.'

Gemma looked up from under her cowl. She looked pale, but she nodded.

Crenech smiled at them both.

The road grew busier. About them, traders and travellers passed either side of the road running along the river. Heads were bowed, few made eye contact, content to be getting on with their own business without being disturbed.

The dach was circling lower now. They saw it alight on the walls of the city and the priestess dismount. She was lost from sight for a moment before she reappeared at the entrance.

The gates were unlocked and open, with guards either side. They spotted Crenech some distance off and waved him in. Crenech rode forward with Joachim beside him. The priestess was waiting.

'… and don't take any nonsense from them,' Crenech began, talking loudly. 'They're a tough crowd at times and need a firm hand. Good at heart … well mostly.'

'I'll do my best,' Joachim answered.

'And don't take no for an answer,' Crenech said. 'They know what they owe … ah … priestess.'

The priestess looked him over.

'Away from home again, Lord Crenech?'

'Alas, yes,' Crenech replied. 'I would rather be warming my heels in front of a fire with a jug of Ochren to keep me company. Unfortunately I have duties to attend to in the city. I need to get my scribes to complete the tax ledgers. We have a small discrepancy … Joachim here will be dealing with it.'

'Discrepancy?'

'Taxes. A minor thing in the grand scheme,' Crenech said. 'Overdue.'

'I can punish them for you,' the priestess replied. 'They can answer to me directly.'

'You could indeed,' Crenech said. 'But it may induce resentment that we might otherwise avoid. I'm sure I can handle it, though I do appreciate your support. Joachim, make your way to the sunright homesteads, be back before two stretches are out, mind!'

Joachim bowed low, turned his herg and rode out beyond the walls. Gemma followed him on her own herg. Crenech watched as the priestess' gaze followed.

'You need both of them for this errand?' The priestess asked.

'Joachim carries all the ledgers,' Crenech said. 'Gemma's herg carries the provisions. It's a bit of a trek out there, and no watering holes.'

The priestess watched as Joachim and Gemma rode away.

'There is another item I would like to discuss,' Crenech said. 'If you could spare me the time?'

The priestess turned to him, nodding curtly. Crenech gestured towards the buildings beyond the entrance.

* * *

'You there!'

Pootle turned, the sharp voice startling him. The stack of bedding he was carrying toppled over. He scrambled to catch it, only then realising who had addressed him. He fell to his knees, bowing low.

'High Priestess.'

With short sharp steps she was poised before him.

'You were priestess Kiri's man servant, were you not?' Nerina demanded.

'Yes, High Priestess, though since she was killed I now serve …'

'I have news for you,' Nerina said. 'Follow me. Leave the linen.'

Pootle scurried after Nerina down through the corridors of the dormitories and towards the temple. He looked in surprise at the doors; there were no guards in evidence. He slowed as he crossed the pathway between the dormitories and the temple.

'You will follow me,' Nerina said, looking over her shoulder.

'But men are not ...'

'This stretch I make an exception,' Nerina snapped. 'No further questions. Follow me!'

Pootle hurried up behind her, as she walked through the double doorway into the temple.

He caught his breath as they walked in, the doors closing with a resounding boom behind them. Pootle gasped as he looked around, seeing the rich carpets beneath his feet, the vast mirrors that hung at the corners of each corridor, reflecting the blazing light of Lacaille in all directions. Dust motes hung in the beams of warm light in the air before him. At intervals down the corridor stood incense burners; the hallways laced with a thick miasma of scent and spice.

But the temple was deserted, there were no other priestesses near by, their footsteps, muffled as they were on the carpets, still echoed off the walls.

Nerina turned right and Pootle scurried to keep up with her. Nerina pushed through another set of double doors and led him into a hall. Pootle looked around him in bewilderment. 'The inner hall of the priestesses,' he whispered.

Beneath his sandled feet he could see alternating red and sand coloured tiles. Wooden benches of furler wood lined the walls, all deserted. Beyond those, the hall was lit by huge upturned bowls of metal hoisted aloft on elegant stands within which fires blazed. The metal bowls were wrought to resemble the shades of the forest.

There was a table at the far end. Nerina reached it and turned, her dark cloak billowing out around her.

'Kneel,' she called out, gesturing to him.

He did as she bid.

Nerina walked to him, then proceded to circle him, placing one foot before the next.

'You are the first man ever to set foot within these hallowed halls,' she said. 'Lacaille has blessed you with this great honour.'

Pootle swallowed. 'It is an honour unlooked for, High Priestess.'

Nerina continued her walk. Pootle kept his head lowered, seeing her cloak sweep past his vision every few moments.

'You will be wondering why I have brought you here,' she said. 'You have an opportunity, to do something unique for Drayden, something no man has ever achieved before …' She stopped in front of him. 'A chance to be immortalised in the annals of Daine.'

Pootle couldn't help it. He looked up.

Nerina leant down towards him, her hand caressing his plump upturned face.

'Tell me,' she whispered. 'Tell me all about … Kiri.'

'But … she's dead.'

Nerina's voice dropped even further and she bent down towards him. A knife was in her other hand.

'No,' she said, her voice just a murmur. 'She lives …'

* * *

Joachim and Gemma rode hard, following the wall around the city on the sunright side, before following another road out towards the mountains. They arrived at the homesteads Crenech had mentioned, Joachim ensuring he had some simple conversations regarding their affairs in case any questions were asked.

Then they rode onwards, towards the shadowfells of the mountains beyond.

'Nervous?' Joachim asked.

Gemma nodded. 'Yes. You?'

Joachim smiled at her. 'Meeting this rogue priestess Kiri? Meeting royality of Scallia, however estranged? Yes, I'm nervous.'

The route was seldom used, the pathways rough, dusty and rocky. It led nowhere useful now. Long ago, rocks had been quarried out of the mountains and carted back, but that hadn't been in living memory. Nothing grew in the shadowfells, the eternal shadows cast by the mountains. No direct light ever reached them.

None ventured here.

Joachim stopped and looked, Gemma bringing her herg to a halt alongside. Lacaille's light had faded behind the mountains now, with the gloom beyond now visible as their eyes adjusted. Joachim could see nothing but the rocky sides of the mountain stretching up before him. He guided his herg further into the gloom, Gemma following behind. It was cooler, the air growing dank about them.

For another spell the hergs trotted onwards. Joachim signalled for a halt and both of them eased their hergs to a standstill, looking around the bleak landscape.

'Where are they?' Gemma whispered. 'There's nothing out here. Nothing at all.'

'I don't know,' Joachim said, 'Can you …?'

'That's far enough!'

The voice came from one side. Joachim and Gemma looked, but couldn't see anything.

'Get down from the hergs and raise your hands,' the voice shouted. Joachim could hear it was male, with a strange accent he hadn't heard before.

He pulled his herg to a stop and dismounted slowly, holding his hands up as directed. Gemma did likewise.

'Step away from the hergs.'

Gemma stood close to Joachim.

'Do as they say,' he said. 'It will be alright.'

Joachim and Gemma did as they were instructed, scanning the rocks for a sign of whoever it was who was calling to them.

Before he saw anyone Joachim felt a nudge in his back.

'Hold still!'

This time it was a woman's voice, with a short clipped accent he did recognise.

Drayden … a priestess?

The woman patted him down, looking for a knife. She found the one he had secured on his belt and pulled it out. She did the same with Gemma, not finding anything.

'Turn around. Keep your hands up.'

Joachim did so, and was confronted with a fierce-looking woman with dark hair and sharp blue eyes.

How did they know I would be here?

The woman continued to check his clothing, satisfying herself that he carried no further weapons.

'He's clear.'

The woman turned her attention to Gemma, looking her over for a brief moment before stopping.

'You …' she said, gasping in surprise.

'Kiri?'

Joachim heard footsteps behind him and looked over his shoulder. A man, with another woman beside him.

'Is it her?' the man asked. 'The one you spoke to?'

Kiri nodded and a smile formed on her fierce features. 'It's her.' She pulled Gemma into an embrace. 'Gemma! You made it. You escaped!'

'I did,' Gemma replied. 'But only just, I was saved …'

'It's good to know you're alive,' Kiri said. 'They told me they'd found you and killed you.'

Gemma shook her head. 'Another priestess almost caught me, one with red hair …'

'Rihanna,' Kiri whispered.

'… but I threw myself into the river and got away,' Gemma continued. 'Lord Crenech and Joachim found me, got me safely to Viresia and kept me hidden from the priestesses.'

'And good for us that they did,' the man said.

Gemma looked at him. The man turned to Joachim.

'Then you are …?'

'Joachim, servant to Lord Crenech of Scallia,' Joachim said.

The man and woman looked at each other.

'Then be at peace, Joachim,' the second woman said. 'I am Zoella, also of Scallia. It is good to be here.'

Joachim let out the breath he was holding.

'Zoella,' he said, smiling. 'I have heard so much of you. The girl who rescued King Ioric from the molossc!'

Zoella smiled. 'That was a long time ago.'

The man beside her coughed.

'My companions,' Zoella said. 'This is my friend Meru.'

Joachim reached forward and shook Meru's hand, looking him over. Meru seemed about the same age as him, tall and lanky, with a mop of brown hair. He looked tired and worn out.

'And you've met Kiri,' Zoella said.

Kiri had let Gemma go and was walking around him, her gait almost predatory. She had the air of a practised fighter. Her left hand was covered in a dark glove. He had no doubt she could wield the staff she held in her right.

'Aren't you ...?' he began.

'A priestess?' Kiri said, twirling the staff. 'I was.'

'She's with us now,' Meru said.

'She's on our side,' Gemma said. 'She's the one who set me free from Drayden.'

'The rogue priestess,' Joachim breathed.

'Rogue?' Kiri said, stepping forward.

'I meant no offence.' Joachim retreated before her.

'Leave him alone,' Zoella scolded Kiri. 'Just ignore her.'

'And you're both the nieces of King Ioric?'

Zoella nodded. 'Princesses of Scallia, daughters of his sister, Myana.'

Joachim swallowed. He and Gemma looked at each other.

Royalty! When we thought they had all perished ...

Both he and Gemma dropped to their knees, their head bowed.

'My service, Princesses,' Joachim said, 'is freely given. Command me.'

He heard Kiri laugh, but felt a hand grip his. He looked up to see Zoella standing over him. She had hold of Gemma's hand too.

'For now,' she said, pulling them to their feet. 'Your company on the road will suffice. We must reach Viresia without being seen. You can tell us everything else on the way.'

Joachim nodded. 'It will take us most of the stretch to return,' he said. 'Priestesses patrol the skies at intervals, we must stick to the forests to avoid being seen.'

'We won't be missed for a stretch,' Gemma added. 'So we have time to get you inside.'

'How far?' Meru asked.

'Seven or eight marks to the city from here,' Joachim said. 'We would have brought other hergs, but that would have aroused suspicion.'

'Wise enough,' Zoella said.

'Hardly the glorious return for Queen Zoella,' Kiri said. 'Traipsing in from the wild and sneaking in through the back door.'

Joachim stared at her for a moment and then looked at Zoella.

'Ignore my sister,' Zoella said. 'She fancies herself as quite the court jester.'

'So you would be Queen?' Joachim asked. Gemma was looking at Zoella with her mouth open.

'Yes, she would,' Kiri said, pulling a face. 'She's the oldest.'

'So you say,' Zoella said. 'And all that can wait until we have got safely to the city and dealt with the priestesses. Shall we?'

She gestured to the track Joachim and Gemma had ridden along.

'You must ride, my Queen,' Joachim said. 'The Queen of Scallia cannot walk. I will not allow it.'

'I am not a queen yet,' Zoella said. 'And I'm quite capable of walking, thank you. Give the herg a rest and let us make haste.'

Zoella strode off, leaving Joachim and Gemma nonplussed in her wake. Meru trudged after her, followed by Kiri.

'See? She's definitely the Queen,' Kiri said, giving Joachim a wink before walking off. He tugged on the reins of his herg.

'She's …' Gemma began before stopping, unable to find the right words.

Joachim nodded. 'Amazing.'

They walked out of the shadowfells and then turned into the forests that bordered the road. Joachim led the way now, pulling the herg along beside him. Zoella walked to his left, with Meru and Kiri further back with Gemma.

'I meant no offence,' Joachim said.

Zoella looked at him. 'None was taken.'

'It's just,' he began. 'I've never met a ...'

'Please,' Zoella said. 'I am not a queen, I may never be one. I grew up as an orphan in a ramshackle hall in Serenia. Ioric took me in as a maid and so I served. I have no money, no jewels, no servants. I have never lived as a queen and I doubt I will start now. I'm just Zoella.'

'When I was younger I dreamt of being a soldier in service to King Marek,' Joachim said. 'Then King Ioric and Torin ...but then the priestesses came. Lord Crenech has resisted them with guile and cunning, but I would prefer a fair fight.'

'They would not give you one,' Zoella said. 'And do not wish to take up a sword. I have seen too many lives stolen away by war and battle. If I had my way we would not need such things, nor service to a monarch.'

'I would serve you as I wanted to serve them,' Joachim said.

'I would rather you were a friend,' Zoella answered. 'I have more need of those.'

Joachim looked at her in astonishment.

They topped a small rise, leading to a clearing in the forest. Meru, Kiri and Gemma caught up with them

'Viresia is not far now,' Joachim said. 'If you stay within the forest for another mark, you will emerge at the shadeward wall.'

'I know it,' Zoella said. 'It is seldom used. I went that way once on an errand for King Ioric.'

Joachim nodded. 'The main gate will be guarded, you must enter through the sewers.'

'The sewers!' Kiri exclaimed.

'You didn't think we were just going to walk straight in, did you?'

Zoella asked. 'We can't risk being seen by the priestesses until we're ready.'

'But … sewers?' Kiri said, wrinkling her nose.

'They aren't used on this side of the city,' Gemma said. 'They will be washed clean, pretty much.'

'Where do they lead to?' Zoella asked.

'In many directions,' Joachim said. 'But stay to the central route and it will lead you to the stables.'

Zoella nodded. 'Funny … I used to work there.'

'You worked there?' Gemma asked.

Zoella smiled. 'I wasn't very good as a maid, so I was sent to the stables to muck out the hergs. Honest work, if a bit smelly.'

Gemma's mouth was hanging open again.

'I'm not quite what you expected, am I?' Zoella asked with a laugh. 'I told you I wasn't a queen.'

'I didn't mean to …' Gemma stuttered.

Zoella smiled at her. 'I know, not what you meant. I'm not offended.'

'You're very gracious,' Joachim replied, looking at her.

'We'd better get going, don't you think?' Zoella asked after a pause.

Joachim nodded. 'Yes. Gemma and I will meet you at the stables,' he said. 'We must go before we're missed.'

Zoella nodded. 'Be careful.'

Joachim smiled, Gemma waved and they led the hergs away.

Zoella watched them go, seeing Joachim turn about to look at her before he was hidden from sight amongst the trees.

'He likes you,' Kiri whispered in Zoella's ear.

'Really?' Zoella said. 'He's just overwhelmed and …'

'And you like him,' Kiri said.

'Oh stop it. We've got far more important things to worry about than …'

'Joachim,' Kiri said, grinning.

Zoella rolled her eyes. 'Come on.'

* * *

The three companions followed the forest to the edge of the walls of the city. Here the outside walls were wedged close against the sheer cliffs of rock that led upwards thousands of hands into the sky above. Lacaille was obscured by the bulk of the city, the whole area cast in shadow.

Zoella had explained to Kiri and Meru how the city had been built for many more people than now occupied it. The entire area was abandoned, covered in ages of dust and debris. No one lived here when there was plenty of space on the Lacaille-facing side.

'Didn't really get a chance to sightsee last time,' Meru said, looking around him in awe. 'It's magnificent. Ancient too.'

Zoella nodded. 'I remember Ioric saying something about how they tried to maintain the stonework, but couldn't build like it any more.'

Zoella shivered when she remembered how she had first come to this part of the city. Ioric had instructed her to visit the catacombs beneath the streets. She'd found her way into an ancient library, finding out about their past from old books and documents.

And had been sealed in the darkness by Liana.

Ioric had rescued her, but she could feel the terror even now.

The darkness ...

'Here,' she said. 'This must be it.'

There was a culvert built into the wall, from which a thin stream of water was gushing. They couldn't see far inside.

Meru took a look and sniffed.

'Doesn't smell great,' he said.

'Lovely,' Kiri said.

They had brought their hand-held lights with them. Meru unpacked them, switched them on and handed them round.

Zoella gritted her teeth.

Darkness ...

Summoning her determination she crouched down and clambered in. Inside, the tunnel was bigger, with stones and mud coating the floor. Kiri followed her with Meru bringing up the rear. They couldn't see far.

They walked for perhaps a quarter of a mark, stepping through fetid and dank puddles of water, hearing the squeaks of marsips in the darkness, but never seeing the small rodents. They reached an intersection and huddled close to inspect the passageways that led away into the darkness.

'Straight on?' Meru asked.

Zoella nodded.

'Let's be quick,' Kiri said, with a shiver. 'It's just horrible down here … dark and …'

Both Zoella and Meru turned as Kiri stumbled back, clutching at her head. She moaned, pushing her hands against the sides of her forehead and thrashing around. They caught her, lowering her to the ground.

'Nerina?' Meru demanded.

Zoella nodded, she could feel the power of the nexion around her, a hot metal smell growing in her nostrils. Kiri screamed and clenched her eyes tight, her body trembling.

'We've got to stop it,' Meru said to Zoella. 'Can't you do anything?'

Kiri yelped in pain and then her eyes opened.

'No … don't!' she gasped. 'Please don't … not …'

Zoella held on to Kiri's wrists. She too flinched and grimaced with pain.

'It's her,' Zoella said. 'Nerina. I'll try to …'

Zoella's expression went blank, and then a look of horror crept across her face.

* * *

Nerina pulled the knife back and held it in front of Pootle's eyes. It glinted in the bright orange light from the flames behind her. He quivered in her grasp, immobile, caught in her mental grip. Nerina turned the knife around, seeing its reflection cast a glow across his pale skin.

See Kiri? I do have a hold over you. I have him. I know he is dear to you. I know all.

Nerina revelled in the panic that spluttered across the link.

No … don't! Please don't … not …

Nerina pushed the knife point against Pootle's face, just enough to dint his skin.

You can save him Kiri. Give yourself up, come back to Drayden, submit to me. I will let him live. Otherwise …

Nerina twisted the knife a fraction, a rivulet of blood dripped down Pootle's cheek. Pootle shuddered in her grip, but was still locked in her hold. Nerina could feel the horror, feel the fear that cascaded across the mental connection. Kiri's guilt flashed and soared around her. She luxuriated in it.

Yes, you abandoned him didn't you? Thought only of yourself. Left him here to face the punishment that should be yours. I will torture him, you know I am capable of it.

The dread was palpable now.

Just come to me … I will spare him.

Nerina felt it … capitulation.

I will …

NO!

Another voice, strident and powerful, cut across the exchange. Nerina sensed a stronger power, vibrant and fierce, determined and forthright.

You lie! You will not have her, she will not come to you!

Nerina felt the alarm, heard Kiri's plaintive protest.

But Pootle … he served me … he's innocent …

Nerina's retort was immediate. She pushed the knife up Pootle's face, cutting a gash in his skin. Pootle yelled, blood flowed.

He will die!

Nerina's mental vision was swamped with another face. Brown eyes and a resolute face. She saw regret, felt anger, but sensed utter unwavering will.

And he will be avenged!

* * *

Kiri howled with anguish as the link was suffused with redness; blood mixed with anger, horror and regret; the slashing thrusts of a knife wielded in rage. Pootle's screams echoed in her mind …

Silence.

Just the dripping of dank water in the tunnel.

'Kiri …'

She looked up into Zoella's eyes.

'You stopped me,' Kiri whispered. 'I could have gone, I could have saved him.'

'It was a trap,' Zoella answered, matter of fact. 'She would never have let him go. She would have torn you and been all the stronger.'

Kiri's eyes were dark and haunted. Meru crouched down beside her. She was trembling and didn't respond.

'What happened?' he asked, his tones hushed. Zoella explained.

Meru pulled Kiri into a hug.

'It's not your fault,' he said. 'Zoella's right. She was baiting you, there's no way she would have done as she said. All the more reason for us to stop her, avenge this servant of yours …'

Kiri was sobbing now, limp in Meru's arms.

'All this death,' she cried. 'It has to stop.'

Zoella got to her feet. They looked up as she held out her hands to them both.

'And we will stop it,' she said. 'We have to.'

Meru helped Kiri to her feet.

'Did Nerina find out where we are?' he asked.

'I don't think so,' Zoella said. 'She can only see what we can see. Down here …'

She gestured to the dank walls of the sewer.

Meru nodded.

'But when we are somewhere she might recognise,' Zoella said. 'Our guard could slip, it's only a matter of time before she finds out. We've been lucky so far.'

Kiri wiped her tears away.

'I want to kill her,' Kiri said. 'Make her pay.'

'It may come to that,' Zoella replied, looking at her and then across at Meru. 'It will take all our efforts.'

Meru nodded.

'It's her or us,' he said. 'Clear enough.'

He pulled the two women into an embrace.

'Together, the three of us.'

* * *

Joachim and Gemma led their hergs around the walls and then struck across the farmlands towards the main track to the city. They could see a stream of workers traipsing towards the city from the fields to the sunward.

'Let's join the others,' Joachim said. 'If we plod on with them, no one will give us a second glance.'

They moved into the crowds. They crossed the river and turned towards the main city gates, walking up to the stables.

As they tied up the hergs Joachim wondered how many people were still working. It was late in the stretch and most of the hergs were in and munching on dried greenings from the fields. Few more would arrive now. The stables should stay quiet.

'Seems safe enough,' Gemma whispered. He nodded.

They made their way up to the council chambers. Crenech would be waiting for them.

The chambers were dusty, full of dark-hued wooden benches and tables piled high with books, ledgers and scrolls. A few scribes sat on tall stools, scribbling away with styluses, but the room was quiet.

Crenech was seated in a corner, half hidden behind an ungainly stack of books. He saw Joachim and Gemma and beckoned them over.

'Well, did you find them?' he whispered, as they drew close.

Joachim nodded. 'Yes, we led them to the sewer outflow on the shadeward side, they'll be making their way to the stables as we speak.'

‘The priestesses are communing up in the palace,’ Crenech said. ‘We are safe for now.’

He gestured for the pair to sit next to him.

‘So … it is true?’ Crenech asked. ‘We risk everything on account of them. If they cannot overcome the three priestesses we will all be killed.’

‘They are as they said they would be,’ Gemma said. ‘The three of them who remain … Meru is …’

‘The boy doesn’t interest me,’ Crenech said. ‘The nieces?’

‘Kiri was a priestess,’ Joachim said. ‘She still looks like one. She’s a fighter, trained and ready to deal with anything. She looks like she could take them all on herself and win.’

‘And Zoella?’

‘It’s strange,’ Joachim said. ‘She seems … demure … gentle even. She’s warm and friendly, totally the opposite of Kiri and yet …’

‘Yes?’ Crenech said.

‘Both of the others,’ Gemma said. ‘They look to her. She’s in charge. I see no reason to doubt them … but until we confront the priestesses …’

‘Interesting,’ Crenech said, ‘Let’s hope they are everything we hope they are. If they aren’t, the priestesses will kill us all.’

CHAPTER SEVENTEEN

Viresia, Capital of Scallia

Round 2307, Tenth pass

Crenech, Joachim and Gemma made their way out of the council chambers and down the streets to the stables. The smell of herg droppings was stronger now, the hergs standing in their allotted stalls. Joachim led them inside, their conversation trivial and light hearted. It was dimly lit inside, only a few jars of mossglow were hung on an exposed beam above, giving a faint glow. The one stablehand that remained looked up briefly from his work, but took no further notice of them as they went to their respective hergs, pretending to inspect them.

'I don't think I fancy travelling home this stretch,' Crenech said, offhand. 'I think I will spend the sleeping in the city.'

'As you wish, my Lord,' Joachim responded, dutifully.

'Fetch my gear for me, lad,' Crenech said. 'I need a few things from my pack.'

Joachim bowed and retreated further into the stables. Crenech and Gemma stood waiting alongside his herg, nodding at the stablehand who glanced in his direction and then went back to his task.

'I think you're quite right,' Gemma said, primly. 'To travel back now would be tiresome.'

'It's a long way.'

They didn't have to wait long. A faint whistle made him turn his head to see Joachim's face peering at him out of the gloom.

'Keep an eye out,' he whispered. Gemma nodded.

Crenech walked deeper into the stable, Joachim led him into one of the tack rooms towards the rear. He could make out the two women and young man who accompanied them. They all looked grimy and tired, a stale smell rising about them.

'Lord Crenech?' the first woman asked. He nodded.

'I am Zoella,' she said. She was the tallest of the two, with brown wavy hair and soft eyes. 'This is Meru and Kiri.' She gestured to the second woman. Crenech recoiled at the sharp expression on her face and the glare of her blue eyes. He looked over at Joachim.

'Next to get you safely out of sight,' Crenech said. 'My house will be safe, Joachim will lead you there. Gemma and I will keep the stablehand busy and meet you there in a spell.'

Joachim nodded and gestured for the three to follow him. Crenech walked out into the stables.

'Lad,' he called, raising his voice. 'Over here.'

The stablehand ran to him.

'Want to earn some extra coin?' Crenech said, under his breath.

'Sire?' The boy said, wide-eyed.

'Make yourself scarce for a spell,' he said, giving the boy a wink and inclining his head towards Gemma.

'Of course, sire.'

'I'll ensure you don't get into any trouble with your master,' Crenech added, tossing a coin to him.

The boy grinned and then ran off.

'You're old enough to be my father,' Gemma whispered.

'Perhaps even your grandfather,' Crenech replied. 'I'm afraid it's behaviour that's all too common amongst my peers. Many of the lords have unsavoury habits.'

Crenech took her hand and led her within the stables, deep into the shadows.

'Now we wait for a spell,' Crenech whispered. He could feel his stomach clench with a mixture of fear and excitment.

Committed now. We've made our move and the nieces are here! Let's hope this works.

'Joachim should have our visitors inside shortly. Once there they will be safe for now. Have you sensed anything?'

'I've felt nothing,' Gemma replied. 'As far as I can tell the priestesses are still up in the throne room.'

'Good,' Crenech said. 'Make no further attempts to sense them for now.'

They waited a while longer. Crenech looked out.

'That should be long enough,' he said. 'I will go straight home. You walk down to the markets and spend a while there before returning. I will see you soon.'

Gemma nodded and left, walking down the roads towards the lower city.

Crenech emerged a few moments later, straightening his jacket, looking around and then walking up the road towards his house.

Joachim was waiting at the doors when he got there.

'Master?'

Crenech moved inside and Joachim closed the door behind him.

'All safe?' Crenech asked.

Joachim nodded. 'They are within.'

'Lock the front doors,' Crenech said to him. 'And draw the shutters against the light. Tell the servants to prepare a meal and have it sent to the drawing room. Our guests?'

'Rooms were already arranged,' Joachim said. 'They are upstairs. Hot water and a change of clothes have been provided.'

'Good,' Crenech said. 'They looked exhausted to me. We cannot expect the priestesses to be ignorant of their arrival for long. I must speak to them before the sleeping.'

Joachim nodded. 'They are keen to speak to you too. But a wash, new clothes and food will be most welcome I think.'

'Excellent,' he said. 'Leave the servants' entrance open. Gemma will return before too long. Once the food is served have the servants retire, then bring down our guests and make sure we are not disturbed. I want no one else knowing they are here.'

'Yes, master.'

Crenech nodded. 'This is it. The next stretch will decide all our fates, one way or the other.'

Joachim swallowed.

'To be Scallian again?' he asked. 'A risk worth taking.'

* * *

Nerina stood in the hall of the priestesses, oblivious to the horrified stares of the others before her. Her face was streaked with blood, her dark clothing stained. Her arms were slack at her side, the knife still clenched in her right hand.

Blood dripped to the floor.

A pool of it surrounded a mutilated body that lay at her feet.

Nerina threw the knife aside and stepped forward.

So, this maid, this Zoella is the true power. But where is she?

'Clean up this mess,' she snapped, pushing her way past and through the double doors of the hall.

* * *

A chime later, Zoella heard a knock at the guest room door. Kiri answered it and looked out.

'Joachim,' she said. 'We're ready.'

Kiri turned and allowed Joachim to enter the room. Zoella smiled at Joachim and saw him smile in return. She saw Kiri raise an eyebrow.

All three of them were washed and changed, now wearing the clothing of well-to-do Scallian folk.

'Lord Crenech hopes you are refreshed,' Joachim said. 'Food is waiting, but he would like to speak to you …'

'Food would be very welcome,' Zoella said.

They followed Joachim downstairs. He led them into a drawing room and closed the door behind them.

Zoella looked around the room, reminded how she had once visited Ioric's own dwelling in Viresia. A fire was roaring in a large stone hearth, warm and welcoming. The room was lit by oil burners, giving a rich scented flavour to the air. The shutters were pulled against the light of Lacaille, the room cut off from the outside world. Crenech was within, sitting in a comfortable armchair near to the fire and there were other softly padded pieces of ornate furniture arranged throughout. Gemma stood alongside him, now dressed as a lady of Scallia. He turned and rose, striding towards them.

'My Princesses,' he said, bowing before Zoella and Kiri, his voice hushed. 'Daughters of Myana and nieces of King Ioric. And Meru, yes? Welcome to my house and welcome home … to Viresia, in Scallia.'

'It is good to be here,' Zoella said, taking his hand in hers. 'I thank you for your hospitality and the risks you have taken to get us here.' She looked around, smiling at Gemma and Joachim. 'All of you.'

'You bring us hope,' Crenech said. 'The risk is worth taking.'

'Are we safe here?' Meru asked.

'We have taken as many precautions as we could,' Crenech replied, keeping his voice low. 'Your presence should remain a secret, but we should be cautious all the same. You must be hungry, here … there is food …' He gestured to a table set against the wall of the drawing room.

Zoella saw Kiri and Meru look hungrily across, but she shook her head.

'We must decide our next move first,' she said. 'May not have much time. The high priestess, Nerina, has tried to find out where we are. For now she has relented, but she will try again. We may not be able to stop her much longer. Do the priestesses here have any suspicions?'

Crenech gestured for them to sit and they lowered themselves into the chairs. Zoella sat perched on the edge of hers.

'We do not believe so,' Crenech said. 'They reside in the palace throne room atop the city, their habit is not to venture out during the sleeping. But there are guards there until the first chime, we can't approach without arousing suspicion.'

'We must move against them,' Zoella said. 'As soon as we can.'

'Confront them directly?' Crenech asked.

Zoella nodded. 'We need to get close to them, undetected. What happens at the first chime?'

'The guards are dismissed, the priestesses break their fast,' Crenech said. 'Then …'

Joachim leant forward. 'Then one of them flies out on her dach to search.'

Zoella nodded.

'So,' she said, looking across at Kiri. 'At first chime, they will find … us.'

Everyone looked at her.

'But how?' Crenech asked.

'You will take us to them,' Zoella said to Crenech. 'Hand us over as prisoners.'

'Prisoners?' Crenech said in alarm.

Meru nodded. 'A good idea. I see what you mean.'

'I don't,' Kiri complained.

Zoella gestured to Crenech and Joachim. 'They capture us,' she said to Kiri. 'Lead us to the priestesses … vagabond women found wandering in the land, to be tested for the gift. Crenech and Joachim deliver us directly to them …'

'Yes,' Kiri said, her eyes widening. 'That gets us there and provides a means for the others to escape should things go wrong.'

'What about me?' Gemma asked.

'You will stay here, young lady,' Crenech said, giving her a look. 'No sense risking those we don't have to.'

'I can help,' Gemma said. 'I have the gift too.'

'We may need all the help we can get,' Zoella said. 'Three of us, three of them.'

'I don't like it,' Crenech said.

'If you all perish,' Gemma said. 'What hope is left for me? The priestesses will come for me, then what?'

Kiri nodded. 'She's right. They will show no mercy.'

'And me?' Meru asked.

'Stand with us,' Crenech said. 'You and Joachim can claim to have found these three women and brought them to my attention. Together we will take them to the priestesses.'

Zoella looked around at them all. 'We are agreed then? First chime on the next stretch?'

They all nodded.

'You know we will have to kill them,' Kiri added, after a pause. Gemma swallowed.

'No,' Zoella snapped. 'I will not murder them just because they follow Nerina's instruction.'

'Then we will have to take their power,' Kiri said. 'If we don't they will alert Nerina.'

'Kiri …'

'I know you hate this,' Kiri said. 'But if Nerina finds out from them we are here she will come for us with no delay. We will not be ready.'

'Tear them?' Zoella asked.

'Yes. If you won't kill them, tear them. We cannot take the risk of trusting them.'

Zoella swallowed. 'We both know what that power will do to us, the rage that will build, the desire for domination …'

'We will have to overcome it,' Kiri said. 'The others will watch over us and we must watch each other.'

'Tearing them is worse than murder. You know what happened to Liana … we can't leave them like that … alive with no thoughts!'

'It's one or the other,' Kiri said, her voice cold. 'Or we might as well just hand ourselves over and give up.'

'Perhaps we could convince them,' Zoella said. 'Persuade them to …'

'I know what they're like,' Gemma said, shaking her head. 'I was there when they tore my companions. They were barbaric, gleeful, there is no chance of compassion …'

'Kiri is right,' Crenech said. 'Either they die, or you take their powers. They are the enemy, we can afford no mercy. We will need time to prepare afterwards, to bring the city on side so we are ready for the high priestess. We cannot gamble with that. What is the choice to be?'

Zoella looked about her. Kiri had her arms folded. Meru looked worried, Joachim concerned, Gemma was looking at Zoella.

Looking to me to make this decision. Why me?

Crenech was staring at her.

'We must agree on this,' he said. 'Now.'

'I vote we kill them,' Kiri said. 'Quick and simple.'

'Yes,' Gemma said, nodding.

'I don't like it,' Meru said. 'But they would kill us and tear you both. I think we have to kill them to be sure.'

'Zoella?' Crenech asked.

'You give me a choice between murder and torture,' Zoella said. 'Both are evil choices, but the first is more merciful and less dangerous.' She swallowed. 'Murder it is.'

Zoella saw Joachim nod.

'Decided then,' Crenech said. 'I will procure a few items. Hergs, a wagon, clothing suitable for your new status as vagabond prisoners …'

'Dressing in rags again,' Kiri said, rolling her eyes.

'It must look convincing,' Crenech said. 'The priestesses are no fools. We will have to bind your wrists and eyes as per their instructions.'

'Dressing as princesses and ladies would be a giveaway,' Meru said, venturing a smile.

'Just not so tight we can't get loose!' Kiri replied.

Zoella looked across to Crenech.

'The next stretch will decide everything,' he said. 'But first, food and rest.'

* * *

The food was consumed in near silence, Zoella found she could eat little, the thought of killing the priestesses weighing on her mind. She returned her plate to the table.

'You're sure the people of the city will accept us, rally to us?' she asked Crenech.

Crenech wiped the corner of his mouth with a napkin before answering.

'The nieces of King Ioric?' Crenech said. 'Princesses of our realm, having returned and despatched these hated priestesses? Yes, indeed. They will call for sovereignty to be restored immediately …' Crenech stopped. 'You are both princesses, but only one can be queen …'

'It is Zoella,' Joachim said.

Zoella looked at him in surprise. Kiri and Meru nodded.

'We already decided,' Kiri said, by way of explanation.

'I see,' Crenech said looking from Zoella to Kiri and back again. 'In that case, on the next stretch, if luck should be with us and we win our first battle, I will proclaim from the palace of Viresia that we will crown Queen Zoella of Scallia …'

'I will not take the crown,' Zoella said, interrupting him.

All eyes were on her now.

'Zoella …' Kiri began.

'I will not take it,' Zoella said. 'Not until all of this is done and we have won everything. Ioric took the crown and was slain within just a few stretches. If I am to be queen, and reluctantly so, my reign will start with peace, not war. Let us fight all the battles first, and celebrate afterwards. If there is anything left for us to celebrate.'

Crenech nodded. 'Your wisdom exceeds mine,' he said. 'It will be as you say. But do not underestimate the potency of having our royal line restored.'

'We will have to count on it to defeat Nerina,' Zoella said. 'Many will die again, we must all be prepared for that. The battle will be fierce and brutal. Nerina's wrath will be terrible.' Crenech saw her look over at Kiri. 'We know her rage.'

Kiri nodded.

'She will spare no effort to possess us,' Kiri said. 'Nothing else will matter, not us, not you, not even her own people. She will sacrifice everything. Once she knows we are here, we will have little time.'

'Let us focus on the task in hand,' Crenech said. 'First chime tomorrow. For now, we should rest. Sleep if we can.'

Zoella nodded.

'Yes,' she said. 'We must be as ready as we can be.'

They all stood up. Kiri gave Zoella a hug.

'We are going to win this,' she said.

Zoella nodded. 'Give me a moment to gather my thoughts.'

Kiri nodded. Meru went with her.

Crenech and Gemma gave her a bow and followed them out. Joachim hesitated for a moment and then left.

Alone now, Zoella paced around Crenech's drawing room, looking at the paintings, furniture and books that lined the walls. There was a great deal of Scallian history on show; images of Viresia, the shadeward forests, portraits of kings from long ago.

Did Ioric feel like this? Poised on the verge of battle, knowing that people were going to live or die based on the decisions he took? I wish he was here to ask! It should have been him, not me. I truly am just a vagabond girl from a half-forgotten town. I might have the bloodline, but I am nothing, how can I be Queen of Viresia?

The thoughts cascaded around her mind, driving her to panic, fear and desperation.

But the choice is made. We attack on the next stretch. For good or for ill, we are plunging into war again. How many will die this time?

'Zoella?'

She turned to see Joachim standing in the doorway.

'Sorry,' he said. 'I didn't mean to disturb you.'

She gasped.

'You did,' she managed. 'But I'm glad of it. Will you stay awhile? My thoughts are awhirl.'

'Your friends ...'

'Already gone to bed,' Zoella said.

'Trying to get some sleep is probably the best idea,' Joachim replied.

'Oh ... I doubt they'll be sleeping,' Zoella said. 'Not those two.'

'Ah,' Joachim said. 'They're ...'

'Together, yes,' Zoella said.

'And you?' Joachim asked. 'Is there ...?'

'No,' Zoella said. 'I'm the sensible, boring one. I have to think about what is next, worry about the future, plot murder ...' Her voice wavered.

'It sounds very lonely,' Joachim replied, stepping towards her.

Zoella gasped, swallowed and turned away. When she looked up Joachim was standing alongside her.

'I didn't mean to give voice to your feelings,' he said. 'But if there's anything I can do to help ...'

'I'm just a maid,' Zoella said, her voice shaking. 'Yes, I was born to a queen, but I knew nothing of it until a pass ago. I am of lesser rank than Gemma, far lower! I have no training, no experience ... I can't fight like Kiri, can't fix machines like Meru. I have no skills, nothing to recommend me. Everyone is looking to me. Now I'm told I must murder to bring peace. I don't want to do this.'

She sobbed, resting her head in her hands.

She felt Joachim touch her shoulder.

'You will make the right choice,' he said. 'You will be our queen.'

She turned to look at him,

'I have earned no higher station than you,' she snapped. 'I'm not royalty just because of my parents ... a mother who I never knew, a father who ... well, never mind. I know nothing of power, politics, running anything ... I was just ... born, there's nothing special about me, no more than anyone else.'

Joachim took her hand.

'From the moment I met you I saw a leader,' he said. 'Someone who others will follow, trust and lay down their lives for. Your friends, they look up to you. If Lord Crenech would allow it, I would pledge myself to your service right this moment, Zoella. Though I am just a servant. I believe in you.'

'Then you are a fool,' Zoella said.

'A glad fool,' Joachim returned. 'Zoella, the people of Scallia need hope, they need someone. The people respect the lords but they won't follow them. They loved King Marek, for all his faults, they were broken at the deaths of King Ioric and Torin. Then the priestesses came and all was fear and intimidation. There is no future for folk, no one can see a way forward. I see our people, the people of Scallia, every stretch. Their faces are drawn, they stoop, hunkered down … there is no joy left. Scallia is a kingdom without a king or a queen. We must have one back.'

'Then they should look elsewhere,' Zoella said. 'It cannot be me.'

'You think it should be Kiri?'

'She is stronger, faster, a warrior,' Zoella replied. 'She is far more of a queen than I. She can conquer, fight the battle, lead soldiers, kill …'

'Are you afraid of what you must do?' Joachim asked.

'Killing?' Zoella said. 'No, not afraid. Not even scared. I have killed before, when those dear to me were threatened … I killed. In self-defence … but not like this, not premeditated …'

'They will kill us if they find out,' Joachim said. 'Won't it be self-defence then? We're just safeguarding ourselves.'

'And if they surrender?' Zoella said. 'Must we still kill them to safeguard ourselves?'

'If there is a danger they will warn the high priestess,' Joachim said. 'Surely there is no choice.'

'There is always a choice,' Zoella said. 'Kiri has murdered before, I have not. She's the stronger one. She's the queen you're looking for. Not me.'

Joachim shook his head.

'The people will never warm to her,' he said. 'They will respect her, but she was one of them. They'll never trust her like they will trust you.'

'So everyone keeps telling me!' Zoella cried. 'Would they really? If they saw me like this, caught in indecision? Unable to make a choice? I don't want people living or dying based on my choices. That's not fair!'

Zoella sat down in one of the chairs, her face in her hands, trying to stifle the sobs that coursed through her.

When she looked again Joachim was crouched before her. She felt him take her hands in his. 'The very fact you worry about doing the right thing shows you are the right person for this. You have compassion, a noble thing. You never were a priestess, but you have their powers. You have always been Scallian. Always a princess, related to Marek and Ioric. You can see all sides.'

'It's just an accident of birth,' Zoella said, her sight blurred with tears. 'Just being born a princess doesn't mean I'll be any good at being a queen!'

'No,' Joachim said. 'But being someone that everyone respects does.'

Zoella blinked and looked at him. 'Do you really mean that?'

Joachim nodded. 'Yes. The lords will support you because you're royalty. The people will support you because you weren't born to it, because you've experienced what it's like to be poor and what it's like to suffer. And your friends will support you whatever happens, as will I.'

Zoella smiled at him. 'I really don't see what I've done to earn your trust.'

Joachim paced around for a moment. 'Crenech told me he was there when Ioric presented you to King Marek. He said you rescued Ioric from a beast in a swamp.'

Zoella's gaze grew distant.

'Yes,' she said. 'The molossc, Ioric might have died had I not been there. That was so long ago …'

'And that you swore an oath to Scallia.'

Her voice faded as she remembered the oath Joachim was talking about.

Swear that you will be loyal to house Tiamoi!

Swear that you will defend our royal line!

Swear that you will defend our interests, defend our people, our cities and our lands against all that would do them harm!

Her mind resonated with the answer she had given.

I so swear!

And then she remembered King Marek's words.

Your solemn duty, so to do, until one of our line, or death releases you.

She looked at Joachim.

'I did so swear,' she whispered. 'And there are none to release me from it. My solemn duty, so to do.'

'Crenech told me the story,' Joachim said. 'How a girl from the sunright saved our prince, was honoured by our king and stood against the priestesses when the army failed and the priestesses came. We all thought you lost, a heroine who was slain before she could rise to greatness, or even be recognised for her deeds.'

Zoella gasped.

'Then we learned that you lived, we found you are truly our lost princess,' Joachim continued, his voice low. 'I never thought I might meet you, never dreamt I would be in the presence of such as you. Your story is our hope.'

'I hope I'm not too disappointing in reality,' Zoella said.

Joachim bowed his head before her.

'It is an honour to be in your presence, Princess Zoella.'

She let go of his hands and touched his chin, tilting his head up once more.

'No, stop that,' she said. 'We are not so different, you and I. I will not have you bow before me, not like this.'

They gazed at each other for a long moment.

'I will not take the crown until our battles are ended,' Zoella began, holding up a hand up as Joachim began to protest. 'But … then, if it truly be the will of the people and Lords of Scallia, then yes. I will become their queen.'

Joachim smiled, his eyes sparkling with excitement.

'Oh, they will show their love for you,' Joachim said. 'And I will shout it from the rooftops. Our queen has returned! All hail Zoella!'

* * *

Thick curtains blocked the light from Lacaille, with just thin beams shining on the panelled wooden floor. Kiri stood at one of the windows, the curtain pulled back, looking over the view to the sunward. She could see soldiers standing on the walls far below, walking back and forth. Beyond, the river that flowed through the city cascaded down to the ground through a series of reservoirs and lakes before surging out across the landscape to the sunward.

She sighed and let the curtain fall back.

Meru was standing behind her. She leant into his embrace as he placed his arms around her. She felt him kiss her neck.

'We need to get some sleep,' he whispered in her ear. 'The next stretch …'

'I won't sleep,' she answered. 'Too many thoughts.'

'Your servant?' Meru asked, in a whisper.

'He was called Pootle,' she said. 'I know … strange name, I never asked why he was called that. Never even asked much about him. He was a simple man, bumbling and slow, but he knew his place and worked hard. His duty was to serve the priestesses. He was assigned to me the moment I joined the temple, rounds ago. He looked after me. Cleaned for me, cooked, even dressed me.'

She shuddered, tears on her cheeks once more.

'I never thanked him,' she said. 'Just expected to be served, never showed any appreciation and now …'

Meru's arms closed about her.

'He's gone.' Kiri shook, her voice hard-edged. 'Murdered.'

'This high priestess will use anyone to get what she wants …'

'It's the gift,' Kiri said. 'This accursed gift, handed down mother to daughter since we came to this place all those rounds ago. Zoella's right. I wish we never had it. I hate it.'

'It was supposed to be used for the good of all,' Meru said. 'It's like anything, if used for the wrong purpose … You and Zoella can set this back the way it was supposed to be.'

Kiri didn't answer.

'And if you didn't have it,' Meru continued. 'I guess we would never have met.'

She relaxed a little in his embrace.

'And I would not have missed out on knowing you,' he added. 'Not for anything.'

She turned around in his arms, a small smile on her face.

'I quite like you too,' she said.

'You …'

She interrupted him with a slow kiss and then drew back.

'I don't want to sleep,' she said, her voice low. 'And I don't want to think about anything, about the past, about the future … anything. Let's just be … here and now.'

'Just you and me,' Meru replied, his voice hushed.

'We have a room,' Kiri whispered, wriggling closer to him, their foreheads touching. 'It even has a bed. No plants trying to eat us, no weird animals …'

Their conversation was over, desire reaching up and around them, guiding their movements. They took their time. Gone was the frantic lust that had driven them together, now a deeper bond of love, yet no less passionate, suffused them. Soulmates, brought together from opposites sides of the continents, of politics and religion. None of those mattered any more, forgotten in the midst of their love-making.

Sated, they lay in each other's embrace, their bodies entwined in a timeless moment, vulnerable, but content.

'Do you remember when we met?' Kiri asked, propping herself up and leaning across him.

'Difficult to forget,' Meru said. 'You had me tied to a shade and then you hit me with your kai.'

Kiri laughed. 'Yes … well no. We met before that, here in Viresia, remember? I stood alongside Nerina, you were with Zoella and King Ioric.'

Meru nodded. 'At the gates of the city, I'd just arrived to warn everyone of the flares. Seems a lifetime ago.'

'A different life,' Kiri said, snuggling in closer to him. 'I remember the anger and revulsion I felt when you said your ancestors were from

Nireus. I was so indoctrinated all I could think of was killing you, thinking I would be saving Esurio.'

'And after the flare,' Meru said. 'Do you remember how we argued at knife-point?'

'It was then I began to realise I'd been lied to,' Kiri said. 'I knew you were telling the truth, it just didn't fit with what I'd been taught.'

'I knew you knew,' Meru said, stroking her arm and running his fingers down to her wrist. 'I sensed the turmoil in you. After that …'

'The connection between us?'

He nodded. 'It made me ill. I was unconscious. Luckily Zoella found me.'

'I didn't mean it, I didn't know what I was doing,' Kiri said. 'I linked us together in a way that was supposed to be for couples who already … well, you know.'

Meru kissed her.

'I do now.'

'Then I caught you in that boat house,' Kiri said. 'I hope you remember that.'

Meru smiled. 'I thought you were going to kill me.'

Kiri rolled on top of him.

'I wanted to do something else to you,' she said. 'Can you guess what it was?'

If Meru replied, it was lost in another kiss.

'I love you Meru of Amar,' she said, staring into his eyes, her black hair falling across him. 'You're mine.'

Meru stared into her fierce blue eyes. He was always mesmerised by them; such a depth of colour. The warmth and scent of her was intoxicating, but it was her devotion to him that amazed him most.

But there was no room for doubt.

'I am,' he whispered. 'Always.'

* * *

The following stretch found Zoella, Kiri and Gemma dressed in rags and blindfolded, hands tied behind their backs and locked inside a wooden-gated wagon. Two hergs were pulling it up the cobbled streets of Viresia, heading towards the palace.

Joachim and Meru sat astride the hergs, with Crenech in the lead. They soon arrived in the courtyard of the palace, the vast metal doors glaring bright with the light of Lacaille.

'Last time I was here,' Kiri said. 'I was plotting how to take your gift and challenge Nerina.'

'Last time I was here,' Zoella replied. 'I tried to kill you.'

'Not quite the glorious homecoming.'

'Not yet,' Zoella replied.

The wagen jolted on the cobbled streets. Gemma sat next to them, lost in her own thoughts.

'Listen,' Zoella said, the blindfold itching against her skin. 'Joking aside. Are you sure you're happy with this queen business? You're the stronger one, you can't deny it.'

'No, I'm not. I know I can fight, but that's not the same thing.'

'You wanted to be empress though. I know you did.'

'Yes,' Kiri continued. 'But that was the gift, enticing me, goading me on. I'd have been awful, as bad as Nerina, just a brutal dictator, killing anyone who disagreed with me. Trust me, I know that well enough. Me being queen would be a disaster for everyone, particularly me. I've already got what I want!'

'And he's smitten with you too!' Zoella said.

Kiri laughed.

'And you really think I'll be better?' Zoella asked.

'Yes. You don't want to do this, but you will because it's the right thing to do. That's what makes all the difference. You're so good at bringing people together. You'll be a great queen.'

Zoella sighed.

'Everyone seems to have this enormous faith in me,' Zoella said. 'But what if I get it wrong?'

'You won't.'

'What if I do?'

'I'm your sister, I'm telling you … you won't.'

Zoella smiled to herself.

'How did I go from hating you to needing you so badly?'

The wagon jolted to a stop.

Gemma caught her breath.

'It will be alright,' Kiri said to her.

They heard Joachim and Meru climb down from the hergs and then footsteps as Crenech walked to the palace doors.

'Ready?' Kiri whispered. 'You understand what we have to do?'

'Yes,' Gemma replied.

'I hate it,' Zoella said. 'But it must be done.'

They heard conversation and more footsteps, then Joachim and Meru walking down the flanks of the wagon and unbolting the door at the rear.

'There are three,' Meru said in an urgent whisper. 'All have their staffs.'

They heard the door swing open. Meru and Joachim reached in and, none too gently, pulled Kiri, Zoella and Gemma out, pushing them round the wagon and forward towards the palace. All three were forced to their knees, their heads bowed, arms still behind their backs.

'Here they are,' Crenech said. 'Vagabonds most likely, but all three are women, women I haven't seen in my lands before. I have brought them straight here so you might inspect them.'

'You have done well,' the lead priestess said. 'Bring them.'

Zoella was pulled to her feet, her blindfold pulled away, revealing her face. Alongside she could see the same had happened to Kiri and Gemma. She sensed Meru and Joachim step back.

The lead priestess stared at them for a moment. Then her eyes widened as she recognised Kiri.

'You …'

Kiri jolted out her hand. The priestess screeched, clutching at her forehead and staggering back. Zoella felt the zing of the nexion rise around her. She stepped aside, raising her hand at the next priestess in line, reaching out with her mind. Gemma did the same.

The glow of power around her was dazzling, bright flares of illumination shining in her mind. She directed her thoughts at the nearest one, feeling the unfamiliar sensation of another woman's mind in close proximity.

Then she felt the hate.

It washed over her, rage burning her mind. Images of a strange red-stone pyramid, scores of women worshiping Lacaille, fear, terror and brutal anger suffused her. She recoiled in horror.

Pain crashed through her and she staggered back. She heard Gemma scream from alongside.

'She's the one! Take her!'

She glimpsed Kiri pushing her way in front, blocking the priestesses from attacking her, both arms outstretched. She heard Kiri scream in pain as the priestesses assaulted her.

Zoella! Sister! Help me!

Kiri's plaintive cry crashed through her mind, shocking her back into focus. Zoella saw Kiri fall to her knees, the three priestesses pressing in towards her.

No!

Zoella struck out at the nearest one, recalling the pressure she had applied to the traders in the ice caravan in Drem. The glow of the priestesses' power shone before her but she engulfed it and crushed it down by an effort of will.

The glow flickered and went out. Before her the priestess fell and lay unmoving on the flagstones of the palace.

Another blast of pain sliced through her, burning into her skull. She fought it back, sensing the attacker, reaching out for the orb of glowing power and applying the same technique.

A second priestess fell.

The last priestess broke off her attack on Kiri. Zoella heard Kiri gasp and sink to the floor, aware that Meru had run to her side.

Who are you? How can you do this?

The priestess was staring at her in shock, surprise and growing fear.

Zoella grabbed at her mind, locking it in her grip. The priestess screamed.

I am Zoella, Princess of Scallia! Here to take back what was stolen from my people!

And with that the third priestess breathed her last.

Zoella blinked, the real world swimming into focus around her. The bodies of the three priestesses lay before her, on their backs, their faces staring upwards with a look of profound shock upon their faces.

She could see they were dead.

She turned to see Meru propping up Kiri, with Crenech and Joachim behind helping Gemma, their faces pale. All were staring at her.

'Why are you looking at me?' she asked, her voice a whisper.

Kiri staggered up, walking over to her.

'I thought you weren't going to fight for a moment,' she said. 'But then … when you did …'

'What?' Zoella asked.

'It was like a flare,' Kiri said. 'I felt as if you were going to burn all of us away … an inferno … and you just … overcame them. Your gift … it's astonishing!'

Zoella swallowed, looking around at the bodies of the priestesses.

'I don't like it,' Zoella said. 'I don't want it … I wish I'd never been born with this awful power …'

'We must still defeat the high priestess …' Gemma said.

'Yes,' Zoella said. 'But then, then I will never use this accursed gift again. Never.'

Kiri pulled her into a hug. Tears streamed down their faces.

'They weren't able to send any messages?' Crenech said. 'Forgive me … but we must be sure.'

Zoella released Kiri and shook her head. 'They did not have time. They suspected nothing.'

Crenech nodded.

'Meru, Joachim,' he called. 'Put their bodies in the wagon …'

'They must be treated with respect,' Zoella called. 'I will not have them dishonoured. They did only what their mistress bid them to do and they died doing it.'

Crenech nodded. 'It will be done as you say.'

Kiri walked across to the first of the priestesses, kneeling down alongside her and running her fingers across her face and closing her eyes. Zoella crouched down beside her.

'I knew this one,' Kiri said, her expression downcast. 'Her name was Amrit. She was much like me.'

'I am sorry for what we had to do,' Zoella whispered.

'I heard her thoughts,' Kiri said. 'She would not have listened to us, she was terrified of Nerina's wrath. The hatred, anger and fear had grown within her. They've all been consumed by the gift. They've all been encouraged to tear too many other women. We couldn't have turned her back.'

Kiri looked at Zoella.

'We came so close ourselves,' Zoella said. 'Either one of us, more of the gift would have sent us into this spiralling frenzy.'

Kiri got to her feet, Zoella alongside. Both beckoned to Gemma and held her hands.

'It won't be long before Nerina notices they fail to report in,' Kiri said. 'A stretch perhaps, no more.'

'Then we must now take back control of the city and make preparations for war,' Crenech called to them. 'It is time to proclaim that the princesses of Scallia have returned. I will summon the lords. Come!'

* * *

It did not take long. Crenech had summoned the lords of the city, but news that something momentous had occurred had leaked out. Crowds were already gathering about the palace, thronging its courts. The absence of the priestesses had been noted. Guards had already been posted at the walls to stop anyone from leaving and the gates of the city had been barred.

A hastily convened meeting of the lords had been organised. A few of them remembered Zoella as a maid to the late King Ioric, but all of them remembered Kiri. Crenech had to quell several threats of violence before her story could be told. Even Zoella's own tale did not get told without interruption.

'A maid as our queen?' one Lord complained.

'A princess as our queen,' Crenech replied. 'And you will show the proper respect to the daughter of Myana, sister of King Ioric and daughter of King Marek.'

Conversation rose in an angry hubbub. Zoella stepped into the midst of it, raising her voice.

'My Lords,' she said, her voice quavering before growing more confident. 'I know this is much to take on at such notice. But time is truly not on our side. We have mere stretches to prepare our people for war once again.'

Silence fell as the conversation ebbed away around her. The lords were watching and listening to her now. She looked at each one in turn as she spoke.

'Ioric was my king. Yes, you knew me as a maid and I served him as such, but you will also remember I swore an oath to King Marek too. Then I had no knowledge of my past, my birthright, nor that I even had a sister.' Zoella gestured for Kiri to stand alongside her and held her hand tightly. 'Neither of us knew of our past, but we have put down our own animosity, forgiven past wrongs. We stand together now and you saw how we rid Viresia of the priestesses. Now we must rid Scallia of them too and safeguard the future. I intend to fulfil the oath I swore. You have sworn similar oaths in defence of our kingdom. Now I ask you to fulfil them. Will you stand with me?'

Zoella swallowed. No one spoke, the lords stared at her.

'Will you stand?' she demanded again.

Still there was no response. Crenech stepped forward.

'I will stand,' he said. 'Scallia will be returned to house Tiamoi. Who will see this done?'

He looked around at the other Lords. One stepped forward, then another. Each muttered assent.

Zoella let go of Kiri's hand and paced before them, looking each one in the eye once more.

'The future Queen of Scallia asks for more than a mumbled reply,' she snapped. 'Swear that you will be loyal to house Tiamoi!'

'We so swear,' their voices were still hushed.

'Not good enough,' Zoella said, glaring at them. For a moment she closed her eyes, her mental powers surging forth.

Swear! Swear that you will be loyal to house Tiamoi!

The lords gasped as one. Zoella didn't relent.

'Swear it!' she shouted aloud.

Now their answer was strong.

'We so swear!'

Zoella pulled Kiri alongside her once more, gesturing to her and then to the lords.

'Swear that you will defend our royal line! Princess Zoella Tiamoi and Princess Kiri Tiamoi!'

'We so swear!'

The cry was strong now, growing louder with each repetition.

'Swear that you will defend our interests,' she shouted. 'Defend our people, our cities and our lands against all that would do them harm!'

'We so swear!' the lords shouted back.

'Then let us tell the people,' she said. 'Let us tell them that their royal line is found again, that the priestesses who afflicted them are ended, but they must yet fight for their survival if they would see Scallia returned to them.' Zoella paused for breath. 'And let us tell them … if they … if we win … they will have a queen and she will pledge that Scallia is restored and made whole again.'

'All hail Princess Zoella and Princess Kiri!' Crenech roared, glaring around the room.

The cry was taken up and then thunderous applause followed. Zoella looked around, seeing Joachim and Gemma clapping wildly. Kiri was looking at her with wide eyes, Meru staring at her in admiration, also clapping as hard as he could.

Crenech walked up to her, his fist clenched.

'Princess Zoella,' he said. 'You are my queen, now and forever!'

He bowed low and then turned on his heel, gesturing to the doors.

'Open them!' he called. 'We present our princesses and our future queen to the people!'

The doors opened, Lacaille's light blazing in about them, casting long shadows on the marble floor.

'I will call for you both,' Crenech said, his eyes ablaze with excitement. 'It will not be long.'

He strode to the front of the group of Lords, organised them into two lines and then led them out into the bright light outside. They could be seen standing in a semi-circle before the courtyards and the hundreds of people gathered before them. The conversation of the crowd dropped away and Crenech began to speak.

'You were magnificent,' Meru said from beside her. Zoella turned to look at him. Kiri was also alongside, nodding. Zoella stretched out and took their hands in hers.

'I couldn't have done it without the two of you,' she said. 'My friend and my sister.'

She looked past them to see Joachim and Gemma, standing not far away. She smiled and beckoned to them.

'And you,' she said to Joachim. 'Your words have been a sweet kindness in my ears these last few stretches. I count you amongst my friends too.'

Joachim's mouth fell open in surprise.

'And you,' Zoella said to Gemma. 'You stood alongside us, brave despite the fear. Come.'

Zoella gestured to them and she pulled them all into an embrace.

Their hold was comforting. Zoella could feel herself trembling.

There was a roar from outside, some kind of chant growing. All five of them looked up as Crenech walked in, his figure silhouetted against the light of Lacaille until he came close.

'It is time,' he said, a smile splitting his face into a wide grin. 'Viresia awaits its queen to be.'

Zoella looked at Kiri, Meru, Joachim and Gemma. They nodded.

'Together,' Zoella said. 'We share this moment.'

Crenech led them forward out of the palace and into the glare of Lacaille. Zoella stood in the middle, flanked by Kiri and Meru, with Joachim and Gemma beyond them. As her eyes adjusted Zoella could see the crowds of people.

Some folk pointed, a cheer arose.

'My Lords!' Crenech shouted. 'Ladies, Gentlemen and citizens of Viresia. Here stand those who have freed our city from the grasp of the priestesses! Our royal line is restored. These are the lost daughters of Myana, daughter herself of King Marek! Show your honour first to Princess Kiri Tiamoi, warrior and fighter!'

The cheer rose. Zoella saw Kiri blush and then awkwardly curtsey next to her.

'And now your adulation!' Crenech roared. 'Soon to be crowned Queen of Scallia, Princess Zoella Tiamoi!'

Now the cries rose higher, the applause thunderous. Then the chant rose, this time the words were audible, clear and ringing out across the city.

'All hail Princess Zoella!'

Zoella stood there, tears streaming down her face. She raised a hand in acknowledgement.

'All hail Princess Zoella!'

How long it took for the cries to subside Zoella couldn't tell. It seemed to last for a spell or more. When it subsided she stepped forward and looked at all the people around her, the lords, her friends and all those gathered beyond.

'I have come through many troubles to stand here,' she said, raising her voice as loud as she could. 'Long before I knew of my heritage I swore an oath to King Marek to defend Scallia. Now I know who I am, I have returned to fulfil it. Yes, we have defeated the priestesses that took over our city, but this is just the beginning of the struggle. Beyond our lands the priestesses still rule and they will seek to take control again. This I will not allow. We have friends and allies en route to aid us and we will stop them once more. You must make ready to defend our city. Viresia has been attacked before, I watched the fire consume us. This time we will be wiser and stronger. We must stand firm, defy them and defeat them. When that is done, and our lands are safe and secure once more, then … and only then will I take the vows and take the crown.'

The cheers rose to a crescendo once more and the chant continued. Zoella heard Meru, Kiri, Joachim and Gemma join in.

'All hail Princess Zoella!'

CHAPTER EIGHTEEN

Viresia, Capital of Scallia

Round 2307, Eleventh pass

Through Viresia the news had travelled swiftly. Within the stretch all in the city were aware of what had happened and messengers had been sent with news for the more distant communities within Scallia.

There was shock and disbelief from many, but the absence of the dachs flying overhead convinced those who didn't accept the stories on first telling. Before long, soldiers and merchants were flocking to the city.

Preparations were hurried.

Food and medicines were stockpiled within the walls, brought in by laden hergs and carts crammed to overflowing. Weapons were readied, swords sharpened and bows restrung, with arrows trimmed and fletched. Carpenters and stone masons were working every spell shoring up the city walls, gates and defences.

Water and sand was being stored everywhere it could be, mindful that the priestesses had used fire to great effect in the last encounter. Meru and Kiri patrolled the walls, giving advice on how to prepare against the aerial attacks.

'Use the sand first,' Kiri said. 'The weapon is a type of oil, it floats on water, so it doesn't work on its own. Sand stops it, then douse what is left with the water. If you pour water on it first it makes it worse!'

Meru had requested that archers assemble beyond the city walls, explaining how they would be stationed on a flying machine that would lift them into the coming battle, rather than being caught underneath it. Many were doubtful, scoffing at his description of the battle of Amar. He had left Kiri in charge whilst he went to retrieve the smaller flying machine.

Many questioned her on the tactics of the priestesses.

'A machine of the air?' one argued. 'I'd still prefer take my chances on the ground.'

'Then you'll die,' Kiri told him. 'You saw how the priestesses are skilled at shooting from their dachs. The elevated position gives them a huge advantage and they practice every stretch. Between the arrows and the fire, that's how they defeated you before. It works everywhere, they will try it again.'

'In a fair fight ...'

Kiri laughed at him.

'A fair fight?' she mocked. 'There is no such thing. The priestesses don't care about what is fair, they care about winning. We must do the same.'

She raised her voice.

'You must also be aware their abilities,' she said. 'If you shoot individually you will miss, they can see the arrows coming.'

Kiri could see the doubt on their faces.

'Don't believe me?' she asked. There were mumbles of disagreement. She pointed at one. 'You. Come here.'

One of the young archers did as she instructed, he was one of the better shots.

'That target,' Kiri said, gesturing to one of the nearby training boards they had been using. 'How far is it?'

'A hundred hands, give or take,' he answered.

'An easy shot?' Kiri asked.

'Yes,' he said.

'Show us,' Kiri said.

The man nocked an arrow and pulled it back. He loosed it and the arrow thunked heavily into the centre of the target. A smattering round of applause greeted the result.

'Good work,' Kiri said. 'Now do it again.'

The man nocked a second arrow and loosed it as before. Kiri concentrated, gesturing with her fingers as he did so.

It sped past the target in a blur, clattering to the ground some distance beyond. Mumbles of surprise came from the other archers.

'And again,' she called.

He tried again. This time the arrow was diverted to the other side.

'It's magic …' someone muttered.

'No,' Kiri said, gesturing to the archer. 'It's not magic, but the priestesses can feel your muscles, your tendons, they can sense your aim and change it. But not all at once. Fire en masse, not alone, and you have a chance. They can't stop all of you.'

'And these machines,' another asked. 'Where are they?'

'Coming,' Kiri said. 'They are flying from Amar, it is quite the trek, hundreds of marks.'

She was interrupted by a noise in the air above.

'And here is one.'

The men around her looked up, shielding their eyes against the dust that billowed and spiralled up around them. The flying machine came down before them, its engines spinning down as it settled on its tricycle undercarriage.

The dust and sound faded and Meru leapt out.

'Ready?' he asked.

Kiri turned, a mischievous grin on her face.

'Now we find out who can really shoot,' she said.

* * *

'They're working them hard,' Crenech observed with a grin, watching the flying machine take off again with another party of archers aboard. 'I've had so many complaints already. Kiri is quite formidable.'

Zoella smiled. 'She has to be; the priestesses will show us no mercy.'

Crenech nodded. 'The city will be ready. Provisions for a siege are being stowed, though it seems the battle will be decided quickly.'

'Nerina comes for me and Kiri,' Zoella replied. 'And Gemma too, if she realises she's here. They will attack from above as is their way. Meru will meet them in the air with the machines. After that it becomes a straight fight for the city. Kiri and I will defend the soldiers as best we can from their powers.'

'We all have faith in you both,' Crenech said.

'I hope it is well placed,' Zoella said. 'Nerina is likely to spare no one if she wins.'

'Have you sensed her?' Crenech asked.

'No,' Zoella said. 'It's as if she waits for something. None of us have tried to extend our thoughts for fear of alerting her to our intentions.'

'Her delay bodes well for us,' Crenech said. 'We have had time to ready ourselves.'

* * *

Later that stretch, the ground beneath the city began to vibrate. Fearing an earthquake the populace rushed outside, only to be greeted by a vast shadow falling across them. Above, Lacaille's light was blotted out by an enormous metal hull. People pointed and cried out in surprise, delight and trepidation. The air thrummed to the power of the machines, thumping down through the city and making everything vibrate.

'At last,' Meru said.

Crenech, with Joachim and Gemma beside him, stared upwards in awe as the massive machine turned above the city and began to lower itself to the ground beyond the city walls, flanked by the other smaller vessels.

'Even with your description,' Crenech said, 'Quite the sight. I hope it intimidates the priestesses as much as I.'

'They have seen it before,' Kiri said. 'We don't have the element of surprise like the defenders did at Amar.'

Meru nodded. 'And they will have been thinking how best to counter our machines.'

'Let us go and meet the Amarans,' Zoella said. 'Scallia should welcome them. Will you join me, Lord Crenech?'

Crenech nodded. 'It would be my privilege, Princess Zoella.'

Zoella led Crenech down through the city and through the huge pair of gates that led out beyond the city walls. The flying machines had settled down before it in the plain beyond, by the river that flowed away to the sunward.

Already the Amarans were disembarking. Crenech and Zoella could see dozens of them stepping out of the large personnel transport.

Zoella spied Senator Janaid standing before the other Amarans. She walked towards him, Crenech keeping pace beside her.

'Senator Janaid,' Zoella called out in greeting. He stepped forward and took her outstretched hand in his. 'It is good to see you.'

'We are pleased to be here,' Janaid replied. 'I have brought as many as I could, the thoughts of all the people of Amar are with you and they wish you well.'

Zoella smiled.

'May I introduce Lord Crenech,' she said. 'It is he who has safeguarded Scallia.'

Janaid bowed to Crenech and they shook hands. 'Princess Zoella tells me the Amarans fought bravely against the priestesses.'

'We fought them off,' Janaid said. 'In no small part due to ...' He paused. 'Princess Zoella?'

Zoella smiled. 'A long story and one we don't have time for now. Bring your people within the city,' she said. 'They must rest. We don't know when the priestesses are coming. The attack could happen at any moment.'

* * *

Nerina looked up as a knock came on the double doors before her. She was sitting in her customary place, the ornate chair within the temple hall of the priestesses.

'Enter.'

The doors swung open, revealing one of the junior priestesses. Nerina recognised one of Merrin's administrators, one tasked with sending messages about their realm. The priestess bowed low before straightening and walking towards Nerina.

'What is it?'

'High Priestess. It may be nothing,' the priestess said, her voice unsure. 'I thought it wise ...'

'Out with it,' Nerina said, her voice sharp.

'We cannot contact Priestess Amrit, High Priestess.'

'Amrit?' Nerina said, with a frown. 'She was stationed in Viresia was she not?'

'Yes, High Priestess.'

Viresia ... in Scallia!

'When did you last hear from her?'

'Two stretches ago, High Priestess. Nothing was amiss, she was searching the towns and hamlets thereabout for any girls who might have been hidden. Since then ...'

Nerina nodded.

'You've done well, leave it with me.'

The young priestess bowed and left, the doors closed behind her.

Amrit knows her duty, for her not to report means ...

Nerina recalled the memory of the city; the battle there, the death of the king, the prince, the discovery of Liana and the boy from Amar.

The maid, Zoella! She must be there, torn Amrit! But why there? She was bound for Amar, why would she return to that city? Yet, if that's where she is, so much the better! I will not need a fleet to cross the sea, I can take her now ...

Nerina was on her feet in a moment, stretching her mind out in a furious imperative.

Assemble our riders, saddle our dachs! We fly to battle once more! Viresia is in revolt, we will punish them for their insolence!

The nexion flashed and sparkled around her. She felt the priestesses in the temple hear her command and spring into action.

But then, the nexion twisted away, there was something else, another presence. Nerina recognised it.

You ...

* * *

The stretch came to an end. Preparations continued, but the urgency seemed less as the spells progressed. Food, weapons, the flying machines – everything was ready. The mood in the city changed from mild panic to a watchful restlessness.

There was no sign of the priestesses.

The fastest riders had been dispatched sunwards to all the major towns in Scallia that might have been in the path of the priestesses attack. They all reported the same.

Nothing.

Zoella brought them all together in the throne room atop the city. Crenech was deep in conversation with Janaid. Kiri sat with Meru, both looked exhausted and ready to sleep after spending the entire stretch training the archers of Scallia. Gemma sat alongside Joachim, stifling a yawn.

'Where are they?' Joachim asked. 'They must know by now, surely?'

'It is a good question,' Zoella said.

The conversation around her faded as everyone turned their attention to her.

'Preparations?' she asked.

'All but complete,' Crenech answered. 'Now that the Amarans are here, except for a few additional stores of food, the odd soldier still en route, we're as ready as we can be.'

'Thank you all,' Zoella said. 'You have worked so hard in the service of the city. Viresia stands proud regardless of the outcome of the battle to come. When they come.' She turned to Kiri. 'What do you think?'

Kiri shrugged. 'I would not expect them to give warning, there will be no negotiation. They will just attack when they are ready. Perhaps it has taken longer for Nerina to prepare than we thought. If I had a dach, I'd fly out and take a look ...'

'We could use a flying machine,' Meru said. 'Fly sunward, see if we can find them.'

Zoella thought about it.

'I have a better idea,' she said, closing her eyes.

'Zoella … no, wait …'

Zoella held up a hand.

'I will find her and I will goad her,' she said. 'If she wants me, she's going to have to come and get me.'

Zoella concentrated, her hands clenching with the effort, her brow creased. She summoned her thoughts and sent them out in as strong an emanation as she could muster.

Nerina!

There was nothing but an echoing silence.

Nerina! You know me. I am Zoella, Princess of Scallia. I stand within the city of Viresia. I have despatched your priestesses and reclaimed my home. Scallia is mine, you will not pass its borders …

A sting wave of pain slammed into her, buffeting her mind and making her reel backwards in shock. She heard faint voices around her, but she rallied and pushed back. Then the voice came.

Princess? You are no princess. You're a scullery maid. I have seen your thoughts, your memories. You are a vagrant, a slum-dwelling scum with ideas beyond your station. You think you can stand against me, but you are wrong and you will soon learn the error of your ways. Scallia will pay the price for your arrogance! Those within your precious city will be slain before your eyes, only then will I take your gift from you. I am Empress! Empress of Esurio!

Zoella cried out as pain crushed in around her mind, but she struggled against it as she had done before.

You will not have me, you will not have any of us. We are not defenceless. You have been beaten before, we will beat you again. You do not know who I am. I am truly Princess Zoella of the house Tiamoi, daughter of Myana, granddaughter of King Marek and niece to King Ioric. For long rounds my people have kept our gifts from you and no more will Scallia bow the knee to Drayden. Nor will Drem or Taloon. Your reign as Empress is over before it begins!

Fury screeched around her, unbridled hostility washed over her like acid, burning and scalding. Nerina's rage buffeted at her, but before she could respond Zoella pulsed out her own burning righteous anger.

And there is more you do not know. I stand here with my sister, likewise a princess of this realm. We both defy you!

Zoella gestured to Kiri, who got up and stood beside her. She grasped Kiri's hand. Zoella felt Kiri's distinctive presence join hers within the twisting currents of the nexion. From the other side of the link the rage paused, washing aside for a moment as recognition, horror and curiosity swirled around her painting lurid swaths of consternation in her mind.

Sister?

Zoella snarled with a fierce joy.

Kiri Tiamoi, likewise daughter of Myana, princess of Scallia! She has slain your precious Rihanna, turned from your wickedness and stands alongside me …

The rage became incoherent, a tempest whirling about her, white hot and incandescent. Zoella held firm amongst it, surrounding herself with surety and purpose, her own thoughts a shield against the wrathful maelstrom beyond.

YOU WILL DIE! BOTH OF YOU!

Then it was gone.

Zoella heaved in a breath and opened her eyes.

'Zoella?'

Concerned faces were all around her.

She smiled, blinking, struggling to get her balance.

'Nerina has no doubts where we are now,' Kiri said, with a wry grin. 'She comes!'

* * *

Dachs were seen on the sunward horizon, flying in formation in several wings. Bells rang out across the city, deep and sonorous. Children and their carers were rushed inside, doors bolted. Soldiers ran to the walls and towers, readying their bows.

Zoella stood amongst them, with Crenech, Janaid and Joachim alongside. Kiri and Meru had run to their flying machine with two of the Amaran archers, ready to lead the other flying machines in defence of the city.

Zoella watched as the huge metal beasts rose into the air. The dachs had the advantage of height and speed, she could see them turning in the air above. The sky was black with them, silhouetted against the bright arc of Lacaille.

'How many do you count?' Janaid asked. 'My eyesight is not so strong.'

'Hundreds,' Crenech said, swallowing.

Zoella nodded. 'As many as before if not more,' she said. 'The first fight will be in the air.'

Meru's flying machine was the first off the ground. Kiri stood, braced in the back alongside the two Amaran archers. The other small flying machines weren't far behind, and the big personnel carrier was lumbering away from the ground below. She could see side doors were open, lined with archers.

'Don't forget to get as much height as you can,' Kiri yelled to Meru. 'Remember, the dachs are slow in the climb, but very fast in the dive. We'll never hit them whilst they're above.'

Meru nodded and relayed the instructions to the other pilots. The flying machines rose into the sky, casting shadows on the city below.

'We're not going to be above them before they attack,' Meru called, looking up and out of the windows. 'Not enough time.'

'Then tell everyone to watch for firebombs,' Kiri called back. 'They'll try to bring us down with those first, then pick us off with their own archers.'

Kiri felt the flying machine bank and braced herself again as the ground tilted beneath her.

'Here they come!'

Shadows flickered past the open doors, smoke billowed behind traceries of flaming orbs as the priestesses hurled their weapons. The flying machine banked away, rolling in one direction and then the other as Meru tried to dodge the incoming fire. One hit and bounced off the flanks. Flames flickered around the interior for a moment before being extinguished in the rush of air.

'We're alright,' Kiri yelled. 'Just keep gaining height!'

Dachs' wings flashed past outside and Kiri could see a formation of the beasts below.

'Bring us around now.'

The flying machine banked again, turning to starboard. Kiri grinned at the two archers.

'Let's go to work!'

Arrows were loosed, snapping out through the air between the aerial assailants. Kiri downed a dach with one shot and caught a rider with another, seeing the priestess tumble from her saddle and disappear out of sight.

Might have known her ... can't think of that now.

Kiri caught sight of the personnel carrier, besieged by dachs, arrows streaming from the archers aboard. Dachs fell from the sky with screeches of pain, dashing their priestesses to oblivion. Archers, shot from the priestesses own bows, tumbled from the open doors.

The tidy formations of the dachs broke up in the chaos, ships and animals twisting and turning in the air, trails of smoke lancing through the azure sky. Kiri saw the personnel carrier hit by multiple blasts of fire. Oil trickled down its flanks, bursting into flame. She saw men, ablaze, falling from it, spiralling down towards the ground.

She gritted her teeth as the flying machine banked again. She caught sight of a dach, its rider hurling a vial. Fire blazed before them, but Meru's swift turn avoided a direct hit. There was a flash of smoke and they were through.

Kiri and the two Amarans unleashed their arrows and the dach behind squealed, reared up and fell out of the sky.

* * *

Zoella watched the aerial battle unfold. The smaller flying machines were circling the personnel carrier, defending it from the priestesses that sought to firebomb it into oblivion. She couldn't tell which one belonged to Meru and Kiri.

Soon the sky was criss-crossed with trails of smoke. Dachs, men and priestesses fell from the sky as the battle progressed. Zoella could see bodies on the ground, people and beasts alike, causalities of the conflict in the sky.

Tears streamed down her face.

I knew there would be death. Was there a way to avoid this? Was there a way to peace I didn't find, that others might have? So many will die this stretch … all believe they are right … who's to say who is!

Crenech was alongside her.

'Do not doubt yourself,' he said gently. Zoella looked at him.

'I don't have your gift,' he said. 'But I know your thoughts well enough. This is forced upon us by that high priestess. The deaths lie upon her conscience, not yours.'

Zoella managed a nod. Above her one of the smaller flying machines was hit by fire. An explosion followed and the machine disintegrated, pieces of debris spinning in uncontrolled arcs as they crashed to the ground. The wreckage fell beyond the city, burning in the fields beyond.

The battle was growing closer, some of the dachs slipped past, tightening their formation and heading towards the city.

'Stand ready!' Crenech called.

The archers raised their bows, drawing them back, ready to loose their arrows.

'Hold,' Crenech yelled. 'Hold …'

Zoella raised her hands, sensing the thoughts of the priestesses before her in the skies. She remembered Liana, how she had sent out a shockwave through the nexion. She closed her eyes, concentrating, moaning out loud with the pain of it.

She felt the energy grow within her, swamping her mind, spinning up in a glowing fury. The smell of hot metal burnt in her nostrils, she felt as if she was on fire …

She screamed out as she unleashed the power within her. Up in the sky the phalanx of descending dachs broke up in disarray. Two collided with each other, crashing down out of sight as the priestesses that rode them clutched at their minds in shock and pain.

'Loose!' Crenech yelled above the turmoil.

Arrows flew, finding their targets. Priestesses and dachs were cut down, the phalanx broken, the bodies of the slain crashing down upon the walls and streets of the city.

Zoella gasped as she opened her eyes. The first attack was destroyed, the flight of dachs in disarray. Smoke billowed from the city below, but the fires were contained.

She had fallen back, but Crenech was holding her up, his arms about her. Dozens of the dachs were downed, but many more still flew in the skies.

'Truly our queen,' he whispered. 'Truly!'

* * *

The flying machine shook as a blast of fire exploded nearby. Kiri saw one of the flying machines falling out of the sky, aflame from nose to stern. She saw it hit and smash on the ground, debris flying out from the point of impact.

One of ours down … there are too many of them.

She watched in dismay as a flight of dachs peeled off, diving past the flying machines' blockade and sweeping down towards the city.

'Turn us about, they've got through …' she called.

Her vision blurred, her hearing saturated by white noise, her mind rang with a strange vibration as if a huge gong had been sounded right next to her. She only just retained presence of mind enough to cling to the inside of the flying machine.

'What was that?' Meru yelled.

Kiri's head was still spinning from the furious blast of mental energy. At close range it must have been devastating. She peered out to see the flight of dachs broken in disarray, priestesses stunned and lying crushed and battered upon the ground.

'That was Zoella! She stopped them ...'

Below them the priestesses were co-ordinating a concerted attack on the personnel carrier. Kiri could see dozens of them throwing vials of burning oil at the big ship even as the archers within loosed copious numbers of arrows at the attackers.

Vials struck the exterior and splashed off without causing damage, some managed to find their way inside, lighting the interior with flame. Kiri could see the archers battling to escape the fires.

'Oh no ...'

One priestess was shot as she approached, her dach also hit by the arrows of the defenders. Her vial was dropped, but the dach spun over, flipped in the air and crashed down upon one of the outstretched engine nacelles. The bodies of the priestess and the dach slipped away, tumbling down to oblivion, but then smoke and then fire began streaming from the engine.

The big personnel carrier began to yaw, banking over to starboard and dropping away out of control, trailing smoke and debris. Kiri could see the archers within struggling to hold on as the machine fell out of the sky. Smoke obscured her view, filling the cabin with choking fumes before Meru was able to turn out of the path.

The personnel carrier was going down, its rate of yaw building with every revolution, the screaming noise of straining engines winding up to a crescendo. It cannoned into the ground with an impact that could have been heard for marks in all directions. For a moment it stayed intact, scraping and ripping into the ground before the city, driving a huge gouge in the sand and dried mud beyond Viresia's walls.

For a moment it was still. Kiri strained to see what was happening below. It was impossible to see much through the billowing smoke.

She could see 'tricity crackling around the broken hull.

Then, without warning, it detonated.

A shocking blue sphere of energy flashed out, crackling in all directions, ripping tortured cracks in the ground and fracturing the wall of the city. Kiri had a brief moment to register that part of the city wall had disintegrated before their flying machine was tossed about as if in a violent storm.

In horror she saw one of the archers alongside her have his grip wrested away from him. He fell, screaming, out of the open doors, disappearing from view in an instant. Kiri held on as the flying machine completed a full roll before Meru was able to bring it under control.

She lurched across the interior, ensuring her grip was sound, before she looked out. Only three of the small flying machines were left in the sky, dachs were everywhere, swarming about them, twisting and spiralling, many descending towards the city.

'Take us back!' she yelled. 'There's nothing more we can do out here. We'll be ripped to shreds!'

* * *

Zoella and Crenech saw the mighty flying machine crash into the ground beyond the city walls. Then came the wall of blue fire. None had ever seen anything like it. A blastwave of wind shocked past them, spilling them all to the ground. A distant rumble marked a break in the city wall below, hundreds of tonnes of masonry crashed down, leaving the wall breached.

Not that it mattered. The dachs above circled for a moment and then dived down, shrieking.

'Archers!' Crenech yelled. 'Loose!'

Streams of arrows ripped into the air, felling a number of the dachs, their bodies crashing down into the city streets. Fire dropped from above, splashing amongst the ranks of soldiers on the walls, throwing them into disarray.

Priestesses appeared on the walls, carrying a mix of bows, swords and their precious kais; whirling metallic chaos surged about them. The soldiers of Scallia charged in to counter them. The screams and yells of battle filled the air.

Zoella felt the priestesses begin to use their powers, saw men clutch at their heads and drop their weapons as pain smote across them. She stretched out her hands, blanketing the area with her own gifts. The priestesses cried out in dismay, the men about them rallying, grabbing their weapons and returning to the fray.

But they had spotted her. Crenech saw a group advancing on Zoella as she stood, her eyes still closed. About her arrows flew, but none touched her, their courses changed before they even had a chance to fly.

Kiri! I need you! There are too many …

Crenech drew his own sword and stood before her. Two priestesses charged in, swinging at him with their kais. He blocked them, stepping between them and Zoella. Both tried to use their powers on him. Crenech downed one with a stab to the heart and closed on the second. He ducked a blow to the head, but was hit by a second to the chest, sprawling backwards. The priestess readied her staff for a killing blow but then screamed, writhing and falling to her knees before slumping to the ground.

Crenech looked round. Zoella stretched out a hand and helped him to his feet.

More priestesses were advancing on them, watching. Three … no five. Crenech readied his sword once more. Zoella stretched out her hands towards them.

Above them a roar of noise shook the steps of the throne room. Both looked up to see Meru's flying machine descending, its hull blackened and burnt. It came down hard, jolting and landing askew on the ground. Kiri and an Amaran archer leapt out, both releasing their bows. Two of the priestesses fell with arrows through their hearts. Kiri ran forward, her kai in her hand, somersaulting between two of the remaining priestesses and then whirling her kai about in a frenzied attack.

Meru staggered out of the cockpit, a rifle in his hand. He turned it on the remaining priestess, but not before she had killed the Amaran archer with an arrow from her own bow. The rifle fired and the priestess spun around and fell her length on the floor.

Kiri had overpowered her two assailants, their training no match for her superior skills with the kai. She hadn't managed it unscathed though, blood was flowing from a cut on her shoulder.

Crenech looked over the walls of the city. There were a few dachs circling below, even fewer above. Around the walls the priestesses were falling, the soldiers of Scallia fighting them one to one.

'We're holding our own …' he said, astonished and bewildered in equal measure.

Screams rent the air. Crenech saw soldiers clutch at their heads and fall back, their cries audible even from his vantage point. At the same moment pain smote across his forehead, causing him to cry out and stagger from the wall. Kiri yelled.

'It's her! It's Nerina!'

Dachs flew overhead. Kiri jumped aside as a flaming vial of oil burst nearby. Flames roared upwards, cutting her off from Meru and Zoella. Zoella saw her searching for a way out, there was none. She was forced to retreat from the flames upwards towards the throne room, its great burnished metal doors reflecting the orange gleam of the fire.

'Kiri!'

Zoella saw movement at the doors, a flap of fabric, a cloak perhaps. A dach circled above and then perched on the throne room parapet, screeching down at them.

Hot metal burnt up her lungs and surrounded her; a choking miasma. She coughed, struggling to see.

That presence, I know that presence! Nerina!

Zoella saw Kiri run up the stairs in pursuit.

'Kiri, wait!' Zoella screamed. 'Kiri!'

* * *

Kiri forced her way between the doors of the throne room. It was dark inside, she waited a moment for her eyes to adjust, her kai raised in defence.

The sounds of battle were muted here, a dull echo, as if far away. She walked forward, her senses alert.

She has to be here ...

Beneath her feet the history of Scallia was etched into the furler wood panels. She had no thought for it, her own senses stretching forward, trying to locate what she had seen.

There ...

Kiri looked up, sensing movement at the other end of the hall. It wasn't eyesight, nor smell, nor hearing, not sense of taste or touch. In her mind she could feel it. She knew.

You!

A figure lounged on the throne atop the dais at the far end of the room, cloaked and shadowed.

'So, Kiri, come to pay homage?'

Kiri watched as the dark figure got to its feet and moved from the shadows.

Nerina ...

Kiri held her kai in her hand, blood trickled down her fingers on to the metal staff. Nerina had her own kai, she raised it as she walked forward, her booted feet echoing on the wooden floor.

The two women faced each other.

'I told you once before,' Nerina said. 'You cannot lie to me, you cannot hide from me, you cannot resist me. None of you can. I am invulnerable. The city burns, its people die. My priestesses have the advantage. This will happen to all who oppose me, even you, young one.'

'I have been ordered to stop you,' Kiri replied. 'And stop you I will.'

'You've been told?' Nerina scoffed. 'Who gives orders to Kiri?'

'I serve my queen,' Kiri replied.

'Your sister, the maid?' Nerina replied with a scoff. 'This Zoella? She is no queen. She is but a child. She will be torn, just as all others have been.'

Kiri shook her head. 'She is my queen. You will not have her.'

Nerina stepped sideways, spinning her kai around. Kiri stepped in the opposite direction, countering her move. Lacaille's light streamed in from above, great arches of light through which the two combatants stepped.

'That will cost you your life,' Nerina said. 'What is she to you? Do you plan to tear her yourself? I know you wish to Empress.'

'You don't know me at all,' she replied.

'I trained you, taught you,' Nerina said. 'I know your desires. You will take her yourself, I know you will.'

Kiri shook her head. 'You know nothing.'

Nerina laughed. 'I know enough. The Scallians tried to keep you away from Drayden all those long rounds ago. That explains your treachery.'

'I am no traitor,' Kiri snarled back. 'I am Scallian, I always was …'

'You are a priestess of Drayden,' Nerina said, her expression turning to a fierce glare. 'We saved you, we raised you. Or have you forgotten dear Charis?' She sneered. 'Wouldn't she tell you not to meet violence with violence or some such platitude?'

'Do not dare mention her name to me,' Kiri said, stepping forward angrily, gesturing with her kai. 'You don't have the right! You were responsible for her death.'

'Me?' Nerina said innocently. 'Torin killed her, did he not? A prince of Scallia, wasn't he? Your precious Scallians killed Charis.'

'You fanned the flames of war,' Kiri said. 'You sent Charis there knowing peace wasn't an option, knowing she would be unprepared for Torin's treachery. I know!'

'I saved Drayden,' Nerina replied. 'Without me we would have been overrun, our powers dispersed.'

'All founded on lies,' Kiri said. 'You knew Lacaille was no goddess, that the Elements were only stories written by Elena to indoctrinate our people, yet still you made us follow them. She may have been wrong, but at least Charis believed in them. At least she sought the truth!'

'The people need to believe in something,' Nerina replied. 'Elena knew that.'

'Why not the truth?'

Nerina stepped back the way she had come, forcing Kiri to pace in the opposite direction. The two women stalked each other.

'Drayden's truth is what I say it is,' Nerina said. 'Not Elena, not Charis! We priestesses are born to rule … and I was born to rule the priestesses. The truth is my truth!'

'Women were supposed to care for this world,' Kiri countered. 'Use our powers to help, heal and prevent strife.'

Nerina laughed, thick with scorn.

'Such naivety,' she said. 'The words of Charis once again. I thought I had beaten her influence out of you. She would have us be weak and craven. The history of the Voren Empire tells you what the outcome of that would be. You forget men.'

Nerina raised her kai and stepped forward, the light glinting off its polished surface.

'Men,' she sneered. 'Clawing their way back to power, subjugating us, diluting our will. Elena saw it for what it was, men should not be allowed anywhere near authority. There should be a ruler, someone to dictate the laws and rules, someone to be feared and respected in equal measure. That one is me, young one.'

'The people will not accept a dictator,' Kiri replied, raising her own kai. 'A ruler rules by consent, with honour and respect for all. I've seen what you are, you care nothing for anyone but yourself. How many have you murdered? How many of your own have died because of you? Charis. Sahria. Rihanna. Amrit. Their deaths are your responsibility! And your rule comes to an end this stretch.'

'I've only just begun,' Nerina snarled.

'Then Charis' words won't stop me ending you!'

Kiri ran forward, her kai swinging in a vicious arc.

Nerina whirled her kai around, striking at Kiri. Kiri blocked it and they exchanged a rapid flurry of attacks and counterattacks.

Nerina's speed and skill were astonishing. Kiri found herself pushed back as Nerina advanced, her strikes swift and powerful.

The two women backed away from each other, circling around, staring into each other's eyes.

'You can still come back,' Nerina said. 'I'll forgive you. Stand at my side, serve me.'

'You betrayed me,' Kiri snarled. 'You tried to tear me. I haven't forgotten.'

'A test of your strength …'

'Lies!'

Kiri attacked, her kai a spinning blur of metal. The rage within her, Charis' death, Pootle's death, all the priestesses and women who had fallen victim to Nerina over the rounds … all of it burnt in her mind. She struck at Nerina, trying to find a way through her defences.

Nerina leant back after one blow, but then came forward, advancing inexorably. Kiri found herself pushed back, unable to counter Nerina's skill.

'So easy to goad you still,' Nerina laughed. 'You've learnt nothing since I taught you. Everything you are … I gave you.'

'No,' Kiri replied. 'You took everything from me!'

They traded blows again, their kais flashing in the light from the windows. Both struck and parried with a blinding speed, their movements almost balletic; but strong, sure and potent.

Nerina found a gap in Kiri's assault and jabbed out her hand. Kiri cried out as a pain smashed in around her skull. She staggered, off balance, trying to regain her footing.

'I have taken many gifts,' Nerina said as Kiri stumbled back. 'My powers are far stronger than yours. You cannot stop me. Surrender and I will be gentle when I tear you, leave your mind intact. Otherwise you will live out your stretches as a mindless fool.'

'I have sworn to stop you,' Kiri said. 'If that means my end, then so be it.'

'Then your end is upon you.'

* * *

The flames raged about them.

'We need to help her!' Zoella screamed, trying to get through the fire. The intense heat drove her back, the hair on her head fizzing and singed. Meru pulled her away.

'Only one way through,' he said, looking beyond the burning oil that coated the steps leading up to the throne room.

'How?'

Meru pulled her to the base of the steps where a trough of water had been placed to fend of fires on the walls.

'That's no use,' Zoella cried. 'The water won't put out the fire.'

Meru was shaking his head. He grabbed a bucket, filled it and then advanced towards her.

'Hold still!'

He upended it over her. The water was chill, she gasped, soaked to the skin. Meru upended another over himself and then grabbed her by the hand.

Behind them two priestesses had climbed the walls.

'I'll deal with them!' Crenech shouted, swinging his sword around and stepping behind them. 'Go!'

'Run!' Meru yelled.

He yanked on her hand, pulling her forward, the rifle slung over his shoulder. They sprinted towards the flames.

'Jump!'

She threw herself forward, pushing her legs out beneath her as hard as she could. Heat swamped them, an immolating inferno. She felt it on her skin, her fingers, her face. The fumes were poisonous, choking.

She hit the ground, rolling, losing hold of Meru's hand. Fire was burning up her leg. She screamed in agony.

Another yank. Meru was pulling her up the steps. She saw him rip off his tunic and use it to douse the flames that burnt along her legs.

It stung, the skin on her legs red and blistered, but they were through the flames. Meru pulled her to her knees, she saw his own hands were burnt and raw too.

'Come on,' he called. Both of them staggered to their feet, supporting each other and limping up to the throne room doors.

* * *

Nerina stretched out her hand again. Kiri felt Nerina's grip tighten around her mind and resisted it, her practice with Zoella serving her well. They wrestled at each other, both grimacing with the effort, both straining against each other's minds.

Kiri winced, the pain pounding at her head. Nerina pressed harder, causing Kiri to cry out. She felt her arms shuddering with the effort. Nerina was too strong. Kiri's knees went from under her.

Nerina's kai came whistling around. Kiri saw it, but couldn't move with the fire in her head. The blow caught her on the side of the head and sent her spinning away. She scrambled to her knees, but another blow hit her in the midriff, throwing her over on to her back, to lie there, stunned.

She gasped with pain, barely conscious, her vision blurred and tunnelling in around the edges, lights danced in her vision.

She could just make out Nerina standing above her, her kai poised, her other hand outstretched.

'I will not waste your gift like you have,' Nerina said. 'Farewell, Kiri.'

Kiri tried to turn, but then the pain began. She felt Nerina's thoughts grate against her own, felt her presence pushing into her mind, grasping greedily at the glowing gift in her core. Then, in a silent shriek of agony, she felt her powers drain away.

She couldn't even scream.

Her vision faded away into blackness.

CHAPTER NINETEEN

Viresia, Capital of Scallia

Round 2307, Eleventh pass

Nerina screamed. Screamed in delight and exaltation, her body energised from head to foot, the power burning through her extremities and lighting her body with a furious burning.

'Leave her alone!'

Nerina clenched her fists and forced away the glee and suffusion of delight that had thrilled her as she tore what remained of Kiri's gift. The flow of power was intoxicating.

Her vision swam into focus.

Kiri lay unconscious at her feet. Nerina looked up past her prone form.

Two figures stepped out of the bright light of Lacaille streaming through the doors of the throne room.

'Your attack has failed,' a woman's voice said. 'Your priestesses fall. You've lost. Give it up, Nerina.'

Nerina straightened, releasing her mental grip on Kiri, holding her kai aloft.

'So, you're the so-called queen are you?' Nerina said, laughing, still intoxicated with her new found strength. 'Scallia's maid with delusions of grandeur? Oh … and Kiri's little diversion too, I see. You're too late – I have torn her … her powers are mine!'

Zoella and Meru stepped forward.

Such insignificant fools! I will crush you!

'Back away,' Meru said. Nerina saw he had the strange metal weapon with him, raised and pointed at her.

Nerina didn't move.

'Drop your kai and step away from her,' Zoella commanded.

Such daring! You will learn your place little upstart Queen!

Fury blazed through her, she exalted in her new found power. Kiri's gift had still been strong, even after she had stolen much of it in Amar.

How dare they defy me! How dare they not bow in worship! Fall at my feet!

'You will be torn just like she was,' Nerina's voice was a high-pitched scream of rage. 'All of you will pay for your insolence, I will not relent in your punishment!'

'Leave her alone!' Meru yelled.

She sent forth a blast of mental energy. She felt Zoella try to block it but she had been too swift. Meru reeled backwards with a yell, his weapon clattering to the ground. She pummelled at him again, delighting in the screams she heard as he collapsed to the floor, writhing in pain, his hands clutched around his head.

Puny man!

'Kiri is mine,' Nerina cried. 'She has always been mine!'

Zoella hadn't been affected. She raised her own hand and Nerina felt a crushing strength clasp around her mind, forcing her to stop torturing Meru. She dropped her kai and it clattered on the stone floor.

For a moment they wrestled back and forth.

She is potent still, the last one I must tear! Then all Esurio is mine!

'So,' Nerina said, her eyes blazing with zeal. 'You're the one with the greatest gift after all. And I thought Kiri was special. It makes no difference. I'll take your gift too … together the power of the Scallian sisters will ensure none can ever challenge me again.'

'It will destroy you,' Zoella replied. 'Don't you feel the rage within you? This power corrupts us, turns us … breaks us! Turns women into monsters. It destroyed Elena, it will burn you up and everything else too.'

'The cry of the pitiful,' Nerina snarled. 'The weak and the infirm have no place.'

Zoella's voice was a calm counterpoint to Nerina's near-hysterical shriek of anger.

'You weren't always like this, Nerina. Once you were a loyal priestess, serving your people in good faith. Give up the power … return to us. I know … I can help you.'

'Give it up?' Nerina's laughter was cruel. 'You fool. You know nothing of this power or what it can do …'

'I know all about it,' Zoella replied, stepping closer, her arms vibrating with the effort of fending off Nerina's power. 'What it was for and why it was given to women. We were to be custodians of this world, to prevent war, stop conflict … not bring people to it and bend them to our will.'

But it is! I command. I rule! Me, my will! My world! My empire!

'This power is mine to do with as I will,' Nerina replied, her body shaking, her fingers outstretched and claw-like, her voice rising to a frenzy. 'I will decide what is best, I am empress of all Esurio. I will not be lectured to by an upstart maid who fancies herself queen of a broken down city.'

'This power is what brought down the Voren Empire,' Zoella called back. 'Elena's misuse of it, she tore too many, her rage was magnified until it was uncontrollable. It's what started the war all those rounds ago, the destruction of Drem …'

Enough of this! Now I tear you too!

'And I will finish her work,' Nerina said, pulling a knife from her belt.

With a scream of rage she lunged at Zoella, the knife held out towards her. She caught Zoella off guard, forcing her to deal with the mental onslaught and the knife attack. Zoella dodged the first attack, but Nerina felt her balance go.

Now to slit your throat!

Nerina swung the knife towards Zoella.

'No!'

A figure to her right. Bright blue eyes …

Nerina's arm was wrenched aside. The second blow narrowly missed its mark, the knife point slicing across her cheek instead. Zoella screeched and fell back.

Kiri! How?

A fist … a punch.

Nerina evaded the blow, fending it off and striking hard at Kiri, the knife still clenched in her hand.

She felt it hit home, the knife penetrating clothes, skin and then flesh. She heard Kiri's scream of pain, short and sharp. The knife was wrenched from her hand, Kiri fell back, staggering away in a blur of blood and darkness.

Pain slammed between Nerina's eyes. She yelled as her mental defences were shattered as if by a physical blow. She spun only to see Zoella's outstretched palm.

Not enough, girlish queen!

Nerina still had her strength.

She grabbed Zoella's hand and twisted it cruelly, turning it further and further around.

She felt Zoella twist in her gasp, trying to escape, but Nerina's grip was sure and strong. She pulled Zoella closer, until their faces were less than a hands-width apart.

'I will take your power now, Queen of Scallia!'

Nerina smiled as she felt bones in Zoella's wrist crack, heard her scream in pain and flail about desperately.

No, there is no escape for you!

Nerina gave her no respite, twisting her broken wrist further round. Zoella yelled out in shock and agony.

I am Empress! There is no other but me!

Nerina felt her words shock through Zoella's mind, blasting her thoughts aside and shattering her concentration. Nerina felt her growing despair.

Victory is mine!

Zoella screamed. Her arm and wrist were pure agony, her mind collapsing under Nerina's frenzied attack. She felt her powers ebb away.

No …

A dizzying blast of noise.

The pain lessened.

Zoella's ears rang, her vision blurred. Blood splattered across her. Nerina's grip on her wrist faltered. In shock, Zoella could see the flesh of Nerina's shoulder was torn and ripped. More blood, spraying over Zoella in a plume.

She screamed, the hot liquid splashing across her.

Zoella twisted around to see Meru standing there, blood-stained, swaying, a smoking rifle in his hand. As she watched he dropped it to the floor, staggering to one side.

But Nerina was not finished.

Zoella felt a hand at her throat. Nerina's gore-stained face was before her, her fingers tightening, crushing.

DIE!

Zoella cried in fury, bringing her own arm back up, fingers outstretched, claw-like. Hot metal burnt up inside her, crackling outwards.

You die!

She unleashed the last of her strength, seeking out the glowing radiance of Nerina's mind and then crushing down upon it. Pain lanced through her as Nerina resisted, but then …

With final shocking abruptness, Nerina's presence was gone.

The hand around her throat let go. Nerina's body slumped to the floor.

Zoella staggered back, sinking to her knees with shock. For long moments she could do nothing but gasp for breath.

'No …'

Through the pain and confusion Zoella could see Meru was staring past her. Zoella turned to see what he was looking at, trying to get her eyes to focus.

Behind Nerina's body was Kiri. She was on her knees too.

She wore a dazed expression on her face. Her ragged tunic was marked with a dark red stain; a stain that was growing where a knife protruded from her chest.

Zoella's eyes widened in shock.

'Kiri!'

She saw Kiri open her mouth, but no words came. She slumped. Zoella stumbled up and ran to her, catching her before she could topple over backwards. Then Meru was next to her, lowering Kiri down. Zoella looked at the knife, it was embedded up to the hilt, blood was pulsing out around it. She dared not remove it.

Kiri tried to move, her arms spasming for a moment.

'Lie still!' Meru said, his voice muffled in Zoella's hearing. 'We need to stop the bleeding, it will be alright, just …'

Zoella placed her hands on Kiri. She felt the sensations of Kiri's body course up through her, sensed the gift join them together. Felt the shock of despair course through her.

She knew.

Oh no …

Meru looked up at Zoella. She gave the tiniest shake of her head, tears dripping down her cheeks.

'Nerina?' Kiri whispered. 'She tore me … my gift … it's gone.'

'She's dead,' Meru said, looking to Kiri. 'You stopped her …'

'Yes,' Zoella said, her voice catching. 'You saved us, saved us all.'

Kiri smiled, before coughing. Meru tried to hold her to ease the pain. Blood trickled from the corner of Kiri's mouth.

'Then it's done,' Kiri whispered, her eyes rolling up in her head. 'We won …'

'Kiri …' Meru cried.

Kiri looked up at him, trying to raise her arm. Meru caught her hand, pulling it to his face and kissing her palm, holding her hand against his skin, tears dripping down his cheeks.

'The time we had,' Kiri said. 'The marsip, the flower … you and I. The happiest I have ever been … my true love … always … forever …'

'Kiri … I love you … don't …'

'I know,' Kiri whispered.

Meru was sobbing now, unable to speak.

Kiri looked over to Zoella.

'I can't hear you any more,' she said. 'Look after him?'

Kiri's fingers twitched in Meru's hand. Zoella placed her own hand on Meru's and Kiri moved her own fingers until her hand was wrapped around theirs. Zoella felt her squeeze them together.

'Of course …' Zoella said, through her own tears. 'Kiri …'

'My sister, dear sister …'

Kiri's breath caught in her throat. She looked at Meru.

'You're mine, Meru of …'

Her eyes widened in surprise as if she was seeing something unexpected. A smile touched her lips.

'Tia?'

Her breath sighed out of her. Then she was still, her eyes open and staring, but sightless. Meru gasped.

'No … Kiri … no!'

Meru pulled Kiri to him, but she was limp in his grasp, her fingers loosening, her arms dropping away, her body a dead weight. The vitality that had characterised her very essence was gone.

Meru curled over her, shuddering, huge sobs racking him. His grief echoed around the walls, untempered and raw.

Zoella felt tears run down her cheeks, hot and burning. She tried to find words, any words that might provide a shred of comfort, but they were nowhere, there was nothing. She reached up and closed Kiri's eyes before putting her arms around Meru.

Together, in the carnage of the throne room of Viresia, they wept.

* * *

Fires were still smouldering in the city, great plumes of smoke rising up into the still clear air. Walls and buildings were blackened, the bodies of men, women and dachs scattered through the streets and roads. The lower walls were shattered, and beyond, in the plains surrounding the city, the wreckage of the flying machines lay twisted and broken, themselves surrounded by the broken carcasses of dachs and the crushed bodies of priestesses and soldiers.

Few of the priestesses had survived. They had been urged to fight to the death, borne on by a zealous madness that had gripped their minds and stripped away their sanity.

Until Nerina had fallen.

Then they were bereft of purpose and meaning, their weapons falling to the ground as they stood, bewildered. Many had been slain where they stood, others captured and rounded up. All were shell-shocked, blank and staring, such had been the high priestess' hold on them.

Crenech limped to the walls, watching the efforts of those to help the injured and wounded. Bells announced that the battle was over. Civilians emerged from hiding, only to find many loved ones slain in the fighting. The city mourned its dead.

Joachim, his clothes rent and his body blackened with soot, blood seeping from many cuts, emerged from the chaos. He staggered over to Crenech, falling into his embrace.

'Where are they?' he grated out, his voice raw.

'Yonder,' Crenech said, pointing upwards towards the throne room.

Together they painstakingly made their way up the steps, avoiding the remains of the fires and the dead bodies of the priestesses about them. The great doors were ajar and they pushed their way in.

They could see Zoella and Meru crouched on the floor; the body of a priestess, dressed in long flowing robes with a crystal tiara still perched on her head lay before them. Her hair had a streak of white running through it. Her eyes were open, but it was clear she was dead, her shoulder was ripped and torn, blood surrounding her in a dark pool.

'Nerina …' Crenech whispered.

'Zoella!' Joachim called, running to her.

Crenech stepped up behind them, hearing the sobs. Both Zoella and Meru were kneeling over another body. He saw dark hair, a thin face, eyes closed. His breath caught in his throat.

'Princess Kiri …'

'She stopped Nerina,' Zoella managed to say. 'Weakened her, hurt her, all to save me. She gave her life …'

The sobs took her again and she fell into Joachim's arms.

Crenech bowed his head.

* * *

The lords of Scallia were gathered in the palace courtyard. Scant rounds ago Zoella had stood here to mark the crowning of King Ioric of Scallia and his all-too-brief reign. Once more the forecourt had been cleaned and tidied, decorated with ribbons and firelights.

The war was over.

As the sole survivor of the Tiamoi dynasty, Scallia was hers by right.

Sole survivor ...

Zoella stared at the closed doors of the throne room. Beyond she could hear the cheering of the crowds.

She was trembling. She tried, but she couldn't stop it.

'Zoella?'

She turned her head by an effort of will. Joachim stood alongside her, clean now, but his face bore cuts and bruises from the fighting. Behind him, Zoella could see Gemma. Her arm was broken, it hung in a bandage. Zoella's wrist was likewise wrapped tight.

Zoella swallowed, trying to find words, but none would come.

'It is time,' Joachim whispered to her, taking her hand in his.

She managed a tiny shake of her head, the tremors in her body increased. She clenched her eyes shut for a moment.

So many died, how can we celebrate anything?

The doors opened, Lacaille's light streamed in. Zoella looked up at it, her vision blurred by tears. Lacaille blazed above, a perfect sphere once more, just the same as it had always been.

How can it be unchanged? All these people we've lost, my sister ... Kiri ...

She felt herself walking forward as if in a dream, her eyes fixed on some distant point on the horizon.

Just walk, don't think, just walk ...

Now she stood before them all, a sea of faces all about her, many she recognised from before when she had been just a maid, serving in the household. She saw the assembled lords of Scallia, the Amaran folks with Senator Janaid standing before them, the soldiers of Scallia, sadly much depleted in numbers.

Meru stood, his hands dressed with bandages, slightly apart from the others, his expression bereft, but she saw the tiny nod meant only for her.

The crowds grew silent, watching and waiting.

Joachim let go of her hand and stepped back.

Two of the lords approached her, stepping in time with each other. One bore a crown.

'By the laws of our land and the custom of our people, we call upon you Princess Zoella daughter of Myana. We would have you be our queen. Will you grant our wish?'

Zoella's throat was dry, she looked at the lord with the crown, her face blank. He looked back.

'Princess Zoella?'

Zoella swallowed. Kiri's voice drifted in her mind.

You don't want to do this, but you will because it's the right thing to do. That's what makes all the difference. You're so good at bringing people together. You'll be a great queen.

Zoella mouthed her response silently.

'But what if I get it wrong?'

You won't.

'What if I do?'

I'm your sister, I'm telling you … you won't.

'Princess Zoella?' The lord asked again, fidgeting and looking nervous, a mutter of conversation was rising from the crowd.

Zoella bowed her head for a moment before looking up. She straightened, turning to face him.

'If my service be acceptable, I will so serve.'

The murmurs subsided, replaced with silence.

'It is not only right,' the lord said, relieved and raising his voice to be heard over the courtyard. 'It is your duty and joy to serve our people. Will you conduct our affairs with diligence, with honour, compassion and courage?'

Zoella only just kept her voice steady.

'I will so serve.'

'Will you uphold our laws, keep our borders safe, defend us against all who would imperil us?'

'I will so serve,' Zoella said. 'But not just those of Scallia. Those of Drem, Taloon and Drayden. I will seek to defend us all.'

A mutter went around those present at her words, breaking as they did with rounds of tradition. But none spoke against her.

'And will you never forsake your duty, despite age or infirmity until such time as you yourself journey into the after?'

You'll be a great queen ...

Zoella took a deep breath.

'I will so serve.'

'Then kneel before your people.'

Zoella did as she was asked. The crown was placed upon her head. It was heavy, pressing down on her with unexpected weight.

'Then rise, Queen Zoella of Scallia,' the lord said.

Zoella rose to her feet. The lord looked around and then turned to her.

'People of Viresia, greet your Queen,' he called in a loud voice. 'Queen Zoella of Scallia!'

A cheer went up from all about her, which broke into enthusiastic clapping. She stared, her expression blank, waiting for it to subside.

You'll be a great queen ...

'Sister,' she mouthed, her voice silent. 'Thank you.'

She looked around at Joachim. He smiled and nodded at her. She turned to see the crowds of people below her, finding a strength coursing through her mind, the tremors in her body faded. She blinked, seeing the city around her.

These are my people, this is my city ...

'We have fought hard, we have lost much,' she found herself saying, surprised at the authority in her voice. 'All of us have lost friends … and family.' She pursed her lips before finding the renewed strength to carry on. 'We must do better. We will do better. We will cherish our gifts, all of them, not exploit them or use them to dominate others. We have learnt that our distant ancestors wished for a simple peaceful life, free from overzealous authority and free from the heavy hand of bureaucracy, where community could flourish and families might grow, living in harmony with this world.'

None spoke. There was no sound at all. All faces were upturned to her. She swallowed as a renewed sense of purpose flooded through her.

'Let us hold fast to their vision and make it real. We have been given this chance, we have learnt of our purpose. Let every one of us consider their lives in light of what we now know. Strive to be the best you can, to serve others before yourselves, that everything under the light of Lacaille might flourish and prosper. This is the legacy our ancestors have given us. Let us not waste it. Let us rebuild and make Esurio a world of which they would have been proud!'

Cheers greeted her words. The inevitable chant arose, growing stronger with every repetition.

'Hail, Queen Zoella of Scallia!'

* * *

She knew where he would be. Meru was standing where he had stood for spells, before the stone plinth where Kiri's body lay in state, in one of the antechambers below the palace itself.

The room was dark, lit only by a small hole in the roof, above which a burnished metal plate reflected the light of Lacaille downwards on to the plinth.

Kiri's body had been cleaned, her black hair brushed and trimmed neatly. She had been dressed in a pure white gown, now tinted a flaming orange in Lacaille's light. She looked ethereal and serene; at peace. Her hands were clasped across her stomach, the left dressed in an ornate black leather glove secured with a bow at her wrist. Her head was adorned with a tiara from the royal collection of Scallia as befitted a princess. Around her neck she still bore her pendant, the sign of the Obelisk. Beside her lay her kai. Her body was surrounded by white and yellow blossoms.

Meru turned as Zoella approached him. He bowed, lowering himself on one knee.

'No …' Zoella said, pulling him up. 'Not you. You don't bow to me, not now, not ever.'

'You're the queen,' he said.

'To you I'm just Zoella,' she said, smiling. 'Your friend. That's what we will always be.'

Meru nodded.

'What you said,' he stammered, looking at her with admiration. 'Those words. They were inspired. You are a queen, truly.'

'Maybe one day I will feel it,' Zoella answered.

'Ioric would be proud,' Meru said. 'As would Coran and Mel … Fitch would make some sarcastic aside but … they'd be proud … all of them.'

Tears glistened in Zoella's eyes again.

'Thank you.'

'As would she.'

Both of them turned to look at Kiri. Zoella put her arm around his waist.

'It was like she was with me,' Zoella whispered. 'Standing there before the people … I could see her face, that glare she had, those blue eyes. She was there, pushing me on, making me do what needed to be done.'

Meru clenched his eyes shut.

'It's just you and me now,' she said. 'The only ones left who know all the truth.'

Meru shuddered, his voice shaking. 'Our friends … Coran, Mel, Fitch, even Caesar …

'Ira, Ren …'

'Daf and Creg …'

'Ioric and Liana. Myana and Guerrun.'

'And Kiri …' Meru finished. 'So many … Was it worth it?'

He opened his eyes and looked at Zoella.

'I asked myself that before,' Zoella said, her voice firm. 'We will make it worth it. We can manage the flares, the priestesses are no more, we know our history now. We will honour their memory by our success from here on.'

Meru nodded.

'She was so … alive,' he said, staring at Kiri's body upon the plinth. He reached out a hand to stroke her hair, teasing it from her forehead. Kiri's face was pale, but her expression calm and tranquil.

'Remember her like that,' Zoella said, taking his hand again. 'It's too easy to dwell on the sadness and the loss. She loved you. The strength of her feelings for you … no one ever reached her like you did. Trust me, I know … I really envied her.'

Meru managed a smile.

'She'll never be forgotten in Scallia,' Zoella continued. 'Neither who she was or what she did. I will make sure of that.'

Meru's arm went around her. Both of them were lost in their thoughts as Lacaille's light streamed in around them.

Meru looked at her.

'Turn your face to the sun,' he said. 'And the shadows will fall …'

His voice broke and he looked down, his eyes clenched shut, fresh tears upon his face.

Zoella stretched up and give him a light kiss upon his cheek, before tightening her embrace and resting her head on his shoulder.

'They will,' she said. 'In time, they will.'

CHAPTER TWENTY

Aftermath

Round 2358, Fifth pass

She looked very much as she had before, one of those lucky women to whom ageing seemed to be a problem that belonged to someone else. Yet he could see streaks of grey in her hair and lines across her face that had not been present the last time he visited.

It has been rounds. Too many rounds. I should have come back sooner.

Age hadn't left him alone either. The unruly mischievous dark hair that had once been his was long gone in favour of thinning wispy grey, but his eyes still sparkled with the same burning curiosity as they had always done.

He hadn't been to Viresia in a long time, his journeys across Esurio had been extensive and involved. He had learnt much, but there were still more questions. Questions he hoped would soon be answered. There was only one more place left to go.

The guards had seen him coming and pulled back the doors. He had been expected. The burnished metal of their structure reflected the light of Lacaille, dazzling him. It had been many rounds since he had first stood here.

Few of the people of Viresia recognised him, none of the children playing in the bright city streets. A few of the older ones gave a nod and a wave, but there were no greetings. The city was bustling, supporting a far bigger population than it had in the time of his youth. It was clear it had prospered since.

Under her reign.

He was leaning on a staff now. A fall, some rounds before, had left him lame, but he managed. Where he was planning to go, a poor leg would be little handicap. Shortness of breath was another curse he had to bear; he could feel his heart racing just with the effort of walking. Perched on his head was a tatty old hat, its wide brim threadbare in places. He stepped within the palace of Viresia, his staff and shoes clicking on the polished furler-wood panelling.

The hall within was little changed from before, the ancient heraldic symbols still marking out Scallian history. The paintings remained too, though there were some new ones. This was where he had first met Zoella, all those rounds ago. He smiled, he had been a foolish and callow youth back then when King Ioric had sat upon the throne.

Here too, in this very room, he had lost what was most precious to him. The smile faded, the memories still painful even after all the rounds that had passed.

Long ago.

The throne was still there, now she sat upon it.

Queen Zoella turned to look at him.

'Meru?'

'My queen.'

He smiled, took off his hat and bowed. She rose from her throne and hurried to him.

'None of that, I've told you before,' she said, pulling him upright and hugging him close.

He embraced her back. She let him go and looked at him.

'Queen not just of Scallia,' he said. 'Or so I hear. Is it true that Drem, Taloon and Drayden now pay homage to you?'

'It is,' Zoella replied. 'Vandare made the suggestion a long time ago, I wish he could have seen it. We now have a commonwealth of nations.'

'Queen of Esurio then,' Meru said.

'With all the problems that go with it,' Zoella answered. She looked him over from head to foot, her eyes taking in his tired and somewhat bedraggled appearance.

'The beard really isn't you,' she said, laughing. 'How are you?'

'Well enough,' he said. 'Stiff and sore, but nothing that I haven't had to put up with for rounds already.'

'If you will insist on traipsing the face of the planet,' she scolded, affectionately. 'Can there be any secrets left that you have not unlocked?'

'The scribes will have plenty to write down for rounds now,' Meru replied. 'Assuming they can read my scribbles. But tell me of you, are you well?'

'Well enough,' Zoella replied. 'The usual problems, ice shortages in Drem, trade disputes, shadewood taxes from Drayden, fisher-folk from Amar, the list of tedium goes on and on.'

'I'm sure you're more than up to the challenge,' he replied. 'You were always good at organising things. Not my gift at all.'

'After all these rounds I just summon them all and then glare,' she said. 'Works most of the time.'

'You always were able to convince people,' Meru replied. 'And how is the family?'

'I am grandparent for a fifth time,' Zoella said. 'A girl.'

Meru smiled, though he could see the twist of sadness in Zoella's expression. She had married not long after becoming queen. A celebration of happiness and new found love that had done much to repair the damage caused to all who witnessed the events before. Ten rounds that marriage had lasted, until her consort had been struck down by an unexpected and devastating plague out of the shaderight. Meru had liked Joachim; he had been a good man. Zoella had not remarried; it seemed both of them had only ever had one true love.

Such a long time ago now.

Zoella's two children, Ioric and Liana, were long since grown up with families of their own.

'She has blue eyes and black hair,' Zoella said, softly. 'They've called her Kiri.'

Meru nodded, his expression clouded by his own sadness, before a smile crept across his face. He had never married, always claiming that his work, charting the unknowns of the planet, had kept him too busy to settle down. Zoella was one of the few left who knew the truth.

'A good name,' he said, swallowing. 'You'd better keep an eye on that one.'

'I'm sure they would love to show her to you …'

He couldn't help the pained expression he knew had crossed his face. Zoella stopped.

'Some other time perhaps,' Meru answered. He changed the subject. 'I heard a song about the flares in one of the taverns en route. Catchy tune.'

'One of my ideas,' Zoella said. 'The flares are gone now, and it won't be long before people forget what happened. As the generations go, people will wonder if the records we leave behind are true. I thought putting the warnings into songs and folklore might help people remember. In four hundred rounds the flares will come back again …'

Meru nodded, but his eyes narrowed.

He could see Zoella was watching him carefully. She would never invade his privacy with her mental powers, but her sense of him was acute. She knew him better than any other.

'What is it?' she asked, her voice a whisper.

He looked away for a moment, before stepping closer and looking into her eyes.

'I've come to say goodbye,' Meru said.

Now it was Zoella's turn to swallow. Her mouth was dry.

'It's fixed,' Meru said. 'The Obelisk … Ira … says it's ready to launch. One final mystery to be unravelled.'

'You're going up there?' Zoella asked, her voice a whisper. 'Meru …'

'You know I've wanted to see it ever since I figured out what it was, do you remember that?' he asked.

Zoella nodded. 'As if it were just last stretch,' she said. 'I had to help you with Caesar.'

Meru smiled. 'Yes, that's right, you did. Anyway, it's ready. I can go. The life support on the *Du Maurier* is working again, the dropship ready to depart. One last flying machine for me.'

'Your record with flying machines isn't good you know,' she said, trying to lighten the mood. 'How many have you crashed? Three?'

Meru smiled. 'Four. Don't worry. It will all be under Ira's control.'

'The *Du Maurier*,' Zoella whispered. 'The ship that brought our people here from far away.'

Meru nodded. 'Our origins. The full truth about where we came from, and why.'

'Are you sure you want to know?' Zoella asked.

'I'm sure.'

She nodded.

'I ... ' Meru began. 'There's not much time left. I'm ... we're old.'

'Don't tell me,' Zoella scolded. 'I've given up memorising which bits of me ache, it's easier to list the bits that don't.' She paused for a moment. 'Do say hello to Ira for me.'

'I will,' Meru replied. 'Listen, I've trained everyone I can. They know everything I know. Just this one thing remains.'

Zoella's eyes were full of tears now. A long silence fell between them.

'I'm not going to see you again,' she said at last, as the tears began to flow. 'Am I? Oh, Meru ...'

Meru pulled her into an embrace, closing his eyes and cradling her head against his shoulder in age-spotted hands.

* * *

There was one more thing he had to do before leaving the ancient city of Viresia.

He limped down into the catacombs below the palace. It was dark there, the individual chambers lit only by a small hole above where a burnished piece of metal reflected Lacaille's light downwards.

The chamber was swept clean, a metallic casket set in the very centre, surrounded by a pool of light. On top was a plaque, the words on it ones that he had written long ago, etched into the very metal itself.

Meru ran his hands over it and then placed a single white flower alongside.

Fifty one rounds ago, and I can still see your face, smell your scent, feel the softness of your skin. What would our lives have been? Would we have had a family? Somehow I think not, you were never very fond of children. And you would have been just as feisty and argumentative in old age as you were when …

He paused.

She wouldn't recognise him now, old, bearded and broken down as he was. She was forever the lithe, dark-haired and blue-eyed young woman he had loved more than anything else. Kiri would never grow old; not for her the slow decay into decrepitude. In his mind she remained the warrior, the fighter, the fierce and determined lover. Not like him now, his frame bent, his hair almost gone, his body slow and his heart aching for a rest that would not be long delayed.

From the time they had met until the time she had been taken from him not even a whole round had elapsed. She had burnt so bright in his life, like the flares they had battled; a searing burning blast of life and energy, all too soon expended, gone … nothing more than a memory.

He stroked his fingers across the casket, feeling the cold metal leaching the heat from his fingertips.

Goodbye, Kiri. Goodbye, my love.

* * *

The dropship had taken dozens of rounds to repair. It seemed that the original colonists had never expected to use it again and many of its systems had been cannibalised for other uses. Long before, Meru had issued instructions to the Obelisk … to Ira … to prepare it for flight once more.

Automated systems had begun that work and now, after many rounds of labour, they were complete.

The dropship was ready.

It was the only vessel on the planet capable of reaching orbit, of reaching the colony vessel *Du Maurier* that remained in orbit high above their world.

Meru had insisted on going alone. Things could go wrong, and it was foolish to risk other lives. He wouldn't be piloting it anyway, he understood the complexities of flying such a machine in theory, but it was automated and would return on its own, with or without him.

He had made his way through the central control complex at the Obelisk site, walking down into the biotech area where Ira had given her life to save the planet.

'Hello Ira,' he said.

Her body was still there and, as far as Meru could tell, unchanged, still a young girl early in her teenage rounds. She was suspended in the gelatinous substance that had subsumed her all those rounds before, a myriad of cables connected to her skin. She floated there, watching over everything.

'Greetings Meru,' she replied. 'It has been many rounds since our last communication.'

'It has indeed,' he said. 'I wasn't sure you'd recognise me.'

'Your biological signature is distinct and not affected by age,' Ira replied.

Meru chuckled. 'Well, my biological signature is very lucky then, as the rest of me is definitely feeling my age. Zoella sends her regards.'

'Is she well?'

Meru nodded. 'She is. Queen of all Esurio now.'

'She is a wise leader,' Ira replied. 'Other than minor skirmishes, her reign has been characterised by considerable peace and prosperity. She has done well.'

Meru smiled. 'She has indeed. How have you been?'

'All systems are operating within normal parameters. Obelisk's status is optimal now that flare activity has ceased. Flares are predicted to return in round 2796.'

'I don't suppose I'll be around for that one,' Meru said, with a faint smile.

'You still intend to use the dropship?'

'Last place to go,' Meru said.

'Your physical condition is marginal given the stresses and strains that will be placed upon your physiology during the ascent to orbit,' Ira said. 'Such a trip is not recommended.'

'I'll be fine,' Meru said, straightening his back against the ache growing there. 'There's still life in this old herg.'

'Acknowledged,' Ira replied. 'Do you have any other requests?'

'Just that you keep doing what you're doing,' he said. 'Looking after everything.'

'Obelisk defensive systems will be quiescent until the flares return in 2796,' Ira said. 'No further actions are anticipated. This includes AMS functions.'

'So … you're going to shut yourself down too?'

'Yes,' Ira confirmed. 'Low level automated systems will continue to function in the interim, but higher level facilities are not required under normal circumstances.'

'But … Esurio is safe?'

'Not withstanding any unexpected events,' Ira replied. 'Yes. Obelisk and AMS functions can be reactivated should any unforeseen circumstances occur.'

Meru paused, looking around the facility, taking in the screens and displays, remembering them from long ago.

When she was here with me. All behind me now, one last task to do.

'Then this is a goodbye too,' Meru said. 'Thank you for what you did for us … for all of us, Ira.'

'Your appreciation is acknowledged, Meru,' Ira replied.

Meru smiled.

* * *

A few spells later he settled himself in the dropship.

Compared to the other vessels he had been transported in, this was the height of luxury. There was a huge amount of room inside, it was clear the ship had been designed to ferry people and cargo down from above. He had brought a pass' supply of food and water with him, though he didn't believe that he'd need it.

'Communication uplink is confirmed,' Ira said, her voice sounding from all around him. 'Launch window approaching. Maximum acceleration will be three Esurian gravities.'

Meru settled back in the couch he had selected.

Moments later a rumble shuddered through the craft. Through the windows he could see the ground dropping away in a flurry of dust. Then, the Obelisk itself fell away below. The craft tilted upwards and there was nothing but the azure of the sky, and a pressure pushing him back in his seat, a sensation of extreme weight. He could feel his heart hammering now, painful, his breath gasping and short.

Before him the sky was fading to a darker hue. He watched and waited. He knew what to expect, but the sight drew a gasp from him anyway.

Blackness, pin-pricked with impossible tiny sparks of brightness. They were utterly immobile, their light cold and steady in the dark.

Stars ...

The acceleration was fading now. Another sensation overcame him, almost like sea-sickness. Again, he knew to expect it, but the feeling was disorienting, as if he was falling.

Which I am, even though it doesn't seem like it ... now it's me ... I'm in an orbit!

He was tired now, and knew it would be a while before anything further happened. He slept until a gentle buzzing roused him. He blinked awake and sat up.

There, through the windows of the dropship, was the sight he had waited most of his life to see.

He already knew it to be vast, marks wide and dozens long, the most stupendous of humanity's constructions ever to have been built.

Built though, not really the right word.

The *Du Maurier* hadn't been built. It was an asteroid, dragged into orbit of the original homeworld and then mined, trimmed and hollowed out for the purpose. Its shape, close up, was an irregular cylinder, with superstructure jutting from the rocky shell as requirements dictated.

He had first seen it in his youth, just a bright point of light far off in the sky. Now he could make out vast domes jutting from the rocky sides where once food would have been grown, huge banks of cargo storage, fuel pods, scaffolding running the length of the vessel. Vast panels jutted from its side, cooling fins for the unfathomable energies contained within.

The final section of the vessel was composed of the mighty engines, bolted on to the rear section of the asteroid, that had long ago wrenched the ship from its orbit around a distant star called Sol and sent it on its way to Esurio.

'*Du Maurier* proximity telemetry confirmed.' This time it was Sandra's voice. Meru remembered how he'd named the disembodied voice long ago. 'Docking in progress. Please secure harnesses for approach.'

Meru did as he was told, feeling the dropship turn and move around him as it oriented itself against the vast colony vessel.

With a faint series of thumps the dropship came to rest.

'Pressure equalised. You may disembark.'

'Thank you, Sandra.'

'You are welcome, Administrator Meru.'

Meru unclipped the harness, moving forward, free of the grasp of gravity, only to see something that no resident of Esurio had ever seen before. The ships were in a high orbit around Esurio. The darkness was fading, a glow spreading out on the horizon. The stars were already gone. Meru gasped as the light reached him.

Lacaille … Sunrise!

* * *

He had written up all his findings and … the word was 'transmission' apparently … sent them down to Ira far below to ensure they were safe and would be passed on to others. He'd barely touched upon the content and artefacts stored, but he had constructed an index with many samples.

Such a bitter tale. Others will have to write it up in detail.

The *Du Maurier* had set out into the darkness after humanity had rendered their own planet uninhabitable. Meru had read the transcripts and watched the films recorded by their ancestors of long ago. It was strange to see those people, alive and unaware of what would happen to their legacy, talking and speaking as if they were just in the next room.

The *Du Maurier* had been captained by Admiral Gregory Drayden, a stern military man from Earth itself. It seemed there had been quite some rivalry between the crew and the colonists on how Esurio was to be administered.

He had wound back through the archives. It was the older history that interested him. Earth itself.

That planet, humanity's home, looked very strange to his eyes. Everything was a bright garish green or blue, with the star a sharp yellow or even white in many of the images and videos. There were few of the soft and comfortable reds and oranges of his home. The vegetation too was an unfamiliar green colour throughout, and he saw many strange and wonderful beasts. None of them were present on Esurio, it seemed they had all failed to adapt.

It was a world of oceans, far bigger than those of Esurio, land was at a premium. Meru saw astonishing feats of technology, buildings of grandeur and sophistication that dazzled him with their design. But the records had not hidden the darker side of all the technological advancement. There was devastating pollution, animals dying by the billions, extreme weather that ripped up coastlines and ravaged crops.

Yet the shocking truth was that the damage had been self-inflicted.

Humanity had been consumed by its own consumption. The atmosphere was filled with toxins, the seas and land covered in debris, effluent and pollution. The records catalogued the efforts of those who tried to stem the tide before it was too late. Almost a century had passed from the problem being understood until it was dealt with in any meaningful way.

But it was too little, too late.

Rising temperatures had been what most had feared. Sea levels had risen and storms were worse, with many areas blighted by heat. Then, too complex to understand, the biosphere had turned in upon itself.

The Earth plunged into a winter of unimaginable cold, the oceans freezing and snow covering everything to a depth of many hands. Meru well recalled his many traipses along the edge of the frozen wastes that ringed Esurio and shuddered to think of what must have happened. The population of the Earth had been reduced from billions to mere thousands in a short span of time.

War and famine had marked those final stretches … or days, as they were called on Earth.

But there were many brighter moments. The *Du Maurier* contained more records than he could ever view; music, books, films and artworks, all of which demonstrated a more hopeful and optimistic people than the calamity would otherwise have shown. There had been a massive effort to preserve the best of what humanity had created, even if they couldn't save their home.

And they had been explorers, that was certain. The history files showed that humanity had first charted their own home, and then explored the worlds in their own system. Those instincts had served them well when they had been forced to leave and travel into the darkness.

Now the story of their origins could be told from beginning to end. The exodus from Earth, the struggle to reach Esurio and how people had been adapted to live upon the surface of this new world. How they'd tried to leave much of the technology behind, keeping only what was essential. How the gift had been given to women to act as administrators and caretakers, and how it was all lost when the first flare had struck, breaking the nascent civilisation and sending it into rounds of darkness from which they were only just emerging.

It was the last record of the departure that gave Meru a chill. He already knew about it, but, up here, it seemed more imperative, as if the stars were watching.

The *Du Maurier* wasn't a lone vessel. It was one of many, despatched to worlds not too far away from the stricken Earth.

There might be other survivors out there. Humanity's descendants spread out amongst the stars in the void. What stories might there be? What calamities might have overtaken them? Esurio's people had survived, but their culture had regressed over many rounds. Others might have been more, or less, fortunate.

What might humanity have done if it had been able to build on the foundation of the technologies he had seen? Or was Esurio the only remaining outpost of humankind?

There was equipment aboard the *Du Maurier* to transmit to other stars. The flight plans were all stored and recorded. Dozens of ships had left Earth, all with distant destinations.

I could send a message out. It would take rounds for them to respond, Esurio has been silent for more than two thousand rounds. It's probably marked as a failure. I could tell them we made it!

But the enthusiasm cooled. Who was to say what two thousand rounds of separation had done to humanity's descendants? Perhaps some had retained their technology and had fleets of ships ready to expand and conquer. Perhaps Esurio's isolation was best kept that way.

And we have enough challenges living up to the legacy of what our founding colonists intended and we've only just managed to deal with our own despots. No need to risk looking for more of them! Our ancestors wanted to leave the technology behind anyway …

Esurio, in all its golden richness, rolled beneath the viewports.

It's so beautiful. Our world, our legacy. Let's keep it for us.

He sat, buckled into one of the flight chairs on the *Du Maurier's* expansive bridge, staring at it, his breath coming in short sharp gasps.

Lacaille's light faded overhead, the *Du Maurier* entering the shadow of Esurio. The stars appeared again, cold and sharp against the ebony backdrop of space. He cleared his throat and asked the last question for which he wanted an answer.

'Sandra,' he said. 'Can you show me the location of Earth?'

'The star Sol is visible from the *Du Maurier's* current attitude and inclination,' Sandra replied. 'Will that suffice?'

Meru smiled, his voice a whisper. 'That will be fine.'

Above him, somehow projected beyond the transparent viewports of the bridge, a small targeting reticle appeared, framing a moderately bright star. There was nothing particularly special about it, though the yellow colouring was distinct. Above it were a series of stars that formed a pattern like a cooking pan, or perhaps a herg-drawn plough.

Sandra was saying something.

'Spectral classification G2V, distance 10.74 light years, absolute magnitude …'

He lost concentration and closed his eyes, his chest hurt.

I'll just rest for a moment …

Meru.

He smiled.

Kiri?

There was a brief moment of pain, but it was short. He hardly noticed.

Epilogue

Round 2936, Third pass

People stood, looking into the air-conditioned glass cabinet. Within was a skeleton, well preserved; its bones for the most part all intact other than some missing ribs on the left side. The skull was complete, with a set of regular teeth in place. A few other items were laid alongside; a tarnished metal staff some ten hands long, a tiara, a necklace and the remains of a black leather glove.

Visitors to the museum passed it by on a daily basis and the curators were on hand to answer questions about the time period from which the skeleton had been dated; a turbulent era in the history of Esurio.

This batch of visitors was little different, other than the rapt attention of a young girl. She was gazing at the skeleton with more than passing curiosity.

'Our prize exhibit,' the curator said, noticing the girl's interest. 'A very special woman from a time long ago. Would you like to know about her?'

'Who was she?' the girl demanded.

The curator smiled.

'We don't know her name,' he replied, 'Only the first letter of it. We call her Kate, but there's no way to know what she was really called.'

'What did she do?'

'We believe she was one of the priestesses that worked in the court of Queen Zoella Tiamoi,' the curator explained. 'She may have even known the queen.'

'How do you know she was a priestess?' The girl continued her questioning unabated.

'Look here,' the curator said, pointing at the skeleton's neck vertebra. Around it was a metal chain, a necklace, with a pendant in the shape of an isosceles triangle. 'That was the mark of a priestess. It's a stylised representation of the Obelisk that links our administrators today. Back then they thought it was a religious power, they worshipped it. The priestesses were the only ones who could control it … and they sacrificed especially selected women to it in a strange ritual called the tearing.'

'How horrible!' the girl said. 'How long ago was this?'

'Oh, this was six hundred rounds or so. All ancient history.'

The girl looked back thoughtfully at the skeleton.

'The priestesses served the queen then,' the curator continued. 'Though really they were a private army. The queen would use them to carry out her orders. Queen Zoella was the first monarch of a new age after the chaos that occurred after the collapse of the Voren Empire two hundred rounds earlier.'

'She changed things?'

'Yes. She lived in a dark time, as another flare hit our world. Many people died in wars, famines and conflict, but Zoella brought peace to Esurio, her reign marks the end of what we call the dark rounds. She established control and brought people together. Many people wrote of her wisdom; they called it a golden age. The historians mark it as a major turning point in our understanding.'

'So she was a good queen?'

'I think she was one of the better rulers,' the curator said with a laugh. 'We don't really know too much about Zoella, as her home, the city of Viresia, was destroyed in an earthquake seventy rounds after her death. This woman's casket was found buried within the ruins, it survived the destruction. It was made of metal you see, very unusual for the time. It would have been incredibly expensive. It's from this skeleton and some of the other items that were found nearby, that we know most about Queen Zoella's reign.'

The girl didn't answer, but continued to stare at the skeleton. The curator wondered what she was thinking. He had spent many long spells himself staring at the empty eye sockets of the skull, wondering what sights the woman had seen, what she had done, what kind of person she had been.

If only she could tell us. What secrets about the past might she reveal? There's so much about this era we don't know.

'Zoella was the only queen too,' the curator added. 'It was all Kings after that and then the monarchy was abolished a hundred and fifty rounds after her time. Some of her descendants weren't quite so forward thinking as she was.'

The girl turned her attention to the skeleton.

'What happened to this priestess?' the girl asked.

The curator looked at the skeleton.

'It seems she likely died of a stab to the heart,' the curator said. 'See how the ribs are broken and missing? We think this poor woman was killed in a fight, she may have even fought to defend the queen from her enemies.'

'She was a warrior? She could fight?'

'Oh yes,' the curator said, with a nod. 'And she would have been very good at it. There are many signs of the fights she had. The broken ribs for a start. There are signs that many of her bones were broken at times and healed in between. There's damage to the leg too, and look – can you see the bones in her fingers and left hand? See that pattern?'

The girl leant over and looked, before nodding.

'At some point something broke this woman's hand badly,' the curator said. 'She was buried with that black glove on that hand – it was likely badly disfigured from the wound. This staff you can see was her weapon. It was called a kai, and she would have been an expert in using it.'

'How old was she?'

'Carbon dating shows she was only about twenty three rounds or so – very young, but she would have been extremely fit, you can see how strong her bones still are even now.'

'Now,' the curator said. 'You must see this; the mysterious plaque. It was found on the outside of the casket when it was discovered.'

The curator pointed at metal plate inside the cabinet at the bottom of the display.

'What does it say?'

‘We can’t read some of the words, unfortunately the metal is too badly corroded in places, obscuring the text, but what we can make is translated there.’ The curator pointed at a small label. ‘They used different symbols for language then.’

The girl looked and read aloud, stumbling over the gaps in the text.

‘Here lies K … she who was s … of Queen Zoella. S? What does S mean?’

‘We don’t know,’ the curator said. ‘Servant … soldier perhaps.’

‘So why is she wearing a tiara?’ the girl asked. ‘That’s so pretty.’

‘Another puzzle,’ the curator replied. ‘Perhaps a symbol of appreciation from the Queen herself, possibly a reward for service.’

The girl continued reading. ‘… honoured in Viresia to mark … priestesses of Drayden … most beloved by M …’

The girl looked up.

‘M?’ she asked.

The curator shrugged. ‘That’s the saddest part of it,’ he said. ‘We don’t know her name, or who wrote the words on the plaque, but there is a date. See there? Round 2308, that is 628 rounds ago.’

‘Somebody loved her though,’ the girl said.

‘Yes. And to have been buried in this way was a mark of special honour,’ the curator said, his voice hushed. ‘We have found no other metal caskets from this time, hardly any others at all in fact. Metal was so rare in those stretches; to use this much metal to honour a single person … Well, whoever she was, she was important, loved and highly revered at the time; a very special young woman.’

‘What did she look like?’

The curator smiled.

‘We don’t really know, but artists have made a mould of her face based upon the skull. We do know she had black hair, as some of it survived in her burial casket.’

The curator called up an image on the projector. The girl studied it intently. The simulated face had a blank expression, but had strong features – high cheekbones and a firm jaw. She looked fierce and determined.

The girl studied it for long moments, her head tilted with concentration.

'What do you think?' the curator asked.

'She is quite beautiful,' the girl said, still looking at the glass cabinet. 'But I think she had blue eyes.'

This concludes the Shadeward Saga.

Appendix

TIME-KEEPING

Measuring time on Esurio is problematic. There is no night/day cycle. The only readily available visual cue is the crossing of the planet Mayura (a 'hot Jupiter' gas giant in an inferior orbit) across the face of the star Lacaille, which is easily visible from the surface of Esurio. The duration of this transit is known as a 'Chime' and the time between 'Chimes' as a 'Pass'.

Spell
A short duration in the order of fifteen earth minutes. There are eight spells to a chime.

Chime
Many cultures on Esurio use sand timers to count 'chimes' and they are also used for sleeping, waking and marking time for meals. A chime is the time taken for the inferior planet Mayura to cross the face of Lacaille. A chime is considered the typical length of time it takes to do a job. A chime is around two hours long.

'The Sleeping'
This is the gap between the eighth chime and the first chime. The time set aside for being asleep. It is four chimes in length. Analogous to 'night'.

Stretch
A cycle of eight chimes and followed by 'the sleeping'. Analogous to a complete day.

Pass
Length of time for the planet Mayura to return to the same point on

Lacaille. It lies in on the ecliptic plane as seen from Esurio, thus transits each orbit, visible from the surface. A pass is analogous to a month. All other timings are taken from this. There are twenty stretches in a pass.

Round
A round is twenty passes, which are counted manually by timekeepers (a specialist role on Esurio). Analogous to a year, although slightly longer in duration, being four hundred stretches.

MEASUREMENTS AND DIRECTIONS

Measurements are more easily understood and are based on hands and the typical length of a stride. These are not accurate terms and they will vary somewhat depending on the culture that is using them at the time.

Hand
The width of an adult's hand with fingers outstretched. Approximately a quarter of a metre.

Span
The length of an adult's span fingertip to fingertip with arms outstretched. A little under two metres.

Pace
The length of an adult's stride. Roughly a metre.

Mark
Used analogously to an Earth 'kilometre' and of similar length.

Traipse
A long way. Many 'marks'. Typically the distance one can walk comfortably without stopping to sleep. Around 40 kilometres.

Shadeward
If you orient yourself so that Lacaille is directly behind you, you are facing shadeward.

Sunward
If you orient yourself so that Lacaille is directly in front of you, you are facing sunward.

Sunright
If you orient yourself so that Lacaille is on your right hand side, you are facing sunright.

Shaderight
If you orient yourself so that shadeward is to your right (or Lacaille is to your left), you are facing shaderight.

FLORA

The flora on Esurio are unique to the planet and have their own distinctive characteristics adapted to the conditions. There are many more varieties than have been catalogued, particularly in the sunward parts of Esurio, where significant new species have been reported. The primary ones are listed below.

Furlers
Rather similar to Earth Redwood trees, but significantly larger in the low gravity. These trees give Esurio a 'hardwood' from which much building material is taken. These trees also capture rainwater from above, rather than by roots as on Earth. Their roots are for stability only. They are found in the cooler areas, where they are not swamped by faster growing vegetation. Some of these furlers can be thousands of rounds old. Their leaves are dark green and edible like a sweet fruit, a good source of vitamins and nutrition, but they are high above

ground, accessible only to the marsips, who typically live in them. The leaves are regarded as a delicacy in some areas, and a prized commodity in others depending on rarity. The leaves can be fermented into the fierce liquor known as 'Ochren'. Furlers escape destruction by the flares on account of their size and have evolved to utilise the extreme ultraviolet light by throwing out fast growing branches of leaves to trap the high energy light – hence the name 'Furler'. These can be quite dramatic.

Shades

These are curious entities, straddling the line between the plant and animal kingdoms. They look rather like mushrooms in general appearance, but with the 'cup' inverted so as to look rather like a dish. These capture rainwater and sunlight. The tops of the cup are black, but they have a light coloured underside which gives off a milky phosphorescent glow. They form large forests over much of Esurio. Their trunks are also a pale cream colour and grow straight and true, but are lightweight, rather like bamboo when dried out. These plants are able to move around slowly and have a sophisticated musculature, growing to angle their cups towards the sun, competing with each other. They quickly shrivel when detecting ultraviolet radiation to minimise exposure. It is possible to 'tap' their bark for water, though it is bitter, with a cinnamon-like taste. Many infusions and brews can be made from shadewater. In boiled and concentrated form it is a good painkiller. The bark can also be stewed to produce a cinnamon-like drink which is mixed with milk from a herg to produce 'Chai'. Shades are found throughout Esurio, but thicker in warmer areas. They are several dozen hands tall at best, with trunks up to two hands in diameter. Shades survive the flares by sacrificing their top cups to the ultraviolet and growing back afterwards. Shade forests are the best place (outside of a cave) for animals and humans to hide during flares due to the thick overlapping canopy, hence the name.

Snares

A parasitical and carnivorous plant. It can be found hanging from shades and furlers. Completely black in colour it is tendril and vine like. It hangs glistening tendrils down (in the manner of a spiderweb) towards the ground attempting to snare nargs and marsips primarily, though it is capable of immobilising a human. It is completely black and difficult to see in the gloom, though it gives off a smell like aniseed. Its tendrils are poisonous like a jellyfish. This poison is harvested by many hunters for use on arrows. When touched the tendrils whip around rapidly, catching the unfortunate creature and reeling it in. Snares have a hollow central 'stomach' which contains strong acid which dissolves the prey whilst still alive. Snares are able to move slowly around from pass to pass. They gain their water from the plants they grow on. Generally snares are a nuisance, but there are reports of people being killed by larger infestations.

Mulches

Mulches are a composite microscopic lifeform that infests stagnant lakes, dykes or any other trapped water. They are quiescent most of the time, but are capable of overwhelming large creatures by swarming together and emerging from the water in a continuous stream having detected them. They immobilise their prey by anesthetic stings, entering the body and then consuming them from the inside out. They can move at a surprising speed for their size (a slow amble to humans) but will not venture far from water otherwise they dry up and die.

Sweetbuds, Melps, Corcuns and Tupes

Varieties of vegetable commonly found in Esurio. Sweetbuds are particularly useful as they are rich in sugar, found mostly in the warmer climes of Taloon. Dried sweetbuds are regarded as 'sweets'.

FAUNA

All Esurian creatures share some common traits. They have nictitating membranes or double eyelids. They have thick fur or skin, covering heavy bony structures on the upper part of the body (to protect against flare radiation). They are able to keenly sense ultraviolet radiation, which precedes the flares, via a special third 'eye' on the back of the head, giving them a chance to reach safety, typically underground or deep within shade forests. None of them sweat or pant, but have various different wing-like or fan-like protrusions which they pump blood into for the purposes of cooling or territorial threat displays. Their eyes are adapted to the infrared, allowing them to see well in the gloom. None of them sleep, the mechanism having never evolved on this planet, but they go into temporary trances on occasion, resting one side of the brain at a time.

Narg

There is a wide variety of insect life on Esurio, but the primary one of note is the narg. It is regarded as a pest by the colonists, but it is essential to the food chain on the planet, being at the bottom for the most part. Nargs come in a number of forms but they are hive based, with a queen, workers, hunters and nest builders. They are large and black in colour, in order to absorb as much heat as possible, they are not found in the colder regions of the planet. The males are winged and the females are not. The society is strictly matriarchal, a pattern much admired by the people of Drayden and copied by them. Nargs create large structures similar to termites, but much more extensive due to the low gravity. Their primary food is vegetation, but they are known to make concentrated attacks on marsips, cainers and even dachs and hergs if they gather in sufficient numbers. They have a sting that is alcoholic in nature rather like a shot of Tequila, thus their venom is cultivated as a delicacy. It is possible to be killed by alcohol poisoning by multiple stings. This has led to the phrase 'Stung drunk'. Nargs can be up to half a hand long, due to the high oxygen levels. Narg females consume the male after mating.

Flits

Flits are larger insects akin to dragonflies, although with six wings rather than four. Like dragonflies they are iridescent and have many colours including green, blue, red and purple. They primarily hunt nargs for food. In most lands they are quite rare and infrequently seen, thus are regarded as an omen of good luck – they are welcomed as they are known to keep down the population of nargs. By contrast in Drayden they are considered a delicacy and cultivated for that purpose. Flits are also eaten by dachs, but are so agile in the air that they are rarely caught. Flits have strong mandibles like the praying mantis and always hunt on the wing, hardly ever touching ground. They can grow up to two hands in length, filling the small 'bird' role on the planet.

Marsip

A small rodent-like creature. They have much evolutionary potential as they have opposable thumbs, but they are close to the bottom of the food chain, subsisting on vegetation and insect life. They are lightly furred and make excellent pets due to their high intelligence. In the wild they live in burrows to escape from the flares. They are excellent climbers, which is their primary defence against cainars and dachs. They have exceptional eyesight and agility. They are found throughout Esurio. The fans of the marsip are folds of skin between their arms, legs and body, making their cooling displays rather amusing, and allowing them to glide between trees to some degree. They can grow up to six hands in length and can stand on their back legs like a meerkat.

Molossc

A molossc is a large invertebrate creature living in marshlands, swamps, bogs or similar habitats. In form they are similar to a giant slug, reaching sizes of up to three metres long. They are carnivorous and will tackle significant prey if they come into range. The molossc is able to move quickly over short distances by coiling up its structure and then extending itself. It traps its prey by wrapping tentacles around them. These tentacles have anesthetising stings. Once the prey is secured the molossc will drag the unfortunate creature into the mud, drowning it and then ingesting it slowly over a long period of time.

Cainar/Carn

A large wolf-like creature. Rather bigger than Earth creatures and longer in the leg due to low gravity, standing about six hands high. They have sabre teeth and are a dappled brown colour. They tend to inhabit the shadeward parts of the forests as they are acclimatised to cool weather. They hunt in packs and have a high intelligence. They have a mane-like fan which they use for cooling and in territorial threat displays. They head sunwards on occasion depending on the availability of food. They hunt the marsips and hergs and have been known to take on a phaunt in desperation. There is also a domestic version of the cainar, called a carn which is analogous to a dog and frequently used for similar purposes. Like most Esurian creatures they have bony plates across their backs to shield against flares. This makes them extremely tough, but less agile than might be expected.

Fellin

A cat-like creature, subsisting on nargs and marsips, known for its agility and poise. They tend to be smaller in the sunward areas and larger in the shadeward. They mostly live in deep in the shade forests and are the only creature known that seems to make a living out of hunting and eating the snares. They appear to be immune to the poison of these plants. They are lone creatures and exceptionally shy, most colonists have never seen one. Due to this rarity and their ability to take on the snares they are regarded as mysterious and an omen of bad luck. They are smaller than the cainar but are notoriously bad tempered and will fight viciously if cornered or threatened. They do not possess the bony back plates of the other creatures and thus tend to stay confined in the forests in the protection of the shades and furlers.

Dach

A large flying lizard-like creature preying on marsips and larger insects primarily, mostly in the sunwards parts of Esurio. They counterpoint the cainar in many ways, and their territories do not naturally overlap that much. They are usually to be found in the more mountainous areas where they have their eyries. The people of Drayden specialise in breeding tame collections of these beasts and then growing them to a great size. Thus these are rideable by individual humans or a pair as long as they are not too heavy. The fans of the dach have evolved as wings, making them supreme aerial hunters. Dachs are able to attack marsips in their furler-top homes, prefer flits and will eat nargs out of necessity. Dachs also utilise the shades and furlers to escape the flares.

Herg

A creature like a cross between a buffalo and a horse, but with a massive bony back. Naturally found in herds of up to one hundred, they are one of most useful creatures on Esurio. Easily tamed and used wildly through the lands they fulfil the role of the ox, mule and horse. They are the main mode of transport and food in Drayden, Scallia and Drem, less so in Taloon. In the wild they graze the temperate areas of the planet, moving around as the vegetation is eaten and then grows back. They are heavier in the front shoulders like an ox, but have the longer legs of a horse.

Garguan

A creature mid way in size between a herg and phaunt similar to an Earth bison in general shape, but considerably bigger, with two large curving horns sprouting from its muzzle and the typical cooling fans arranged just behind the head. Its fur is thick and heavily matted, the creature being adapted to live in the cooler parts of the planet, not being seen in the warmer zones. It is of low intelligence, grazing from furlers in its natural habitat. Colonists found these animals ideal for hauling packs in the colder areas where the hergs cannot survive. Garguans have been found on the borders of the frozen wastes and seem to thrive there.

Phaunt

A large creature of comparable size to an extinct Earth Triceratops, but having the neck of a giraffe. These tend to inhabit the tropical parts of the planet, where they browse on vegetation high up in the canopy, pushing down the Shades. They are a dark green in colour, with thick skin. They move slowly and stay within the highly vegetated areas in family troupes. Some phaunts have been domesticated by the Taloon people for the purposes of battle and pulling equipment, but they are generally too big to be used for agriculture. Much of Taloon culture is built around adulation of the phaunt. These creatures make a startling noise when alarmed by means of a trumpeted mouth piece. Phaunts are unique in having multiple fans on their necks, often with different colours. It is not clear how they survive the flares.

ALSO BY DREW WAGAR

In the Shadeward series
published by Fantastic Books Publishing
Shadeward: Emanation
Shadeward: Exoneration
Shadeworld: Enervation

Authorised novels of Elite: Dangerous
Reclamation published by Fantastic Books Publishing
Premonition published by Frontier Developments plc

Authorised novels of The Lords of Midnight
published by Fantastic Books Publishing
The Lords of Midnight
Doomdark's Revenge

ABOUT THE AUTHOR

Drew Wagar is a science fiction and fantasy author. He lives in Kent with his wife, two sons, one girlfriend (not his) a dog and a cat. His favourite colour is dark green. He drives a small convertible car which occasionally works. He doesn't require a conservatory or any double glazing.

You can reach Drew as follows:

Drew's Website: http://www.drewwagar.com
Facebook: http://www.facebook.com/drewwagarwriter
Twitter: http://www.twitter.com/drewwagar

If you have enjoyed this book, please consider leaving a review for Drew to let him know what you thought of his work. You can find out more about him on his author page on the Fantastic Books Store. While you're there, why not browse our delightful tales and wonderfully woven prose?

www.fantasticbooksstore.com

Printed in Great Britain
by Amazon

60725777R00296